BY D. L. SORIA

The Cottage Around the Corner
Thief Liar Lady

FOR YOUNG ADULTS
(As Destiny Soria)

Iron Cast
Beneath the Citadel
Fire with Fire

THE COTTAGE AROUND THE CORNER

THE COTTAGE AROUND THE CORNER

A NOVEL

D. L. SORIA

DEL REY

NEW YORK

A Del Rey Trade Paperback Original

Copyright © 2024 by Destiny Soria

Published in the United States by Del Rey,
an imprint of Random House, a division of
Penguin Random House LLC, New York.

DEL REY and the CIRCLE colophon are registered trademarks
of Penguin Random House LLC.

LIBRARY OF CONGRESS CATALOGING-IN-PUBLICATION DATA
Names: Soria, Destiny, author.
Title: The cottage around the corner: a novel / D.L. Soria.
Description: New York: Del Rey, 2024.
Identifiers: LCCN 2024022413 | ISBN 9780593358108 (trade paperback;
acid-free paper) | ISBN 9780593358092 (ebook)
Subjects: LCGFT: Fantasy fiction. | Novels.
Classification: LCC PS3619.O752 C68 2024 |
DDC 813/.6—dc23/eng/20240517
LC record available at https://lccn.loc.gov/2024022413

Printed in the United States of America on acid-free paper

randomhousebooks.com

2 4 6 8 9 7 5 3 1

Book design by Alexis Flynn

For David and Amanda:
You make Middle Child Syndrome worth it.

THE
COTTAGE
AROUND
THE CORNER

CHAPTER ONE

I was being stalked by an enchanted broom. It had been shuffling around the shop for weeks, delighting the customers and driving me crazy. I only had myself to blame. A month ago, I'd insisted on *The Sword in the Stone* for our family movie night, and when Merlin magically animated the kitchen to clean itself, my parents took it as a challenge. (There is always a great deal of wine involved in family movie night.)

I barely managed to convince them that flying dishes were a bad idea, so the broom was a consolation prize. As the only one of us sober enough to be trusted with a blade, I used my boline to carve the runes into the broom handle while Mim gave instructions over my shoulder. Even when she was drunk, her spellwork was unparalleled. Mama, who at her most sober still found runes too fiddly for her taste, had chosen to contribute by dancing around and singing the evil Madam Mim's song from the film. Our Mim was unamused.

I had hoped the next day's hangover would dull the excitement and they would decommission it, but instead I found the broom to be my new companion in the shop. My parents insisted that the novelty would be good for business, and I couldn't deny that the customers enjoyed its whimsical dancing down the aisles while they browsed. I would have been more impressed if it had kept the floors clean, instead of just getting in the way while I went about my chores.

This particular Saturday morning, it was more underfoot than usual. I'd come downstairs an hour early to set up a spell, and the broom dogged my heels while I gathered ingredients, until finally I slipped into the work room and shut the door. While I set out a shallow clay bowl, a saltcellar, and a glass bottle of Florida Water, I could hear the broom scratching at the door like a forlorn puppy. I couldn't believe a nonsentient aggregate of wood and straw had me feeling sorry for it.

By the time I finished setting up, the broom had given up on the door to continue its ambling circuit around the shop, and I was finally able to concentrate. The worktable was piled with paperwork and random inventory that needed to be reshelved, so I knelt on the floor in front of the bowl. Decades of Sparrow family spells had imbued the floorboards and walls of the stock room with a permanent smell of smoke and burnt herbs that most customers found unpalatable but to me was the scent of home.

First, I took a length of thin red ribbon from my pocket and tied it around my wrist in preparation for the casting, and then I turned my attention to the bowl, which was about the size of a dinner plate. I spooned in salt until there was a thin layer covering the bottom.

I flipped through the pages of the leather-bound book next to my knee. The spine was so well-worn that it rested open without any trouble when I found the page I needed. Mama had taught me the white fire limpia when I was in high school, but I still liked to read over the instructions I'd penned into my grimoire at fourteen, to reassure myself that I wasn't going to make any terrible mistakes. As if after thousands of iterations, I was one day going to accidentally use sugar instead of salt or forget how to light a match.

I settled back on my heels and closed my eyes to meditate. My family had a few different cleansing and protection spells that we performed periodically to benefit Chanterelle Cottage, but this was a special one-off. We'd been forced to keep the shop closed yesterday, after waking up to find that someone had broken the transom window and reached inside to unlock the front door. You'd think three witches under one roof would be enough of a theft deterrent—it had been for the past two centuries. Even in this day and age, Owl's Hollow was the sort of small town where people left their purses unattended and kids were allowed to roam unsupervised. Our sheriff spent all his time writing parking tickets and taking naps in his office.

Once we'd taken stock of the damage, we didn't even bother calling the sheriff to report the break-in, because the loss was nowhere near our insurance deductible. The cash register, surprisingly, had not been touched, and only a couple hundred dollars' worth of merchandise had been stolen: some spell jars, wands, books, and all but a few of our specialty hand-packed tea bags. The incident was more odd than troubling, as long as I didn't dwell on the thought of a stranger rifling through the shop while my parents and I slept upstairs. But that thought had been hard to put out of my head with negative energy permeating the shop, seeping into the edge of my consciousness last night while I tossed and turned. Hence the early-morning cleansing ritual.

I realized that my meditation had morphed into obsessing about the burglary, and I took a deep breath to recenter myself. Mentally, I gathered all the anger and fear and confusion. I picked up the bottle of Florida Water and poured some into the bowl, imagining that I was pouring out all my negative emotions with it.

I lit a match and tossed it in. As the flame burned, I picked up the bowl and made my way out of the work room. I expected to be ambushed by the broom—not ideal when I was holding a live flame—but it was oscillating in the corner by the cauldrons.

I walked up and down the aisles, letting the limpia cleanse the bad energy left behind by the burglary. The walk was meditative in itself, as I basked in the comfort of familiar surroundings.

Chanterelle Cottage was not just my job—it was my birthplace and my lifelong home. The walnut floors were scratched and stained with generations' worth of use. Overhead, dried herbs and various wards and blessings hung from the exposed wood beams. The shelves and bins were haphazardly packed with the tools and ingredients of our trade, as well as items meant to make magic more accessible to mundane folk.

We sold a little bit of everything here, not least of all the spellwork that couldn't be captured in jars or tea bags. We specialized in small cures, good-luck charms, and blessing crops. The sort of little things that made a big difference in a town like Owl's Hollow. We usually left the flashy work like telekinesis, transmutation, and summoning to magecraft firms, which were overpriced and overrated but better suited to ostentatious displays of magic.

Thinking about mages was darkening my mood again. I didn't want to ruin the limpia before it was even finished, so instead I did my best to calm myself by envisioning a pure, bright light expanding to fill the shop and our home. As the light grew, so did my sense of peace, until at last the foreboding was edged out by a deep sense of serenity.

As the fire burned out, I heard voices and footsteps coming

down the stairs. I set the bowl on the front counter. It must be almost time to open, so I would have to tidy up later.

"Morning!" Mim was the definition of bright-eyed and bushy-tailed. She had curled her honey-blond hair like a forties pinup star today, and her floral sheath dress hugged her thick curves. Her daisy earrings were truly enormous.

Behind her, Mama made a vague grunting noise that was the night-owl version of "Good morning." Her jaw cracked with a yawn, and she clutched her travel mug of coffee like a lifeline. She was dressed more formally than usual, presumably for their appointment at the bank. But that is not to say she was particularly formal. Her dark jeans were rip-free, and her black shirt was only one size too big. In the past few years, streaks of silver had appeared in her dark brown hair, which she enjoyed calling evidence of her advanced and superior wisdom, even though she was only two years older than Mim.

"Tonight," I said, in lieu of a greeting, "we are having s'mores, and I'm using that broom as kindling." I jerked my thumb toward my nemesis, which was wobbling around uselessly by the wand display.

"What has Broomhilde ever done to you?" Mim asked.

On cue, the thrashing handle knocked several wands to the floor.

"Don't be jealous, Charlie," said Mama. "You're still our favorite child."

"I'm your only child." I stole a sip of her coffee. "And I'm not jealous of a broom."

"Speaking of," said Mim, as she went to scoop up the wands and redirect the broom that I guessed we were calling Broomhilde now. I didn't like that it had a name. You can't throw things with names onto a bonfire. "Tandy DiAngelo has been wanting to take a look at it, so she might stop by today."

"And if she does, you should tell her to kick rocks," Mama said.

"No." Mim shook a wand scoldingly at Mama. "I told her it was fine."

"She just wants to try to make a better version that she can brag about," Mama muttered. She was not normally opposed to sharing spellwork—the witch community of Owl's Hollow was small and tight-knit. But Tandy was an exception.

"She can try," Mim said mildly. She was clearly not concerned about being bested by Tandy, a suburban socialite who specialized mostly in crystals and curating her Instagram aesthetic.

I didn't like Tandy all that much either, but her nosiness served a useful purpose in the local witch community, keeping everyone apprised of everyone else's business, discouraging anyone from dabbling in magic outside their ability. The last thing we needed was another incident like the time in Los Angeles when a witch attempting a nose job on a prominent actress accidentally switched the woman's mouth and eyes. Or the time in D.C. when a coven's spell gone haywire turned all the cherry blossoms Day-Glo orange. Both times mages had been hired to fix the spells—and you can bet they made a big fucking deal about it in the press. A publicity nightmare for those of us witches just trying to make a humble living. There aren't any central governing bodies for witches like the Mage Institute, which has its perks but also its downfalls. Not every witch is as responsible with their magic as they ought to be. And that's how you end up with Day-Glo cherry blossoms and nose jobs from hell.

"I'll let her have a look," I said, and in response to the face Mama pulled, I added, "and I'll make sure Broomhilde smacks her in the ass on the way out."

"And that's exactly why you're my favorite daughter." Mama

raised her coffee toward me in a toast, and I stole another sip. She liked her brew black as tar, but I wasn't picky today, considering I was running on a couple hours of fitful sleep and the temporary buzz of magic.

Mim had finished restoring the wand display and returned to the counter. She peered into the empty clay bowl curiously.

"I knew it felt different in here." She breathed in deeply, like the cleansing spell was something she could smell in the air. Maybe she could. Mim had a keener sixth sense than most, picking up on auras that most witches never noticed. "No one can burn out negative energy as thoroughly as you, Charlie."

A disproportionate amount of joy fluttered in my chest at the praise. I was annoyed at my own propensity to hoard compliments about my work like a business professional dragon, as if I hadn't been doing this for over a decade now. And the white fire limpia was amateur stuff, not exactly evidence of greatness. But still I clutched her words close.

"You've always been a genius at cleansing," Mama said. "We knew you were a natural when you were drawing sacred circles in the sandbox at six years old."

"Pretty sure I was just drawing circles," I said. "And anyway, this limpia was weaker than I hoped. I wasn't focused enough. Mama should probably redo it later."

My parents exchanged a look that I couldn't decipher, and Mim looked like she wanted to say something more, but before she could, the cuckoo clock behind the counter chirped eight o'clock. We all startled.

"Isn't your appointment at eight-thirty?" I asked. "You're going to be late."

"Yes, we mustn't anger the Master of Coin," Mama said.

"He's called a loan officer," said Mim. "And we have time. The appointment isn't until nine."

"You said it was eight-thirty," Mama said, affronted, probably at the realization that she missed out on thirty extra minutes of sleep.

"Did I?" Mim said innocently, shooting me a little grin. "My mistake."

I bit back my own grin and busied myself behind the counter. Mim often told Mama an earlier time for important appointments, to combat her natural propensity for rolling out the door at the last possible minute.

"I married you so I could be a hot trophy wife." Mama slouched over the counter in dramatic fashion. "I'm supposed to be lounging on a chaise, being fed grapes, not groveling to boring old men in suits."

"We're not groveling," Mim said, stroking Mama's hair sympathetically. "And I promise to buy you grapes after."

"I accept your terms." Mama raised her head and made a pitiful face. "But only if they are aged twenty years and squeezed into a glass bottle."

Side by side, they struck a cozy picture. Mama's golden brown skin and effortless edge (even when forced to wake up at ungodly hours, she never skipped a fierce eyeliner) were perfectly complemented by porcelain-skinned and pink-cheeked Mim, who was a rainbow of pastels from head to toe. The sight of them together invoked a glowing feeling of *home* in my chest, strong enough to rival my magic's invigorating buzz.

"Good luck with the Master of Coin," I said, smiling. "I need to open up."

"We should probably head out anyway." Mama exuded an air of long suffering. "I need at least eight shots of overpriced espresso."

"Are you going to be all right by yourself today?" Mim's forehead was wrinkled slightly in consternation. I knew she was asking because we usually tried to have two people on the floor on Saturdays, but the question unexpectedly stung. Like she was doubting my ability to run the shop at all, even though I'd been working behind the counter full time since I returned home from college almost a decade ago.

"I'm fine," I said, shaking off the twinge of insecurity. I rounded the counter and headed for the door, so she couldn't see my face. "It should be a pretty quiet day."

"Let's hope you're wrong," Mim said. "How else can I afford to ply my trophy wife with grapes and espresso? She's going to leave me for Tandy DiAngelo."

Mama snorted.

"Babe, I will grovel at the feet of a thousand old men in suits before that day ever comes."

"Besides," I said, "who would get Broomhilde in the divorce?"

"We'll let her choose," Mama said. "We'll stand equidistant from her and see who she comes to first."

"You'll only find a way to cheat," said Mim, nudging her toward the door.

"I would never." Mama put a hand to her chest in mock indignation, then caught my eye and stage-whispered, "The trick is to hide dust bunnies in your pocket."

They were both giggling by the time they made it onto the front porch. I waved them off, then flipped our *Closed* sign to *Open*. (Well, technically it was a sign that said *The Witch Is Out* and *The Witch Is In,* complete with a cartoon of a stereotypical pointy-hatted witch on a broom. A flea market find that my parents both thought hilarious, despite my attempts to convince them otherwise.)

I wasn't in the mood to clean up the back room or to dig out the cloves, rue, and angelica root I needed for a protection floor wash to replace all that banished negative energy with positivity. Instead, I wandered around the shop, nudging spell jars back into place on the shelves and taking note of which herbs were running low. Other than the cardboard taped over the broken transom window, all traces of the burglary had been cleared away, but that didn't mean the shop was neat. It never was, which was part of the charm.

Even so, I busied myself with the display of crystals that was messy beyond the point of charming, as per usual. Mim thought they should be organized according to effect and Mama thought they should be organized according to color, and the result was always a haphazard jumble with the handwritten labels sticking out all over the place.

I hummed a mindless tune and lost myself in the Sisyphean task. I wasn't even halfway done when the little brass bell on the counter picked itself up and gave three clear rings. I nearly jumped out of my skin. The bell was a new addition in response to the burglary. Last night we had spelled it to sound whenever someone came within ten feet of the shop. Mim had argued for a real security system, but Mama hated technology with a passion bordering on ludicrous, and Mama had wanted a guard dog, but Mim was afraid it would scare her cat. I suggested the charmed bell as a compromise. Besides, it would give tourists a good thrill.

I was pleased to see that the bell worked properly when the door opened a few seconds later. I had been the one to craft the spell, though I'd used Mim's runework on Broomhilde as a rough guide.

I half expected the sound to be signaling my parents' return. Part of the reason Mama was always running late was that she inevitably left something important behind—her wallet, her phone, occasionally her shoes. But the man who entered was a complete stranger, which is rare in a small town like ours. We got tourists from time to time, detouring from their ultimate destination when they saw our colorful sign along the main highway: *Wonderful Witchcraft for Wonderful Prices.* The sign had been there for nearly half a century, though it was less effective every passing year. Witches had experienced their heyday in the eighties, when fascination with the occult was at an all-time high, but nowadays people tended toward the fast convenience of magecraft.

Fortunately, as with many other aspects of the eighties, we were coming back into vogue. Just not fast enough to reliably pay all the bills.

Drive-by tourists were usually in flip-flops and T-shirts, camera phones at the ready. This man was in a suit—expensive by the looks of it, not that I know much about suits. No tie, and the first few buttons of his shirt were undone, making me wonder if this was his version of casual.

"Hi," I said, donning my customer service smile. I started to wave, then realized I was still clutching two handfuls of random crystals. I quickly dumped them back into the display, which looked exactly the same as when I had started—possibly worse.

"Hello." His hands were shoved into his pockets as he wandered in, surveying the shop with a look that seemed more critical than curious. I looked around at the homey, slapdash assortment of tables and shelves, all covered in merchandise. With the collections of herbs, bones, and other odds and ends that might appear random to the untrained eye, I could see that the Cottage more closely resembled a witch's hut in a fantasy film than a place of business. Certainly we were nothing like the sleek, contemporary offices where mages plied their trade.

"Welcome to Chanterelle Cottage." My tone was still polite, but a chill had crept in. For some reason his flat perusal of the shop was making me defensive. I much preferred the awestruck whispers or nervous chatting of tourists, even if they snapped too many pictures and couldn't stop touching things.

Broomhilde chose that moment to come twitching down the center aisle. She knocked a spell jar off the shelf, and I lunged to catch it before it shattered. When I straightened up, I caught a pleasant, woodsy aroma—eucalyptus maybe—and breathed it in before realizing that I was smelling *him* because I was entirely too close, with only a few unprofessional inches between us. I stepped back hurriedly and busied myself returning the jar to its place, willing the sudden heat in my cheeks to dissipate. If the man was disturbed by my invasion—and inhalation—of his personal space, he didn't show it. He watched with bemusement as the broom swept merrily between us.

"Doesn't seem like the most practical use of magic," he said. He wasn't wrong, but I prepared to defend Broomhilde anyway. I was the only one allowed to insult my broom-sibling.

Before I could reply, Broomhilde started sweeping at his shoes with vigor, even though they were spotless and polished to perfection. I snatched her handle before it could jab his eye out and dragged her to the open door of the stock room. I threw the broom inside and yanked the door shut. I took a second to compose myself, trying not to think about the mess she was going to make of the salt and Florida Water, and then I turned back around.

"Can I help you with something?" The question did not come out nearly as composed as I'd hoped. Damn.

His eyebrows rose slightly. He was white, with short dark hair and bangs that fell across his forehead in a way that looked effortless but undoubtedly took a lot of work every morning. Overall, I found him attractive in that urbane, aristocratic way where you can't decide if you want to seduce them or send them to the guillotine.

"Do you own the shop?" he asked, and I blinked out of my reverie. Double damn, I was definitely not supposed to be thinking about seducing customers. Or decapitating them, for that matter.

"My parents do." I offered what I hoped was a friendly smile as I made my way behind the counter, a position that would hopefully restore my equilibrium. Mama had told me before that if resting bitch face were a thing—which it isn't because it's an offensive, sexist construct—I would definitely have it. But I really was trying to be friendly. Not only could we not afford to lose customers to poor service, but I was oddly flattered that he thought I was the owner.

That day under my apron I was wearing my typical attire of loose flannel shirt, jean shorts, and my worn-out brown leather boots. Farm-girl hipster chic, Mim liked to call it. (The "chic" designation was sheer generosity on her part.) I had inherited Mama's genes, but unfortunately none of her skill with the eyeliner pen. And even though I had taken the time to straighten my hair to a sleek shine that morning, I had promptly pulled it into a messy top bun and sweated it into a frizzy mess while working the limpia.

Most people took one look at me and assumed I was just the shop girl. They always wanted to know where the real witches were.

Supposedly, you should dress for the job you want. Sometimes I wondered, if I dressed more like a boss, would my parents finally start to see me as a potential partner in the business? There was nothing wrong with being a shop girl, but I was a witch, first and foremost, and the Cottage was my life. I wanted to invest in it accordingly.

There was probably a "boss witch" aesthetic I could emulate. I made a mental note to google it later, and maybe some eyeliner tutorials for good measure.

"The Sparrows," the man said musingly. "Are you Charlotte?"

I blinked in surprise, but it wasn't too weird for someone to know the name of the family of witches who owned Chanterelle Cottage. Anyone in town could have told him.

"That's me," I said, rallying myself. "Everyone calls me Charlie."

I extended my hand across the counter, and he came over to shake it. He had a nice grip, firm but not painful.

"Sterling Fitzgerald," he said.

It was my turn to raise an eyebrow.

"Sterling? That's . . ."

"Pretentious, I know."

"I was going to say interesting," I lied feebly.

He smiled, and for all the cool air of criticism he'd exuded upon entering, it was a nice smile. Nice suit, nice handshake, nice smile, nice face. As I pulled my hand away, I had to resist the urge to smooth down my hair. Not that it would do any good in this humidity.

"Everyone calls me Fitz," he said.

"I guess that's slightly less pretentious than Sterling."

His smile widened, and I grinned back, more at ease now that the ice had been broken. Resting bitch face or not, I was a people person. There was a reason I didn't mind working the front of the shop most of the time, fielding all the day-to-day customer service antics while my moms focused more on spell-work.

"I think this is the part where I say you must be new in town," I said.

"Is it that obvious?"

"Let's just say the closest place that sells suits is the Men's Wearhouse three towns away."

"I moved here last week from Boston. Someone told me about your shop, so I thought I'd come check it out."

"We sell products for witches and laypeople alike." I paused, but if he'd caught my invitation for him to tell me which category he fell into, he didn't acquiesce. "Spell and potion ingredients, charms, minor spell jars. For anything more complicated, we provide free consultations. Satisfaction guaranteed."

It was a spiel I could rattle off in my sleep. He was watching me with a faint amusement that made me itch. I wasn't as good at reading auras as Mim was, but there was definitely something off about his. Like a drop of ink diffusing in an otherwise clear pool.

"Can you do tarot readings?" He nodded toward the hand-written sign at my elbow, which offered forty-dollar readings, no appointment required.

"I can."

"Are you any good?"

"Only one way to find out."

There was an undeniable smirk playing around his lips, which I ignored as I pushed aside the clay bowl and retrieved my deck from under the counter. I kept my cards in a mango wood box that was hand-carved with the tree of life. Before I opened the lid, I took a second to release the irritation that had begun festering in my gut. I set aside the selenite that I stored with the cards to keep them clear of negative energy, then spread a black silk cloth over the wooden countertop. I'd cleansed the deck a couple nights ago with the full moon and hadn't used them since, so they were fresh and ready.

"Do you have any questions in particular you'd like answered?" I asked.

"Like when am I going to die?"

I shook my head.

"'If' and 'when' questions are no good. The future isn't set in stone. It's constantly evolving based on our decisions."

"That sounds like a convenient way to let you off the hook for any predictions that don't come true."

I had a feeling he was trying to get a rise out of me, and I wasn't about to oblige.

"Try 'how' or 'what' instead."

He appeared to give this some thought.

"I'm starting a new job on Monday," he said. "That's why I

moved here. Can you tell me how it's going to work out for me?"

"Okay." I wondered what type of job would convince someone like him to move from Boston to Owl's Hollow. Maybe the cards would be generous and give me some specifics.

Focusing on that, I shuffled the cards and fanned them out facedown across the black silk. The deck had been passed down from my grandmother on Mim's side. They were a soft cream color with simple black illustrations accented with gold. Well loved and well worn.

"Pick out ten cards," I said.

He selected his cards, and I swept the rest of the deck back into the box. I laid out the cards using the Celtic Cross spread. Two cards in the center, a horizontal laid over a vertical, four cards around them in a cross pattern, then the last four vertically down the right side.

He watched all of this with that same vague air of amusement, and I had to concentrate on keeping that provocation from leaking into the deck. When I was sure my mind was intent only on the reading, I flipped the cards in the order I'd placed them. I scanned the images, gathering some general impressions while I fiddled absently with the red ribbon on my wrist. The cards were evenly split between upright and reversed, but even so I was getting a dark impression from the spread. A prickling instinct like the seconds before a lightning strike.

I decided to keep that to myself until I'd parsed out the individual cards. It wasn't always helpful to tell the client everything you were gleaning from the spread. I tapped the vertical card in the center.

"This is the Querent." I slid away the horizontal card covering it, so that he could see the full picture. He leaned down to get a better look, resting his forearms on the countertop. "It tells about your current state of being. Who you are." The Emperor, upright. I tapped the card again, mostly in thought, while I mused over the illustration of a throne with a sword and scepter crossed over the center.

"So who am I?" His voice was low, and I realized how close we were, with only three feet of counter space between us. Warmth bloomed up my neck.

"You're not just starting a new job." To my chagrin, there was a noticeable quiver in my voice. I powered through it. "You're the boss. The owner, if I had to guess."

"I thought the cards meant you didn't have to guess."

I ignored him—though I did note with some satisfaction that he hadn't contradicted me—and tapped the second card in the center.

"The Crossing tells us what opposing forces will be against you. Five of Wands, reversed, suggesting competition, ambition, and untrustworthiness." That gnawing unrest in my gut had intensified, but I couldn't quite wrap my head around it. I let my instinct guide me, like I'd been taught. "Competition is going to be your main problem, but I wouldn't underestimate the other two."

I caught a flicker of surprise on his features, which puzzled me even more. None of those were particularly odd problems to face when you were starting a new business. If anything, I would have expected him to point out how generic a prediction it was. I decided to take advantage of his silence and forge onward.

"Next card is the Foundation, and it addresses the origin of your question." I rested a finger on the Star, reversed. "You're insecure about the new venture, even though you're qualified. Something is causing you to doubt yourself."

I had fallen into the groove of the reading now, which was my favorite place to be. The cards sang to me like a choir in perfect harmony, granting me images and feelings that I'd learned over the years to hone into predictions. Fitz seemed to have lost his sardonic edge. I couldn't tell if it was because my words were resonating with him or because he was getting bored.

"Next is the Recent Past, which is exactly what it sounds like. This is the upright Eight of Cups, which speaks of disillusionment, of walking away from the past and into a new beginning. Whatever you left behind in Boston, you don't want it to follow you here." I hesitated, wondering if he would have something to say to that, but his features were stone as he stared down at the spread. Not so much as a twinge to give away what he was thinking. "Up next is the Crown. This tells us what possibilities might be in store, depending on how you handle the present. Good news is that the Nine of Pentacles represents love, fortune, and success. Bad news is that it's far from a certainty—it always depends on the decisions you make. The rest of the spread will help shed some light on what might influence your decisions."

"And does it tell you whether consulting an oracle is a good or bad decision?" he asked, and I was strangely relieved by the return of his dry humor, even if he still wasn't making eye contact.

"Could be a little of both." I touched the next card. "The Future is also pretty self-explanatory. It's similar to the Crown, but more . . . independent of your individual choices."

I hesitated, studying the drawing of a robed woman standing between two pillars. The High Priestess in reverse.

"Let me guess," he said, leaning closer to study the card. "This one is not a promise of love, fortune, and success."

"In reverse, the High Priestess represents secrets and lies." I fidgeted. At least we were getting to the core of this uneasiness in my chest. "Be careful of who you trust." *And other people need to be careful of trusting you.* I left the rest unsaid, because I couldn't be certain it was a truth from the card or a thought from my own mind.

"My father has told me that plenty of times for free."

"Next card tells us about your current emotional state," I said, not rising to the bait. I picked up the reversed Queen of Swords and smiled to myself. "Cynicism, inaccessibility, and a sharp tongue. What a shock."

"Shouldn't you be nicer to a paying customer?"

"I can only share what the cards are telling me," I replied innocently. "Take it up with them."

"You've yet to tell me anything that couldn't be picked up from an amateur cold reading."

Hot indignation prickled along my back. I was half a second away from gathering up my cards and tossing him out of the store.

"If you're so sure I'm a fraud, then why did you want a reading in the first place?" My buzz from the limpia and my parents' earlier praise had faded completely, as if Sterling Fitzgerald's unimpressed demeanor had leached it away.

He shrugged.

"I was hoping you would prove me wrong."

Fine, two could play at that game. I snatched up the next card.

"External Forces. This tells me about the influences on your life and relationships. The Ten of Swords, upright." I glared at it, demanding it give up its secrets. A sick foreboding twined through me as the image clarified itself in my mind. "Someone you loved betrayed you. That's why you left Boston. You thought you could trust them, and they stabbed you in the back."

I looked up, half hoping I was wrong. This cruel double-edged blade of betrayal and loss was not something I'd wish on anyone. Even this city-slick asshole.

But the moment our gazes locked, I knew I wasn't wrong. It was all there, everything I was sensing, everything the card had shown me. A life-shattering, world-ending sort of pain. The kind that drives you away from everything you thought you knew, in search of someplace—anyplace—that's safe from the heartache.

"I'm sorry." My voice sounded faraway to my own ears.

He blinked and came back to himself. That cool, disinterested expression slid back into place. He checked his watch.

"Unfortunately, I have to go," he said. "I'm running late for a meeting in town."

"There are two more cards." The reading wasn't complete without the full spread to tie all the disparate pieces together and give him a clearer picture of how he might shape his future.

"You'll have to let me know if there's anything of dire importance." He fished two twenties out of his wallet, but I raised my hand to stop him.

"This one's on me." I wasn't sure why I said that—he could clearly afford it. But I felt bad about how the reading had gone, even though I'd only said what the cards revealed to me. I guess I just felt bad for *him*.

He put the bills on the counter anyway. His tight smile didn't quite meet his eyes.

"It was nice to meet you, Charlie. I'm sure I'll see you around."

Before I found my voice to reply, he was already out the door.

I stared after him for a few seconds, then studied the remaining two cards. For Hopes and Desires, there was the upright Three of Swords: freedom, liberation, a way out. That made sense, given what he was leaving behind in Boston. Last of all was the Outcome, based on the path he was currently on. A nude figure encircled by a ribbon, holding a wand in each hand. The World in reverse.

Emptiness and disappointment.

I wondered if that counted as being of dire importance. Something told me Fitz was no stranger to either of those. He'd left behind a miasma of negative energy that promised to give me a headache if I lingered in it too long. So much for my limpia.

With a jolt, I remembered the unnatural disaster I'd let loose on the remnants of my spell ingredients, and I raced to the back room. As I feared, Broomhilde had very helpfully scattered the salt across the floor. My apprehension about Fitz's tarot was forgotten as I stormed off in search of a real, proper broom.

"You're my least favorite sibling," I called over my shoulder.

In response, Broomhilde knocked over the bottle of Florida Water and kept right on sweeping.

CHAPTER TWO

I made macaroni and cheese from a box for dinner, because it had turned out to be that sort of day. My parents decided to run some errands and have a date night after their meeting at the bank, so I was alone except for Mim's cat Sophie, a massive gray Norwegian forest cat who excelled at nudging things off countertops to distract me, then stealing bites of my food.

Tandy didn't stop by after all, which was a reprieve for me but a loss for the Cottage, since she had a platinum card that she loved to pull out when she visited. After Sterling Fitzgerald, the only other customers all day were a couple of teenage girls. When they found out we didn't sell magic to minors—or perform love spells—they left in a huff, but not before one of them informed me that she would just hire a mage because witches were old news anyway. I don't know what she expected me to do with that information. As they stalked out, I resisted the urge to hex them, not necessarily for moral reasons but because black magic always gives me hives.

The annual summer lull seemed to be lasting longer every year. Typically business picked up around this time in late July, as people returned from vacations and started preparations for the school year. But we'd yet to see the usual uptick, which was worrying. Mim handled the bookkeeping, but I was pretty sure our profit margin couldn't withstand many more days like today.

The ringing bell announced my parents' return. I finished up the last bite of macaroni and pushed the bowl aside for Sophie to lick clean.

"We bring the gift of cheesecake," Mama announced once they made it up the stairs. She set a plastic carry-out container and fork in front of me with a flourish.

"Celebration cheesecake?" I asked, but my hopes were immediately dashed by the expressions on their faces. "So consolation cheesecake, then."

"The loan officer wasn't impressed by our proposal." Mim kicked off her shoes and yanked out her giant daisy earrings before sinking into the chair next to me. Sophie jumped immediately into her lap and began purring aggressively.

"Bastard suggested we cast ourselves a money spell," Mama said. "Like it's that easy."

It was a perfect opportunity for the suggestion that was perpetually on my mind, and I decided to seize it.

"We don't need a money spell. We don't need to restructure the loan either. You know I've got the capital to buy into the business."

I tried to maintain a calm, assertive air, but it was hard when the stakes were so high for me. I'd been saving the money for this exact purpose since high school, and with the help of some modestly successful investments and an inheritance from my grandparents, I had close to thirty thousand dollars. The saving was the easy part. Convincing my parents to accept the money had turned out to be the real challenge.

To be fair, I hadn't exactly proven myself an ideal business partner recently, but I didn't want to think about that right now.

They exchanged one of their patented cryptic glances, but I didn't need to be privy to their silent conversation to know what the answer was going to be. I knew I should be used to it by now, but my heart sank anyway.

"We'll have to think about it," Mama said.

"You've been saying that for years now." I tried to keep my tone even, as if through sheer equanimity I could convince them I was ready for this next step.

"I know," Mim said, scratching behind Sophie's ear. "But we don't think it's a good time, baby."

I squeezed the bridge of my nose and took a calming breath. It was the same reason they always gave, when they could be convinced to give one. *Not a good time.* I knew it was code for other concerns that they didn't want to share with me. They didn't think I knew what I was doing. They didn't think I was ready for the responsibility. How could I blame them, after the incident with the fairy ring?

Nearly a year ago, the homeowner association of the wealthiest suburb in Owl's Hollow had come to the Cottage with a job that paid more than we typically earned in six months. (I shudder to think how much those suburbanites pay in HOA fees.) Some kind of fungus or disease had ravaged all the lawns in the neighborhood, thwarting the best efforts of their landscapers. The commission wasn't just to clear the pestilence but to spell every yard to remain perpetually green and trimmed. For magic of that size and scope, they normally would have gone straight to a magecraft firm in the city, but Tandy DiAngelo was on the board, and she insisted that witches could do the job better and cheaper.

She would have been right, except that Mim and Mama were on a rare vacation, and I was harebrained enough to think I could pull it off by myself. I was spectacularly, detrimentally wrong.

After that, I couldn't blame my parents for not wanting me as an equal partner.

"I know I messed up last year." I stared down at my cheesecake and fiddled with the plastic fork. My stomach was twisted into knots. "But if you let me—"

"This isn't about the fairy ring." Mim gave my shoulder a squeeze. "You made a mistake, but you're an incredibly talented witch. We've never doubted that. You were sewing poppet charms when you were ten years old."

"Our little prodigy." Mama smiled fondly.

I squirmed in my seat. When they started using words like "prodigy" and "gifted," I was always struck by the same mix of embarrassment and chagrin. I didn't like being reminded that I had once been a witch of endless potential and had instead grown into . . . me.

"You don't have to worry about the Cottage." Mim gave my shoulder another squeeze. "We'll figure it out."

"Besides," Mama said, stealing my fork and a bite of cheesecake. "Ruby channeled her inner Karen and got us an appointment in October with the vice president of the bank to plead our case. I'm sure we'll be able to talk him around."

Their propensity for trying to shield me from business woes, as if I were still running around with skinned knees and pigtails, pretending to talk to goblins and gnomes, made me want to scream, equanimity be damned. Instead I changed the subject.

"Hey, do you know of any new businesses opening in town?"

"Looking for a new job?" Mama wriggled her eyebrows at me.

"How else are we going to afford to repair all the damage done by your second-favorite child?" I asked. *And why shouldn't I look for a new job, if you're determined to keep me as a cashier forever?* "Actually, I did a reading for a client today. He's the owner of a new business, but he didn't say what."

Not that I could blame Fitz for not sticking around for idle chitchat after I'd tossed what must be a painful memory into his face. In retrospect, I probably should have shown a bit more tact. I'd let my annoyance at his smug dismissal of tarot get the better of me. Not my most professional reading.

"I haven't heard of anything," said Mim. "But I did hear Mayor Smithers is officially retiring. Apparently his wife threatened to divorce him unless he quit and moved with her to the Maldives like they've been planning for years."

"The Maldives," Mama said dreamily, stealing another bite of my cheesecake. "Now, there's a good retirement plan."

"We're going to have to rob the bank on our next visit if we want to afford a retirement of any kind." Mim moved ever so slightly, and Sophie expressed her affront with an outraged meow before darting under the table and down the hallway.

"Does this mean Bonnie will take over as mayor?" I snatched my fork back from Mama before she could finish off my dessert.

"At least until they can have a special election."

I wondered if Sterling Fitzgerald had political aspirations. I hadn't gotten that vibe—from him or the cards—but it wasn't like tarot (or my intuition for that matter) was a foolproof science.

"She'll probably run," said Mim, "and she'd definitely win. Everyone loves her."

"Hope so," I said. Bonnie and I were good friends, and more important, she was a friend of witchcraft. As deputy mayor, she sided with us every year when we had to renew our license to practice magic, which was contested annually by a small group of anti-magic residents. Not everyone liked the idea of folks like us plying our trade. Bonnie as mayor would be a very good thing, and despite my parents' insistence that everything would be fine, my gut told me that we needed all the help we could get.

CHAPTER THREE

I rode my bike into town the next day, which is less idyllic than
it sounds, since it was three miles and hilly. But Mim had taken
the car to visit a friend, and I had never bothered to buy my own
since I rarely had reason to leave Owl's Hollow. The problem is
that the ride used to be a lot easier when I was in my twenties,
and the late summer weather was still hot more often than it
was mild.

Once I reached Main Street, I was dripping with sweat, and
not in a hot-beach-babe kind of way. The strip was crowded
with folks in their Sunday best, heading to Madge's Café or The
Blue Spoon for lunch. Owl's Hollow isn't particularly religious,
but we do have a little church on top of the hill overlooking the
old cemetery. The white chapel with its steeple and rosy stained-
glass windows started off Baptist but has become more nonde-
nominational over the years in an effort to retain a congregation.
(Most Baptists had kept their hard-line view on witchcraft and
magic, even as it became mainstream, but more modern
churches have looser restrictions around the craft. I was informed by Pastor Dale at the farmer's market one morning,

when we were stuck in line together waiting to buy strawber-
ries, that as long as I didn't ascribe my magic to Satan or pagan
deities, then I was still welcome in his flock. What a relief.)

I returned a few greetings from the sidewalk as I pedaled up
the street but didn't slow down—mostly because I was afraid if
I lost my momentum, I wouldn't make it up the final hill to my
destination. Main Street ends in a cobblestone roundabout that
encircles a patch of green grass popular for picnics. The town
hall, with its classic red brick and white pillars, is the centerpiece of the municipal plaza, nestled in between the library and
the post office.

I took a second to redo my ponytail, then leaned my bicycle
against the rack and headed inside. My powder blue Electra
Townie was one of my most prized possessions, but with the
protection sigil carved on the underside of the seat, I never
bothered with a cable lock. If anyone but me tried to take it for
a ride, they wouldn't make it far before the wheels locked up
and the handlebars became red-hot.

Even though the town hall was closed on Sundays, when I'd
texted Bonnie the night before she'd promised to leave the door
unlocked for me. I wasn't surprised when she told me she'd be
working. There was probably a lot of preparation to be done in
the wake of Mayor Smithers's retirement. I found Bonnie in her
office, more dressed-down than usual in jeans and a pink chif-
fon blouse. Her beautiful black curls were pushed off her face
with a floral headscarf. Six years ago, she'd become the first
Black woman in the history of Owl's Hollow to be elected to
the town council, and only the second member who was openly
queer. The achievement was both exciting and a little depress-
ing, considering the fact that in 1942, the citizens famously
elected a local chicken to the council, for laughs.

Bonnie had been making history ever since with each new
step up the political ladder. I'd always known she would make it

to the mayor's office someday, so the news about Smithers's early retirement was beyond thrilling. Hence my sweaty journey into town especially to congratulate her.

"Excuse me," I said, knocking on her open door. "I have a complaint about the disgraceful state of our park benches, and I demand to speak to the mayor."

She grinned and stood up.

"Well, I've got another couple of days until it's official, but I'll put you at the top of my list."

"Seriously, though, congratulations." I gave her a hug, though I kept enough distance between us to save her from my sweat. "I'm so excited for you. Are you nervous?"

"Less than I thought I'd be." She gestured for me to sit down. "But talk to me again after I've sworn my oath."

"Let me take you to brunch to celebrate. My treat."

"Only if you've got a spell up your sleeve that can empty my inbox."

"You have that already: it's called Delete All," I said. She gave a short laugh that was edged with the mania of someone who's been in the trenches of new notifications for far too long. "Come on, you still have to eat."

"Raincheck," she promised. "But there's something I've been meaning to talk to you about, so I'm glad you came by."

Her features were pinched as she scooped up her pen and started fiddling with it. Bonnie was usually pretty good at keeping her emotions under wraps—comes with being a politician, I guess—but I was able to read her moods for the most part. We'd been friends ever since our single disastrous date many years ago. She was happily married now, and she and her wife Jen loved nothing more than to tease me about how I'd chosen the night of our date to discover I was allergic to kombucha, and Bonnie had to rush me to the hospital for my sudden severe case of hives. For some reason they found a witch being allergic to kombucha hilarious. Ironically, that was the night she'd met Jen, an ER doctor, though they still refused to give me any credit for their happy union.

"What's up?" I asked.

"Don't get mad," she said. "I would have told you sooner, but I was kind of hoping it would end up falling through. There's a new business opening this week where the furniture store used to be. It's called Maven Enterprises."

"Okay." My gut churned with an echo of the foreboding I'd gotten the day before, while reading Sterling Fitzgerald's tarot.

"They're mages," she said with a wince.

"Oh." I blinked. "That is . . . not ideal."

"I told the mayor I didn't think it was a good idea." She twirled her pen wildly through her fingers. "But he didn't have a choice. Someone on the council sponsored their application, so he had to issue the temporary magic permit. In ninety days, there will be a full vote, but until then they're open for business."

"Who sponsored their application?" I demanded.

She fidgeted.

"Well, I guess it's public information. It was Larry Munch."

"Munch?" I echoed unbelievingly. The oldest council member was the town's premier anti-magic crusader. He spent all his spare time finding obscure, markedly unscientific studies about the dangers of magic use and writing raving op-eds for the local paper.

"I know," said Bonnie. "I thought for sure it was some kind of scam until the clerk called him and confirmed."

"He's up to something." I didn't think for a second that Munch had changed his tune. More likely he was trying to hurt the Cottage and figured that since he couldn't get our license revoked, running us out of business was the next best thing.

"Like I said, it's only ninety days," Bonnie said. "Then he'll have to get it through a community forum and council vote."

"Thanks for letting me know." I stood up abruptly. "I'll let you get back to work."

"You're not going over there, are you?"

"Where?" I asked innocently.

"You can't go harassing new businesses—even if they are mages."

"You make it sound like I'm headed over there with a torch and pitchfork. There's nothing wrong with one business owner extending a friendly hello to another. Now you should really get to work on those park benches."

"No hexes," she called after me. I saluted her on my way out.

The old furniture shop was only a few streets away, so I made it there in a couple minutes on my bike. Honestly, I didn't even expect they would be open. My plan was to get in some angry glaring from the sidewalk—maybe snoop through a window or two. The glass storefront had been replaced with mirrored glass, reflecting my own red-faced visage back at me. *MAVEN* was printed in a black, classic font above the door, with the "*A*" replaced by the alchemical symbol for air—a triangle transected by a horizontal line.

"Tacky," I muttered to myself. Mages didn't have anything to do with alchemy or the elements. They were egoists, obsessed with the concept of self, divorced from the natural world or other humans. Mim called their magic a type of anarchy. No rules, no discipline, no reliance on tradition or cooperation. That was why the Mage Institute had to be established, because who knew what havoc they would wreak otherwise.

The door was open, with a box fan sitting in front, blowing air outward. The interior was dim compared to the stark daylight, but I could make out a receptionist's desk with two legs and a pair of black ankle boots propped on it. I almost talked myself out of doing anything stupid, but in the end my curiosity got the better of me. Like I'd told Bonnie—nothing wrong with a neighborly hello.

I propped my bike against the brick wall of the building next door and sidled inside. I was greeted by the strong odor of fresh paint, which explained the fan. With the dark wood floors, matte gray walls, sleek leather chairs, and a black metal lighting fixture that looked more like a piece of modern art, it was as if I had stepped into a completely different town. Owl's Hollow waiting rooms tended more toward plastic chairs and cheap pendant lights. The dentist's office was considered the fanciest in town, on account of their huge tropical fish tank set into the wall.

No fish tanks here. The young white woman behind the desk—owner of the ankle boots—was wearing earbuds and preoccupied by her tablet. She sported crimson-dyed hair, perfect wing-tipped eyeliner, and an understated silver nose ring. When she caught sight of me, she pulled out her earbuds and swung her feet to the ground.

"Hiya," she said brightly. "We're not open till tomorrow, but I can set an appointment for you if you'd like."

I made a conscious effort to keep my face neutral and my voice calmly polite.

"No thanks. I saw the door open, and I was curious." I looked around, but they were underselling the whole magic aspect of the business. No signs, no paraphernalia, nothing to differentiate this from your typical corporate office. "So you guys are mages?"

"That's us," she said. "Sorry about the smell. The painters just finished yesterday. I'm Elinor." She stood and extended her hand over the desk. I didn't want to venture any deeper into enemy territory, but I couldn't exactly ignore her without being a total bitch. Besides, she seemed nice enough. Maybe she wasn't a mage herself.

"Charlie," I said, shaking her hand.

Elinor was a couple inches taller than me, willowy and chic in a black silk romper with a silver triple-moon necklace. To be honest, she embodied the boss witch aesthetic much more than I did, in my jean cutoffs and wrinkled Taylor Swift shirt that was a size too big because technically I usually slept in it. If I'd known I would be seeing anyone but Bonnie that day—much less my de facto rivals—I would have put in a little more effort.

"You sure you don't need an appointment for anything?" she asked. "Our prices are very reasonable." She flashed the same grin that I wore myself when I was courting customers. Instead of annoying me, it inspired a kinship with her that was entirely against my will.

"I'm sure," I said, trying to figure out how I could explain who I was without it sounding like I had come to spy on them, which of course had been my sole intention.

"No worries." She gave a dismissive wave, apparently deeming her obligation to the company discharged. "We're hosting a block party–type thing at the park on Friday night, to introduce ourselves to everyone. Free food, free booze, games for the kids, the whole nine yards. You should totally come—hang on, I have the flyers around here somewhere."

She opened a drawer and started digging around. I wanted to give a polite excuse and make my escape, but before I could say anything, another voice came from the corridor beyond the desk.

"Hey, El, have you seen my wallet?"

"I imagine it's in your pocket, where it always is," she said without pausing her search.

"If it was in my pocket, I wouldn't be—Charlie." Sterling Fitzgerald stopped short and stared at me in undisguised surprise. As for me, I wasn't shocked in the least. Tarot may not be an exact science, but I would've had to be pretty thick to not put two and two together. I'll admit it was still the slightest bit disconcerting to be face-to-face with him again, this time on his turf instead of mine. His stupid expensive suit and smug superiority from yesterday made so much more sense now.

"Hello," I said, in what I hoped was a coolly relaxed tone. "I thought I'd swing by and welcome you to the neighborhood."

"You guys have met?" Elinor looked between us curiously.

"Yesterday." Fitz had recovered from the momentary lapse of his unruffled mien. He was wearing a tie today, though the knot was loose, as if he'd been tugging on it. Jacketless, with his sleeves rolled up to his elbows, he looked slightly more casual but not any less sophisticated.

"He came into my shop for a tarot reading." I was trying to maintain my mellow composure, but I was the tiniest bit intimidated in this plush office, with two mages who looked as if they had actually spent some time in front of the mirror this morning. I tugged on the hem of my sweat-damp T-shirt. The unwelcome rush of self-consciousness made me petty. "He failed to mention the real reason he was in town."

"In my defense," said Fitz, leaning on the edge of the reception desk, with a faint smile tugging on his lips, "I thought your cards might be a little more helpful in that regard."

Before I could swing back with a cutting remark about there not being an arcana for jackasses, Elinor chimed in.

"Wait, you're one of the Chanterelle Cottage witches?" she asked. Rather than the disdain I might have expected, she clapped her hands together with unironic glee. "That's so cool."

"Um, thanks," I said.

"I read that article in *Vanity Fair* about your parents. Total icons."

The article had been a spotlight on small-town witches across the country, one of the few pieces of modern journalism that didn't paint local shops like the Cottage as a dying industry. Mim and Mama had been only two of at least ten witches interviewed. I wasn't sure if it was sweet or creepy that Elinor remembered them.

"I've been wanting to meet them for ages," she went on. "Fitzy, you should've told me you were going." She whacked him on the shoulder.

"I refuse to enable your minor celebrity stalking." He rubbed his arm and gave her a look but was otherwise unperturbed by her low-key fangirling.

I'd never considered Mim or Mama to be celebrities, minor or otherwise. And Elinor being nice to me was seriously undercutting my efforts to be an imperious bitch.

"Well, I need to get going," I said, inching backward.

"Wait!" Elinor ripped a few folders out of her drawer and had strewn half the contents across the desk before she found what she was looking for. A bright yellow flyer announcing a free community picnic on Friday, sponsored by Maven Enterprises. "You guys *have* to come. Please?"

I took the flyer but was caught off guard by her continued fervency, since she now knew who I was. Was she somehow unaware of what their new business could mean for the Cottage? Had centuries of bitter rivalry between mages and witches somehow escaped her notice? I couldn't help a questioning glance at Fitz, who was in the process of rolling his eyes. Jerk.

"Sure, we'll try," I said, just to spite him.

"Awesome." She was beaming. She gave Fitz a little shove— apparently his expression had not gone unnoticed. "Don't let my shithead brother scare you off. There's a reason we keep him in his office and away from the customers."

"I thought that was because I'm the one who does all the actual work," he said mildly.

Automatically, I studied their faces for signs of familial simi-larities. I thought I could see it a little in the nose, and they both had the same primrose blue eyes. And there was no missing the comfortable rapport that can only come from knowing some-one your whole life. When I was a kid, I used to pester my moms for a sibling, but they always joked that they'd gotten a perfect daughter on the first try, so there was no sense in trying again. Of course, when I was older, I'd realized the costs in-volved with the multiple failed rounds of intrauterine insemi-nation followed by the in vitro that finally brought me into existence. Even with Mim and Mama keeping me in the dark about family finances, I was able to do the math.

If Broomhilde was any indication of how annoying a human sibling could be, then maybe I was better off.

I waved the flyer at Elinor in a silent farewell and made my escape. On my way out, I heard them arguing about Fitz's wal-let, which apparently *had* been in his pocket the whole time. I tried and failed not to smile, then had to give myself a stern talking-to as I pedaled away. It was a smart idea to become ac-quainted with the new competition—keep your enemies closer and all that. But fraternizing was strictly off the table. There could be no friendship in war, and without a doubt that was where we were all headed.

CHAPTER FOUR

When I made it home, Mim and the car were still gone, and Mama was pacing the living room on her phone, talking animatedly in Spanish to her family.

I gave her a wave that went unnoticed and poured myself a glass of cold water. Sophie was mewing pitifully by her empty food bowl. She was notorious for tricking her way into more food, but also Mama *did* forget to feed her sometimes. Perhaps sensing my indecision, Sophie flopped onto her back to show me her fluffy belly while staring at me with her enormous green eyes. Even knowing her game, I was helpless to resist the cute factor. I opened a can of food and scraped it into her bowl. I tried to pet her, but now that she had no further use for me, she swatted me away.

"Rude," I told her. She kept eating but turned to show me her ass.

I brought my water into my bedroom and shut the door. As much as I wanted to lie in bed and obsess about the fate of the Cottage, I decided to turn my energy toward something more productive. I brought out a shoebox hidden in the back of my closet beneath a pile of sweaters.

There was a desk in my room—a gorgeous antique that had belonged to my grandfather on Mim's side—but it was perpetually covered in an assortment of crystals, scribbled notes on spells that had yet to be transcribed into my grimoire, and half-read books that I had every intention of finishing. My laptop lived on the floor next to my bed, and most of my real work was done on the woven rug in the center of the room. I yanked off my boots, pulled a throw pillow from the bed to sit on, and settled down cross-legged to open the box.

The orange origami butterflies, hand-painted with black veining, had turned out exactly how I wanted them. I had another box with the paper and paint, and I'd been adding more whenever I had free time. I was up to about fifty paper monarchs now, although I was hoping to double that before my parents' anniversary in October.

While I was pleased with the appearance of their gift, the actual execution of my idea left something to be desired. I'd been trying for months to breathe some artificial life into the butterflies, to finagle them into fluttering around in a vaguely natural way. Hell, at this point, I'd settle for unnatural. No matter what spells I tried or how firmly I set my intentions, they remained motionless scraps of paper. Heaven help me, I'd even asked Tandy DiAngelo to pass my conundrum around her contacts, but none of the suggestions by my fellow witches produced any results.

Unlike mages, who can summon magic spontaneously (hence their eternal superiority complex), witches depend on spellwork to draw upon the magic around us. It's all about maintaining balance with the world, both the natural and the spiritual. Don't get me wrong—I'd never wish to be a mage. They don't have to respect magic to use it, and that breeds not only recklessness and arrogance but also a high rate of burnout. Whereas witches can use magic to cleanse and rejuvenate both mind and body, mages can only use it extrinsically. Mama once explained to me that it was like being the world's greatest masseuse. Other people love you for it, but you can never give yourself a massage.

In times like these, I'll admit I was a little jealous that I couldn't snap my fingers and bring my butterflies to life. In the same way that the good-fortune spells my family regularly used for the Cottage didn't translate directly to winning the lottery, I couldn't simply will the paper to fly. I had to figure out the right balance of spellwork and intention—what trade I could make with the universe to coax the magic into being.

I spent a while halfheartedly prodding a butterfly with my oak wand tipped in iridescent blue-green labradorite (good for transformation), but unsurprisingly there were no results. My heart wasn't in it today. I gave up and flopped onto my back, staring up at the glow-in-the-dark stars that had been on my ceiling since I was a kid. Every time I tried to focus, my mind would drift back to the tarot reading yesterday, parsing through the cards and their meanings, especially the one that had caused Fitz to leave so abruptly. The Ten of Swords. Betrayal by someone he loved. Unfortunately, I doubted that my curiosity for more details would ever be sated, unless one of Owl's Hollow's gossip hounds found the trail. I certainly wasn't going to be getting close enough to the Fitzgeralds to find out for myself.

A knock on the door. *Shit.*

"One second!" I scooped up the butterflies and shoved them back into the box, then slid that under my bed. "Come in."

Mama entered. She was wearing her favorite ratty jeans and faded Dartmouth shirt (no one in my family had attended Dartmouth). Clearly, I came by my fashion sense honestly.

"Yoga or meditation?" she asked, looking down at me skeptically.

"Calisthenics," I said. "What's up? How's the family?"

She offered a small, mirthless smile.

"They're good. Doesn't look like we'll be able to visit this year."

Mama had three brothers, a sister, and a host of extended family in Texas. We had visited every summer when I was a kid, though I'd stopped joining my parents when I went to college. After my abuela passed, the visits grew more infrequent. Mama would have liked to see them more, but the timing—and money—didn't always work out. Though this time, the reason might have more to do with how badly I'd fucked up last year when they'd left me in charge of the shop.

I ejected that possibility from my mind before it could take root. I wasn't going to hijack Mama's feelings with my own self-pity.

"I'm sorry," I said. "That sucks."

She slumped onto the edge of my bed.

"That's what technology is for, I guess."

"You hate technology."

"What can I say? I'm a martyr for mi familia." Her tone was light but lacked her usual good humor. Guilt pricked me. Now that I thought about it, I hadn't joined them on the Texas pilgrimage in years. I didn't know Mama's side of the family well, and I knew she wished that I was more in touch with my Mexican roots. Sometimes I did too, but that part of my ancestry was so distant from my everyday life that it usually seemed irrelevant.

"Let's start a travel fund jar," I said. "Next year all three of us can go. We'll close the Cottage and make a vacation of it."

She perked up visibly, and the tightness in my chest loosened. I didn't exactly love the idea of spending my vacation with a bunch of relatives I barely knew, but I would get the Mexican flag tattooed on my ass if it would make Mama happy.

"I like that idea." She hopped up and flashed a genuine smile. "I was thinking breakfast for dinner tonight. You want to whip up some pancakes?"

"Sure."

She started to leave, then paused, studying me with renewed skepticism.

"Something's wrong," she said. "Tell me."

I'd never been able to slip anything past her. Which hardly seemed fair, since she'd once taken a week to notice when Mim dyed a blue streak in her hair. I decided not to expound on my white-half-guilt. We had a more pressing problem.

"A mage firm opened up in town."

"*What.*" Mama sank back onto my bed, mouth agape and pancakes forgotten.

I nodded grimly and relayed everything Bonnie had told me about Larry Munch and the temporary magic license. I left out the fact that I'd read a mage's tarot yesterday. Not because it was a secret—I just didn't want to get into it. Also, even though I had confidence in my ability and knew my reading had been accurate, I still couldn't help but feel that the encounter had left me with egg on my face.

"I hate everything," Mama announced, when I'd finished. Not exactly the reassurance I might have hoped for. "And we're having margaritas with our pancakes."

"Obviously." I climbed to my feet and followed her into the kitchen. I started pulling out ingredients while she poured us each a pregame shot of tequila.

We clinked our glasses in a miserable toast and threw them back. I was about to pour a second when Mim came flying through the door in a flurry of frenetic energy.

"Stop everything," she cried. "I have news."

"If it's about the mages," Mama said dryly, "we already know."

"No, it's about Tandy DiAngelo."

"What happened?" Mama and I both asked at the same time.

"Wait, what about mages?"

"There's a new magecraft firm in town," I said. "What about Tandy?"

"You're kidding me." Mim frowned. "I sensed a bad wind blowing, but I hoped it was because bell-bottoms were coming back in style."

"*Mim.*"

"Oh, right. Tandy. Someone turned her into a chicken."

CHAPTER FIVE

Of all the witches in the tristate area, we Sparrow women would've probably been Tandy's last choice for her saviors. I'm pretty sure that after my colossal fuckup with the HOA's commission, she had lost any of the grudging respect she had for my abilities, and by extension my teachers, Mim and Mama. Unluckily for her, we were the only other witches whose names her husband had ever bothered to learn, so we were the ones who got the call.

The DiAngelos lived in a regal white colonial that was funded by Carl's moderately successful used-car dealership. I noted (with more than a little resentment) that their lawn, along with every other lawn in the neighborhood, was emerald green and perfectly trimmed. There was a definite air of Stepford about the place. I'm of the firm belief that feminism means women should be able to live however they want without judgment, but I'd be lying if I said that Tandy's lifestyle of choice didn't make me cringe. It was composed mostly of pastel yoga attire, yappy Pomeranians, and a penchant for referring to her two children exclusively as "my darling little angels."

It was dusk by the time my moms and I arrived. The two darling little angels had been packed away to Grandma's house for the night. Tandy was currently clucking around the spare bedroom, which had been converted into her private yoga studio and altar room. The three of us filed inside with Carl, who had brought a bowl of shredded lettuce in hopes of appeasing her. We all stared for a good ten seconds, because of course Tandy couldn't just be regular-type poultry. The chicken strutting around was gray with a huge white bouffant of feathers on its head, resembling an oversized British barrister's wig.

"Oh my god," Mama whispered, as she raised her phone to snap a picture. I swear there were tears pooling in her eyes. "This is the best day of my life."

"You have a wife and daughter," Mim reminded her.

"I said what I said."

Carl let out a baffled noise between affront and despair.

"Don't worry," I told him, talking over my parents. "She's going to be fine."

"You've seen something like this before?" he asked, with a new note of hopefulness.

I glanced at my parents, who both gave a little shake of their heads. Full transmutation wasn't the kind of magic you came across often, especially involving humans. Witchcraft wasn't suited for it, unless you dug deep into the kind of black magic hexes that reasonable witches with any sense of self-preservation steered clear of. And using that kind of powerful magic against a living being would get a mage blackballed by the Institute immediately.

"She's going to be fine," I repeated to Carl. I lacked conviction, but it was the best I could offer.

The doorbell rang.

"That'll be Harriet and Mark," said Mim.

"Who?" Carl asked. "How many witches did you invite into my house?"

"Only the Wharburtons," Mim assured him.

"But Lucas Hansen will probably show up," Mama said. "He usually does."

"I don't know any of these people," Carl grumbled as he followed us downstairs. I wasn't sure how he'd managed to be married to Tandy for so long without meeting the three other witches who lived in Owl's Hollow. I got the impression he didn't concern himself much with that part of Tandy's life.

"We need their help with the spell." I did not add that first we needed their help brainstorming a spell that might work. My parents and I had been spitballing the whole drive over here, and we still didn't have any foolproof ideas.

Mark and Harriet Wharburton were a retired couple who mostly used their craft around the house and garden. They spent over half the year in an RV, visiting their children and grandchildren, who were spread across the country. Mark was especially skilled with garden magic, so he usually came by every spring to give our bed of herbs a little boost.

As predicted, Lucas Hansen wandered up the driveway behind the Wharburtons, with no indication of how he'd gotten here or how he'd even known to come. His voicemail was always full, and he never read text messages, so Mim hadn't bothered sending one.

Lucas was somewhere in his midforties and considered himself a drifter by choice. He was forever sporting shaggy brown hair past his shoulders, tangled with briars and wildflowers in a style that may or may not have been purposeful. He kept his long beard in three braids and wore a shapeless gray smock, ratty jeans, and brown sandals so that he perpetually looked like he was walking off a cult compound. He was eerily in tune with nature and claimed to regularly perform astral projection. No one thought he was a liar, but he also did a lot of mushrooms, so his astral trips may have had more to do with that than witchcraft.

Carl was clearly distressed at the giant old RV parked in his driveway and the number of witches crowding into his foyer, and at the sight of Lucas he seemed ready to put his foot down. But Mim suggested he pour himself a drink while we worked and herded the rest of us upstairs before he could protest. We shut ourselves in the yoga room.

The six of us gathered in a circle around Tandy, watching in silence while she pecked disdainfully at the bowl of lettuce. We weren't a coven—too much organization was required for that, plus no one wanted to risk Tandy being officially in charge of anything. And Tandy, of course, looked down her nose at Lucas and considered the Wharburtons too old to be relevant. But we were the not-quite-coven she was stuck with, so she would have to get over herself, assuming we ever managed to transmute her back into herself again.

I shied away from that line of thinking. Half of witchcraft was the belief that your magic would succeed. I didn't want to resign us to failure before we'd even begun.

"Oh dear," said Harriet. "Do we know who's done this to her?"

"No idea," said Mim.

"I'm sure we could come up with a list of people who would *want* to do this to her," Mama said unhelpfully.

"I've never seen anything like this before." Mark stooped down with some difficulty to get a closer look. "Do you think she understands us?"

"Tandy, cluck twice if you can understand us," Mama said. Chicken Tandy ignored her, which wasn't incontrovertible proof, since Tandy might also ignore Mama out of spite, even in her current predicament.

"Consciousness is secondary," Lucas said. It took us all a little while to realize that he had no intention of continuing or explaining himself.

"Right." Mim clapped her hands together. "The one thing I do know about transmutation is that the longer the object—or person, I guess—is changed, the harder it is to change them back. So we should get to work."

We had packed into the car's trunk any ingredients we thought might possibly come in handy, and the Wharburtons had an impressive array of herbs in their camper. Lucas's contribution was a handful of unidentified mushrooms from his pocket, which Mim assured him—despite Mama's protests—that he could keep for himself. After some snooping, I also found that the big white cabinet in the yoga room was stocked with essentials in neatly organized bins. (Tandy clearly had some kind of labelmaker fetish.)

We all had our grimoires on hand, of course, and after a lot of flipping pages and comparing notes, we decided on a few spells to try. Carl was sitting in his living room watching television. He glared at us as we tromped up and down the stairs with armloads of witchy paraphernalia but otherwise left us to our devices. I liked him less and less as the night went on but told myself that everyone deals with their emotions differently. He must have been worried about his wife, in his own way.

We tried a few different variations on healing and cleansing spells and anti-curse rituals. Every time we started a new spell, I could tell before we'd even finished that it wasn't going to work. If half of witchcraft was belief, then the other half was intuition. And my intuition told me that we weren't coming at this from the right angle. Simply flooding Chicken Tandy with white magic wasn't going to do the trick.

After a couple hours, we were all reaching a level of frustration that was not conducive to any kind of purifying spellwork.

The yoga room was crowded and hot and stank of chicken shit. When Carl made the mistake of sticking his head into the room to ask if we were done yet, he was lucky to escape without a hex.

I was beginning to think we were in over our heads and that maybe this was a task better suited for Maven Enterprises. I knew I wasn't the only one.

But that had to be the frustration talking, not my intuition. I refused to believe that the universe was nudging me to go crawling to Sterling Fitzgerald for help. The witches of Owl's Hollow were perfectly capable of looking after their own.

As Mim and Mama bickered about whether the phase of the moon might be hindering our efforts, I left the room to clear my head. The upstairs hallway was lined with family photographs, each one professionally posed and edited to be magazine perfect. Tandy, Carl, and the two darling little angels beamed back at me, first in matching Christmas sweaters, then wearing all white on the beach, and finally in their Sunday best, hands stretched toward the sky as a shower of autumn leaves fell around them.

At the end of the hallway was a smaller picture in a home-made wooden frame covered in kid's finger paint. The photograph was a candid shot, a little blurry, of a much younger Tandy and Carl standing in front of this house. Carl was holding a *Sold* sign aloft with a proud grin, and Tandy was smiling down at the infant in her arms.

It occurred to me then what all our failed spellwork had been missing.

I raced back into the yoga room and flipped through the early pages of my grimoire until I found the notes for a ritual I'd created when I was in high school, and my friend Katie's beloved dog had gone missing. Using that as a reference, I started sketching out a new ritual, tweaking it here and there for our current situation, based on all the knowledge I'd picked up in the years since.

Mim and Mama, their argument forgotten, peered over my shoulder while I worked. It didn't take them long to catch on to what I was thinking.

"Genius," Mama said. I tried to ignore the flurry of inter-mingled pride and anxiety in my chest and focus on what I was doing.

"The Wunjo rune here instead of Eihwaz, I think," said Mim, pointing. "Then it's perfect."

I made the correction and held up my grimoire.

"One of you should do it." The last thing we needed was for me to mess up the spell and turn Tandy back into a human with a beak or other chicken-y characteristics, no matter how much Mama might enjoy the idea.

"Nonsense," said Mim. "You're the one who came up with it."

"But—"

"Don't argue with your mother," Mama said. "It's your spell. You're doing it."

I was tempted to ask what she was going to do if I kept arguing—ground me? But I resisted.

"How can we help?" Harriet asked, once I'd explained my line of thinking to them. All of us got to work, with the exception of Lucas, who was hand-feeding Tandy sunflower seeds in the corner and talking to her quite seriously about the virtues of veganism.

I laid down a salt circle in the middle of the room and placed white candles at the four cardinal directions. Meanwhile, Harriet lit a charcoal disc in a small cauldron while Mark searched our supplies for a jar of myrrh resin. Mama mixed together a paste of bay leaves, salt, rowan berries, and moon water, then Mim went to fetch Carl from the living room.

Lucas held Tandy for me so that I could use the paste to trace the angular *P* of the Wunjo rune onto her crest. Wunjo was the Futhark rune of joy, representing the ties of family, friends, and community. Mim returned with Carl, and I directed him to stand in the center of the sacred circle. I took Tandy from Lucas and plopped her into her bewildered husband's arms.

"Tell me what a typical day looks like for Tandy," I said.

Carl blinked at me.

"What does that have to do with anything?"

"Trust me, it's important."

"Um, well, I guess she—uh—does yoga? Sometimes? The kids go to school—but I guess it's summer now, so not that. Yesterday we had pork roast for dinner."

Behind him, Mim and Mama exchanged a glance. I tried to keep my tone pleasant and customer-friendly.

"Anything else? What does her daily routine look like? Does she have hobbies other than yoga that she enjoys?" My ritual was a call to home, an appeal to whatever part of Tandy remained to come back to her true self.

"I—I guess she cleans," said Carl. "We got a new laundry machine so she . . . likes that, I guess."

I stared at him, and he stared back at me, helpless. Dear god, the man had no concept of what his wife's life looked like outside of cooking and cleaning for him. For the first time, I began to feel sympathy for Tandy DiAngelo. I knew that informing him he was a shit husband wasn't going to do us any good, but also I couldn't exactly call Tandy home if I had no concept of what her home looked like. *Hey, Tandy, it's time to come home to your clueless husband and make him another pork roast.*

"Here, Charlie." Mim handed me her phone. She'd pulled up Tandy's Instagram. I scrolled through the recent pictures, trying to build up a better image of the woman in my mind. I was right that she had a lot of wannabe influencer shots of yoga poses, altar setups, and her children—both human and canine. But she'd also been taking regular photos of a stray cat she was trying to lure in with treats so she could take it to the vet for a checkup. She had been reading the Magic Tree House book series to her son every night and teaching her older daughter the meanings of different crystals. Her stories from that day were filled with several videos of her and her kids cannonballing into their pool, laughing gleefully. A warmth spread through my chest.

I dug the red ribbon out of my pocket and tied it around my wrist. Mama gave me a small smile when she saw the ribbon. She was the one who had taught me how to protect myself from absorbing negative energy while I was casting, and it was a method she'd learned from her mother, who'd learned from *her* mother. She pressed a malachite stone into my hand. It was a deep forest green, banded with lighter shades and sharpened into a point to direct energy.

"Okay, hold her still," I told Carl. I leaned down to make eye contact as best I could with the beady black eyes. I took a deep breath and attempted a tone that was both strict and kind. "Tandy, I know it has been a confusing day for you, but it's time for you to come back to yourself." As I spoke, I glanced at the smoke from the myrrh resin smoldering in the cauldron. It was drifting in a clockwise circle, almost due south now.

"You need to come back to yourself," I repeated slowly, squeezing the stone. "Nicholas needs to know how the book ends, and Millie needs someone to teach her the difference between jade and jasper. You need to come back to yourself, so you can wake up in the morning, have a chai latte, do your favorite yoga routine, and open up a fresh can of tuna for Dickens the tomcat."

The smoke was aimed south now. I closed my eyes and ruminated on the magic that flowed all around us, through my veins, through the stone in my hand. Focus. Intention. *Tandy, it's time to come home.*

A sharp, cold wind filled the room, blowing out the candles and chilling the sweat that dripped down the back of my neck. For a second, confusion reigned, and I was terrified that I'd messed it up, that I'd somehow made things worse. Then my brain caught up with what I was seeing. Tandy was sprawled over her husband's lap, her blond hair disheveled in a wild poof not unlike her chicken crest. She coughed and spat out a couple gray feathers.

"What the hell," she cried, looking around at all of us. Her face was frozen in shocked outrage. She tried to climb to her feet but fell right back over, knocking Carl back down with her. The pair of them scrambled around awkwardly on the floor, until we managed to get them both upright and stable. Mama couldn't stop snickering, which only further fanned Tandy's indignation. She dusted off her color-coordinated Lululemon outfit and leveled another glare, this time at me specifically.

"What did you do to me?" she demanded.

"You were a chicken." I kept my voice as polite and detached as possible, as I had no doubt any hint of gloating would only exacerbate her mood. "I changed you back."

"You're welcome," Mama said pointedly.

"A . . . a . . . *what*." Tandy whirled on her husband, searching for an explanation. He could only shrug helplessly.

"I don't know," he said. "I called Lisa, and she told me to call Sharon, and Sharon told me to call the Sparrows."

"You told *Sharon*?" Tandy seemed more aghast at that than at the concept of being a chicken for half the day. "Carl, you *know* she's been gunning for my position in the PTA."

"Well, I didn't know what else to do." He threw up his arms

in exasperation. "It's not like I have an instruction manual for this shit. I swear to god, Tandy—never mind. I'm going to bed."

He stormed out. Tandy stared after him in stunned silence. When she remembered the rest of us were there, I saw her struggle to replace her hurt expression with one of haughty indifference.

"I suppose I should thank you." Her voice was the tiniest bit wobbly.

"You damn well should," said Mama. Mim elbowed her.

"No problem," I said, trying to sound breezy. "We witches have to stick together."

"Are you all right, hon?" Harriet asked, rubbing her back.

Tandy made a noncommittal noise.

"If you'll just send me an invoice," she said.

"Don't worry about it," I said. Mama tried to interrupt, and even Mim looked ready to protest. I kept talking over them. "I'm glad you're okay."

Tandy crossed her arms. I could tell she was trying to figure out what my angle was. I wasn't even sure myself. All I knew was that I had pity stirring in my chest, and it didn't have anything to do with her being a chicken.

"All the same," she said. But she didn't have a follow-up.

"I don't suppose you know who might've done this to you," I said.

"Probably Sharon," said Mama, unhelpful as usual.

"Thanks, but I'll deal with this from here," Tandy said. "You've done enough."

I know I told her not to worry about thanking or paying me, but I'll admit her chilliness was disconcerting and almost irritating enough to dash away the pity. I knew she still blamed me for making her look bad in front of the homeowner association. Harnessing the power of a fairy ring is next-level witchcraft—

Tandy sure as hell wouldn't have been able to pull it off either—but that didn't mitigate my failure to save suburbia from the indignity of brown lawns. The HOA had taken their business to a magecraft firm that had delivered the desired results, but for twice the money. In Tandy's opinion, I'd sullied the good name of witches everywhere with my incompetence. It would take more than a free transmutation to win back her good graces.

She helped us pack up the candles and other supplies in silence. As she led us back to the front door, I caught sight of Carl stomping up the stairs with a beer in hand. Even Mama managed to bite back any smug parting words as we all filed onto the porch. Tandy offered a stiff goodbye, then shut herself back inside.

We waved off the Wharburtons and Lucas, who tried to refuse a ride but was helpless in the face of Harriet's grandmotherly insistence. Mim, Mama, and I climbed into our car, but Mim didn't start it right away. We sat in silence for a while, until the front porch light flickered off.

"You did good, Charlie." Mim shot me a look in the rearview mirror.

Happiness swelled in my chest. My parents weren't exactly stingy with praise, but that didn't stop me from tucking every positive word into my heart, creating a nest to protect it from bruising whenever they told me, yet again, that they didn't want me to have any ownership in the Cottage.

"Thanks," I managed. Immediately my stomach grumbled, and I realized that we'd never gotten around to making pancakes. Either my moms heard it from the front seat, or they were getting similar reminders.

"Takeout for dinner?" Mim asked.

"Anything but chicken," said Mama.

CHAPTER SIX

I had no intention of taking up Elinor on her invitation to the community picnic, but Mama saw the crumpled flyer I'd left on the table, and she insisted that passing up free food was a mortal sin. Mim was skeptical at first, but then she decided that it was a good idea to show our faces around the event and remind the townsfolk who we were. No sense in letting the mages have all the free publicity.

I couldn't decide whose reasoning was more persuasive, but in the end I came along. I didn't want Sterling Fitzgerald to think that he had intimidated me into staying away. Owl's Hollow had been my town first.

And, in the interest of transparency, I'll admit that the final factor in my decision to go was because the rain spell I cast the morning of the picnic only resulted in a light drizzle that dried up well before the event started. I wasn't sure if it was shoddy spellwork on my part or if one of the mages had skill with manipulating weather. In fact, I wasn't even sure that there was more than one mage. I hadn't seen or heard of anyone at Maven Enterprises besides Elinor and Fitz, and I didn't know if Elinor was a mage or not. Like witchcraft, it sometimes ran in families, but it wasn't always predictable.

Anyway, with the heavens themselves rebelling against me, I decided that I might as well take advantage of the free food. Determined not to present myself as a hot mess a third time in a row, I took much longer than usual choosing my outfit before we headed into town.

I settled on a saffron sundress covered in little white birds. Instead of my old boots, I wore my brown and navy oxfords. I styled my hair in an artfully messy bun, then spent entirely too long copying a "summery eye makeup" tutorial on YouTube. The finishing touch was my gold Caravaca de la Cruz pendant. An heirloom from my abuela, the crucifix with a second horizontal bar served as a talisman for good luck and protection against evil.

I wasn't religious, and neither were my parents, but many aspects of witchcraft were inescapably linked to some form of religion. The elements of Brujería that Mama had picked up from her mother and grandmother were a complex fusion of magic, spirituality, Indigenous practices, and Catholic colonialism. Mim's ancestors traced back to the polytheism and mysticism of Celtic Druids, whose true history was swallowed by early Christianity. Like me, my craft was a patchwork of the Sparrow and Vega ancestries.

My parents were both waiting for me in the living room when I finally emerged, which was rare. Normally Mama was the one making us late.

"You look cute," Mim said, as she grabbed her bag. She seemed happily surprised, and I immediately took offense. It wasn't like my default appearance was that of a bridge troll.

Mama just seemed skeptical as she eyed my attire.

"Who are you trying to impress?"

"Pastor Dale." I breezed past them toward the stairs. "I'm hoping to lure him away from his wife into a life of sin and scandal."

Mama snorted but didn't press it further. Not that I cared either way, because I wasn't trying to impress anyone.

We were almost an hour late to the park, and the picnic was already in full swing. At least two hundred townsfolk had shown up and were playing cornhole and horseshoes or chatting around picnic tables. There was even a bright red and yellow bouncy castle set up for the screaming children. Damn, Maven had gone all out. On top of everything, the food was catered by Madge's Café and the portable bar setup had a sign for The Blue Spoon. I wouldn't have expected mages to be considerate enough to hire local vendors. That was sure to earn them extra points with the citizens. Double damn.

The food line was long, so my moms went to stand in it while I fetched drinks for me and Mama. As advertised, everything was free, even when I asked the bartender to make my margarita a double. I dug around my purse and was happy to find a few dollar bills crumpled at the bottom that I could stick into the tip jar. Clutching my plastic cup with its lime wedge and Mama's can of beer, I turned and made it two steps before tripping on an exposed root. I flew face-first into someone's chest.

"Shit, I'm sorry!" I tried to regain my balance and only succeeded in spilling the rest of my margarita down his shirt. He grabbed my elbows to steady me, and I looked up to find myself once again inches away from Sterling Fitzgerald.

"You know," he said pleasantly, "if you're already too drunk to walk a straight line, maybe you should stick to one at a time."

"I'm not drunk." I was too flustered to come up with anything even remotely clever. I found my feet and put a respectable distance between us. The front of his (likely designer) button-down shirt was soaked. "I'm so sorry." I gestured help-lessly, but my hands were still full, and I didn't even have a nap-kin.

He glanced down and blinked, as if he'd just noticed that he was covered in margarita.

"Don't worry about it," he said.

"Let me get a napkin."

"Charlie, it's fine." He brushed a hand down the front of his shirt, and the wet stain evaporated without a trace. Fucking *mages*.

"Well, that's useful," I said, regaining some edge now that I was back on solid ground.

"Very." He grinned, and I couldn't decide whether it was smug or not, which only irritated me more. "Let me get you another drink. Margarita?"

"Yes," I said. "Wait, no, you don't have to—"

But he'd already moved past me to wave down the bartender. I wasn't sure why I was protesting, since the drinks were free—although technically he was still the one paying. There were three other people at the bar, so I rested my elbows on the counter next to him to wait.

"You look nice today," he said.

"Stop that." I gave him a sideways look.

"Stop what?"

"Stop being friendly. It's annoying."

He tilted his head to look at me, eyes bright under arched brows.

"Would you prefer me to be rude?"

"Actually, yes." I used a cocktail napkin to wipe some residual margarita off my hand. "I don't know why you're pretending we're friends, but we're not. We're competitors. You're trying to run me out of business, and I'm going to do everything I can to make sure that you don't get that permanent license."

He studied my face, his own expression inscrutable. A blush threatened to creep up my neck, and I tried to contain it with sheer force of will.

"If you're trying to compete with me," he said, "then maybe you shouldn't have read my tarot to tell me how to succeed."

What did he mean, if I was *trying* to compete with him? As if he and his swanky boutique were in a completely different league than the Cottage.

"You lied to me about who you were," I returned coolly.

"I never lied."

I decided not to dignify his semantics with a response. The bartender slid a cup over to me, and I snatched it up.

"Thanks for the drink," I said to Fitz, my sarcasm more cutting than I intended. I didn't know why he got under my skin (well, okay, I could think of several reasons), but usually I wasn't this prickly, even with people I hated. Killing with kindness was the way my parents had raised me, even though Mama didn't always follow her own advice. My rare conversations with Larry Munch were sweet enough to give us both cavities. But with Fitz, my well of kindness was dry as a bone. It didn't help that he wasn't ruffled by my rudeness. At least if he would act hurt, my conscience might get the better of me.

"You don't think that Maven and Chanterelle Cottage can coexist?" he asked, with a sincerity that had to be for show. There was no way he came here thinking that his sleek, convenient brand of magic wouldn't be in direct competition with the Cottage's rustic traditions. The amount of magical assistance needed in a town like Owl's Hollow was limited, and the disposable income even more so.

"About as well as Fox Books and The Shop Around the Corner did," I replied.

"I see." He didn't bat an eye. "And am I the smarmy sociopath or the gullible ingenue in this scenario?"

"Tom Hanks was not a smarmy sociopath," I cried, immediately losing the cool indifference I'd been aiming for.

"Are you sure we're talking about the same movie?" He leaned his back against the bar, and his lips quirked into something dangerously approaching a smirk. "You do know that the cozy little shop is the one that closed, right?"

I was as tongue-tied as Kathleen Kelly was when Joe Fox belittled her existence. I forced myself to take a sip of my drink, just to give myself something to do. I sputtered as the tang of lime and fire of tequila washed down the back of my throat. The bartender had remembered to make it a double.

"The Cottage isn't going anywhere," I coughed out. "We've been open for almost two centuries, and we're not going to be run out of business by your pretentious, overpriced company."

"I guess we know what the competition is that you saw in your tarot reading," he said, unperturbed by my characterization. "Although I don't think having clean floors and a dress code makes Maven Enterprises pretentious. Some might argue that's the bare minimum for a place of business."

My cheeks heated. Our floors were *clean*. Or at least as clean as we could get two-hundred-year-old wood. And, despite the occasional daydream about a boss witch aesthetic, I wasn't going to start swanning around in a suit and heels like some kind of executive. My days consisted of down-and-dirty spellwork and restocking shelves, not board meetings and twiddling my thumbs behind a desk.

"In case you haven't noticed, Owl's Hollow isn't anything like Boston."

"I'm aware," he said dryly. "In Boston when you want to find a shop, you can search for it in Google Maps. You don't have to follow increasingly terrible and obscure signage through endless back roads. And that's to say nothing of your travesty of a billboard on the main highway."

Damn that tacky billboard. The eighties had been the height of witchcraft, but it had not been the height of advertising design. Still, it was fine for *me* to hate the peeling old sign. No one else was allowed to insult it, least of all Sterling Fucking Fitzgerald.

"That sign is vintage." I tossed a lock of hair away from my face. "And I'll have you know the town loves us exactly how we are."

"You're probably right." The smile that had been playing at his lips materialized fully as he surveyed the park full of townsfolk currently enjoying themselves on Maven Enterprises' dime. Laughter and the sound of gleefully shrieking children filled the air. "I'm sure bribing them with free booze and food would never sway their affections."

"Now you're just being a dick." I ignored the faint flutter in my chest when he turned that smile on me. Behind those bright eyes and the charming dimple nestled in his left cheek was a mage trying to destroy my entire world.

"You did tell me I should be ruder," he replied.

I glared at him for a second but realized that if I kept arguing I would be giving him exactly what he wanted. I had no intention of obliging.

"I should get this to my mom." I lifted the beer in a farewell salute and headed for the food line, where Mama and Mim were near the front. Hopefully it didn't look too much like I was running away.

I handed Mama the can and sipped my own drink, resolutely not looking back over my shoulder to see if Fitz was watching me. Surely he had better things to do. I know I did.

"What was that all about?" Mim's voice was nearly a whisper.

"What?"

"You were talking to the owner of Maven, Starling What's-His-Name."

"Sterling Fitzgerald."

"Someone said you threw your drink on him." Mama sounded more pleased by the prospect than a parental figure should.

"I tripped," I said, indignant. Then I cast a nervous look around to find that lots of people were *not* looking at me in a very obvious way. I fiddled with my cross pendant. "People are saying I did it on purpose?"

That wasn't going to reflect well on our business in the least, if folks thought I was going around tossing drinks on my competitor—the same competitor who had paid for the dinner I was about to consume.

"Don't worry about it." Mama picked up a paper plate and analyzed the buffet spread with the concentration of an athlete at the starting line. "I don't think many people saw."

Be that as it may, by the time we'd finished our dinner, I was under the strong impression that people were staring in the direction of our picnic table and whispering among themselves. I told myself I was being paranoid, but then Bonnie came and plopped down next to me.

"So did you at least have a good reason to throw your drink in Sterling Fitzgerald's face?" she asked.

"Goddammit," I muttered.

"It was an accident." Mama's leap to my defense would have been more appreciated if she hadn't coupled it with air quotes and a theatrical wink.

Before Bonnie could reply, Jen came up from behind and draped her arms around Bonnie.

"Oh my god, Charlie," she said, resting her chin on her wife's shoulder. "Did you really—"

"No," I snapped. "I tripped." It came out louder than I intended, but maybe that wasn't a bad thing. Hopefully some of the gossipers would overhear and start spreading that around instead. Doubtful.

Jen giggled. She was still in her seafoam green scrubs, with her ash-blond hair up in a tight bun.

"Whatever you say." She gave Bonnie a quick peck on the cheek. "Sweetheart, Councilman Redgrave asked me to tell you that he's looking for you. Something about his designated parking space."

Bonnie groaned and climbed to her feet with the air of someone headed to their execution.

"Can't you tell him you're off duty?" I asked.

"There's no such thing," she said morosely.

"I'll come interrupt you with an important phone call in exactly five minutes," Jen promised, sliding into Bonnie's vacant seat.

"You're a lifesaver." Bonnie kissed the top of her wife's head, squared her shoulders, and marched off.

"Okay, but was it really an accident?" Jen asked me, without missing a beat.

I pointedly ignored her and gulped down the last of my margarita. I was going to need a refill soon, but I wasn't sure I was tipsy enough to brave the walk to the bar. It was a catch-22.

Mim came nobly to my aid. "I'm sure it was."

"But also if it wasn't, then he definitely deserved it," said Mama.

Jen giggled again.

"Well, you'd better get your story straight, because isn't that his sister headed this way?"

Elinor was indeed coming in our direction, clutching a diet soda. She was effortlessly chic again in a silky black asymmetrical dress with spaghetti straps. Beneath a floppy black hat, her red hair fell in beachy waves around her bare shoulders. Honestly, she would've been exactly my type, except that she looked like she was barely out of college. *Not* that I would ever consider dating a mage of any age or gender.

"Hello." She included all four of us in her sweeping glance, even though it was obvious that she was more interested in her favorite minor celebrities than me or Jen. "I'm Elinor Fitzgerald."

"Hi, Elinor," Mim said politely. "I'm Ruby. This is my wife, Alicia. I think you and Charlie have met?"

Elinor nodded and gave me and Jen a little wave.

"Hi, Charlie. Hi—Jen, right? Bonnie introduced us at town hall the other day."

"I remember," Jen said. It would be hard for anyone to forget meeting Elinor.

"I've been so excited to meet you two," Elinor said to my moms, as if she couldn't bear to wait another second. "Your essays in *Prism* magazine on the modern usage of fairy rings in powerful workings were so inspirational. I wrote my senior thesis on the topic."

"You did?" Mama asked, and any standoffish urges she may have had dissolved immediately. She was not a tough egg to crack. Mim liked to joke that there were two surefire ways into her heart: her pride and her stomach.

"Are you . . . not a mage, then?" Mim asked, with a tiny, confused frown. I was glad that she asked, since I hadn't been able to figure it out for myself.

"Oh, I am," Elinor said breezily, as if she saw no contradiction in a mage doing their thesis work on witchcraft—at least, in a way that didn't denigrate it. "I mean, I'm still an amateur. Fitzy does all the magic work. I'm in charge of accounting and marketing and all the other things he's terrible at."

"Ah." Mim was at a loss for what else to say.

"This was my brainchild," Elinor went on, gesturing to the picnic festivities around us. "If Fitz had his way, he'd never leave the office. People aren't his strong suit."

"I couldn't tell," I said wryly. It just slipped out. Mim gave me a look, while Mama hid her mirth with a sip of beer. Jen slapped a hand over her own mouth to stop a laugh.

Elinor didn't seem offended in the least.

"I know, right?" she said with a chuckle. "I've been dying to come visit Chanterelle Cottage, but we've been so busy. I was furious with Fitz for going without me last week."

Mama and Mim both shot me a look then. I had completely forgotten to tell them about his tarot reading.

"Stop by anytime," Mim said. "Charlie works the front of the shop, but Alicia and I are usually around somewhere."

"I definitely will." Elinor was beaming. "I'd love to pick your brain about how the species of mushroom affects the efficacy. One of my professors disagreed with my hypothesis and I need to know which of us is right."

"Sure," Mama said, oblivious to *my* look.

"Awesome." Someone across the park caught Elinor's attention. "Oh, I've got to thank Madge for the amazing food. Hope you guys have a great night!"

She drifted away, glad-handing people as she went, the consummate hostess.

"Isn't she precious?" Jen asked.

"Beautiful aura," said Mim. I couldn't help but think that complimenting a mage's aura was a betrayal of her fellow witches, even if it was true.

"She brought Bonnie the most beautiful orchid for her office," said Jen. "It's been spelled to never need tending."

My moms and I exchanged a glance, discomfited by the reminder of what we were competing against. Jen realized her faux pas a couple seconds later.

"Oh—um, I should go save Bonnie." She gave an apologetic grimace and rushed off.

"Well," Mim said into the silence, but she didn't seem to know what she wanted to follow up with.

I glanced longingly toward the bar, but the route was blocked by Fitz and Juniper Lee, one of the three hair stylists in town. She was laughing at something he'd said, and he was smiling back at her with no hint of a smirk. Juniper was stunningly gorgeous and tragically straight and went into the city every weekend to give free haircuts to people in need. She was presumably not saying anything rude or sarcastic. And she definitely hadn't spilled anything on him.

I frowned at the turn of my own thoughts and dragged my attention back to the table, where Mim and Mama were currently arguing about whether fly agaric mushrooms were native to the Southern Hemisphere.

"Can we go home now?" I asked abruptly.

They both paused and looked at me in surprise.

"Sure, I guess." Mama caught Mim's eye, and she nodded. "Everything all right, mija?"

"I don't feel good." I carefully did not look in the direction I was itching to look. "Maybe the food's not sitting well with the alcohol."

"Let me say bye to Paul and DeeDee," Mim rose to her feet. "I want to see how that Herkimer diamond talisman they ordered is working for them."

I stood up and straightened my dress, not acknowledging Mama's concerned stare.

"We're going to be okay," she told me. "You know that, right? The Cottage is going to be fine. This isn't the first time we've had competition."

But it was the first time mages had moved to town. We were in a different ball game now. A whole different stadium. I didn't attempt to put any of my roiling anxieties into words. Instead, I pasted a grin on my face.

"I'm not worried. They won't know what hit them."

CHAPTER SEVEN

It had only been a week since Maven Enterprises' grand societal debut, and the Cottage was already suffering from the squeeze of capitalism. I had hoped that the exorbitant prices of magecraft would discourage most of the townsfolk, but Tandy had done a little snooping and found that not only were they already booked up for the next month, but their rates were also competitive with ours. Of course. How else were they going to drive us out of business? The second the Cottage was shuttered, I had no doubt those rates would skyrocket.

But in October, the council would vote on whether to grant them a permanent magic license. If enough councilors sided with us and decided that a shiny new magecraft firm wasn't as important to Owl's Hollow as the survival of Chanterelle Cottage, then Maven's temporary license wouldn't be renewed, and Sterling Fitzgerald would be forced to take his overpriced suits and underpriced magic elsewhere.

I lay awake in bed on Saturday morning, contemplating the chances of the council voting against Maven and what steps we could take to help that decision along. My rule over the past few days, as worry about the Cottage's future had started pulling me out of sleep earlier and earlier, was that I was only allowed to obsess until my alarm went off. This morning, instead of my alarm, my raging thoughts were interrupted by Mim calling for me and Mama.

I reached for my phone on the bedside table, but something was wrong with the display. The clock wasn't showing up. I left it and rolled out of bed. I met Mama in the hall. Judging by her bleary eyes and general confusion, she had been sleeping soundly, which was more a testament to the effectiveness of her prescription sleep meds than to her level of concern for the Cottage. We padded into the kitchen together.

"I wanted to make strudel," Mim said.

"Okay." I couldn't think of anything else to say. Half my brain was still in bed, running the hamster wheel of familiar worries.

"Babe, please tell me you didn't wake us up to tell us that," Mama said.

"Look." Mim pushed the open cookbook across the countertop toward us. It was a thick floral binder that had belonged to her mother and was stuffed to the brim with several generations' worth of recipes. The page she showed us was blank. There were lines on the card, but nothing written on it.

"You can't find the recipe?" I asked. Wordlessly, Mim flipped to the next recipe. I frowned down at what appeared to be a page ripped from a magazine. There was a picture of some kind of soup, along with tiny icons of a clock, oven, and measuring spoons like you typically see in printed recipes. But there was no text.

I flipped to the next page, and the next. Some had pictures, but none of them had any words or numbers, printed or handwritten.

"What . . ." I struggled for coherency. "The hell?"

Mama grabbed the binder and turned a few pages herself. She slammed it shut, then reopened it, as if hoping it would reset itself like a laptop. Nothing.

"There's more." Mama pointed over the sink, where normally there hung a kitschy metal sign that said, *"No Bitchin' in My Kitchen."* A white elephant gift that Mama had committed to wholeheartedly. It was blank. Not exactly a loss but nonetheless perturbing.

I turned and stumbled toward one of the bookshelves. We had a huge collection of novels, memoirs, and various tomes on witchcraft. Only empty spines stared back at me.

"This isn't possible," Mama murmured.

I ran back to my room, my stomach flipping over and over with mounting dread. I opened my book of shadows to a random page, willing it to be normal, willing it to be somehow unaffected. Other than the various sketches I had drawn of sigils or candle placements, the entire book was blank. A lifetime of work, vanished.

"Fuck," I shouted. I went back to my bedside table and snatched up my phone. No time or date was displayed on the lock screen. The facial recognition worked, and the app icons were all present, but without any accompanying labels. My text messages were nameless and wordless, empty bubbles of green and blue except for the occasional emoji. The keypad was blank as well, other than the pound sign, asterisk, and call symbol. Numbly, I walked back into the kitchen.

"This is bad," Mim said, unnecessarily. "Do you think it's just us?"

Before Mama or I could answer, the bell from the shop, which we brought up to the living room every night, started ringing itself. It had been a while since I'd had to read an analog clock, but according to the one over the microwave, it was two hours before we were supposed to open.

"I'm gonna guess no," I said, then trudged back to my bedroom to get dressed.

Barely an hour later, we were downtown with everyone who was awake within a ten-mile radius. At first, we had gathered uncertainly in the grassy quad outside the town hall. Pastor Dale had tried in vain to convince everyone to hike up the hill to the church to join him in prayer and sermon, until someone pointed out that the Bibles and hymnals were blank too. He gave up after that. Once Bonnie and the council members arrived, things took on a more official air and we assembled in the forum, which was standing room only.

For a while we were all left to our own devices, complaining about the lack of air conditioning and speculating among ourselves, while the council and mayor discussed the issue in the closed chambers beyond. Someone had driven around that morning and found that all the signs and billboards were also blank, all the way to the official town border. The world beyond that was unaffected, though nothing carried across the border returned to normal.

Every printed word and number in Owl's Hollow—and *only* Owl's Hollow—had simply dropped out of existence overnight.

For the most part the crowded room, though buzzing with nerves and frenetic energy, remained under control. That is, until the Fitzgeralds came in. It wasn't like they made a big show of their arrival, only slipped in through the back door. But the second someone caught sight of them, the buzz in the room reached a fever pitch. Suddenly it was pandemonium. From what I could make out, half the room was convinced they were responsible, while the other half was convinced that they were our only salvation. Either way, they were now the focal point of a large and demanding crowd.

"Well, shit," said Mama. From our spot against the side wall, we had a pretty decent view of the ruckus.

"Yeah," I said.

Mim was, as always, the only one of us with any instinct for helpfulness.

"I'm going to get Bonnie," she said, and squeezed her way through the crowd toward the council chambers.

Elinor must have just rolled out of bed like everyone else, but she managed to make her messy bun and outfit of tank top, leggings, and Vans look chic. Fitz, unsurprisingly, was in his usual dress shirt and slacks with his hair neatly combed, as if he'd already been up for hours. He was only missing his tie.

Elinor fielded the questions being hurled at them, standing in front of her brother in a posture that was both defiant and oddly protective. Fitz seemed perfectly content with letting her do all the talking. Elinor *had* said he wasn't a people person.

"Where are you going?" Mama asked me. I hadn't realized that I'd taken a couple steps forward.

"Nowhere," I said, falling back beside her.

Elinor was holding her own for the most part, even as Eddie Hightower, who made his living occasionally mowing lawns and always cashing his mother's Social Security checks, was growing increasingly agitated. He stepped closer to Elinor so he could tower over her while he shouted about government conspiracies and something called the magic mafia. He was obviously drunk—whether he'd gotten that way this morning or it was leftover from the night before was anyone's guess.

Uncowed, Elinor glared right back up at Eddie, but Fitz put a hand on her shoulder and tugged her back a step, saying something to Eddie that I couldn't make out.

Whatever it was, it pissed Eddie off even more. When Elinor tried to make him back away, Eddie pushed her aside roughly, intent on her brother. But before he could move another muscle, Fitz threw up his hand. He didn't touch Eddie. Didn't even come close. But Eddie landed flat on his back and slid a few feet across the polished floor like a giant bowling pin.

"Shit," I heard Mama say behind me, with genuine concern this time. I was already sprinting across the room. When people wouldn't move out of my way fast enough, I jumped up to run along the metal folding chairs, leaping over the laps of the few people who were still seated.

Eddie was struggling to his feet when I reached them. No one had stepped forward to lend him a hand, although it was hard to tell if it was because they feared him or Fitz. Elinor was already upright, rubbing her elbow even as she assured her brother she wasn't hurt. I had the distant, eminently sensible thought that if I kept my mouth shut and backed away, the townsfolk would probably turn on the mages right here and now. Magic was all fun and games until it wasn't anymore. Witches could hex people, but that was behind closed doors and therefore easy to ignore. Only mages could fling people bodily across a room without touching them.

I could leave the Fitzgeralds to face the crowd alone, and all my problems would be solved without me having to do a thing.

I've never been accused of being a particularly sensible person.

"For heaven's sake, Eddie," I said, loudly enough for everyone's benefit. I sidled between him and the mages. "Didn't you get arrested last year for touching women without their permission? Sheriff, surely he's on his third strike by now?"

Sheriff Daniels, who was especially useless for a law enforcement officer, had been watching the proceedings with slack-jawed bewilderment, but my question snapped him out of it. He nodded vigorously and elbowed his way forward to grab Eddie by the collar and haul him the rest of the way up.

"Let's go, Eddie. You can sleep this off in the drunk tank. Sorry about the trouble, miss." He tipped his hat to Elinor and shuffled toward the door, pushing a protesting Eddie ahead of him.

"You all saw that," Eddie howled. "He used magic on me!"

"We all saw you knock down Elinor," I said, in a charitable tone like you might use with a belligerent toddler. "Then we saw you fall flat on your ass. Are you sure you aren't just too drunk to stay upright?"

I expected him to yell at me. I did not expect him to twist out of the sheriff's grasp and go for my throat. Or at least, I could only assume that's where he was going, because he took two steps and fell flat on his face this time. It's possible he really was too drunk to stay upright and had tripped on his own feet— that was what it seemed like to everyone else. I glanced over my shoulder at Fitz, who shoved both hands into his pockets and looked askance, and I wasn't so sure.

Eddie, while not exactly humbled, was at least shocked into a dazed silence as Sheriff Daniels dragged him to his feet a second time and propelled him out the door, chewing him out the whole way.

My knees wobbled a little as the rush of adrenaline promptly abandoned me, but I recovered enough to herd Elinor and Fitz out the side door, before anyone else could decide to start yelling.

"Are you okay?" I asked, ostensibly to them both, even though I couldn't quite bring myself to look at Fitz. I'd never seen magic used that way before. In fact, the most I'd ever seen of magecraft up close was when I was a kid at the state fair, and a mage in a ridiculous top hat juggled fireballs. It had been such an over-the-top display that it was hard to think of that magic as being useful for anything but entertainment. Nothing like the effort-less power that Fitz had displayed.

"I'm fine," Elinor said, a little tetchy. I decided not to hold it against her. "Why does everyone think we had something to do with this?"

"Um, I guess the timing is kind of . . . coincidental?"

"What is that supposed to mean?" she demanded, and I raised my hands in immediate surrender.

"Chill. I don't think you did it." Up until that point, some part of me *did* think they were responsible, but the righteous indignation on Elinor's face was enough to convince me other-wise. "But magically hurling folks around isn't exactly going to help your case," I couldn't resist adding, with a pointed glance at Fitz.

"That asshole deserved it," Elinor said. It was a staunch dec-laration so unlike her usual blithe cheeriness that it caught me off guard.

"No, Charlie's right," Fitz said—another surprise. He ran a hand through his hair, leaving it mussed in a way that I refused to find sexy, given the circumstances. "I didn't even mean to do it. Just a reflex, I guess."

A reflex to protect his sister, I thought. And maybe me? But that was more evidence suggesting the verdict of *sexy*, and I forcibly steered my thoughts clear of the speculation. The no-tion of being indebted to a mage was too discomfiting to con-sider. Eddie definitely tripped the second time.

"If you hadn't done it, I would have." Elinor folded her arms.

A hint of indulgent fondness crossed her brother's face, like Mim used to give me when I was a kid and insisted I could make breakfast on my own, ten minutes before I turned the kitchen into a disaster zone. Elinor herself had said she was an amateur, and the magic that had sent Eddie flying was not novice level. Fitz didn't seem inclined to point that out, and Elinor didn't seem in the mood to take it gracefully at any rate.

"He did deserve it," I said. "Eddie is a dick. Trust me, no one's going to hold it against you."

As to why I first helped my business rivals out of a thorny situation and was now reassuring them, I could only surmise that I was losing my mind. The door to the forum opened, and I whirled, half expecting the mob to be following us into the corridor. It was Mama.

"Oh good, you're still here," she said. "Come on, the council wants to talk to you."

"Who?" I asked.

"All of you."

The council chamber was outfitted in nineties style with a fake mahogany conference table, creaky leather swivel chairs, shiny cream wallpaper, and a worn carpet patterned with abstract shapes. All six members were in attendance, along with Bonnie at the head of the table.

"Please tell me someone knows what the hell is going on," she said, without preamble, after me, my parents, and the Fitzgeralds had all lined up in front of the projector screen like we were about to give a group book report.

The five of us exchanged glances, no one wanting to admit the obvious. At last, Mim sighed and bit the bullet.

"We've never seen anything like it before," she said.

"Neither have we," said Fitz.

"But," Mama cut in, "with some time—"

"How much time?" demanded Larry Munch. "This is a nightmare. Honestly, what is the point of magic if you can't even—"

"Thank you, Larry," Bonnie interrupted politely but firmly. She looked at the five of us. The stress of the morning had etched new lines into her features. The retired Mayor Smithers and his wife had already jetted off to the Maldives, so this problem was entirely hers. "We appreciate that this is not exactly precedented, but we're asking you to find a solution as soon as possible. We're willing to pay three grand to whoever can fix it, provided you can prove to the council's satisfaction that the solution was your doing."

Three thousand dollars? My heart skipped a beat. That would make a huge difference for us. I looked over at my parents, and they were obviously thinking the same thing.

"Five thousand." Fitz's tone was stolidly resolute.

I blinked and looked at him but couldn't glean anything about what he was thinking from his smooth, implacable exterior. Bonnie was also shocked by the counteroffer, but she recovered quickly.

"That's exorbitant," she said.

"No, it's not." There was no aggression or belligerence in Fitz's demeanor. He was the very essence of calm and collected. I couldn't even bring myself to haggle at yard sales. "Whatever magic this is, it's affecting the entire town. Any spell of that magnitude, regardless of its nature, would easily cost you twice that. Five thousand is more than fair."

I couldn't tell if Bonnie was about to laugh off his demand or yell at him. In the end she only clasped her hands and waited while the councilors began exchanging whispers around the table. Finally Councilwoman Hibbert whispered the consensus into Bonnie's ear. She nodded.

"Five thousand it is," she said. "But only to the party that can prove they are responsible for reversing the spell. Now, unless there are any questions, we're going to make a public announcement."

She stood up and straightened her blazer, which she'd thrown on over a wrinkled blouse and jeans. It was the most casual I'd ever seen her in a professional setting, and despite the extenuating circumstances—and the fact that several of the council members were even less presentable—I'm sure it was driving her crazy.

I wanted to say something, but no words formed. If the council agreed to pay five grand, it wasn't like I was going to argue for less. Even if the whole thing left a bad taste in my mouth.

We all filed out of the council chamber in silence. Mama and Mim headed back into the forum to hear what the official announcement to the citizens would entail. I was also curious how Bonnie was going to put a positive and reassuring spin on this situation. The disappearance of any written communication—digital or print—was not exactly a minor inconvenience in this day and age.

The Fitzgeralds didn't seem interested in what the party line was going to be, and they were already headed toward the parking lot, deep in murmured conversation. Probably strategizing how to fix this mess. Or how to squeeze the town for more money.

After a few seconds of hesitation at the door to the forum, I ran to catch up with them.

"What was that?" I demanded.

"What was what?" Fitz asked. Neither of them had slowed down, so I fell into step beside him.

"You can't waltz in here and start extorting Bonnie for money."

"Not Bonnie, the government," he said. We'd reached the

door, and he pushed it open and stood aside for his sister to exit. I exited too but turned around on the sidewalk to glare at him. "And I didn't extort anyone. They were lowballing us. I wouldn't be surprised if they had already agreed to go as high as ten grand."

I gaped. *Ten grand?*

"You can't know that." I floundered for my lost poise.

"Shouldn't you be thanking me?" He flashed one of his trademark smirk-smiles.

"For what?" I teetered between outrage and disbelief. "Making us all look like money-grubbing charlatans?"

"For negotiating a fair wage." His smile faded, and he looked genuinely bemused by my reaction. "Do you always insist on charging so much less than what your work is worth? It's a wonder you've stayed in business this long."

I stared back at him, trying to come up with a retort, because clearly, he was wrong. Clearly, he was twisting things around to suit his mercenary worldview.

"If it bothers you so much," Fitz said into my stunned silence, "you can go back in there and demand to work for pennies."

"Only someone who grew up with a silver spoon in his mouth would consider three thousand dollars *pennies.*" I injected as much disdain into my tone as I could, but he'd rattled my conviction.

Instead of being insulted, he gave another smile, softer this time.

"Fair enough," he said, "but my point stands."

My righteous indignation had run out of steam in the face of his sangfroid, and I couldn't remember what my argument was. Luckily, Elinor interrupted before I was forced to do anything drastic, like admit he was right.

"Fitzy, come on." She was yanking on the passenger door of

a black Mercedes that was out of place among the old pickup trucks and budget sedans. "It's hot out here."

"Coming," he called back. He watched me for a few more seconds, like he was trying to figure something out. Then he shoved his hands into his pockets and walked past me toward the car. He cast one final glance over his shoulder as he went. "Good luck."

And I couldn't help but feel that the unspoken addendum was: *You're going to need it.*

CHAPTER EIGHT

We closed the shop and holed up in the back room. The Wharburtons and Lucas stopped by for a while to offer various suggestions—none of which were particularly helpful. They were all skilled witches in their own right, but their craft was *too* focused. They lacked the breadth of experience that came from using magic to solve other people's problems for decades. As it seemed unlikely that Mark's flora expertise, the comfort and sleep spells that Harriet knitted into her blankets, or Lucas's (supposed) astral projections were going to aid in the problem at hand, none of them had much to offer other than vague suggestions and half-baked ideas. Finally, sensing that their presence was more distracting than useful, they took their leave.

If only Tandy could take a hint as gracefully. She had hovered over me, Mim, and Mama like a disapproving schoolteacher while we passed ideas back and forth, until finally Mim had diplomatically suggested that maybe she should go see what she could gather on the mages' progress. I guess the thought of being a spy was thrilling enough to tempt her away from her self-appointed role of supervisor, because Tandy had finally left. She promised to return in a few hours. Honestly it was more like a threat, but at least with her gone, we could breathe.

First, we cast a sacred circle to give ourselves a safe space to focus, free from any unwanted interference from outside energies or forces (including Broomhilde, who was wedged between a cabinet and the wall to keep her sequestered). I grabbed a feather to represent the element of air and a candle to represent fire and placed them on the east and south sides of the room. At the same time, Mim set a cup of water and a vial of sand to the west and north. Mama took her onyx-handled athame and stood in the center. With the knife extended, she spun slowly in a clockwise circle, pointing to each element in turn.

I always loved the way Mama looked when she did spellwork. There was a calm transcendence that overtook her and seemed to emanate from within, so that her amber skin glowed and her eyes sparked like fire. Mim often claimed that she'd fallen in love with her the first time she saw her cast a spell.

Once the circle was in place, we sat cross-legged on the floor and began to brainstorm. My parents and I had been a team for my whole life. Mim and Mama had an intimate bond of understanding between them that made them a power couple when it came to the craft, and they had raised me as the third point of the triangle. We could communicate through half-formulated thoughts and obscure references. In many ways our minds interconnected as easily as our magic when we cast spells together. Usually, it made us unstoppable.

But the current curse plaguing Owl's Hollow eluded even our combined expertise.

I tried reading the cards. My deck wasn't labeled anyway, but the Roman numerals at the top of each card had vanished. The reversed Magician kept showing up, which made sense, as the problem at hand was certainly the result of dark powers at work.

The Hermit in reverse suggested isolation or loneliness. The Nine of Swords signified anxiety, depression, nightmares, and other such cheery stuff. Despite the presence of "dark powers," none of the cleansing spells we tried on any books or papers made a difference. We even pieced together a spell from our collective memories for banishing evil from an object, but nothing changed.

Mim read her runes, but with the same frustratingly opaque results as the tarot. It was almost like the universe didn't want us to know who or what was responsible for the curse, or how we could reverse it.

Or maybe whoever was behind it had some kind of magic in place to cover their tracks. It seemed like the sort of thing a mage would do. At the town hall, I'd believed that the Fitzgeralds had nothing to do with it. But it *was* a huge coincidence that two weeks after they arrived, the town was struck by an unprecedented show of magic. And if the mages were the ones to reverse the curse, they would be the saviors of the town, which practically guaranteed that their license would be renewed.

Of course, a similar argument could be made about my family. Proving witchcraft as the superior magic would do wonders for our business and make it that much harder for Maven to win the council's votes in October.

I decided that at this juncture, pointing fingers was less productive than getting to the bottom of the curse.

"What about that ritual your grandmother did that one time—with the buried book?" Mama asked Mim. She was rapping her knuckles in absent rhythm on her knees.

"It was a journal," Mim said. "I think she was trying to summon what had been written on some pages that were ripped out after the owner died."

"Did it work?" I asked.

"Maybe. I can't remember." Mim sighed. "All my notes on it are in my grimoire."

That was the real crux of the problem. We had a lot of experience and ideas between us, but when it came to the nitty-gritty details of spellwork—we each depended on our own book of shadows to preserve the knowledge. There were dozens of spells I could do from memory, as well as divination and a few cleansing rituals, but none of them were of a magnitude that might help us figure out how to bring the words back to Owl's Hollow.

"Memory spell?" I suggested.

"I guess we could try," Mim said glumly.

"This is pointless," Mama said, putting Mim's obvious pessimism into words. "We could cast spells and set up rituals all night long without any progress. It's a needle in a haystack. We need to figure out the root cause."

"We've already tried that." Mim gestured toward the tarot spread and scattered runes.

"I've got an idea." I climbed to my feet and went through to the front of the store. The obsidian scrying mirror tucked away on one of the shelves had been in stock for a while. It was an expensive piece, not the sort of thing tourists or casual witches purchased, which were the bulk of our clientele. I slid it carefully out of its wooden box and unwrapped the white cloth we kept it wrapped in, for safety. It was about the size of a dinner plate and polished to a gleam.

I carried it into the back room and was greeted by looks of skepticism. Mim had never been any good at scrying, and Mama said that doing it always gave her horrible nightmares, so she stayed away from it. I'd done it a few times with varying degrees of success, so surely it was worth a try.

"I hate that thing." Mama shuddered as I placed it gently on the floor. "It's creepy as fuck. I wish we'd never bought it."

"Are you sure you want to try?" Mim asked. I knew the concern in her voice wasn't because she thought I couldn't do it, but because scrying wasn't a harmless divination like tarot or runes. Peering beyond the physical realm was a practice that could turn ugly fast. When you were looking into the glass, you could never be sure what might be looking back at you.

"I'll be okay," I said, with what I hoped was an encouraging smile. In the sacred circle, with my parents close at hand, the potential dangers were not as daunting as they might have been otherwise.

Mim pressed her lips together but nodded and fetched me two thick white candles. I placed them on either side of the glass and lit them, then settled on my knees in front of it so that I could peer down.

"Stick to the past and present," Mim said, with uncharacteristic sternness. "Don't try to learn anything about the future. It's different from asking the cards or the tea leaves. The universe doesn't give answers for free, and by the time you find what you're looking for, you might already be lost for good."

"No future, got it," I said.

"Ready?"

"Ready."

She switched off the light and sat down again, though not too close. I needed to be able to achieve perfect concentration. It would have been better for them to leave the room entirely, but even if I'd wanted to do this alone, I knew Mim wouldn't agree.

I fidgeted until I was comfortable, placing my hands on the ground so I could lean forward without losing my balance.

"If you need to stop," Mama said, "don't forget to close it down."

I nodded, already half-lost in my deep, steady breathing. I let my vision unfocus so that mentally I could fall into the void of dark glass. For a long time, I swam in darkness, my mind drifting aimlessly in search of a tether. The trick with scrying was to not try to impose your will upon the universe. It was much easier—and safer—to float along the current and pick up what tidbits you could along the way.

Finally, an image coalesced from shadows. Some kind of animal, maybe? It dissolved back into darkness before it had fully clarified, but more images followed in succession, too murky for me to pick out any details. A weather-worn gravestone. The town hall. An assortment of sports equipment. All mundane, all useless.

I drifted away, but then my focus was yanked sideways, like I'd been caught on a fishing hook. I found myself immersed in a new scene, hazy and dripping with shadows. It was an office, furnished simply with a desk, lamp, and some shelves. There were stacks of paper boxes against the wall, threatening to topple over. Some books were spread around the floor, lying open with empty pages. I willed the image into sharper focus. Scrying wasn't exact, but I could at least trust that whatever I was seeing was important somehow. I wasn't going to find myself looking at some random person in a random office somewhere, working on billing spreadsheets or whatever.

And sure enough, the scene slowly clarified to reveal Sterling Fitzgerald. I would have expected to find him hard at work, puzzling over the curse. Instead, he was unpacking books and organizing them on the shelves. There was no telling what criteria he was using, since they were all blank.

Why was I seeing this? Was it proof that he *was* behind the curse, and so he didn't need to put any effort into figuring out how to reverse it? Maybe he didn't care one way or another—although in that case, why did he bother haggling for a higher offer from the council?

Maybe he was just a terrible procrastinator.

My grip on the scene was slipping, and I tried to dig in, to get a better look. When he was alone there was a quality to his demeanor that I hadn't seen before. A sort of detached melancholy.

He froze with a book extended halfway to the shelf and glanced toward the ceiling.

"You know," he said conversationally. His voice was as clear in my head as if he'd been standing beside me. I hadn't seen anyone enter the office. Was he talking to himself? "It's rude to spy."

Before I could react, I was flung out of the scene and back into the Cottage. My head whirled and my senses screamed in confusion as I tried to get my bearings. At first, I thought it was somehow Fitz's doing, but then I realized that Tandy had burst into the back room. Her interruption had dragged me prematurely from the session.

"Charlie, the glass," Mim said.

I nodded through my disorientation and set my palm flat on the glass.

We're done, I thought, directing my intention with all the force I could muster. I blew out the candles.

"Goddammit, Tandy," cried Mama, once she was sure I'd closed off the spell. "What the hell is the matter with you?"

Tandy looked between me and the obsidian glass, realizing the disruption she'd caused with her unannounced entry. Not that she would deign to apologize.

"Maybe you should put up a sign or something," she said. "How was I supposed to know?"

"Are you okay?" Mim asked me, her voice warm with concern.

I nodded again, wordlessly. I needed some time to recenter myself after such a jarring return to reality. Mama ran to get me a glass of water from the sink in the back corner. I swallowed it down in three gulps. By then Tandy had gotten antsy and was pacing back and forth, teetering on impractical neon pink stilettos.

"Maven already knows how to reverse the curse."

"Seriously?" I set my glass on the floor with a thud.

"The office is closed, but I caught the receptionist when she was walking to the café to pick up lunch. I forget her name, Lucy or Laura or something."

"Her name is Elinor."

"Whatever." Tandy dismissed my correction with a wave, and I fought the urge to roll my eyes. "Get this, the mage is her brother!"

"Literally everyone knows that," Mama said. "Just get on with it."

"Well, did you also know that—"

"That Elinor is a mage? Yes, everyone knows that too."

Tandy sniffed indignantly at Mama's disparagement of her spying skills.

"You know, I went through a lot of trouble getting this information. The least you could do is—"

"*Tandy.*"

"Fine! I asked if they'd figured out who was responsible yet, and she said they had no idea, but her brother would be able to fix it anyway."

"When?" Mim asked in disbelief.

"She said I could expect it to be resolved before dinner. I asked why they hadn't fixed it already, if they knew how, and she said he needs to rest first. I guess that means he's off taking a nap while the rest of us suffer."

"Suffer" was a strong word, but there was no use telling Tandy to dial down the dramatics. I wondered if organizing books was Fitz's version of rest. It made sense that the magnitude of magic involved in a town-wide spell would require him to build up his

strength, and he'd already expended himself that morning tossing Eddie around. I realized I had no concept of how much
energy various degrees of magecraft required. It wasn't like I'd
ever known a mage well enough to ask.

"I still think they're the ones behind it," Tandy went on. "I
say we call up the town council and demand they investigate
this."

"We don't have any evidence," Mim said. "They would just
call us sour grapes. The best thing we can do right now is try to
solve it ourselves, before the mages have the chance."

"So, what have you got?" Tandy gestured at our assortment of
witchy paraphernalia. Our silence told her in no uncertain
terms that the answer was a big fat nothing. "Are you searching
for the cause of the problem so we can use the fairy ring?"

The mention of the fairy ring triggered an eruption of hot
shame inside me. It had been wilted and useless ever since my
failed spell last year had drained it of its power. I couldn't bring
myself to look at my parents, who no doubt would have had the
same thought as Tandy, but thanks to me, our most powerful
tool wasn't even an option. Tandy knew that I'd fucked up the
spell for the HOA, but she didn't know the whole story.

"The fairy ring is currently out of commission," Mim said
lightly.

"What happened to it? I know it's technically on your property, but that doesn't mean you—"

"Leave it alone, Tandy," Mama snapped. The harshness of her
tone shocked even Tandy into a few moments of blessed silence.
She blinked and glared at Mama, obviously ready to escalate
matters with a sharp retort, but then she glanced at Mim and
me, and I guess our expressions made her realize that she'd
stepped in something that was better left alone. She threw up
her hands in mute surrender.

Relief washed over me, followed by a wave of fatigue. I lay

back on the floor, too tired to remain upright, and stared idly at the exposed wood beams of the ceiling. If only there were a way to recharge the fairy ring ourselves, rather than wait for it to regenerate naturally, a process that could take years. In their series of essays on the topic, my parents had hypothesized that there might be a way to do just that, though modern witchcraft had yet to crack it, if it was even possible.

My head was starting to throb, but I wasn't sure if it was the strain of scrying, my guilt over damaging what was probably our best shot at fixing this, or the incessant way Tandy was clack-clack-clacking around on her heels.

"Even without the fairy ring, this would be a lot easier if we had some kind of guidance." Mim tugged her book of shadows into her lap and stroked it sadly. It had a tawny moleskin cover with creamy unlined pages that were overflowing with various dried herbs, pasted pictures, and random notes on napkins shoved inside for safekeeping. Like my book, all her illustrations and pictures were in place, but no words detailing any spellwork that might help.

"It's disgraceful," Tandy said. "I've been saying for years that we need to start teaching witches how to cast more intuitively. Mages have private tutors and academies where they send their kids. And meanwhile we can't even heal a wart without following instructions."

"Speak for yourself," I said with a frown. There was plenty I could do without the help of my grimoire, though admittedly I usually consulted it anyway, to be safe. "This is a lot more complicated than a wart. We can't be expected to remember every obscure piece of spellwork we've ever come across."

"And if it was so easy for the mages, they would have fixed it already," said Mama, her chin jutting out in defiance, obviously ready for a fight. Even slouched on the floor in her ripped jeans and baggy T-shirt, with Tandy looming over her in four-inch heels, she wasn't someone you'd want to mess with. Tandy took a step back, out of range.

"School," Mim said thoughtfully. Our attention swiveled to her.

"What about it?" Tandy asked.

Mim looked at me.

"Remember when you were in high school, and you got suspended for calling Mr. Hearst a fascist?"

"I think my exact words were 'fascist fucking pig.' I stand by them."

"You were mad because he gave you detention for passing notes in class."

"I was mad because he had no *proof* I was passing notes," I countered, as the old well of adolescent outrage refilled. "I never handed Kim anything. I only—*oh*."

Mim grinned at me. It had been one of my first successful complex spells. I'd charmed two pens so that when I wrote on a piece of paper on my desk, the words would appear on the paper on Kim's desk, then vice versa. I was insanely proud of my work. So were my moms, for that matter. I hadn't even gotten punished for the detention (although the subsequent suspension did merit a stern talking-to about not calling teachers fascist pigs to their faces, regardless of how true the designation may or may not be).

"Please tell me you remember how you did it," Mim said.

"I think I might." It was near the beginning of my grimoire, a page that was soft and worn from years of my fingers tracing over it, reliving the glory of that simpler time, when I was still a gifted witch of limitless potential, when magic was nothing but a source of celebration. Before I'd let anyone down.

"Could be a good jumping-off point," said Mama. "If we could figure out how to adjust the spell to reprint words on paper that were already there, then multiply it on a larger scale."

A much, much larger scale. My heart fell at the thought. Even if we managed to bring back the words in one book—how were we ever going to replicate that for every single word in town?

"It's a start," Mim said to me, seeing my flash of pessimism.

"Right." I marshaled my determination. We were the Sparrows. We performed the impossible every day of the week. "I need a pen, a regular mirror, and five—no, seven—pieces of howlite."

Tandy dug a pen out of her purse while Mim and Mama fetched the rest from the front of the shop. I scrounged around in my own bag until I found my key ring. I removed the silver leaf-shaped talisman from the ring. The two halves of the leaf flipped open, revealing a small but sharp blade. The boline was what I used for cutting twine and harvesting herbs.

I took Tandy's pen—a heavy fake silver one like you'd find in graduation boxed sets, although this one had no engraving.

"Does this have any sentimental value?" I asked.

"No," she said, then squawked as I started to carve a series of tiny symbols along the barrel. "But it *was* expensive!"

"Sorry," I said, but mostly ignored her as I concentrated on remembering the correct runes.

Ansuz for communication, Uruz for the transfer of energy, and Ehwaz to bind the two together. The Futhark runes weren't used by all witches, but they were the tradition in Mim's family, so I'd memorized them at a young age. At least this was one thing I didn't need my grimoire for.

My parents returned, and I slid the obsidian mirror away to make room for the bigger, gilt-edged mirror that Mama laid down in front of me. Mim handed me the white stones, veined with gray like trailing smoke. It took me a while to remember the correct placement of the howlite across the mirror's surface. I knew the grid shape was a combination of the three runes, but

I had to sketch out several possibilities before I found the one that seemed right. Fortunately, any marks we made on paper remained, as long as they didn't form any language. My grid sketches were safe, but if I wrote even the letter "*A*" it would dissolve immediately into nothing.

I placed the stones in their pattern with the pen at the center. The magic was a sense memory coming back to me. Excitement flurried in my stomach as I lit one of the white candles and placed it next to the mirror. There was no high like the anticipation of new magic.

The actual casting of the spell only took about a minute. Strangely enough, not being able to double-check my work with my grimoire made it easier. I had no choice but to be confident in my skill. I'd already done the difficult part in high school—all the late nights of trial and error until it was perfect. Now that I knew how to channel the magic correctly, it was just a matter of setting my intention and directing it toward the pen.

I blew out the candle when I was done and scooped up the pen, too excited to linger. I handed Mama a blank sheet of paper and kept one for myself.

Concentrating on Mama's page, I wrote my name on mine. *Charlotte Isabel Sparrow.*

The words on my paper dissolved . . . and reappeared on the sheet in Mama's hands.

We all gasped in delight. Tandy even clapped her hands together gleefully. But no sooner had we gotten our hopes up than the words disappeared again.

"Dammit," I cried, flinging down the pen.

"This is progress," Mim said. "We need to dissect your spell and see if we can get around the curse. If we can figure that out, then—"

The chorus of "Single Ladies" blared, making us all jump. Tandy fished her cellphone out of her purse and hit the green icon to answer. "Hello? Oh, hi, Julie. Did you . . . are you sure? . . . yeah . . . uh-huh. No, I'm with them right now. We'll be there in ten minutes."

She flung her phone back into her bag like it had personally wronged her.

"The mages are ready to reverse the spell. Apparently, Bonnie has been trying to call you, in case you wanted to be there when they do it."

We'd all silenced our phones so we could better concentrate. I'd really hoped we would have a few more hours before Fitz was ready to make his move. Dismay curdled in my chest. I told myself he hadn't succeeded yet. If reversing the spell proved trickier than he anticipated, we might still have a chance.

But immediately I felt guilty for even thinking that. I should want the town to be delivered from this curse as soon as possible, regardless of who got the glory.

Mama hopped up and brushed off her jeans, not that the effort improved their appearance.

"Let's go, then," she said, her tone flat. "Tandy, you're driving."

CHAPTER NINE

Even though Bonnie had only invited me and my parents to the little assembly in the council chambers, Tandy insinuated herself quite forcefully into our midst. No one—not even the mayor—had the energy to turn her away. Other than us, only the council members and the Fitzgeralds were present. Larry Munch tried to insist that the "demonstration," as he called it, be held in public. I think he liked the idea of all the townsfolk seeing the mages *he* brought to Owl's Hollow solve the current crisis. Maybe he had his sights set on the mayoral seat.

The other council members were split on the idea, and Bonnie was not keen, but to my surprise it was Fitz who put his foot down, stating calmly that he didn't work in front of audiences. Larry Munch was visibly disgruntled, but it wasn't like he could argue.

As it turned out, there wasn't much of a show to impress an audience anyway. I'd known some mages who plied their trade with unnecessary pizzazz, but even though I'd only seen him use magic once, I somehow knew that Fitz wouldn't be one of them. He was standing at the head of the council table with

Elinor to his left. She gnawed on a fingernail while she watched her brother, uncharacteristic anxiety written all over her features. Fitz put both hands on the table and bowed his head as if in prayer.

Tandy was not-so-surreptitiously filming with her phone, and Mim snatched it away from her. Tandy let out a strangled sound of protest but wasn't about to raise a fuss in the silence. Fitz didn't give any indication that he'd noticed.

Several random books, newspapers, and magazines had been spread across the table. Everyone was staring at the blank pages in anticipation, but I couldn't stop watching the mage himself. His eyes were closed and his features oddly relaxed in a way that was detached rather than serene. It was almost like he wasn't there at all.

After nearly a minute of tense silence, a visible shudder ran through his body, but he still didn't make a sound. Then he opened his eyes. A cacophony of murmurs and gasps erupted around the table. I knew without looking that he'd done exactly what he said he would do. His gaze met mine from across the room. I wondered if he could read any of my roiling emotions as I struggled to keep my expression neutral. Relief that the crisis was over coupled with disappointment that it was the mages who had fixed it. Anger that the solution was so simple and easy for him, when we'd worked all day without an inch of progress. Shame at my own childish resentment. Loss at the thought of that five grand going to Maven Enterprises, when it was Chanterelle Cottage that needed it the most. But who was to blame for that? Not Fitz, as loath as I was to admit it.

His own expression was curiously void of the smugness I would have expected. Instead, there was heaviness around his eyes and tension around his mouth. He looked . . . tired. He was still resting with both hands on the table. His attention slid away from me as Elinor leaned over his shoulder and whispered something urgently into his ear. He shook his head and straightened up, but slowly, like he wasn't sure if he could manage it. Elinor hovered with obvious distress. She hissed something else into his ear, and he grimaced. Whatever he replied didn't mollify her in the least because she crossed her arms and glared at him.

Phones had started ringing. Around the town, people were discovering that numbers and words had resumed their rightful place in the print and digital realms. I pulled out my own phone, though I hardly needed confirmation. The time and date were displayed on the lock screen. All my apps and messages were back to normal. I wished that I'd brought my grimoire with me—not because I had any reason to think that it wasn't restored, but it would have made me feel better to flip through it and take in all the comforting scribbles and notes from a lifetime of study.

"I think I speak for everyone when I offer our sincerest gratitude, Mr. Fitzgerald," Bonnie said, in her robust, civil servant voice.

"No gratitude necessary," he replied. There was a definite strain in his normally measured tone. "Just the payment we agreed upon."

Some of the councilors exchanged glances and meaningful whispers at that. I wondered if they'd expected him to make a noble gesture and tell them to keep the money or donate it to charity or something. I felt a traitorous pang of defensiveness on his behalf. After all, they'd been the ones to offer payment in the first place. Did they expect him to work for free?

But still, under the weight of the judgmental stares, I probably would have been guilted into blurting out that payment wasn't necessary. Fitz didn't seem to care about the shifting sentiment from awe to bitterness—or even notice.

Bonnie nodded stiffly.

"Of course," she said. "If you'll stop by the clerk's office to-morrow, I'll make sure your check is waiting for you."

"Thank you." Fitz turned to leave, obviously not interested in basking in any residual excitement from his fantastical feat. I watched him and Elinor go. He might have been limping, but they were out the door before I could tell for sure.

"Well, that's that," Mama said.

"Don't look so forlorn." Mim wrapped an arm around each of our shoulders. "Sure, the money would have been nice, but the important thing is that everything is as it should be. On Monday we'll be open for business again."

She was so cheerful that I could almost believe that all the Cottage needed was a good day of business to turn everything around. Mim was the accountant for the shop, and she tended to keep money concerns under her hat, but I'd peeked at some of the spreadsheets on her computer before. You didn't need to be an accountant to understand that when more money was going out than coming in, the business was in trouble.

Bonnie came over to talk to us. I tried to keep up with the conversation—which was peppered with occasional self-important remarks from Tandy—but my mind kept wandering. I excused myself and slipped out the door into the corridor. I caught up with the Fitzgeralds in the parking lot. The glow of dusk had enveloped the sky, casting everything in a haze of dreamy orange and pink. Elinor was in the process of wrestling the keys from her brother, insisting that *she* was driving and there was nothing he could do about it. She'd managed to grab them and was dangling them in the air with a triumphant "Aha!" when they noticed me.

"Hi," I said, when neither of them spoke. I was suddenly self-conscious and not sure why I'd followed them. I didn't have anything to say.

"Hi," said Elinor. She realized she was still holding the keys aloft and dropped her arm quickly. "We're just heading home." The car doors unlocked with a beep.

I waited for Fitz to say something, but he only regarded me with that frustratingly calm demeanor. Now that I knew what to look for, though, I could see the hints of exhaustion from his effort in the council chamber. In stark contrast to the sherbet colors of sunset, his aura was gray, almost colorless. He was leaning with his hip and arm against the car, as if he couldn't quite stand up straight. Maybe it had been unfair of me to assume that reversing the curse on the town had been easy for him.

"Okay," I said, shuffling uncertainly. A flush had begun to spread up the back of my neck and toward my ears and cheeks. "I just wanted to say, um, congratulations, I guess."

There. Now no one could ever accuse me of being unable to gracefully accept defeat.

"For what?" Fitz asked blankly.

Oh, for fuck's sake, was he really going to make me admit it out loud? *You won, I lost.* I tried to convince myself to say it and get it over with, but while I could manage graceful acceptance, humility was a whole different beast.

"If you're going to be a jerk about it, then never mind," I said, with a surge of righteous petulance. After all, if our positions had been reversed, I doubted he would have been gracious about it either. But on the other hand, losing your temper in a public parking lot is not a good look for anyone. I ground my back teeth to prevent any further outbursts.

His brow wrinkled—maybe he had expected more kowtowing in the wake of his brilliant accomplishment. I turned on my heel and headed back inside. It seemed like the most dignified course of action.

"Charlie, wait." His tone was so confused and sapped of its usual salt and vinegar that I wondered exactly how much his magic today had cost *him*. I hesitated, on the verge of turning back around, to hear him out, but I forced myself to keep walking. I was already racked with more than my fair share of guilt. First my failed spell in the fairy ring had lost us a huge payday, and now I'd let this five-thousand-dollar reward slip through my fingers. I'd pitted my witchcraft against his magecraft, and I'd come up short. Maybe I'd been a gifted witch as a child, but clearly I'd squandered the potential.

I refused to feel sorry for Fitz, on top of everything. If that made me a sore loser, then so be it.

CHAPTER TEN

In the weeks following what the local paper had dramatically dubbed the Whiteout, no one ever uncovered any clues on what or who might have caused the bizarre calamity. My parents and I did our own digging, when we had the time, but honestly, the crisis having passed, it seemed less and less important as the days went on. Our main focus was keeping the shop afloat. We had a slight uptick in customers after the incident, with a demand for protection charms and wards against negative energy, but it was a pittance compared to the boom in business that Maven Enterprises experienced once word of Sterling Fitzgerald's feat had spread around town.

A few outside media outlets had even picked up the story, earning Maven a spot on the network news. I'd looked up the clip online, telling myself it was professional curiosity, even though I knew very well it was a hate-watch to fuel my bitterness toward my rivals. It was not a riveting segment, considering that Fitz had refused an interview and Elinor only gave a brief, friendly statement about how happy they were that they could help the community. Elinor had said she was in charge of marketing, and I wondered if she was sore at her brother for wasting the prime publicity.

Aside from that little interlude, along with one or two late-night, wine-fueled Google searches, I refused to give the Fitzgeralds any space in my head. The shop was my only concern. (Also, there was disappointingly little about Fitz on the Internet, other than the fact that he was actually Sterling Fitzgerald III. The second Sterling was the dominant subject of almost every news article, web page, and social media post that I could find. He ran a hugely successful magecraft firm in Boston, which, best I could tell, he'd inherited from the first Sterling. Aside from that, he was well known for causing scandals at parties, such as having sex with the governor's daughter in a coat closet, giving one of the Red Sox two left hands after an argument, and setting fire to his yacht rather than cede it to his ex-wife during their messy divorce twenty years prior. If I were Fitz, I would have wanted to escape Boston too.)

Sometimes at night I could hear my parents up late at the kitchen table, poring over bills and spreadsheets and murmuring in worried tones. But every time I tried to broach the subject, they presented a united front in saying that we were fine, the shop was fine, everything was fine. Other than pitching a fit, I wasn't sure how to convince them to tell me the truth. And even if they did, what would that change? I already knew the shop was struggling, and I was already doing everything I possibly could to make sure we stayed afloat—or everything my parents would let me do, since every time I suggested investing my own capital in the business, they shut me down.

The fear crept in that my failures had already doomed the Cottage, and blocking me from being an equal partner was my parents' attempt at damage control. They had been on vacation when I took the commission from Tandy's homeowner association. I should have convinced the HOA to wait until they returned, or at least I should have consulted them over the phone, but they had left me in charge of the shop. I thought if I could handle the job and earn that payday on my own, they would have no choice but to admit that I was ready to be a partner in the business. I was desperate to prove myself, but in the end I only succeeded in proving myself a liability.

I was lucky they even let me run the cash register anymore.

Of course, my parents never so much as hinted at anything that dire. If anything, they bent over backward trying to reassure me that they didn't hold the fairy ring incident against me. I was catastrophizing, but logic didn't prevent me from diving into the helpless spiral of self-pity every night before I slept and every morning before I started my day.

It was the last Friday in August, three weeks after the White-out, and I was standing at the front counter in the shop with my laptop open, putting some final touches on a flyer design for a BOGO special on charms and spell jars. I hated the tackiness of it, but we needed to move product, and everyone loves a good sale.

My cell rang, and I answered without looking away from my work, tucking the phone between my shoulder and ear.

"Hello, Charlie. It's Fitz."

My brain took a couple of seconds to catch up with the words, and even then, it refused to offer me any sort of polite greeting.

"How did you get my number?" I asked instead.

"I read your mind."

I startled and the phone slipped off my shoulder. I scrambled to catch it, knocking a box of hag stones off the counter in the process. They skittered across the floor. I swore under my breath and managed to get the phone back to my ear. Fitz was chuckling.

"Relax," he said. "If you don't want people to have your number, then you shouldn't list it on your website."

Dammit. I'd been telling Mim for ages that we needed a separate line for the shop, but she insisted that listing our mobile numbers was perfectly adequate and much friendlier, besides. I took a second to collect myself and regain at least some of my dignity.

"And to what do I owe the pleasure?" I hadn't seen or spoken to him since that evening in the parking lot. (Unless you counted the handful of pictures I'd seen in my Google searches, which I did not.) In fact, I'd made it my mission in life to never go anywhere near Maven Enterprises again. "If you need another tarot reading, I'm afraid the rates have gone up."

"I have a referral for you."

"A what?" Of all the things I might have expected to hear—gloating, veiled insults, a challenge to duel at dawn—that was not one of them.

"I've got a young man in the office named Anthony Hawthorn. Somehow his mother has been turned into a ferret."

"Unfortunate," I said, still unsure where this was going.

"I've been told you're an expert at transmuting humans."

"I mean, I wouldn't say expert."

A pause.

"Have you ever turned anyone from an animal back into a human?" he asked.

"Yes. Once."

"Seeing as I've never met anyone who's managed it at all, I'd consider you an expert."

I was a little flattered, even though it wasn't exactly a compliment. But it would take more than a stroke of my ego to soothe my raging skepticism at this phone call.

"It took you less than a day to reverse a town-wide curse," I said, careful to keep any residual bitterness from seeping into my tone. "Surely you can manage this."

"I probably could."

A strange mix of vindication and disappointment swirled in my chest.

"We don't need your pity referrals." I gripped the phone tighter in an effort to keep myself calm. "We're not a charity case."

Another pause.

"I don't know what you want me to say, Charlie." His voice was quieter now, with an edge of weariness.

"I want you to be honest with me."

"Honestly, I wouldn't dare pity you. Honestly, I've never done this sort of magic before, and I don't see any reason to try, and possibly make it worse, when I know for a fact that you can do it right. Is that a good enough reason, or would you like me to grovel? This kid is sixteen years old. He needs his mother back in one piece."

My heart pounded so hard against my ribs that I was certain Fitz could hear it through the phone. Yet again, he'd said the last thing I would have expected. I'd never known a mage to admit that a witch could do a job better.

"Send him over," I said, my voice cracking. I cleared my throat. "I can help him right away."

I ended the call and closed my laptop. There was no sense in pretending I could focus on flyers right now. I headed to the back room to set up as much of the spell as I could before Anthony and his mother arrived. I made a mental note that we were running low on moon water and myrrh.

Less than half an hour later, the bell on the front counter signaled the approach of a car. I went outside to greet them. To my surprise, it was a black Mercedes that rolled up the winding drive. Immediately and unwillingly, I started taking stock of my appearance. I was in my typical work attire of jean shorts and a loose green and black plaid button-down, open over a gray tank top. I'd rushed my makeup that morning and had sweated most of it off by now. I probably looked exactly the same as the first time Fitz had visited the Cottage—stained apron and all.

I managed to purge myself of self-consciousness by the time the car was parked. Fitz stepped out, looking much the same as the first time I'd seen him too. He pushed his sunglasses onto his head and grinned at me. A hot wave rolled down my back that had nothing to do with the late-summer temperature. I averted my attention and focused on seeming both professional and approachable, for the sake of the kid who was climbing out of the passenger seat. Anthony was a gangly white kid with shaggy blond hair and a chin full of acne. He stared at the cottage in trepidation while clutching a cardboard box to his chest. There were several holes cut into the side and lid, so I presumed that his mother was in there.

"Hi, Anthony," I said with a friendly wave. "I'm Charlie. You can come on in."

Anthony studied me apprehensively, as if he expected at any moment I was going to hop on a broomstick and soar away, cackling. He looked beseechingly at Fitz, who gave him an encouraging nod. Personally, I thought I was much less intimidating than Fitz, with his impeccably tailored suit and his expensive car and his languid confidence and his stupidly deep blue eyes that never seemed to flinch away, even when I was glaring daggers at him.

But there was no accounting for taste.

I led them inside, where it was a little cooler than outdoors, but not by much thanks to our restricted budget.

"You can wait out here," I said pointedly to Fitz, as I guided Anthony toward the back room.

"Wait." Anthony stopped in his tracks and looked helplessly from me to Fitz. "You said you'd be with me the whole time."

"It's nothing scary," I assured him. "And it only takes about twenty minutes."

"I'm not scared," he said, with all the mustered indignation of youth. But he clutched the box a little tighter and still didn't move.

"I'll be right out here." Fitz gave him a gentle pat on the back. "You can trust Charlie."

Anthony eyed me again, as if searching for evidence that that was true. Dammit, he looked so terrified that now I felt like the bad guy. I guess witnessing your mother turn into a ferret and visiting first a mage then a witch, all in the same day, was not something a sixteen-year-old should be expected to handle alone. And if he'd decided, for whatever bizarre reason, that Fitz was his ally in all this, then so be it.

"Fine, you can come in," I told Fitz. "But no commentary."

His mouth twitched in what I was sure was going to be a smirk before he wisely caught himself.

"My lips are sealed," he said.

The ritual went more or less the same as the first time. Fortunately, Anthony knew more about his mother than Carl Di-Angelo had known about his wife. Once I'd tied the red ribbon around my wrist and lit the candles and incense, he calmed down enough to tell me her name and her daily routine. He kept his composure while describing her off-key singing while she made breakfast, how she spun around idly in her chair while on the phone for her remote marketing job, and the way she insisted on watching him play videogames but would never stop asking questions because she had no idea what was going on. His voice grew thick and watery when he explained that they'd had a fight the night before because he had never finished his summer reading for school.

I needed to focus on my spellwork, but first I reached out to lay my hand softly over his.

"She's going to be okay. I promise."

Maybe it was foolish to make a promise about something as

fickle as magic, but I couldn't help it. Chewing on his bottom lip, Anthony nodded, and at my signal he pulled the tawny brown ferret out of the box, cradling her snugly in his arms.

He set her down in the center of the circle, keeping his careful hold on her wriggling torso as I traced the rune onto her back with the herb paste I'd concocted earlier. I clasped the malachite in my hand and began to concentrate on the call to home.

After so many years of practice, my focus was usually superb, but I couldn't stop my mind from drifting toward the interloper in the corner of the room. True to his word, Fitz had remained silent throughout the process, offering only an encouraging smile whenever Anthony shot him a nervous look. That didn't keep my wayward mind from keying in to his every slight shift, wondering what he was thinking and second-guessing my every move.

The smoke from the candles and the incense had begun to waft in a lazy clockwise motion. I gripped the warm malachite so hard that the ridges dug into my skin. *Focus.* I'd made a promise to Anthony, and I wasn't about to break it because I couldn't keep my head on straight.

I closed my eyes, letting my jangling nerves and racing thoughts settle into a cool, dark center inside me. I reached outward for the familiar buzz of the magic on my skin and in my veins. It would never stop being one of the most beautiful feelings in the world.

When I opened my eyes, the smoke was floating due south. I bent down until I was face-to-face with the twitching Morgan Hawthorn. In a kind but firm tone, I called her home. The exact words I used seemed almost inconsequential, as the magic pulsed in rhythm with the flames inside our sacred circle of salt and candles. Mama had told me once that the casting of some spells resonates with your soul more deeply than others. Sometimes it's to do with the nature of the spell, or the person you're casting for, or just the perfect alignment of the stars and planets, but when you reach that stunning synchrony with the universe, it's like diving headfirst into the invisible flow of magic all around us. It's like breathing in stardust and breathing out galaxies. A power that both drowns and revives you.

I don't know why, because it was so rote in the beginning, but my spell for Anthony's mother carried me into that place. I must have completed the call to home. I remember setting my intention and speaking the words, but I don't remember anything that I said. I blinked, and Morgan was kneeling in front of me, her son sprawled behind her in a state of rapturous shock.

"Mom," he cried, diving forward and nearly tackling her with a hug.

There was a good bit of hugging and confusion, until Anthony calmed enough that Morgan could sit up straight and look around with consternation. She was a petite white woman, with sharp features that lent her a natural severity. Anthony did his best to explain how she'd ended up here (and where "here" was). As the full situation dawned on her, she began to look more and more upset, which was to be expected.

"You're totally fine now," I said.

Her manner darkened as she studied me. She was in her workout clothes and tennis shoes, with her golden hair pulled into a high ponytail. The transformation had probably occurred right before she left for her morning run.

"And what do you think you're doing, using your witchcraft on me without my permission?" There was no curiosity in her tone, only a cold, restrained fury.

"You . . . were a ferret." I wasn't sure what else to say. I glanced toward Fitz, but he seemed as perplexed as I was by Morgan's animosity.

"Mom," Anthony whispered, his face flushed with teenage mortification.

"Maybe we should head back to the front." I climbed to my feet.

Anthony helped his mother up, and the four of us moved into the shop. I stepped behind the counter and pulled out the ledger to jot down the details.

"And how much do you think I owe you for this *spell* of yours?" Morgan asked, with a disdainful emphasis that made it clear she considered my work on par with highway robbery or baby panda killing.

The high from the ritual was draining away fast in the face of her distinct lack of gratitude—or even civility.

"It's five hundred dollars," I said with a practiced smile, determined to ride this out like a professional. I pulled out the clipboard below the counter with the new-client information sheets and passed it over to her with a pen. "If you would fill this out, I'll be happy to bill you. And we do offer installment plans, if that's easier."

From her designer workout attire, I suspected that she and Anthony were not living hand to mouth. I probably could have gotten away with charging more. No doubt Fitz's services would have been at least three times as much. But price gouging was a line I was not willing to cross, no matter how desperate the times. Or how obnoxious the customer.

"That's outrageous." She crossed her arms with an imperious scowl.

"Mom, I said we'd pay," Anthony insisted.

"You're sixteen," she said. "Legally you can't promise anything of the sort."

"Mrs. Hawthorn," I said, squeezing my hands together on the countertop. "I assure you our services are—"

"I'm going to have to discuss this with my lawyer," she interrupted. "I don't think you can charge me for an untested, unregulated procedure that I didn't even consent to. I don't want magic anywhere near me or my son. It's volatile and dangerous and there have been cases of excessive use causing epilepsy, cancer, and permanent immune system damage."

During her entire diatribe, Anthony was looking steadily more embarrassed. By the end, he couldn't even look at me. I'd come across a few people like Morgan Hawthorn in my time—when they find out you're a witch, they can't help lecturing you about all the research they've done on how poisonous magic is and the incentive that big magecraft firms and coven conglomerates have to ensure that society remains dependent on them. I understood the distrust some folks harbored, and I didn't care if someone wanted to avoid magic, but I didn't appreciate when they felt the need to preach at me about all the harm I'm supposedly inflicting on the world.

"If you would prefer to remain a ferret," said Fitz from his position by the front door, "Charlie can probably reverse the reversal of the curse." His hands were in his pockets, and his posture and tone were that of utter leisure.

I shot him a glare. As far as I was concerned, the no-commentary rule was still in effect. The last thing I needed was him inflicting his big-city charm on my clients. Even clients who didn't want to be here in the first place. If I'd known Morgan was so anti-magic, I would have thought twice about casting the spell. But the unfortunate reality was that no matter how much you despised magic, there were some instances where it was the only solution. There are no medical procedures or home remedies that can cure you from transmutation.

"Please ignore him, ma'am. He's not affiliated with the Cottage," I told Morgan, slipping on my calm, commiserative customer service persona. "I understand your concerns, and I'm sorry that I wasn't able to obtain your verbal permission for the spell. However, you were incapacitated, and I had every reason to believe you needed immediate aid, so consent was implied.

Feel free to consult your attorney. Like I said, I'm happy to bill you, if that's most convenient."

I pushed the clipboard a couple inches closer to her. Though I was reasonably sure she couldn't sue, I wasn't as certain that we could compel her to pay us—not that we would take her to court over five hundred bucks if it came to that anyway. Hopefully my superior customer service skills would win her over. My rictus grin was starting to hurt my jaw, but my small-town charm paid off. Though her expression remained pure mutiny, Morgan snatched up the pen and scribbled down the bare minimum of her contact information, including an email but no phone number or address. In the checkbox asking if she'd like to receive coupons and marketing promotions, she wrote a big, unnecessary *NO*.

She threw the pen back onto the counter and took her son protectively by the arm.

"Anthony, where's your phone? We're calling a cab."

"Fitz said he would—"

"Anthony!"

He grimaced and dug out his cellphone while his mom herded him out the front door. She kept as wide a berth as possible from Fitz, as if he were going to turn her back into a ferret at any second. It was obvious from her darting eyes and hunched shoulders that she couldn't wait to be free from the diseased air of the witchcraft shop.

I notated her line on the ledger with *Unpaid*, then rounded the counter to watch them go. With Anthony in tow, Mrs. Hawthorn marched down the front steps, through the parking lot, and toward the main road. She must have decided she wanted to wait for a cab as far away from here as possible. Good riddance.

Fitz and I exchanged a look. The strain and exhaustion that had weighed on him so visibly the last time I'd seen him was gone without a trace. Three weeks must have been enough time for him to recover from whatever lifting the curse had cost him, although according to Tandy, they had been solidly booked ever since, so he couldn't have taken much of a break.

Without a word we stepped together onto the porch. The garish sunlight was blinding on the pale gravel of the parking lot, and the grass and shrubbery around the edges shone a deep emerald.

"That was . . . something else," said Fitz.

"Yeah." While unpleasant, Morgan Hawthorn wasn't the worst customer experience I'd had in my life. Not anywhere close.

"I don't suppose you'd let me pay their fee," said Fitz, a little cautiously.

I frowned.

"What? Why?"

"I talked you into taking the job. If I'd known her opinion on magic, I never would have—"

"I took the job because I wanted to take the job. She's not the first person to try to stiff us, and she won't be the last. I can handle it—I *did* handle it."

"You sure did." He wore a vague smile. "That was nice spell-work, by the way."

"Thanks," I said suspiciously, giving him side-eye. For some reason compliments from him never gave me the warm fuzzies. "And?"

"And what?"

"Normally when we talk, you have some suggestion for how to better conduct my business."

"Come on, I'm not that bad," he said. I replied with only a pointed look, and he raised his hands in surrender. "All right, fine. I won't make any more suggestions about your business. Will you stop looking at me like that?"

"Like what?"

"Like you want to murder me and feed my remains to your cat."

"How do you know we have a cat?"

"Don't all witches have a cat?"

I caught the edge of a smile on his lips and realized he was winding me up. A favorite pastime of his, it seemed.

"We do have a cat," I said with my own smile, "but Sophie wouldn't deign to eat the likes of you. She has a much more refined palate."

"What a relief."

"That doesn't mean I've decided against murdering you." I rested my arms on the whitewashed wood railing of the porch and studied him with mock seriousness. "Or maybe just hexing you."

"I'll take my chances." He leaned against the railing next to me, and I was reminded of the evening of the picnic and our conversation while we waited at the bar after the unfortunate margarita incident.

"Why do you think Tom Hanks was a sociopath?" I asked. He blinked at me, and I realized that the rabbit-leaping of my thoughts might need a little more explanation than that. "His character in *You've Got Mail*. You said he was a sociopath. Why?"

Fitz blinked again, then finally seemed to catch up with my question. He pulled his sunglasses off his head and fiddled with them between his fingers, squinting out at the thick clusters of trees that shielded the rest of the world from view.

"He was lying to her for almost the entire movie. Literally from the first time they met."

"F-O-X," I said, absently quoting the scene. *You've Got Mail*, while only tangentially a Christmas movie, was nonetheless a holiday favorite in my house. I'd seen it at least once a year since I was a toddler.

"He was pretty much an unrepentant asshole the whole

time," Fitz went on. "He only started acting like a decent human when he realized that she wouldn't give him the time of day otherwise. Even then his only redeeming quality was that he was Tom Hanks."

"He was funny," I said. "And he was good with kids."

"With his family at least. For all we know he was a monster to other people's kids."

I might have expected the offbeat opinion of one of my favorite romantic leads of all time to rub me the wrong way, but instead I found myself grinning.

"Is there a reason why you have a treatise on the evils of Joe Fox?"

"Shopgirl deserved better," he said ruefully, then slanted a glance in my direction. "My sisters watched it a lot after my parents divorced. It was their comfort movie, I guess. After the hundredth viewing, the love story starts to lose its shine."

The casual mention of what had, by all media accounts, been a nuclear war of a divorce caught me a little off guard. But we hardly knew each other. It wasn't like he was going to share his life story in detail.

"You have another sister?" I asked, pretending like I hadn't already read about her online. It seemed like a safe enough subject.

"My older sister Victoria. She's back in Boston with her husband."

I nodded, aware of the awkwardness that had descended between us, now that we were no longer sniping at each other. Small talk was truly the worst. I found myself wishing he would say something obnoxious so that I could bite back.

Fitz picked idly at the flaking paint on the railing.

"This could use a fresh coat," he said, almost to himself.

How obliging of him. I tried my best to sound annoyed instead of jubilant.

"You really can't help yourself, can you?"

"What?" He tilted his head to look at me.

"We do have a suggestion box inside, if you'd like to make a list of all your complaints."

"I'm trying to be helpful." He flicked a loose paint chip onto the ground below. "Chanterelle Cottage is a remarkable business, but you run it like a lemonade stand. Your store layout is confusing, your merchandising is lackluster, and your branding is nonexistent."

I smacked his hand before he could peel off another chip. He was lucky I didn't smack the back of his head for good measure. He wasn't saying anything I didn't already know, on some level, and had even brought up with Mim and Mama on occasion. But I was allowed to critique the Cottage. He was not.

"We have a billboard." It was the only expletive-free response I could think of.

"Which perfectly illustrates my point. That billboard is from the seventies."

"1986," I muttered. "Are you done yet?"

"You know, it wouldn't kill you to take some of my advice. Might help your bottom line. It's not like I don't know what I'm talking about."

"Oh please." I spotted a charcoal smudge on the back of my hand and wiped it against my apron. "I've been at this as long as you have—if not longer. Just because you're smart and talented and wildly successful doesn't mean you're always right."

Fitz searched my face while I spoke, sparking a tingle on the back of my neck. I hoped there weren't any other charcoal smudges on me. A tiny quirk appeared at the corner of his mouth. He looked almost pleased.

"Thank you."

"I'm insulting you," I said, incredulous.

"I know." The quirk spread into a smile, revealing his dimple. "You're terrible at it."

"Great, now you're telling me how to insult you better." I swiped a stray piece of hair behind my ear and headed back into the shop, unable to take another second of that steady gaze.

Fitz followed me inside, not catching the hint—or, more likely, choosing to ignore it.

"I don't think you're being fair." He propped his elbows on the counter while I stepped behind it and pretended to straighten up. "I'm just being neighborly."

"We aren't neighbors."

"Figuratively speaking."

"I'm not convinced you know the meaning of that word."

"Figuratively?"

"Neighborly." I found a half-burned energy-cleansing candle I'd forgotten was shoved under the counter and pulled it out. That was exactly what the shop needed after Morgan Hawthorn's visit. "Constant criticism is not one of the requisites. Honestly, I don't know how your sister can stand it. You must be a nightmare of a boss."

I glanced up in time to see something bleak cross his features. Not anger, more like . . . chagrin. But in the next second, he had resumed his normal deadpan, and I wasn't entirely sure I hadn't imagined it.

"I offer great benefits," he said.

"I'm sure." I pushed the candle toward him. "How about you make yourself useful? I'm out of matches."

"Happy to." He brushed his fingers over the top of the wick. Nothing happened. He frowned and tried again.

I rested my chin on my palms, biting back a giggle.

"Something wrong?" I asked innocently.

"No." He redoubled his focus, but a third attempt yielded only more of the same.

"Well, magic is hard." I produced a matchbook. "Maybe you need more practice."

He shot me a withering look as I lit the candle and blew out the match.

"You know what." I tapped my chin, as if something were occurring to me. "I wonder if it has something to do with no one but Sparrows being able to use magic on the Cottage grounds?"

"I wonder," he said in a dry tone.

"Silly me."

"I'll take that as my cue to leave you alone," Fitz said as he retrieved his keys from his pocket and headed toward the door. He paused on the threshold, turning back to regard me with his usual impossible-to-read countenance. "It was nice to see you again, Charlie."

"Same." I was surprised to find that I meant it.

"Can I call you later?"

I was frozen with bewilderment. My brain scrambled, trying to figure out if this was some kind of joke or trick, trying to figure out if I wanted to talk to him again.

"No," I said finally, only to regret it a second later. For the sake of my dignity and what little good sense I possessed, I decided to stick to my guns.

"Okay." He seemed utterly unruffled by the rejection. "Have a good one."

He departed without so much as a backward glance, and I was left oddly disgruntled and irritatingly aware that I had no one to blame but myself. But I was certainly not going to chase after him. As I heard the engine revving, I pulled out my phone and added Fitz's name to his number. So I could ignore him if he ever did call again, I told myself sternly. I almost believed it.

CHAPTER ELEVEN

Mama had mixed up some chili that morning to simmer in the crockpot throughout the day, so the entire upstairs of the Cottage smelled wonderfully of mouthwatering spices. We had dinner in the living room, balancing our bowls on our knees, so we could watch an old horror movie because Mim insisted that it was practically September, which was practically the same as October, and so the season of scary movies was upon us. For all her bright flowery dresses and cutesy statement jewelry, Mim really had a thing for gore and hair-raising thrills.

Mama, for all her swagger and leather jackets, spent the entirety of horror movies with her face buried in Mim's shoulder. Honestly, the two of them were almost more entertaining than the movie itself. Once they'd gone to bed (with Mama insisting she wouldn't sleep a wink and Mim promising to make it up to her and me pretending to gag while they kissed), I shut myself in my own room and pulled out the box of paper butterflies. I'd finished cutting and folding nearly a hundred, but I was still no closer to cracking the spell to give them artificial life. My parents' anniversary was less than two months away, so the pressure was on.

I tried a few different variations on a wind spell I had, testing different crystals I'd borrowed from the shop. I took painstaking notes of each failure in my grimoire, the way I'd been taught. Failures were as important as successes when it came to creating new spells. The problem was that my failures now spanned an entire two pages. I flipped to a new one and stared down at the creamy blank page for a long while, contemplating what details I might be overlooking or what other avenues I should try.

I was so zoned into my own thoughts that it took me several seconds to realize that inked words were appearing on the page, materializing in neat, crisp handwriting.

I can't help but feel that you would have told Joe Fox he could call you.

Once the initial shock wore off, irritation buzzed under my skin, coupled with the realization that I was grinning from ear to ear. It was confusing, to say the least. I tried to convince myself I should ignore him but only lasted about two seconds before I hopped up to scrounge around my desk for Tandy's silver pen. I'd tossed it there after the Whiteout and promptly forgotten about it. Since the carved runes were undamaged, I could only assume that it still worked. I'd show Fitz that even though my methods were more involved, I had no problem keeping up with his magic.

Maybe I have a thing for unrepentant assholes, I wrote beneath his words, not bothering to be careful with my shabby penmanship. Once I'd finished, my words vanished, to reappear (hopefully) on whatever piece of paper was in front of him.

I stared in unblinking anticipation at the page until I realized I was holding my breath and clutching the pen so tightly that my fingers ached. I forced myself to relax. At long last, more words began to appear, letter by letter as if I were seeing them as he wrote.

I'll keep that in mind.

I bit my lip to kill my obnoxious grin and decided to take my time with replying. I packed the butterflies neatly away, changed into my pajamas, brushed my teeth, washed my face, and got comfortable on my bed, sitting cross-legged with my book of shadows on my lap.

You have to admit that this is a little creepy, I wrote. *Next am I going to find you spying through my window?*

I wondered if he would make me wait for a reply too, but it was only a few seconds before the letters began to appear.

You're the one who's been spying.

I hesitated. Did he mean the scrying? He'd said something at the time, but I assumed he was talking to someone entering the room. I twirled the pen between my fingers, then decided denial was the best option.

That is slander, sir. Despite myself, a tiny smile formed. *Or does this count as libel?*

So the witch named Tandy who keeps dropping in and annoying the hell out of Elinor isn't a friend of yours?

Ah, Tandy. I shook my head. I should have known she wasn't as subtle as she insisted she was.

I wouldn't say friend. More like a reluctant colleague. And she's just nosy.

Well, technically, my moms and I *had* asked her to spy on Maven once, but that was to get her out of our hair, and we definitely hadn't asked her to keep doing it—which is not to say that we refused her continued updates on the status of their business. But I wasn't about to admit that to Fitz.

If you say so. But I can't be held responsible for what my sister says or does if Tandy calls her Elly-kins one more time.

I snorted a laugh. Tandy must've finally learned Elinor's name, sort of.

Noted. But to be fair, it's not like there are any deep secrets to be gleaned from standing around your lobby and annoying Elinor. Hardly counts as spying.

Despite myself, I was filled with a fizzy lightness. There was something strangely intimate about this way of communicating. More detached than talking, sure, but also more personal than texting. We were trading back and forth not only our handwritten words, but our magic as well.

True, came his reply. *All the dark and powerful secrets are kept locked away in my office.*

There's nothing dark and powerful about standing around and organizing books. The moment I penned the last word, I realized my mistake. His response came immediately, like he'd been waiting for my slip.

Busted. I could almost read his smirk in the word. *I KNEW it was you.*

My cheeks flamed, and I was glad we weren't face-to-face.

It wasn't on purpose. I can't help where the scrying session takes me.

You're terrible at apologizing.

You first.

For what?

You lied to me on the day we met.

I didn't lie to you.

That's exactly what Joe Fox said to Kathleen Kelly.

I was writing so fast that my words were barely legible at this point. If I was growing sleepy before, that had been purged out of me, replaced with the same thrumming electricity that filled me every time Fitz and I sparred.

Fair point, he wrote. *I'm sorry I didn't tell you who I was the first time we met.*

I was a little surprised that he actually apologized. Before I could reply, he was writing again.

Do you like me less, now that you know I'm not an unrepentant asshole?

The notion that he wanted me to like him sent another spark through my chest.

You may not be unrepentant, but I'm not so sure about the asshole part.

Not only was he trying to drive my family out of business, but he also criticized that business every chance he got.

You're the one who told me to stop being friendly. Meanwhile, you've insulted me more times than I can count and thrown a margarita on me.

I TRIPPED.

My point stands. If we're keeping a tally, then currently you owe me.

So what do you want?

I tapped my pen impatiently on the edge of my grimoire. It took him almost three minutes to reply—not that I was counting.

Let me take you to dinner tomorrow.

My heart stuttered in my chest. Was he being serious? Surely it was some kind of joke, and the punch line would come after I agreed. If I agreed, that is. I didn't want to go to dinner with him, did I? That was a big leap from vaguely insulting banter. He was still my competition. I chewed on the pen, formulating a dozen different replies. Finally, I settled on the simple and obvious.

No.

I kind of hoped he wouldn't reply, because I wasn't sure how strong my resolve was. But then the thought of the conversation ending there filled me with dismay. My pen was poised to write something else—I wasn't sure what—when letters appeared where I was about to write.

Lunch?

I knew I should write another "*No*," but I hated the idea of such a flat dismissal. It was so disingenuous, considering how tempted I was to say yes.

I can't, I wrote, thankful that I had a decent excuse. *I'm going to the farmer's market on Main in the a.m. to buy some supplies for the shop, then I have to do inventory. It'll take most of the day.*

Technically the shopping only took a couple hours, and then Mim and Mama did the inventory while I lounged around in their vicinity munching on roasted pecans or whatever treat I'd picked up at the market. But he didn't need to know that. I was gnawing on the pen again while I waited for a reply. At this rate, I'd decimate the carved runes and render it useless.

Perfect, I'll drive. What time?

I was smiling again, despite myself. I lowered the pen to write that it hadn't been an invitation, but I wavered. Was there any harm in a day trip to the market? It wasn't a date. I pressed the pen to paper.

Pick me up at nine.

CHAPTER TWELVE

When I woke the next morning, it was pouring rain, and I couldn't decide if the possibility of canceling the trip to the market with Fitz was a disappointment or a relief. But the weather app on my phone promised clear skies in the next hour. Whether or not Mother Nature was doing me a favor, only time would tell.

Instead of my usual messy bun, I painstakingly straightened my hair. Mim had a special magic concoction she used to keep her hair from frizzing, even in the worst humidity, so I stole a little to rub into my roots. I stared into my open closet for a while, trying to decide on what to wear. Normally I didn't wear anything special on trips to the farmer's market, but this morning I found myself gravitating toward the cuter pieces in my wardrobe.

I changed no fewer than three times before I finally forced myself to settle on something or risk being late. I was tying a scarf in my hair as a headband when Mama drifted in through my open doorway, yawning. She was still in her pajamas.

"Going to the market today?" she asked.

"Yeah," I said. "I won't need the car after all. A . . . friend is driving me."

Even half-asleep, Mama seized on my hesitation like a hawk on a mouse. She scrutinized my attire, which was casual, but still nicer than my usual fare.

"I see," she said. I finished tying my headscarf, desperate to avoid her eyes. "And would this friend of yours happen to be tall and handsome and a mage?"

How the hell did she always know these things?

"No," I said, but much too late and too weak to be believable. Mama gave a giddy little shriek.

"I'm telling your mother," she cried, then raced down the hall. I chased after her, but she slid into the kitchen before me, where Mim was brewing a pot of tea. "Ruby, you'll never believe it. Our beloved and traitorous daughter is going on a date with a *mage*."

"It's not a date." I gave Mama a light shove as she made a dramatic show of fanning herself with her hand like she was having the vapors. "He's just giving me a ride."

"Honey, we only live three miles from town," she told me, planting a hand on her hip. "If he offered to come out here just to drive you three miles, then it's a date."

"I'm thirty-two years old." I crossed my arms and glared. "I do not need my mother to tell me whether or not I'm going on a date."

"If that were true, we'd have a freezer full of leftover wedding cake by now."

"I hate you," I said, but was undermined by my own smile.

In contrast to Mama's amused mischief, Mim was stirring her tea while watching me ponderously.

"Are you sure this is a good idea?" she asked. It wasn't an accusation but a genuine question. Heat flared up my back, because no, I wasn't sure at all.

"It's not a date," I repeated.

Mim eyed me for a moment longer, then nodded.

"Okay, but wear your protection sigil. If he tries anything—"

"Oh my god." I buried my head in my hands. "I am not sixteen, and this is not the prom. Please stop."

"When is he getting here?" Mama demanded. "I want to sit on the front porch in a rocking chair with my shotgun across my lap."

"You don't have a shotgun," I said.

"Or a rocking chair," said Mim.

Fitz arrived at nine o'clock on the nose, and I was waiting for him on the front porch, sans my parents, a rocking chair, or a shotgun. It had taken me nearly ten minutes of cajoling to convince them not to come downstairs and embarrass me, which they dearly wanted to do. They were both probably standing with their noses pressed unsubtly to one of the upstairs windows, and I could only hope that Fitz didn't look up.

The rain had slowed to a faint drizzle, so I didn't bother with an umbrella. Fitz opened the passenger door for me, and as I slid inside, I heard my phone buzz in my bag with a text message. I knew without looking that it was Mama saying, *I told you it was a date.* I resisted the urge to lean forward and shoot them the bird through the windshield.

I'd never seen him in actual casual clothes before, but today he was wearing dark jeans and a plain, fitted T-shirt, and god help me, he looked just as good in that as he did in a suit. Possibly better, because now I had an unobstructed view of his trim waist, the lean muscles in his arms, and the way his dark hair curled a little at the nape of his neck.

To distract myself, I started playing with his space-age car's touchscreen and plethora of buttons and switches. Fitz tried in vain to hide his distress as I upset the perfect balance of his interior. He lasted less than a minute.

"Good god," he said, "are you compelled to touch every shiny object you see, or is it my property in particular?"

"Sorry," I said, without much conviction, but I did sit on my hands in an attempt to behave myself. "You probably regret offering to drive now, don't you?"

"I'm getting there." He shot me a wry look. "But as long as you don't find a self-destruct button in here, I think we'll be okay."

"I'll just have to find myself some shiny things at the market to amuse myself."

"Do you buy all your inventory there?"

I hesitated, trying to figure out if it was a leading question that he was going to follow with more unwanted business advice. But his tone didn't suggest anything more than idle curiosity.

"No," I said carefully. "We have a few vendors who only sell at the market. It rotates between towns, so it's only here once a month."

Getting added to the market's rotation had been a big coup for Owl's Hollow and Bonnie's first major win as deputy mayor. She'd gone with me a few times to the market in other towns and realized the benefit of all that disposable income being funneled onto Main Street. Once she set her mind to the task, it had only been a few months before the grand opening in Owl's Hollow. It certainly made my sourcing trips more convenient. We were usually open on Saturdays, but on market day every month we closed the shop so I could purchase supplies and my parents could do inventory.

Fitz nodded while he navigated through the four-way stops at the edge of town. There were more cars on the road today than the rest of the month combined.

When he didn't start lecturing me on inventory management or whatever, I relaxed some.

"I also have to test every single free sample," I added. "It's serious business."

"Sounds like it."

The awkward lull that followed left me itching for distraction again, even though we were only a couple minutes away. My left hand escaped from beneath my thigh, and I reached to press one of the few buttons I hadn't managed to test earlier. An orange light flickered on.

"You're incorrigible." Fitz sounded more amused than aggravated, though he did move my hand back to my lap and hit the button a couple more times until the light went off.

With effort, I ignored the shivery sensation that had run up my arm at his touch. My body was inexplicably reverting to teenage hormone levels, but I was going to keep a stiff upper lip. So help me, I would not give my parents the satisfaction of being right.

"Was that the self-destruct?" I asked.

"Seat warmer," he said. "*My* seat warmer."

"Well, maybe the manufacturer should label their six million buttons more clearly."

"I'll write a letter. In the meantime, you could try keeping your hands to yourself."

"What fun would that be?" I didn't realize until the words left my mouth how they could be construed as flirtatious—downright suggestive even. I risked a glance in his direction, but he was still focused on the road. He had a nice profile, which was not something I'd ever thought about a person before. Further evidence that my brain was short-circuiting. He didn't say anything to indicate that he'd construed my comment as innuendo, but his grip on the steering wheel had tightened. Or maybe I was imagining that.

Fitz parked in his reserved spot in the alley behind Maven Enterprises, which was only a few blocks away from Main. We had to make a quick detour to his office, because he hadn't been able to find his wallet at home. After a fruitless search, he ended up calling Elinor to ask if she'd seen it. She told him it was probably in his pocket, where it always was. He told her it definitely was not. (It was.) And then we were on our way.

Though the sky was congested with thick gray clouds, the rain had stopped, and occasional beams of sunlight streamed through. The day wasn't a scorcher, but it was muggy enough that I'd probably have to pull my hair up before we were through. What a waste of my straightening efforts.

"Looks like the weather is clearing up," I said, to fill the awkward silence between us as we walked.

"Really?" he asked. "You've spent most of our acquaintance insulting me and *now* you want to start doing the whole friendly small talk thing?"

So much for social niceties.

"Well," I said, "if you don't want small talk, then that only leaves us two options. Either I can insult you some more—"

"Pass."

"Then all that remains are the big, existential questions."

"I suspect there's a middle ground you're ignoring."

I ignored *that* and forged onward.

"What do you want more than anything in the world?"

"Right now? Coffee." He nodded toward Madge's Café on the corner, and we crossed the street. Through the wall of windows, I could see that there was an actual line at the counter. Unheard of.

"Coffee is not nearly existential enough," I said. "Try again."

"World peace."

"That's cheating." I bumped my shoulder against his. "Everyone wants that."

"You don't get to add rules after the fact." He bumped me right back. He was grinning as he held open the café door, and that damn dimple of his was on display. I was struck by the urge to brush my fingers across it.

This trip might have been a bad idea after all.

I scurried inside, letting the welcome burst of air conditioning clear my head.

"What about you?" Fitz asked, once we'd taken our place in line. "I don't think I should be the only one who has to wax existential."

I tried to think up something as ubiquitous as world peace, but in the end, I stuck with the truth.

"I want to be an equal partner in the family business. I have the money, but my parents don't think it's a good idea."

"Why not?" A tiny frown etched a line between his brows.

"You'd have to ask them." I tried to keep my voice light, but I was beginning to suspect this whole "existential conversation" thing was a mistake. Theme of the day, apparently. "Probably has something to do with my felony convictions."

"Wait, what?"

"Kidding." I wouldn't let myself nudge his shoulder again, as much as I wanted to. "As far as you know, anyway."

"Your parents strike me as the type of people who wouldn't be fazed by a few minor felonies."

"You're probably right." I had every intention of leaving it at that, but the words tumbled out before I could stop them. "They don't think I'm ready for the responsibility. I messed up a customer's spell a while back—a big one. It did some damage and lost us a lot of money."

The confession immediately lifted a weight off my chest that I hadn't even noticed before. I took a deep breath, confused by my own relief. I had admitted one of my biggest mistakes to my business rival. I should have been mortified at my own vulnerability.

But for some reason, sharing it with Fitz wasn't mortifying in the least. I was certain he wouldn't think of me any differently, which was a completely illogical conviction. I barely knew him.

I watched for his reaction from the corner of my eye, but he wasn't the easiest person to read. All the more reason why I shouldn't be laying myself bare in this coffee shop line.

He was quiet for a while, and I plucked nervously at the hair elastic around my wrist. Maybe it would be for the best if he said something insulting about me or my witchcraft. Then I could hate him, and we could go back to being bitter rivals instead of whatever we were doing right now.

"Let me guess," he said finally. "You accidentally hexed someone to perpetually feel like they have to sneeze."

A shaky laugh escaped me.

"Not quite. That's a pretty good idea for a hex, though."

"Swapped the covers of all the books in the Cottage?"

"Now who's incorrigible?" I said, but I was smiling. Hearing him make light of my failed spellwork was strangely freeing, like he was putting it into perspective. Suddenly the shame that had been festering in a dark, secret place inside me was a little less secret, a little less powerful. My parents had told me before that draining the fairy ring wasn't the end of the world, but this was the first time I'd been able to believe it.

Once it came time for us to order, as penance for the traitorous thoughts I kept having about touching him, and to prove once and for all to myself—and Mama—that this wasn't a date, I absolutely refused to let Fitz pay for my drink. He seemed bemused by my vehemence but otherwise didn't offer any objection. I knew a five-dollar frappuccino wasn't the most reasonable hill to die on, but I still counted it a victory.

I did realize belatedly that he'd never answered my original question about what he wanted most in the world. So much for deep and meaningful conversation.

The market was a smorgasbord of farmers, witches, local artisans, and food trucks, all lined up along both sides of Main Street and the two parallel streets, which were pedestrian only for the day. The market had opened over an hour ago, but thanks to the rain, the early birds were showing up at the same time as the later arrivals, and it was more crowded than usual. A man and woman on a small stage near the top of the street were strumming guitars and crooning a ballad into microphones, while a handful of patrons swayed to the music.

The rows of colorful tents and stalls gave me a rush that hit better than caffeine. My trips to the market were one of my favorite parts of my job, second only to spellcasting for customers. My parents and I had been regular patrons even before the market came to Owl's Hollow, ever since I was a baby cradled in a sling across Mama's chest. They still accompanied me occasionally, but the market didn't hold the same fascination for them.

As we neared, I was struck by the insecurity that comes when you share your favorite book or movie with someone and are waiting to hear their opinion. I sneaked a look at Fitz to gauge his reaction to the riot of color and commerce stretched out before us. I was worried I'd find a hint of disdain for the rustic pastimes of the common rabble, but instead I saw that he was smiling. A real smile, not the smirk he'd worn the first day I met him. Warm satisfaction spread through my chest.

There were three or four regular sellers where I always sourced the supplies we needed for the shop, but that never stopped me from wandering the aisles in search of new and interesting treasures. We stopped at a booth offering free samples of different salsa flavors and each took a tortilla chip from the bowl to spoon our selections onto. Fitz made a face at his.

"Not a fan of—" I leaned in to read the label. "Mango Chili Explosion?"

Fitz checked to make sure the owner was distracted by another customer, then shook his head.

"It tastes like a mango curled up and died in it."

"Try this one." I scooped some Cilantro Celebration onto a new chip for him, then yanked it back before he could take it. "Wait, you're not one of those people who think cilantro tastes like soap, are you?"

"Is that a thing?"

"It's a thing." I handed him the chip.

"That's tragic." He took a bite and nodded his approval. "Much better."

I picked up one of the jars to find the handwritten price tag on the side.

"Worth thirty dollars a jar?"

"Maybe not," he said, and we made our escape before the owner could reel us in.

We hit up a few more stalls with free samples but found nothing worth writing home about. I did learn that Fitz was allergic to coconut, which prompted me to tell the story of my disastrous date with Bonnie and her subsequent happily-ever-after.

"I told her and Jen that they ought to thank me in their wedding vows," I said, "but for some reason that didn't make it in."

"Please tell me you at least got extra cake."

"No, but they offered kombucha tea as one of the drink options at the reception and thought that was hilarious."

"They could have at least had an ice sculpture of you as their centerpiece. Or set you up with someone to return the favor."

There was nothing in his tone to suggest what he was thinking, but I was struck by the notion that I'd spent the past few minutes talking about my date with a woman, and I wondered if he'd misconstrued my refusal to go to dinner with him. It wasn't like it mattered, because I *wasn't* interested in him that way, but I also needed to set the record straight for reasons I didn't plan on exploring anytime soon.

"I'm bisexual," I blurted, a bit too loudly. *Smooth, Charlie.* "I mean, just so you . . . know."

Very smooth. He stared at me for a few seconds, brows slanted slightly in confusion.

"Okay," he said, after an awkward pause, like he couldn't think of anything to say. I suppose that was a fair reaction to someone abruptly flinging their sexual identity at you in casual conversation.

"Sorry, that was random." I was cringing so hard on the inside that I considered pulling one of my tote bags over my head.

He looked like he was about to say something, but then he stopped short and frowned at something over my shoulder. Without warning, he grabbed my arm and yanked me toward him. A split second later, a deluge of water dumped over the spot where I'd been standing.

My mind scrambled to catch up with what had happened. At first, I couldn't process anything but the fact that my shoulder was pressed hard against Fitz's chest and my hip against his thigh. His grip on my arm was firm but gentle. He smelled faintly of coffee beans and laundry detergent.

I looked up, and despite our proximity, I was still somehow startled to find his face so near. His surprise mirrored mine, like he wasn't quite sure how we'd gotten here either. He released my arm but didn't step back.

Behind me, the vendor that had been in the process of adjusting his tent apologized profusely to the passersby whose shoes he'd accidentally soaked. He hadn't realized that his sagging canopy was swamped with rainwater. Luckily for me, Fitz had.

Now that the flood had passed, we were standing in the way of people trying to access the vendor's stall. (His gorgeous collection of glazed pottery had survived the mishap no worse for wear.) I led the way farther down the street, to a quieter section where a man handing out religious pamphlets about the evils of witchcraft had managed to drive away most of the foot traffic.

"That was—" I cut off, trying to put my racing thoughts into some semblance of order. My heart was thumping madly with adrenaline I didn't fully comprehend. Getting doused with water would have sucked, but it wasn't exactly a life-or-death situation. "Thank you."

"No problem." His throat pulsed with a swallow, and he glanced down. I realized I was still holding his hand, and I dropped it, hoping my expression didn't betray how my skin effervesced at his touch. God, I really was like a horny teenager. "You should probably avoid any more suspiciously drooping tents. My reflexes aren't always that good."

"Clearly," I said, "or you would have fewer margaritas spilled on you."

"Maybe." He ran a hand through his hair, leaving a disheveled mess in its wake. There was a glint of mischief in his eye. "Or maybe I figured that you spilling a drink on me was a good excuse to talk to you."

My heart, which had settled to a quiet strum in my chest, leaped into my throat. I was trying desperately to keep my cool composure, but it wasn't working.

"The hour of repentance is upon us," cried the man with the pamphlets, making his way over to us to wave one in my face. "Have you given any thought to where you'll go when you die?"

"Oh yes," I said pleasantly. "Straight to hell if I'm lucky. Hail

Satan." I freed the pentacle necklace from beneath my shirt to wave at him. It had nothing to do with hell or Satan, and in fact had a protection sigil carved on the reverse (yes, I let Mim talk me into wearing it, just in case). But judging by the man's wide-eyed panic as he stumbled backward to get away from me, he didn't know anything about magic symbols.

"'Thou shalt not suffer a witch to live,'" he quoted, which would have been more frightening if his voice weren't shaking as hard as his legs. He earned himself several harsh looks with that—the market was a mainstay in the witch community. An elderly Latina woman in a nearby booth pointed a bony finger at him and hissed something in Spanish that I'm sure he thought was a Bruja curse. (In fact, she told him to fuck off.) He hightailed it out of there, clutching his pamphlets to his chest like some kind of armor against our wickedness.

Maybe he would have preferred my Caravaca de la Cruz. I slipped my pentacle back under my shirt and realized that Fitz was staring at me.

"What?" I demanded.

A grin split his lips, and he shook his head.

"Nothing. You're . . . surprising, that's all."

I wanted to ask if that was supposed to be a compliment, but I also didn't want him to think that I cared either way. At any rate, it was probably time to do the shopping I'd come here to do.

I bought more moon water and myrrh, amethyst and jade crystals in various shapes (our bestsellers), various oils and tea blends, and some new hand-carved wands. Because I bought in higher quantities than the average customer, and my family had been buying from them for years, the sellers always gave us enough of a discount that we could turn a profit in the shop. There were ways to source cheaper product, but cheaper usually meant worse quality, and the Cottage never dealt in inferior goods. It was a matter of principle. Plus, we used our products in our own rituals, and impure oils or unethically sourced herbs could damage spellwork.

I was nervous that Fitz would get bored quickly, but he took everything in stride, joking around with the sellers while I made my decisions and occasionally asking me what a specific item was for. It was strange for a mage to show interest in witchcraft, but I found it hard to hold on to my anti-mage sentiments when I was talking to Fitz. He listened like he cared what I had to say, not like he was being polite. And I found myself caring what he had to say as well.

He wandered off only once, while I was admiring a gorgeous tarot deck that one of the booths had on display, and returned with two paper cups filled with ice-cold, fresh-squeezed lemonade. His eyes glimmered with laughter as he told me how the person in front of him in line had confounded the poor vendor by demanding a lemonade that was citrus-free. I laughed with him, and as the tart sweetness filled my mouth and the cool condensation from the cup dripped down my hand and the newly emerged sun overhead warmed me from head to toe, I was finally convinced that this not-date had been a bad idea. But I couldn't bring myself to care.

CHAPTER THIRTEEN

It was past noon by the time Fitz dropped me back at home. We'd ended up buying lunch from one of the food trucks at the market and sitting on a damp curb to eat, paper plates balanced on our knees. I kept thinking we would run out of things to talk about and sink back into awkward silence, but we never did.

By the time we were sitting in the gravel lot in front of the Cottage, the car idling quietly, I was bone-deep tired, but content.

"It's a beautiful old house." Fitz was gazing up at the Cottage, at the gabled roof with its gingerbread trim, the whimsically ornate brackets, and the hooded bay windows. The foundation of the house was original, but various renovations had spruced up the appearance over the years. The last one was at least fifty years ago, though.

"It is," I agreed, but I was mesmerized by the way the afternoon light washed over his features, casting his pale skin in a rich glow and glinting in his eyes like the sun on ocean waves. "Can I ask you something?"

Those eyes flickered in my direction.

"Sounds ominous, but sure."

"What brought you to Owl's Hollow?" I picked at a loose thread on the hem of my shirt. "I mean, I love it here, but coming from Boston, you aren't exactly climbing the career ladder."

"Believe it or not, I care about more than making money."

"That's not what I meant," I said defensively, even though maybe it was. A little.

"My father owns a big magecraft firm, and I worked there for a while, but he—" Fitz hesitated, a shadow flitting across his expression. His fingers tapped idly on the steering wheel. "He was a shitty boss. I told some contacts I was looking for something different, and one of them put me in touch with Larry Munch. He said he'd been trying to bring the town's magic market into the modern era and offered to sponsor our license."

I snorted, and Fitz shot me a look. "What?"

"Larry Munch hates magic," I said. "He's been trying to put the Cottage out of business for years. I guess he figured some direct competition was his best chance."

Fitz frowned, the lines between his brows deepening as the full implications settled in.

"Well, that's disappointing," he said at last.

"You're telling me."

He twisted to face me, his hand moving as if to touch my leg, but he stopped short and rested it on the gearshift instead.

"I didn't know." The lines of concern in his forehead were like fissures, and I fought the urge to smooth them away. "I mean, I knew about Chanterelle Cottage, but I didn't know that was the reason Munch wanted us in Owl's Hollow."

I had no reason to disbelieve him, even though yesterday that wouldn't have stopped me from assuming the worst. A lot could change in a day.

"Don't worry about it." I managed a halfhearted grin that probably more closely resembled a grimace. "It's just business, right?"

The lines didn't dissipate, and he searched my face for a few moments in silence. I wasn't sure what he was looking for, or if he found it.

"You know," he said, in a mild tone, "if you were truly diabolical, now would be the time to guilt me into shutting down Maven."

I was tempted to ask him if that would work but changed my mind.

"I don't want to guilt you into anything." I gathered up my purchases from the floorboard. "There's going to be a vote on your license in October, and I'm going to beat you fair and square."

I had the date circled on my calendar in red ink. After his unmitigated success with the Whiteout, it was looking less and less likely that the council would vote against Maven, but I was determined to keep that stiff upper lip. I opened the door—or tried to, anyway. It was locked and remained locked even when I hit several buttons in succession.

A sound came from the driver's side that was dangerously close to a snicker, and I shot Fitz a glare.

"It's not that complicated," he said. "Have you never been in a car before?"

"I've been in a normal car with a normal number of buttons." I yanked the handle with gusto, but that didn't do the trick either. "Your stupid space car has clearly developed sentience and hates me for some reason."

"It probably got tired of you turning on the seat warmers in eighty-degree weather." But he took pity on me and reached across my lap to hit the correct button, which I swore was one I'd already tried.

For a few seconds, our bodies were dangerously close again. I caught a whiff of something sharp and fresh—eucalyptus maybe? I wanted to breathe in his scent more deeply, but I resisted. I didn't want to cap off this not-date by being creepy.

I opened the door, trying not to appear too eager to escape.

"No," I said, when Fitz started to open his. "Don't get out. If my parents catch sight of you, they will descend."

"Charlie, are you ashamed of me?" The glimmer was back in his eyes, the frown gone without a trace. I didn't miss it.

"I'm protecting you." I patted his shoulder, the only touch I was going to allow myself. "Trust me on this."

I climbed out, knowing if I lingered much longer that one or both of my parents would come outside anyway. I was already going to be getting the third degree on what exactly we were doing sitting in the car this long.

But before I shut the door, something else occurred to me, and I leaned back down.

"You know, I told you what I want more than anything, but you never gave me a real answer." I rested my forearm against the car. The black metal was hot, but after the constant, icy blast of state-of-the-art air conditioning against my sweat-dampened skin, it felt nice.

"Am I not allowed to want world peace?"

"You're allowed to want whatever you want," I said. "I'm just curious what that is."

His mouth twitched into a tiny smile, but there was something almost rueful about it.

"When I know, you'll be the first person I tell." He slid his sunglasses down from the top of his head. "Bye, Charlie."

"Bye, Fitz. Thanks for the ride." I knocked the door shut with my hip, gave him a wave, and headed onto the porch. It wasn't until I locked the door behind me that I heard the engine rev and the tires crunch on the gravel.

I set my bags behind the counter, deciding I'd unpack them later when I had more energy. Broomhilde was sashaying up one of the aisles, so I dragged a couple chairs from the work room to block off the space behind the counter. The last thing I needed was for my least favorite sibling to start knocking around my new purchases.

"I'm on to your game," I told the broom. Then I wondered when exactly I'd started to lose my mind.

I trudged up the steps and found my moms at the kitchen table with a laptop open, piles of bills and several half-finished cups of tea surrounding them. They were in the middle of a tense discussion that cut off the moment I entered.

"How was the not-date?" Mama asked.

"Fine," I said, slipping off my shoes and tossing my bag down by the door. "What's up?"

It was hard to miss the look they exchanged.

"Nothing, catching up on some paperwork." Mim wasn't convincing in the least. "You want some lunch before we start on inventory? I think we've got a frozen pizza."

"Already ate." I sat down at the table with them. "Are you going to tell me what's going on?"

"What do you mean?" Mim asked, at the same time Mama said, "Nothing's going on."

"This isn't fair." I glared between them, irritation trickling hotly down my spine. "You can't keep me in the dark forever. I know something's going on with the finances, so why won't you just tell me?"

They both averted their gazes. Mama nudged her mug a few inches to the left with one finger. Mim straightened a stack of papers.

"Well?" I demanded.

"Okay, fine," said Mama.

"Ali," began Mim.

"No, she's right. It's not fair." Mama pinched the bridge of her nose. "We're close to bankruptcy."

My stomach twisted, though I'd already suspected as much. "How close?"

"A month. Two, if we're lucky." Mim sighed heavily. "The roof repairs after that storm last year put us in a hole, and sales have been down for longer than that. And now with Maven Enterprises . . ." She trailed off.

I chewed on the inside of my cheek. Maven Enterprises, whose owner I'd spent the day laughing and goofing off with, while my moms sat at home and worked to delay the inevitable.

"Why didn't you tell me before?" I asked, because turning the blame outward was so much easier than bearing it myself.

"We should have." Mama twisted her fingers together on the table. "You have to understand that it's hard for parents to admit failure to their kids—even when the kids are grown up."

"You're not failures." I was horrified by the mere suggestion. "It's a bad patch. If you'll let me—"

"We're not taking your money," Mama said, with a sharp edge of impatience.

Tears welled, and I blinked rapidly. It was more frustration than anything. The uniquely helpless kind of frustration that only parents can evoke. I didn't want to argue right now. If I pushed too hard, they might tell me the real reason I couldn't buy in—that they didn't trust me or think I was ready. I wasn't sure I could handle that.

"There has to be something *else* we can do." My tone was a little testy, but otherwise I kept my cool.

"We're trying, baby, but it's a snowball running downhill," Mim said. "It'll take more than an uptick in business to fix this."

"There has to be something," I repeated stubbornly. I stood up. "Promise me you won't keep something like this from me again."

They exchanged a weary glance.

"Please," I said. How could I do anything to help the business if I didn't even know what was going on?

"Okay, promise," said Mama. Mim nodded.

It didn't make me feel better exactly—there were far too many emotions jangling in my chest for that. But I did feel like I could breathe again.

"I'm going to take a shower." I backed toward the hallway. The thought of helping with inventory and pretending like everything was fine seemed like too daunting a task at the moment. "I'm all sweaty."

"Okay." Mim's attention had drifted back to the computer screen. I hated the heaviness in her features, tugging on the laugh lines and pooling in dark circles beneath her eyes. Mama had laid her head down on her arms, like she didn't even have the energy to stay upright anymore.

There was a dense, aching knot in my throat, and I fled to my room before it could turn into tears. I paced for a few minutes, my mind whirling uselessly through all the things that couldn't help us now. Sales, advertisements, new product—none of that would do any good. And even if we did manage to convince the council not to renew Maven's magic license, would that be too little, too late?

At last, I couldn't think anymore and retreated to the shower. The hot water soothed some of the weariness in my muscles, if not the racing of my thoughts. When I was finished, I combed through the wet tangles of my hair, then slipped into an oversized Duke University T-shirt, the cotton made soft with wear. I'd had a good time at my alma mater. I even kept in touch with several friends I'd made there, but attending university had been more to appease my parents, who were worried that staying in Owl's Hollow was somehow holding me back. I'd hoped that going away to school and traveling for a while after graduation would ease their concerns. I moved back to Owl's Hollow because it was my home. I never wanted to make one anywhere else.

My parents had started letting me work part-time in the shop when I was sixteen. Since my first taste of magic as a service, as a solution for people who didn't have anywhere else to turn, I'd had my eye on the prize. I'd saved every penny I could. I wanted to be part owner of Chanterelle Cottage on the basis of my own hard work and dedication. I wanted to earn it.

Ever since I'd returned from college and my parents had (kindly, but firmly) denied my first request to purchase a stake in the Cottage, I'd been collecting praise and approval and heaping it all on an invisible scale. I was convinced there had to be a tipping point. There had to be a moment when their reluctance was finally outweighed by how good I was with customers, how clever I was at marketing tactics, how skilled I was with spells, how dedicated I was to my work. And when that day came, I would finally—*finally*—have everything I wanted.

The incident with the fairy ring had set me back, maybe too far. Not for the first time, I burned with the desire to turn back the clock, to somehow go back in time and smack Past Charlie on the back of the head and tell her that she had no business trying to take on such a complicated commission by herself.

Permanently altering the molecular composition of grass in an entire neighborhood was bigger magic than one witch could command under normal circumstances, but the secret weapon growing in the woods behind the shop had given me unearned confidence. I'd never cast a spell in a fairy ring before—it was a tool strictly reserved for seasoned witches—but I thought I was ready. I really did. The mushrooms that gave Chanterelle Cottage its name were in full bloom, meaning the magnifying power of the ring was at peak efficacy.

I'd painstakingly designed a ritual and followed it to the letter. The fairy ring did its part and amplified my magic exponentially, but the surfeit of raw power did nothing except wither the mushrooms, and all the grass on the Cottage's property besides.

When they returned from their vacation, Mim and Mama weren't angry, but they were unhappy that I'd drained the ring's power with nothing to show for it. What I hadn't known at the time—what a better, more experienced witch would have known—was that binding wild magic like the fairy ring to a particular spell required more than a clever ritual. You needed perfect clarity in not only your intentions but your understanding of the problem's source. And what did I know about fungal lawn diseases? (Even though, scientifically speaking, that was what a fairy ring was.)

One phone call to my parents would have told me that my ritual couldn't work until I had more information about the problem I was trying to solve, but I hadn't made the call. Instead, my failure had lost us a small fortune and a powerful magical tool. There was no telling how long it would take for the mushrooms of the fairy ring to regenerate their former power. Maybe a couple years. Maybe longer.

By the time I redeemed myself, there might not even be a business left to buy into.

If we declared bankruptcy, would we lose the Cottage? The thought of my ancestral home passing into the hands of some indifferent bank or developer raised another sob in my throat. I fought it back and grabbed the butterfly box from the closet. I settled on my bed, resting my back against the headboard, my legs tucked under the blankets even though I wasn't cold. I placed a pillow over my lap and scooped out a couple paper butterflies to lay across it.

I stared at their lifeless shapes for a long time, my mind wandering down dark alleys even as I tried to concentrate on what I could possibly do to make these damn monarchs fly. Vexation fisted in my chest. What was the point of magic if it couldn't be wielded to make a difference where it mattered most? I could turn a chicken back into a human, but I couldn't make money appear in our bank account. I could see the future in a handful of cards, but I couldn't make customers flock to the store in droves.

I couldn't outmaneuver the mages, not when all they had to do was snap their fingers and bend the world to their liking.

The universe was finicky when it came to balance. Witches might have more control than most over its whims, but at the end of the day, we couldn't outrun our own fates any more than the next person.

I picked up one of the butterflies, poising it carefully on my fingertip. Even if I couldn't make them fly, I knew my parents would appreciate the effort. But it was my own expectations that I hated failing. In this, in the business, and in every other part of my life, if I had higher expectations for myself than anyone else did, then I was the only one who would ever be disappointed.

There was a thump on my bedside table, and I startled. The butterfly fell gracefully back down to the pillow with its brethren. I searched for the source of the sound and realized my grimoire had fallen open to a blank page. Or at least it used to be blank. Now there was writing appearing on it in a familiar hand.

Anthony left a message. His mother is doing fine. Cranky, but still human.

I chewed fretfully on the tip of my thumb, trying to decide if I should respond or not. I shouldn't be encouraging this strange form of interaction Fitz and I shared, but on the other hand, it would be rude to ignore him, right? And wasn't I trying to be nicer?

I dug around until I found where the silver pen had fallen to the floor between the bed and the table. Sweeping the butterflies back into their box, I brought my book onto my lap and began to write.

Thanks for letting me know.

There. Nice and straightforward, with no invitation to continue the conversation. He did not take the hint.

Hypothetically, what would you say if I asked you to dinner again?

I bit my lip, pen hovering above the paper in dreadful indecision. The problem was that I really, really wanted to say yes. I liked Fitz. I liked spending time with him. I liked his droll insights and the sound of his laugh. I liked learning new things about him, as if I were unwrapping a present on Christmas morning. I wanted him to like me too.

But if I was going to save Chanterelle Cottage, I couldn't waste any time dating someone—least of all the man whose company was driving us faster into bankruptcy. It wasn't fair to my parents, or to him, or even to me. Thoroughly whipped by my own logic, I put the pen to paper.

No.

A long, long pause.

I'll save myself the heartache, then.

I waited for almost a full minute, though I wasn't sure what I was waiting for. Keen regret filled me at the thought that this might be the last I heard from him, other than maybe awkward, empty hellos on the street. But why couldn't we find the middle ground between strangers and dating? Today had been nice, aside from the resurgence of my teenage hormones. Couldn't we keep floating along that same current?

And then:

I've been thinking

As the letters appeared on the page, my stomach flipped. Shit, this was the part where he said something devastatingly sensible like we should keep things strictly professional or something devastatingly dickish like calling me a tease or bitch or the other litany of insults certain men reserve for women who won't sleep with them. I didn't think Fitz would fall into the latter category, but you never can tell. I squeezed my eyes shut for a few seconds, too afraid I'd see something I couldn't unsee.

When I finally plucked up the courage to open my eyes, I read:

I've been thinking that cover-swapped books are a little pedestrian for you. My new theory is that you made it rain slugs. Or possibly scorpions.

A laugh bubbled in my throat, drawing with it a tear from the corner of my eye, courtesy of the past hour's roller coaster of emotions. I wiped it away with the back of my hand.

You're getting colder, I wrote.

Grew your cat to the size of a barn?

She would've already taken over the world if that were the case.

I, for one, welcome the arrival of our new feline overlord.

I closed my grimoire and hugged it to my chest, wavering again between the need to laugh and cry. A tricky balance.

CHAPTER FOURTEEN

It was the second week of September, and the people in Owl's Hollow were turning into animals.

The transmutation struck randomly and without warning. One minute a man was pushing a grocery cart through the parking lot and the next minute a chinchilla was running around in circles. One second a woman was kissing her spouse, and the next second she had a gecko clinging to her lips.

It was pandemonium.

Once word spread that we had successfully reversed the transmutation twice before, the Cottage was mobbed with citizens toting animals, from a tiny dormouse in someone's pocket to a groaning cow being tugged at the end of a jump rope. I might have wondered if the mages were similarly overrun, but I barely had time to breathe, much less worry about Fitz and Elinor. Fitz had said that he could probably reverse the spell on his own—I guessed now we would find out.

We enlisted the help of Mark and Harriet in staging the spellwork and resetting it for the next client. Mama and Mim hadn't tried the spell themselves until that morning, but they each managed it on the first try, so we were able to set up three different salt circles: in the back room, in the corner of the shop where we'd pushed aside some tables and shelves to make space, and in the dilapidated gazebo in the far corner of the backyard. Lucas was there too, but he wasn't much help, since he'd clearly had some mushrooms before his arrival and was wandering around thanking people for their essences. Tandy, of course, had enlisted herself as the manager of the whole operation, and we, of course, didn't have time to argue with her. I had to admit, she was pretty useful in terms of keeping things organized. She stalked back and forth on the front porch, calling numbers and ordering people and their furry, slimy, or scaled loved ones to settle down, now, settle down.

By midday I was parched and starving and exhausted. Witchcraft doesn't suck the energy from you the way magecraft does, but corralling goats and birds and even at one point a small alligator was stressful work. I had a few nicks and scratches, but so far nothing too detrimental. And all our rituals had been a success.

Of course, that didn't help much, considering there were at least another thirty people waiting, with more arriving every hour. It was quickly becoming clear that we couldn't keep up with the demand. Sooner or later, something would have to give.

"Charlie, phone for you." Harriet found me inside when I ducked in for a drink of water and a handful of crackers. I took the cellphone from her and propped it on my shoulder while I poured myself a second glass.

"Hello?"

"Thank god, I thought I was going to have to drive over there myself." It was Bonnie, frazzled and out of sorts. No surprise there.

"Is Jen okay?" I asked.

"She's fine. She's at work. Looks like yet again this madness is confined to the borders of Owl's Hollow."

I guessed that was a good thing, but as I peered out the kitchen window at the crowd of anxious people and animals, I was not encouraged.

"I can't really talk right now. We have our hands full here."

"I need you to come to the town hall."

"What? Now? I can't."

"Charlie, three of the council members are animals, and Larry Munch is about to have a fucking aneurysm. I can't deal with this by myself. Please? I'm asking as your friend, not the mayor."

Dammit.

"Okay," I said. "I'll be there in fifteen minutes."

I grabbed my bag and keys and ran downstairs to get a tote bag and stuff it full of candles, salt, and everything else the ritual required. I could hear Mim in the middle of her ritual in the corner of the shop, and I wasn't sure if Mama was busy in the gazebo. Instead I found Tandy and told her what was going on. She wasn't happy in the least that I was shutting down one of her "stations," thereby ruining her expert system, but it wasn't like she could do much to stop me as I sprinted off the porch and hopped into the car.

There were complaints from people who had been waiting for a while and from animals who had no idea what was going on, but I ignored them and backed out of the drive as fast as the crowd would let me.

At the town hall, I expected to find a black Mercedes in the parking lot, but it was conspicuously absent. Maybe instead of coming from home, they had walked from the office? It occurred to me that I didn't know where the Fitzgeralds lived, or if they even lived together. But that was hardly important right now.

Bonnie and the council were ensconced in their chambers, as if blocking themselves away from the outside world would protect them from the rampant magic. There was a blue parrot squawking on the back of a leather chair that Bonnie informed me was Councilman Emerson and a guinea pig in a box that was Councilman Huang. Councilwoman Hibbert was a grumpy-looking bobcat in the corner that hissed whenever anyone looked in her direction but otherwise didn't move.

"Finally," declared Councilman Munch when I arrived. I wished fervently that he would turn into some kind of insect and get eaten by another resident.

"Thanks for coming." Bonnie pulled me into a brief hug. She was in a nice suit and blouse, but it was stained on the front, presumably from some animal or another, and she'd shed her shoes in favor of the comfort and ease of bare feet. That was how I knew we were in crisis mode—as if it hadn't been perfectly obvious before. "Please tell me you can help us out here."

The other councilors eyed me eagerly. It didn't seem fair to give them preferential treatment, considering the line of people waiting at the Cottage. On the other hand, it was the council's job to come up with a plan of action during this kind of upheaval, and they couldn't very well do that when half of them were animals.

"Yes," I said. "I need some space to work with. Maybe on the stage in the forum?"

Bonnie nodded, and we went out together.

"Thank you again, Charlie," she said, while I was setting up the salt and candles and lighting the charcoal disc in my miniature cauldron. "Seriously, I owe you big time."

Money, I thought. *I charge money for my services.*

"I figured you would have called the Fitzgeralds too," I said aloud. "Are they on their way?"

Bonnie hesitated, then glanced around, as if speaking their name might have summoned them.

"I didn't call them. I heard that several townsfolk went over there and were cured, although I think most people are going to the Cottage."

"We're cheaper," I said with a mordant smile. It didn't surprise me that Fitz was able to pull off the reversal, though I did wonder how much effort it required of him. After reversing the last curse, he'd barely been able to remain upright. True, that had been a town-wide spell, but magic involving the human body was also notoriously tricky. "Aren't you going to see if they can stop whatever this is for good?"

"I was hoping you'd be able to stop it," she said. "You and the other witches. Honestly, I don't know if I trust the Fitzgeralds."

"You don't?" I paused halfway through lighting the candles and peered up at her. She hadn't seemed hesitant about trusting them when she offered a five grand reward for solving the last crisis.

"This is the second curse in a row that's affected the entire town," she said. "The first was only weeks after they arrived, and they were the only ones who could fix it. After this . . . I don't know, it seems like too much of a coincidence."

"That's crazy. Fitz and Elinor wouldn't do something like this."

"You're defending them?" She stared at me in shock. "I figured you'd be the first in line to accuse them."

She had a point. It didn't make much sense to be defending my competitors, especially when Bonnie was right—it was one hell of a coincidence. But then again, the more I'd gotten to know Fitz and Elinor over the past couple weeks, the more I realized that they weren't here to screw people over for money. They cared about their clients, and even if most of those used to be *my* clients, I had to respect that.

I tried to keep a professional distance from them—or from Fitz in particular. I'd managed for the most part, and he'd never repeated his offer to take me to dinner. But he also didn't seem inclined to hold it against me, and every time we crossed paths it was like we'd never left the farmer's market. Everything was easy between us, and it was nice. It was the middle ground I'd wanted. I always kept my hands to myself and a safe distance between us, so it wasn't like I was betraying my decision to not get romantically entangled with him. And he sent a couple more referrals our way—folks who wanted the comfort that a good charm or spell jar could bring better than an expensive, impersonal flash of magic—so it was easy to convince myself that staying on good terms with him was good for business.

"I don't think they have anything to do with it." I didn't have anything more concrete than that to offer. I continued lighting the candles.

"Regardless, we need you to figure out what the hell is going on in this town and stop it," Bonnie said. "We're willing to pay. Five thousand, like before."

"Ten thousand," I said without thinking.

Bonnie recoiled slightly, as if I'd slapped her.

"What?"

I finished with the last candle and stood up, dusting some stray salt off my knees. The look of dismay on Bonnie's face immediately invoked some guilt. But I remembered what Fitz had said about them being willing to pay a much higher amount than they offered initially. And he was right that a town-wide reversal like this would easily run at least fifteen thousand, if not twenty, if they sought help outside Owl's Hollow.

"It's a fair price," I said, willing myself to sound calm and reasonable, like Fitz had. Transmutation of humans was much more fraught and complicated than the magic behind the Whiteout.

"You're kidding me." Bonnie shook her head. "Since when do you care about money? Those mages are starting to rub off on you."

Frustration coiled around my lungs, hot and thorny.

"I care about money because goodwill doesn't pay the damn bills," I snapped. "This is my *job*."

"I thought we were friends."

"We are, and if you or Jen were in trouble, I'd help you in a second and I wouldn't dream of asking for a dime." My pulse was pounding in my ears, and I tried to relax and recenter. "But right now, you're the mayor, and you and the council are asking me to do a job. I deserve to be paid for my work."

Bonnie regarded me in silence. I didn't need our long history to know that she was peeved. I hated that I was adding to her stress but not enough to back down.

"You know, I could go to the mages with this offer," she said, in a cold tone that was entirely unlike the Bonnie I knew. This was a politician talking. "They might be willing to take the five grand."

Was she really trying to bluff me right now? My frustration flared into anger, but I matched my tone to hers. Cold for cold.

"Then you should do that. I'll get out of your hair." I stooped down and blew out one candle, then another. Bonnie cut in before I reached the third.

"Wait, goddammit, wait." She rubbed her temples. "Okay, fine. Ten thousand dollars. But the same stipulations apply. You have to prove that you're the ones who fixed it."

Instead of relief, a new wave of anger washed over me. She *did* have authorization for ten thousand, and still she'd tried to talk me down to half that. It was the government's money, not hers. And she knew that it was a fair price.

I picked up a lit candle to reignite the others. It wasn't worth arguing about, at least not while we were in the middle of this magic pandemic.

"Bring me Councilman Huang first," I said sullenly. "He'll be the easiest to deal with."

Bonnie lingered for a few seconds, and I thought—hoped— she was going to apologize, but she just nodded and returned to the council chambers. I dug around in my purse until I found the little velvet satchel where I kept a couple crystals, in case of emergency. I plucked out the quartz and squeezed it between my palms, willing the negative energy to flow out of me. The magic responded. I wasn't back to normal, but I was reinvigorated enough to keep going.

It was going to be a long day.

CHAPTER FIFTEEN

When I finished at the town hall (and informed them that if any other councilors fell victim, they would have to come to the Cottage like everyone else), I sat in my car in the parking lot for several minutes, trying to clear my head.

I had a new scratch from Councilwoman Hibbert along my forearm. It wasn't bleeding too badly, and we'd dug out an old first-aid kit from one of the councilors' offices to bandage it, but I needed to get home and disinfect it.

First, I had a stop to make.

Even though it was early afternoon, the town was mostly deserted. Everyone was either huddled at home or waiting at the Cottage for their cure. I parked on the street in front of Maven Enterprises and stepped into the air conditioning. It was more or less the same as I'd last seen it, except the paint smell was gone and canvases of obscure modern art were displayed on the walls.

"I'm sorry," said Elinor when I entered, without looking up, "we aren't—" She saw it was me and jumped to her feet. "Oh, Charlie, thank god."

She came around the desk to pull me into an even heartier embrace than Bonnie had.

"Wow," I said. "Not sure I deserve that warm a welcome."

She waved a hand as if to brush away my self-deprecation.

"It's been hell here today—I mean, I know it's probably a hundred times worse at Chanterelle Cottage—but like, there's not a lot I can do, and Fitz is such a stubborn ass, and—" Here she leaned in close and lowered her voice to a furtive whisper. "—if he knew I was turning people away he'd go nuts, but I care about him even if he doesn't care about himself so it's not like I have a choice."

I was stumbling along with her words, trying to make sense of them, but my mind refused to put the pieces together. Fuck, I was tired.

"Elinor." I put my hands on her shoulders, eminently calm because I didn't have the energy to be anything else. "I have no idea what on earth you're talking about."

She stared at me for a few seconds, as if *she* had no idea what *I* was talking about. Then she took a deep breath and tugged me over to sit in the leather chairs along the wall.

"Let me try again," she said. "I thought Fitzy would have told you more about the way he works, but I guess I should've known better. When a mage uses magic, we have to use our own energy to channel it, not like how you can use rituals and crystals and stuff like that."

"I know that much."

"On the night of the Whiteout or whatever they're calling it, when Fitz reversed the curse, I don't know if you saw how much it took out of him, but he slept for almost forty-eight hours straight after that. For a while I thought I might have to take him to the hospital."

"Really?" I asked, and she nodded somberly. I'd known magic

took energy, and it was clear that he'd been spent that night, but I hadn't realized how bad it was.

"He recovered okay, but now this shit with the animals is happening, and at first, we weren't even sure he'd be able to reverse it—to be honest I was kind of hoping he wouldn't. I would have been happier leaving all the hard work to you guys this time around, no offense."

"None taken."

"But anyway, once he knew he *could* do it, of course he felt like he *had* to do it for everyone who showed up. We tried to send them your way at first, but I guess the wait was too long and they were desperate."

"So what's wrong?"

"Well, as you might have guessed, transmuting a human from an animal is a little more difficult than your average spell." She grimaced darkly. "We've only had nine people so far, but he's dead on his feet, and I can't convince him to stop. Honestly, I don't know how you guys have been curing so many people. A friend of mine said you'd gone through almost a hundred before lunch."

"There are three of us working." I rubbed the back of my neck. I hadn't even realized it was that many, although I was sure Tandy was keeping meticulous count. Despite my grandstanding with Bonnie, we wouldn't end up charging the folk who came by. I knew a lot would insist on paying, but most couldn't afford it and it seemed wrong to profit off this crisis. Unless, of course, the government was footing the bill. That was what taxes were for, right? "And like you said, we don't have to put our own energy into it the way mages do."

Elinor sighed and slouched a little in her seat. Her usually vivid aura had dimmed noticeably.

"I've turned away a couple people so far, but he's going to catch on soon, and then he's going to be right back at it." She tilted her head to look at me, eyes bright and hopeful. "Maybe you can try to talk some sense into him?"

I gave a short, incredulous laugh.

"Why do you think he'd listen to me if he won't listen to you?"

"I'm his kid sister. It's in his genes not to listen to me." She slouched lower and closed her eyes. Today she was wearing a silky black midriff shirt and black jeans (she never seemed to wear any other color), but the shirt was wrinkled—perhaps from all the miserable slouching—and her sloppy bun had two different pens sticking out of it, like she kept forgetting she was putting them there. "This is all Dad's fault," she mumbled.

"Why?" She and Fitz never talked about either of their parents, except the briefest of mentions. Anytime I brought them up with Fitz, he would smoothly deflect or change the subject. He clearly had a lot of practice avoiding the topic. I'd read up on the various scandals Sterling Fitzgerald II was famous for, but with the media you never knew how much was sensationalized.

"He's a fucking asshole, that's why," she snapped. I drew back in shock at her vehemence. She opened her eyes and noticed my expression. "Sorry. I mean, he is, but you don't care about any of that."

"It's all right," I said. "You can tell me, if you want." I tried not to sound like I was desperately curious to hear more, though of course I was.

She let out another sigh.

"Dad is one of those obnoxious shoulder-to-the-wheel alpha males, and all he ever talks about is how you have to keep your nose to the grindstone and work hard and that's the only way to make anything of yourself—never seemed to occur to him that since he inherited the whole business from his father, he didn't actually have to do all that much grinding to get where he is. I

mean, you know the type, right?" She glanced at me, and I nodded. She went on. "He's a raging sexist, of course, so he pretty
much ignored me and Victoria when we were growing up,
which was fine by me, but Fitz got the worst of it. Even when
we were kids, Dad was riding him constantly, telling him he
wasn't trying hard enough, yelling at him for no reason, finding
every weakness he could and picking at it. It was . . . awful."

She wiped at her eyes with her palms, even though she didn't
seem to be crying.

"Sounds like it," I said softly. I didn't know what else I could
say.

"Our mom was an alcoholic and not a very nice person herself, so she wasn't any help. Vicky and I tried to run interference
when we could. She's the oldest, so she could sometimes get
Dad to back off. And I had more leeway than the other two
because I was the youngest, so I spent a lot of my time getting
into trouble because it didn't bother me so much when Dad
yelled at me. I already knew he didn't give a shit about me, and
I didn't give a shit about him, so most of the time it was more
like a twisted game than anything else, to see how much I could
embarrass him. And if he was yelling at me, he was leaving Fitz
alone." She cast me a sideways glance and flashed a mirthless
smile. "I know it sounds heroic *now*, but it's not like I understood it all back then. It's taken me years of therapy to put it
into perspective like this."

"Still seems pretty heroic to me." There was a tiny waver in
my voice, and I swallowed hard to keep the creeping tears at
bay. None of this was my trauma, so crying about it when she
was so composed seemed kind of selfish.

She shook her head wearily.

"Whatever. The three of us survived together." Her hands
squeezed into fists. "Fitz was still working at the family business, though, right up until—well, it doesn't matter. The point is

that he only recently got out from under Dad's thumb for real, and sometimes he still thinks he has something to prove. That whatever he's doing, it's not good enough. And so that's how we end up with him passed out for forty-eight hours straight and me freaking the fuck out."

I studied her profile in silence. It was the first time I'd seen a side of her that wasn't upbeat and unflappable. How much of that was part of the new game she had to play, trying to convince herself that the past was the past and it didn't matter anymore?

"Is Fitz in his office?" I asked.

She looked at me with a new gleam of hope and nodded.

"I'll go talk to him," I said. "But I can't promise he'll listen to me."

She nodded again, more fervently.

"Thank you so much." She hopped up to give me another hug before nudging me down the hallway. "The door on the left."

I knocked and heard his muffled "Come in." I entered, though I left the door open behind me. My little concession to propriety.

"Charlie," he said in surprise.

"Hi," I said. At first he looked perfectly fine, and I thought that maybe Elinor was overreacting. When I got a little closer, though, I could immediately tell that something was wrong. His face was wan, his features drawn. There was a slump to his shoulders that wasn't normally there, like he couldn't quite keep himself upright. He reached up to run a hand through his hair, and I could see it trembling from across the room.

"Is everything okay?" he asked. I knew he meant with me in particular, because obviously everything was not okay in general.

"Could be worse," I said, truthfully enough. "Your sister tells me you're being a stubborn ass."

"Is that so?" His gaze flicked toward the open door, and I caught a glimpse of brotherly irritation across his face. I would have laughed, under different circumstances. "She worries too much. I'm fine."

Now I did laugh, but it was hollow. His desk was mostly bare—there wasn't a lot of paperwork involved in magecraft. And the boxes I'd seen in my scrying glass must have all been unpacked. The tall bookshelves were stacked neatly with books and a few picture frames. I saw a couple of Elinor, and another of a woman and a man that must have been Victoria and her husband.

"Well, you look like hell." I rounded the desk and hopped up to sit on the edge.

He leaned back in his chair, observing me with a bemusement that seemed at war with his exhaustion.

"I'm fine," he said again. Stubbornly. "You're hurt." He reached out to take my hand, frowning at the white bandage wrapped around my forearm. A few spots of red had leaked through, but I was pretty sure it had stopped bleeding. I'd all but forgotten about it.

"Councilwoman Hibbert makes a mean bobcat." I tried to slip my hand free, but he held on, his thumb running along the edge of the wrapping. Goosebumps raced up my arm and the back of my neck at his gentle touch.

"If it's not too deep, I can heal it," he said.

"Absolutely not." This time I gave a firm yank, and he released me. He blinked up at me in owlish surprise. "I came in here to convince you to take a break. I'm not letting you waste any energy on me."

"Waste?" he echoed, as if the word offended him. "You're hurt. Just let me—"

He reached for my arm again, and I slapped his hand away.

"I'm aware of that, thank you." I twisted sideways on the

desk, so my arm was out of his reach. "You're clearly exhausted. No one's going to suffer if you get some rest. We can handle any new cases at the Cottage."

"We don't know how many more cases there will be before this ends," he said, crossing his arms. "If it ever does."

"Which means there will be plenty of people for you to help once you've rested up," I said sweetly.

He scowled at me, and I knew I'd convinced him.

"I'll take a break if you let me heal your arm."

"Take a break first, then maybe I'll let you," I countered.

"You're worse than Elinor." He glared at my arm, like the bandage had personally insulted him. "I thought the protection sigil you wear was supposed to prevent things like this."

I touched the thin outline of my pentacle under my shirt.

"For your information, the councilwoman was going for my throat, so I'd say the sigil did its job." He looked ill at that prospect, and I slid to my feet. "I'm telling Elinor you've agreed to close the office until tomorrow."

"*Tomorrow?* No." He started to climb to his feet, but his knees must've given out because he fell straight back into his chair. He grimaced. "I'll be better in a couple hours."

"Then by tomorrow you'll be great," I said, heading out the door.

"You know, you can't tell me what to do," he called after me. "It's *my* business."

"Then do what you want," I shot back. "But when I get gangrene in my arm and die a tragic death, it's going to be your fault."

He swore at me, and I laughed on my way back to the front. He was going to be fine. Now I had to get back to the Cottage and deal with whatever was waiting for me there.

CHAPTER SIXTEEN

We worked through the night, but townsfolk and their animal loved ones kept coming. We tried sleeping in shifts, a couple hours at a time, but by dawn we'd run through our reserves, in both body and inventory. The other witches had done their best to keep us stocked, but there's only so much myrrh resin to be found in the middle of the night. I was pretty sure we'd run through most of the town's salt supply as well. We'd tried reusing salt and incense for multiple spells, but it was no good. The magic that had transformed these poor people was too strong to be assuaged with secondhand ingredients.

There were still at least a dozen people camped out in our parking lot, and I had no doubt more would be coming. Whatever this curse was, it was raging through the town at a breakneck pace. We'd already had one person fall victim to it twice, first as a lizard, then as a pig.

I never thought I'd be grateful to Tandy DiAngelo, but after we explained the situation to her, she broke the news to the crowd for us in a crisp, no-nonsense tone that brooked no argument. Normally we would have wanted to talk to our customers ourselves, but my parents and I were dead on our feet.

We all needed a few hours of sleep. We'd sent Mark and Harriet home hours ago to get some rest. (God only knows where Lucas had ended up. He was probably out among the crowd, communing with the animals.) I knew Tandy had to be exhausted too, even though she showed no interest in returning home. In fact, she invited herself to take a nap on our couch.

Once the crowd was assured that we wouldn't abandon them indefinitely, most decided to stay where they were. Our parking lot and front yard had begun to look like the world's strangest music festival, sans musicians and with a lot more exotic animals. People had brought coolers for snacks, beach umbrellas for shade, and blankets and camping chairs to sit on. Word had spread rapidly through the town that even though the witches at Chanterelle Cottage could reverse the magic, there was a long wait involved, so people had begun to arrive prepared. At some point someone had even ordered a huge stack of pizzas and was selling it by the slice. Enterprising.

The four of us sat around the kitchen table to divide up a phone list of contacts to call for more supplies. Mim had begun to dig through our pantry, searching for food that would take the least amount of effort to prepare, when the bell on the coffee table began to jangle. Mama had wiped it free of its enchantment yesterday when all of this started, otherwise it would have been ringing continuously as people arrived.

We all stared at it in confusion.

"I guess I'll check downstairs." I didn't have the mental fortitude to consider anything more complicated. I dragged myself to my feet with a groan and went down into the empty shop. I unlocked the front door to look outside and was surprised to find two large brown paper bags, folded neatly closed. I crouched down and caught the warm smell of freshly baked bread, chased by the mouthwatering scent of bacon. There was a folded note stapled to one of the bags, and I gently tore it free. A message in black ink, written in a familiar hand:

Thought you might need this. I did take the night off, so please refrain from getting gangrene to spite me. —Fitz

A smile crept across my face. There was a second message scribbled beneath his in red ink, the handwriting loopy and large.

And tell Ruby and Alicia I said hi.—Elinor

I carried the bounty upstairs and set it on the table.

"What's this?" Mim asked in surprise, as I started pulling out the food. The white boxes and plastic containers all had the Madge's Café logo on them. I handed her the note, and she read it, with Mama looking over her shoulder.

"Gangrene?" Mama shot me a puzzled look.

"An inside joke." I tried and failed to suppress my telltale smile. My parents exchanged a glance that on a normal day would have been the harbinger of an awkward talk. Luckily Tandy was here (never thought I'd think *those* words), and we were all too burned out for conversation at any rate.

There were hot bagels with cream cheese, bacon, scrambled eggs, hash browns, and some of Madge's famous fried apples. A few minutes ago, I might have said I was too sleepy to have much of an appetite, but now I was ravenous. We all ate our fill, passing around the containers for seconds and, in Mama's case, thirds. Other than that, we didn't talk much, except to agree that we'd set our alarms for noon.

Tandy curled up on the couch in the living room, while we packed up the leftovers to store in the fridge. In less than a minute she was snoring softly.

"Why hasn't she gone home?" I whispered to Mim. "What about her kids?"

"She told me they were staying with their grandparents for a couple weeks," she whispered back, casting a pitying glance in Tandy's direction. "Carl is the only one at home."

She didn't have to say any more. I could guess the rest for myself. In Tandy's shoes, I doubted I'd want to go back home either. I wondered if Carl had called to check up on her—or if he'd even noticed she was missing. Probably he would when he woke up and there was no breakfast waiting for him on the table.

I didn't have any energy to spare sympathizing with Tandy, so I trudged down the hall to my room. I collapsed face-first on my bed, barely remembering to kick off my shoes. I could hear rustling below my floorboards, and it took me a few seconds to realize it was Broomhilde bumbling around the shop. Great, all I needed was one more mess to clean up.

I yearned for sleep. Though my body was exhausted and my eyelids too heavy to stay open, my brain was still running at full throttle. We couldn't keep going like this, and what if the curse, whatever it was, kept cycling through the townsfolk? Soon enough there would be more animals than people, and if we didn't know anything about the person we were trying to cure, we couldn't properly call them home. Even now, there had to be citizens in animal form who were running around town in panic or hiding in terror, because they hadn't been lucky enough to transform near someone who could wrangle them.

My mind flipped through possibilities. In some ways it was as hopeless as the day of the Whiteout, but at least in this case, we knew how to fix the problem on an individual level. Now it was a matter of expanding that solution to the town—and stopping it from happening again.

I drifted off once or twice, but each time I snapped back awake with a tiny piece of the puzzle. Until finally, at a quarter till noon, I had a firm idea of what needed to be done. I rolled out of bed, dizzy with drowsiness but unwilling to succumb. I turned to a few different pages in my grimoire, checking my memory against the relevant passages. Then I opened the almanac app on my phone to find the phase of that night's moon. Waning gibbous. Ideal for cleansing and the undoing of bindings and curses.

A thrill ran through me. The alignment was a sign from the universe that I was on the right track. But first I had one more thing to check.

I found the last page of my notes to Fitz and started a new line with the silver pen.

Are you there?

I knew I could call him, but for some reason this was more . . . real. More meaningful. And to be honest, I didn't know if I'd be able to convince myself to ask him what I had to ask over the phone. It was hard enough already.

My phone alarm went off, making me nearly jump out of my skin. I turned it off. Fitz's reply came within the minute.

Yes.

Thank you for breakfast. You'll be happy to know that I'm gangrene-free.

When we had a spare second, Mim had lathered my arm with some of her special magic-infused cream, and after about ten minutes the scratch was a barely noticeable pink line. In an hour or so it would be gone. Witchcraft couldn't reset a bone or anything drastic like that, but flesh wounds from grumpy humans-turned-bobcats didn't stand a chance.

That's a relief, Fitz wrote.

I hesitated, then forced myself to keep writing.

I'm going to ask you a question, and I need you to be completely honest.

I've never lied to you before.

True, he hadn't—his convenient omission on the first day we

met notwithstanding. My question was one I hated to ask, because the thought of ten thousand dollars in our bank account was enough to make me cry with joy. But I kept thinking of what Fitz had said to me over the phone, on the day he'd referred Anthony Hawthorn to me. He didn't want to risk making things worse when he knew I could do it right.

As much as I hated to admit my own fallibility, I was in the same position now, and I owed it to Owl's Hollow to swallow my pride.

Are you able to reverse the magic on the whole town the way you did during the Whiteout and stop more people from transmuting?

Elinor had said that changing people back from animal form was more taxing than the average spell, but I didn't know if the summoning of the words was considered an average spell, or how much more complicated it was. I had an idea for how to save the town, but it was only an idea. If Fitz could for sure make things right, then I wasn't going to stand in his way, even if it meant I lost the Cottage that ten-grand reward.

Maybe, he replied.

I bit my lip. It was clear what he wasn't saying. Now was the time to see if he could be honest about it.

Without it killing you?

A long, breathless pause.

No.

I couldn't tell if it was disappointment or relief flooding my veins. Maybe a bit of both. He was writing again.

Can you?

I weighed my answer. Truth or bravado. I decided to repay his honesty in kind.

I think so, but I'm not sure. Meet us at the graveyard at eleven tonight to find out.

CHAPTER SEVENTEEN

It didn't take long to bring Mim and Mama onboard with my idea. At that point my plan fit together so flawlessly that I doubted anyone could have dampened my excitement. To my surprise, Tandy was onboard as well, without even a dose of condescension. In fact, by the time I finished laying out my explanation, her face was cracked open with a grin. "Now *that* is witchcraft," she declared.

We decided that since we had more supplies being delivered today, we would change back as many people as we could, while still reserving some ingredients for the night ahead.

Among the three of us, we cast the ritual about a hundred more times that day. In hopes that the other witches could help lighten the load, my parents had temporarily deactivated the spell that prevented anyone from using magic on our property. Mark and Harriet were reluctant to try, in case something went wrong, but with some coaxing, they each made a valiant attempt with no success. Tandy was more eager than the Wharburtons but equally unsuccessful. She couldn't master the call to home, and—other than the pigeon she was working on flailing madly until it tired itself out—nothing happened. Lucas showed up for a while but wandered away again before anyone could ask him. We reset the spell on the property, unwilling to leave the Cottage exposed for longer than necessary—not that the enchantment could help our current predicament. It only prevented any non-Sparrow witches and mages on the property from using magic; it couldn't disrupt spells that were cast from afar or curses that were already in place when the victims arrived.

After her failure, I expected Tandy to go home in a funk after all, but she only announced that her craft might be less practical, but it was also more esoteric than that of the average witch. With that, she recommitted herself to the role of administrator with gusto.

Around dinnertime we sent the remaining customers home, assuring them that we were working on a permanent solution that would hopefully take effect before morning. I wasn't sure if they believed us or not, but they left without an uprising. We also tied a rope across the top of the driveway with a sign to keep anyone else from showing up.

Harriet and Mark brought over two cheesy chicken casseroles for dinner. (The leftovers from Madge's had been devoured for lunch.) Lucas returned as well, as he often did when food was involved, and the seven of us strategized. Around eight P.M. we disbanded with plans to meet up at the cemetery. Tandy went home, although she didn't look particularly excited about it, claiming the need for a shower and a yoga session to prepare herself.

As tired as we were, my parents and I couldn't settle down enough to rest. Instead, Mama and I hovered over Mim, eating ice cream from the carton, while she applied our cut of the ten-thousand-dollar reward to our current financial situation. We'd been planning to split it seven ways, of course, but Mark and

Harriet both refused to take a dime, stating they were quite comfortable in retirement and would rather it go to keeping the Cottage afloat. Lucas had given a vague statement about the ruination of the soul under capitalism that I gathered meant he wasn't interested in cash either. To our surprise, though Tandy did want compensation, she only wanted one-seventh, to reflect what the original cut would've been.

The generosity was overwhelming, and Mim teared up more than once. I might have been more moved if I weren't so racked with anxiety that my plan wasn't even going to work, and all of this would be moot. What if we were counting our cheesy chicken casseroles before they hatched?

According to Mim's calculations, the reward money would keep us afloat through the end of the year, if we were careful. It wasn't much of a reprieve, but it was something. A little spark of hope amid all the stress. If we could pull this off.

At eleven that night, we all gathered in the cemetery. It was near the church, but it was public property, so we didn't have to worry about Pastor Dale kicking us out. Midnight was a time for endings and beginnings, but also for spells bringing positive change, which was ideal for what we hoped to accomplish. The time and moon phase were the easy parts, though.

There were no streetlights nearby, and only Tandy had thought to bring a flashlight, so the rest of us had to use the lights on our phones while we worked. I wasn't sure if Fitz would come, but he and Elinor both arrived a few minutes after us, offering their assistance, to the suspicion of everyone else. Mama was afraid they were trying to muscle in on our spell-work, but I assured her that wasn't the case. She was slightly mollified when Elinor came over to talk to her and Mim, telling them that her old professor had been wonderfully distraught at finding out Elinor was right and he was wrong about the mushroom species in fairy rings.

I made my way over to Fitz, hugging my grimoire to my chest. He must've come straight from the office, because he was wearing his usual slacks and button-down. His maroon silk tie hung loose around his collar.

"If you want to make yourself useful," I said, in lieu of a greeting, "you could hold this for me while I work. It seems wrong to balance it on top of someone's gravestone."

I held out the leather-bound book. Handing over my most precious possession to a mage was probably reckless, but I knew I could trust Fitz with it.

"Sounds difficult, but I'll try my best," he said, his small smile visible even in the shadows created by my phone light. He obligingly held the book open while I flipped to the right page and studied the notes that the seven of us had cobbled together at dinner. It was time to begin.

First, we cast our sacred circle, about fifty feet in diameter, in the exact center of the graveyard. We couldn't risk damaging the earth by using salt to delineate the circle, so we just placed objects to symbolize the elements at the four cardinal directions. The graves in the middle were close to two hundred years old, so we weren't treading on any recent plots, but there was still an eerie sense of unease as we picked our way around tombstones. The creepy location was not for aesthetic reasons. Graveyard dirt formed a link between the physical and spiritual world, making it a powerful conduit. And for the magnitude of spellwork we were hoping to perform, an entire cemetery's worth of dirt was necessary. We were standing at the intersection of Owl's Hollow's past, present, and future. I couldn't think of a more meaningful place to channel the magic we hoped would save it.

Next came the candles. Typically, white and black would be used for purification and protection, but we decided that when it came to a working of this nature, the symbolism would matter less than the power of the flame itself. We'd brought every candle we had in stock, which, after burning as many as we had for two straight days, wasn't many. Tandy and the Wharburtons had a few they brought from home, and Lucas produced one half-melted pillar from his ratty backpack. Still, once we'd arranged them around the circle and lit them, my gut told me that it wasn't enough.

I could tell without asking that Mama and Mim agreed. A witch's instinct is one of their most useful tools.

"Shit," I said to myself, while I glared at my own notes in the book of shadows that Fitz was still patiently holding. "I should have thought of this earlier."

I fiddled anxiously with my Caravaca cross, wondering if we were dead in the water before we'd even begun. Despite my glaring, the grimoire did not magically reveal the answer to the conundrum.

"Maybe they can help," said Fitz. I looked up, and he tilted his head left. A procession of candlelight was winding up the path from the main road. I squinted into the dark and moved closer to stand by my parents, trying to decipher what I was seeing.

"That's Bonnie and Jen," said Mim.

"And there's Paul and DeeDee Schafer," said Mama. "And the Vickers."

As the people drew closer, I recognized most of them as townsfolk. And they were all carrying lit candles of various shapes and sizes.

"How did they know?" I asked, stunned. I'd informed Bonnie, of course, in case she and the council wanted to bear witness, but she hadn't said anything about making it a public event.

"I may have made a few calls." Tandy sidled up next to me.

Her self-satisfied tone was less grating than usual. "I thought we might need some reinforcements."

One by one the citizens came forward, handing off their candle to one of us witches so that we could place it in the circle. When Bonnie handed me hers, she leaned forward to whisper in my ear.

"I'm sorry about before. I was being an asshole, and you had every right to ask for what you're owed. I shouldn't have offered you less in the first place."

"You were doing your job," I said, pulling her into a one-armed hug, "and I was doing mine. We don't have to make a big deal out of it."

"Good luck. I'm rooting for you, and not just because it will make me look good in front of the voters."

I laughed, and she went to stand beside her wife. We kept the citizens a safe distance from the circle, not wanting to risk any accidental interference. Elinor was extremely helpful with that, cheerily guiding everyone into position while we finished setting up.

I stood back next to Fitz while the last candles were being placed. The flickering flames cast light and shadow in a hypnotic dance against the chipped and weathered gravestones of citizens past. This was right. The people of Owl's Hollow participating in their own salvation.

"Do you have everything you need?" Fitz asked.

"Almost," I said. "We need some stormwater. It's best for spells requiring a lot of power and focused energy."

"Where are you going to get that?"

"Where else?" I looked skyward. It was a cloudless night, with the moon and stars in full view. Fitz was clearly skeptical as he followed my line of sight, but he didn't say anything.

I went to join the others. Mark and Harriet had agreed to

work the weather magic. They were experienced in calling down localized rain for the benefit of their gardens and the farm one of their sons owned out west. Tandy, Lucas, Mama, Mim, and I took up our positions around the circumference of the circle. I was standing in front of the bell we'd used to represent air. Around my feet, candles burned, giving the entire circle an amber hue.

Mark and Harriet knelt in the center, between two graves. Harriet used her athame to carve the rune for Hagalaz into the ground, while Mark used his to carve Laguz. Hail and water. Symbols to invoke the unbridled chaos of nature.

Together, they carved Algiz, the rune of life. A symbol of protection to balance out the storm.

They put away their knives and each took a piece of white quartz from their pockets. They clasped hands, facing each other over the sigils, and bowed their heads. I couldn't hear their chant, but I could feel the rhythm, building on itself and rising toward the sky. It was less than five minutes before the first droplet of rain splashed on my forehead, followed by a second on my nose. Lightning split open the sky, temporarily casting the graveyard in a light as bright as day. Thunder cracked so loud that I swear the ground trembled. Rain fell faster now, until it was pouring down in sheets, soaking everything and everyone to the bone.

I thought the citizens might run for cover, but no one moved. As the lightning and thunder clapped again, I figured I couldn't blame them. It was one hell of a show.

Mark stood up, helping his wife to her feet. They clung together, giving each other watery smiles, then plodded to the edge of the circle. Not a single one of the candles had gone out, and that gave me a smidgen more courage. We were on the right path.

I cast a glance around the circle at each of my fellow witches, even though it was hard to make them out clearly in the downpour. None of us knew the exact source or nature of the curse that had spread across Owl's Hollow. In hopes of breaking it, we needed to cleanse the entire town in one fell swoop. I reached into my pocket and pulled out a smooth piece of black jade that nestled snugly in my left palm. The others would be pulling out their own preferred crystals, freshly charged and ready to direct our intentions.

As one, we raised our right hands and began to trace the zigzag lines of Eihwaz, the rune of the yew tree. A signifier of life and death and the inescapable path between them. A rune for transformation and new beginnings.

I squeezed my black jade tightly in my other hand while I traced the rune, over and over again. With each stroke in the air, I set my intention as firmly as I could. Break the curse. Cure the people. Save the town.

For a while I felt nothing, not even the faintest tingle of magic. I refused to give up. I pushed my will into the universe with all the spiritual force I could muster, reminding it that I could be stubborn too. The witches of Owl's Hollow weren't going to back down.

When the magic first flared in my chest, it was so overpowering I thought I might combust right there on the spot. It twined around my lungs and spiraled around my muscles, filling every iota of my body with its glistering strength. I'd never experienced magic so consuming, so explosive—but then again, I'd never cast a spell of this magnitude before, in conjunction with six other witches. It was a ritual of pure power.

The magic raced across my skin and burned behind my eyeballs, and then it was not only inside me, it was all around me, skittering through raindrops with wild abandon, charging the stormwater with our intentions.

I knew, even before I heard the delighted shouts of the few

citizens who had brought along their animal loved ones, that we'd done it. The curse, whatever its origin, had been washed away by a cleansing flood.

The seven of us, sensing our work was complete, all lowered our hands. With a whoosh of wind, the candles all went dark. Despite the continuing rain, there still wasn't a cloud in the sky, and the night was radiant with moonlight, ethereal and other-worldly in its brilliance. I tucked my stone back into my pocket, just in time to be nearly tackled by both my parents in a wet, warm embrace. People were cheering. Mim was laughing and crying at the same time, her tears mingling with the raindrops.

"Holy shit," Mama kept saying, squeezing me so tightly I thought she might break something. "Holy shit, Charlie. You really are my favorite daughter."

"Glad to hear it," I coughed into her hair. She finally released me, so she could crush Mim with a similar embrace.

I soaked up the euphoria along with the rainwater. I envisioned my imaginary scale tipping ever further in my favor. What was one ruined fairy ring compared to a victory of this magnitude?

The townsfolk all rushed in to join the celebration, eager to shake our hands and slap our backs and tell us they never doubted for a minute that it was the witches of Owl's Hollow who would save the day.

Someone pushed a thermos cup of lukewarm tea into my hand, and I sipped at it for a while and let myself be tossed around the roiling crowd, like a buoy on the ocean. Eventually I ducked and weaved until I'd freed myself from the throes.

And there was Fitz, standing alone outside the crowd, holding my book of shadows tightly to his chest. Despite the storm raging around us, he looked perfectly dry. I moved closer to him, and with a small gasp, I stepped into the calm of his invisible umbrella. I was waterlogged, with rain clinging to my hair, dripping from my clothes, and draining down my face in rivulets. I still clutched the half-full thermos cup in my right hand. Fitz was staring at me. The blue of his irises was wonderfully dark, but also radiant, like starlight dancing on deep water.

"You did it," he said. His voice was placid beneath the tumultuous rush of rain.

"I did it." The buzz of the magic was hot beneath my skin, flowing through my veins and emanating through my pores. It was supposedly a high like no other, but tonight I suspected that I could climb even higher. I took another step forward to Fitz, closing the last of the gap between us. My sudden nearness surprised him, but he didn't move away. Then I slid my free hand behind his neck, pulled his face down to mine, and kissed him.

Sweet and uncomplicated joy surged within me, threatening to burst through my chest. Despite being shielded from the elements, he tasted like rainwater and lightning and wind. He tasted like magic. A tiny sliver of reality pierced my mind. I was a witch, and this was a mage. This was *the* mage. The rival who had the power to destroy the heart of everything I held dear.

I lurched backward and, without any clear thought or decision, snatched my grimoire back from him, then tossed the rest of my tea into his face.

"What was that for?" He swiped a hand across his eyes and looked down at his wet fingers, as if to reassure himself that had actually happened.

I was as shocked at myself as he was.

"You kissed me." The accusation was the only answer supplied by my addled mind.

"*You* kissed *me*."

"You kissed me back," I said, in stubborn defense of my own irrationality. He blinked at me again in bewilderment. He'd once called me surprising, and I hadn't been sure if it was a compliment or not. I sure hoped it was, because a new clarity was dawning on me, brushing reality aside like a nuisance. I didn't care that he was my rival. I didn't care that he was a mage. At the moment, I didn't care about anything outside our cocoon of calm in the midst of the storm.

Fitz was still regarding me with a mix of astonishment and fascination. He scrubbed his sleeve across his face, though he missed a single droplet that traced its way toward his clavicle.

"Well?" I demanded impatiently. "Are you going to kiss me again or not?"

His eyebrows shot almost to his hairline.

"Are you going to throw something else at me if I do?" he asked. A reasonable question.

"Maybe." A not-so-reasonable reply.

He considered me with an air of contemplation that was mismatched with the electricity that arced between us, drawing us closer by degrees until our faces were inches apart. I was locked in to his gaze, unable to pull back now, even if I wanted to. But I definitely did not want to.

"Worth it," he decided at last, his words barely a breath against my lips.

Our mouths met again, fierce and hot and full of need. My book of shadows was pressed between us, a compendium of my craft, but Fitz was the enigma that I wanted to solve, a mystery to be unraveled, a present to be unwrapped, until I knew every part of him as intimately as I knew my own spellwork. A flash of lightning lit up the world for a brief moment, followed by rolling thunder. Our tongues and lips moved together in a rhythm we both already knew by heart. We were perfectly in sync, perfectly balanced. Safe in our little pocket of the universe.

CHAPTER EIGHTEEN

I decided that since I'd now kissed Fitz, thrown tea on him, and kissed him again in front of half the town, it was only fair to finally let him take me to dinner. I insisted on The Blue Spoon, because I was afraid that left to his own devices, he would take me to some horribly upscale place out of town with bathroom attendants and jeweled flatware and god knows what else. I did not have any dresses appropriate for that sort of venue.

The Blue Spoon was Owl's Hollow's fanciest restaurant, meaning there were cloth napkins and bread baskets. Every once in a while, they even had a pianist playing in the corner, although tonight was generic classical music from the wall-mounted speakers. Despite Mama's extremely unwelcome suggestion that I show more cleavage, I'd worn my emerald cotton sundress with the 1950's fit-and-flare silhouette. It was knee length with thick straps—the picture of tasteful modesty. Mim let me borrow her gold necklace with the sunburst pendant, inset with tiny diamonds that she insisted were real but Mama had told me once were definitely cubic zirconia. Regardless, I thought it elevated my look to a classiness befitting a first date.

First date. All the work that went into my outfit was so that I could keep my thoughts from spinning around and around that exact notion. My parents expressed no opinion on the matter (other than Mama's cleavage lobbying), but I knew they couldn't be thrilled with my decision to go out with the mage who might end up running us out of business. I was far from comfortable with it myself. But after all, it was just a date, and we were thousands of dollars richer now, with a healthy dose of gratitude from the citizens besides. Things were looking up for the Cottage. It wasn't like a little harmless flirting would change that.

When I first caught sight of Fitz outside the restaurant (I'd refused to let him pick me up again), I began second-guessing my ability to restrain myself to harmless flirting. He was the perfect balance of understated elegance and effortless informality, in an impeccably fitted black suit but no tie, the first few buttons of his shirt undone, giving me a glimpse of the pale hollow of his throat, the sharp ridges of his clavicles. It wasn't like I hadn't seen him like this before—in fact this was almost exactly how he'd looked the day we first met. But tonight was different for some reason. Maybe because I was finally letting myself see him as something other than a customer or a threat to my livelihood.

Distracted as I was by my own ill-behaved libido, it took me several seconds to register that he'd told me I looked beautiful. Heat flared in my cheeks as I forced myself to meet his eyes.

"Thanks," I managed. Thank god—or more accurately, Mama's genes—that my skin tone did not show blushes easily.

"Is everything all right?" His tone revealed nothing, but there was a ghost of a smile playing in his features, like he'd guessed exactly what was distracting me. Fortunately, I do not find smugness attractive (at least most of the time), so I was able to regain control of my senses.

"I'm great," I said with my own smile. "I'm wondering if they'll have fresh garlic bread tonight."

"Here's hoping." He was obviously not fooled.

He opened the door for me, and we stepped inside the artfully dim interior. There was never a need for reservations at The Blue Spoon, but he'd made one anyway, and we got a nice table in front of one of the bay windows. I knew a lot of people in town, so it was hardly a stretch to imagine that I'd recognize someone else in the restaurant, but the fact that Pastor Dale and his wife Martha were sitting two tables away from us was a little bit of a mood killer.

I would have gladly pretended not to see them, but Dale caught my eye and waved, then said something to his wife, so she looked up from her menu and waved too.

"That's the pastor, right?" Fitz asked, once we'd all finished our waving.

"Yeah," I said. "He's a nice guy, although I'm still kind of worried he's going to sneak up on me with a spray bottle and surprise baptize me."

Fitz nearly spat out his water with a laugh but managed to swallow it down.

"He stopped by the office when we first opened," he said. "I was with a client, but Elinor said he gave her a confusing speech about the dangers of biblical literalism and how magic is evidence of God. Then he invited us to church."

"That won't be the last you hear from him about that, but you can keep him at bay if you show up for Christmas and Easter services."

"Good to know." He perused his menu for a bit, then looked up. "You grew up here, right?"

"Born and raised," I said proudly. "The Sparrows have owned Chanterelle Cottage for six generations."

"That's impressive."

I searched his expression for any irony, but he seemed genuine.

"You grew up in Boston?" I asked.

He nodded.

"My grandfather started the magecraft firm that my father owns now. I guess we both got roped into the family business."

"I wouldn't say I got roped into it." I studied the dinner specials, trying to decide if I was in the mood for chicken or seafood. "I love working with my family in the Cottage. I've never wanted to do anything else."

I glanced up to find him watching me in fascination, as if it had never occurred to him that someone might *want* to work with their parents. Remembering what Elinor had told me about their father, I couldn't blame him.

"Did you start at the firm right out of college?" I asked. It seemed a safe enough question.

"Officially." He looked back down at the menu. "Tell me what it was like growing up in the Cottage."

I gnawed on the inside of my cheek. I had hoped for more than one word about his life in Boston, but I didn't want to push him to talk about things he'd rather not, so I decided to let it drop.

Conversation with Fitz was somehow both intimate and superficial. He was such a good listener, so earnest and focused on everything I said, that I found myself telling him things I usually kept to myself. How when I was a kid, I used to sneak down into the shop's back room at night to practice spells. How I'd spent most of my adolescence identifying as a lesbian, until I realized I had a crush on a boy and kissed him under the bleachers at a football game, then cried for hours in Mim's lap because I was so confused and overwhelmed. How sometimes I worried that Mim and Mama were sick of me and wished I would move out so they could be empty nesters in peace—though of course they'd never given me any reason to think that.

I still hadn't told him the nature of the big spell I'd botched, mostly because I enjoyed hearing his guesses. The latest conjecture was that I'd turned our car into a pumpkin.

When he was listening to me ramble about random snippets of my life, he had an intensity that made me feel like everything I said was the most important thing in the world, as if the rest of the universe had dimmed, and the two of us were the single bright spot in the center of it all. It was intoxicating.

But even so, as the evening went on, I realized that though he was never exactly secretive, he also never dipped further than the surface level of his own life. I learned that he'd played lacrosse in high school, that he'd gotten his MBA at Harvard, and that his first use of magic was at six years old, when he inadvertently transformed the family's entire dinner into ice cream.

I got the vague impression that he had loved lacrosse and hated Harvard, but he never technically said that. He offered no hint about how his parents had reacted to his first foray into magic, or even how he himself had felt about it. Despite all his honesty, Fitz was a difficult person to know.

It frustrated me—made me want to chip away at his smooth exterior and find out what was beneath—but I knew it wasn't fair of me to demand more than he was willing to give. I apparently had no filter on a first date, but that didn't mean he had to reciprocate by laying bare his entire history to someone he barely knew.

I did my best to follow his lead and keep the conversation from straying anywhere too vulnerable. It was easier once the food came, and we could divert our attention to that. I'd ordered the shrimp linguine. It was good, but then Fitz let me try one of the truffle fries that came with his gourmet burger, and I immediately wished I'd ordered that instead. That was the worst thing about dates; at least when I was with my family I could eat freely from their plates. I think I probably inherited it from Mama, who was infamous for refusing to order dessert and then eating most of mine and Mim's.

Our discussion turned, perhaps inevitably, to the magic troubles in Owl's Hollow. The local paper had dubbed the most recent incident the Animal Pox. We'd both been researching possible causes of large-scale curses without much luck. One time all the cars in several major cities turned red overnight, but it turned out to be a marketing campaign funded by a big auto insurance company, and the cars went back to normal the next day. God only knows how much they shelled out to mages for *that*. And of course there was the famous incident at NYU when a coven of witches cast a campus-wide hex that made the penises of would-be rapists shrivel up and fall off. There was a huge backlash against the university when the women were expelled, and a public GoFundMe gave them full rides to any other college of their choice. We had a newspaper picture of the coven tacked up in the back room of the Cottage for inspiration.

What those large-scale incidents had in common was that they took a group of magic users to pull off. I found it hard to imagine what an entire group of mages or witches could have against Owl's Hollow. A random disgruntled individual made more sense, but I didn't think one person could pull off magic of this magnitude.

"I don't know," Fitz said. "A young mage with enough latent power could possibly cause a town-wide disruption. It might explain how random the incidents are, if it was accidental."

Now that I thought about it, there was a certain ludicrousness to the troubles befalling the town, not unlike turning an entire family dinner into ice cream, though on a much bigger scale.

There were a handful of famous cases where young mages came into their power in a public or destructive way. It was why schools offered classes specifically for magecraft and witchcraft, to teach kids to be responsible and not hurt anyone. When it came to mages in particular, if there wasn't another mage in the family who could be a mentor, most families who could afford it hired a tutor. The Big Brothers Big Sisters program had even launched a subsidiary solely for mages.

The bottom line was that a young mage was infinitely more dangerous than a young witch. When it came to witchcraft, sometimes your spells could go wrong or have unintended consequences—like, say, killing an acre of grass or turning a car into a pumpkin—but you couldn't *accidentally* affect an entire town.

"Would a kid be able to use that much magic without seriously injuring themself?" I asked, chasing the last shrimp with my fork. "When you fixed the Whiteout, Elinor said she nearly had to take you to the hospital."

"Elinor overreacts."

I jabbed my speared shrimp in his direction.

"So you *weren't* unconscious for forty-eight hours straight?"

He flashed a grimace that answered my question. "Regardless, a younger mage would have a lot more energy to spare."

I nodded thoughtfully. It made sense. Mages lost their capacity for magic as they aged. A mage in their sixties might have developed perfect control, but they wouldn't have the stamina they had in their youth. The inverse correlation between skill and power was the reason there were no supervillain mages running around with the ability to explode entire cities.

"Still," I said, surveying my empty plate with some sorrow,

"first the Whiteout, then the Animal Pox—I find it hard to believe that even a young mage could cause both of those without needing to be hospitalized."

Giving in to my lowbrow urges, I swiped my finger through the remaining lemon butter sauce on my plate and sucked it clean with no little satisfaction. Then I glanced up to find that Fitz's gaze had snagged on my mouth. The spark in his heavy-lidded eyes was the exact opposite of disgust at my table manners. Between the dim restaurant lighting and the last vestiges of dusk against the bay windows, his pupils were already dilated, but now the blue had been almost completely devoured by black.

A strange giddiness raced up my spine, but I lowered my hand. I wasn't going to sit here and make a seductive spectacle of myself with the pastor and his wife in full view. Fitz cleared his throat.

"You're probably right."

I didn't even remember what I'd said. He took a sip of wine, then stared ponderously into the red liquid, as if it might give him the answers. I found myself contemplating the curve of his fingers around the delicate crystal stem. He held the glass the way you were supposed to, the way I'd always been too afraid to try for fear of dropping or spilling it. (The Sparrows were a wine-in-mugs kind of family.)

Why did I find the position of his hand on that glass unbearably sexy? Next thing you know I'd be fanning myself over the starch in his collar or the shine of his shoes. At some point I'd stopped finding the small manifestations of his affluence to be pretentious. Now they were just fragments of the whole, and the more I got to know him, the more irresistible I found every new piece I discovered.

I cleared my throat as well, conscious of a new heat creeping across my body in some unvirtuous places.

"I guess there's nothing to do but wait for another catastrophe, and hope that whatever it is, we can fix it."

"Maybe there won't be another one."

"Or maybe the next one will be even worse," I said glumly, ripping off a chunk of bread to dip in the sauce. I wasn't sure if that was polite table manners or not, but it was more respectable than my finger.

"And here I thought I was the cynical one," he said. "Can't you read the cards?"

"I have, but they're not making a lot of sense. The readings are all too vague."

"What a shock."

In response I flicked the sauce-drenched bread chunk at him. It hit him right on the nose, and he marveled at me while I stifled a giggle.

"I guess I deserved that." He wiped the spot of sauce away with his napkin.

"I'm taking another fry as recompense," I told him, snatching one from his plate. The second taste did nothing to curb my craving. Damn, they were delicious.

"I think the fact that I've refrained from any comments about your business practices for the entire night should earn me some goodwill." He scooped up another fry.

I realized I was watching the fry instead of him and shifted my attention up.

"I know it must have been so difficult for you," I said, in a somber tone. "You're truly a—" Something bumped into me from behind, so hard that I lurched forward. I had been in the process of bringing my glass to my lips, and most of the wine went all over Fitz.

"Oh no, I'm so sorry," came a voice behind me. I turned in my seat to find an elderly man looking horrified. He'd been trying to stand up, caught his foot on the table leg, and lost his already precarious balance. He looked so fragile that I was glad he'd fallen on me instead of the floor.

"Don't worry about it," I said, "I'm fine. Are you okay?"

He nodded, still clearly in distress as his wife tottered over to his side, followed by the alarmed hostess.

"But what about . . . ?" The old man cast a rheumy glance at Fitz.

"He's fine too," I said.

"Happens all the time," Fitz said wryly, brushing the napkin down his face. At least it was white wine.

Once we'd finally convinced the old man that he could stop apologizing and that he didn't need to pay for dry cleaning, he and his wife left. The hostess brought us more napkins and promised us a free dessert as well.

"Could we have another order of truffle fries instead?" I asked, ignoring Fitz's snort of laughter. The hostess looked confounded but nodded and hurried off.

"You could have had the rest of mine," Fitz said.

"They're covered in wine now," I pointed out.

"And whose fault is that? You realize this is the third time I've ended up wearing your beverage?"

I might have felt worse if he hadn't been suppressing a smile, and if he hadn't just given up on the napkin in favor of magic. The way he could use it so mindlessly, so indifferently, was still an uncanny sight. Magic for me was ritual and tradition and intention. There wasn't anything quick or convenient about it.

"I'm sorry about the tea," I said. "But the margarita was an accident, and the wine clearly wasn't my fault."

"You don't seem like the type to waste perfectly good alcohol," he conceded. "I accept your terrible apology." His smile, when it finally emerged, was pure charm, and the dimple made another appearance.

I hadn't had much to drink, but it was enough that my (admittedly unimpressive) inhibitions were dwindling perilously low. The problem was that I'd jumped the gun with Fitz too soon, and it was difficult to rein myself in. I'd already made out with him in the pouring rain, and now we'd taken a step backward into first-date territory. It was uniquely frustrating.

I was saved from myself by the hostess bringing us the plate of truffle fries, along with the bill, which she informed us reflected a discount for our troubles. The nice thing about local restaurants was the local hospitality. I didn't bother reaching for the bill, because I knew there was no way Fitz would let me take it anyway. Plus, I was busy with my bounty of truffle fries.

"You know," I said, scooping up a couple and dipping them in the ramekin of aioli. "If throwing a drink on you reaps rewards like this, I can't promise I'll be able to abstain in the future."

"Maybe next time my reflexes will be better." He glanced up from his perusal of the check. "Then it really will be a waste of alcohol."

"Not sure I could live with myself in that case." I offered him a fry, and he shook his head.

He reached for his wallet, then frowned. I watched in amusement as he checked all his pockets, his frown growing more and more pronounced until finally he gave up.

"Shit," he muttered.

"Something wrong?"

"Can't find my wallet," he said, clearly less amused than I was. "Hold on, let me ask El about it."

He tried her number twice with no answer, then slumped back in his chair in defeat, rubbing a weary hand down his face.

"Are you sure it's not in your pocket?" I teased. "It usually is."

"No, it's not." He downed the rest of his wine in one gulp.

"Elinor's favorite new way of practicing her magic is disappearing my wallet whenever she gets a chance, then making it reappear when I ask her about it. She thinks I don't know."

I hadn't expected *that*. I'd known Elinor considered herself an amateur mage, but I'd never wondered how she might go about honing her skills.

"Why don't you tell her to stop?"

He scratched his forehead and looked askance, almost as if he were embarrassed.

"I don't know, she seems to get a kick out of it." He slid his phone back into his pocket. "I don't want to ruin it for her."

"Okay," I said slowly, "that might be the cutest thing I've ever heard."

"I'm glad you think so." He shook his head and looked mournfully at the check he couldn't pay. "Damned inconvenient sometimes, though."

"Am I going to do irreversible damage to your manly pride if I pick up the bill?" I reached across the table to pluck it from his hand, then dug my own wallet out of my purse.

"Quite possibly."

A thought struck me. I let the idea ruminate while I picked out my credit card and placed it with the check on the edge of the table. Then I leaned in, resting my chin on my palms.

"And what if I use this opportunity to also extort a favor out of you?"

He rested his arms on the table and leaned in as well. Under the table, our knees brushed together. There was a glint in his eye that made me squirm.

"Sounds scandalous," he murmured.

I was struck by a whole new litany of ideas for extorting him that would have made Pastor Dale reconsider allowing me to step foot in his church ever again. It took great effort to reel in my lurid imagination, but I needed to stay on task. My parents' anniversary was coming up fast.

"I need you to do some magic for me." I opted for a business-like tone. "It shouldn't be too difficult." I wasn't sure why it hadn't occurred to me before that Fitz would be able to animate the paper butterflies when I could not—well, that wasn't true. I knew exactly why it hadn't occurred to me: the thought of admitting failure and asking a mage for help would have been anathema to me even a few hours earlier. But after tonight, I thought I might be able to stomach it, if Fitz was the mage in question. Plus, I was desperate and running out of time.

If Fitz had been hoping for something less pedestrian, he didn't show it. He regarded me with a slight tilt of his head, his mouth twitching with one of his signature smirk-smiles.

"You realize that the price of this dinner would normally be about enough for me to magically tie one of your shoes?"

"Not even both?"

"Definitely not both."

God, mages were horribly overpriced. No wonder he could afford all those nice suits.

"Well, these are my terms." I leaned back and spread my hands, palms up, in a gesture of finality. "If you don't want to accept, then maybe they'll let you wash the dishes."

"I suspect I'd be terrible at that." His smile widened, revealing another flicker of that dimple. "Fine, you get one magical freebie, but I'm not assassinating anyone for you."

"Oh, I've been doing my own assassinations for years," I said, with a careless wave. "Plenty of hexes to choose from."

His laugh, so unguardedly genuine, sparked inside me like a match to kindling. And even though I knew it was a bad idea, I let it burn.

CHAPTER NINETEEN

The rest of September flew by. After our heroic exploit in the graveyard, witches received a huge boost of publicity and appreciation. There was even a short period where it looked like the story of the Whiteout and the Animal Pox might go viral online. On social media, #OwlsHollow trended for a few hours. But then a mage in Florida grew an alligator to the size of a tractor trailer, and the Internet moved on to its next dopamine hit.

Fitz and I went on more dates. I kept thinking that something would happen, that he would say or do something to make me come to my senses and quit wanting to spend time with him. But the moment never came. And the more I liked him, the more trouble I knew I was in.

The second Sunday in October, I woke up with an odd pressure on my chest. I'd fallen asleep with my book of shadows open on top of me. It had been happening a lot lately. Fitz and I would stay up until all hours writing back and forth. That silver pen was getting twice as much use as my cellphone these days.

I rolled over and saw on the clock that it was half past eight. I sat bolt upright and had a minor heart attack before remembering the shop was closed today. I'd been late to open the shop more than once in the past several weeks, thanks to my late nights. Every time I promised myself it would be the last, but then Fitz would write something clever, and I would find myself reaching for the pen, bedtime be damned.

We were having dinner at his house tonight. I was curious to see where he lived, even though I still refused to let him anywhere near my abode above the Cottage. My parents couldn't be trusted not to embarrass me beyond recovery. Plus, their anniversary party was in a week, so it was time to bite the bullet and call in my favor with the origami butterflies.

After breakfast, my parents cajoled me to join them in a Disney Channel Halloween movie marathon, but I insisted on spending a few hours downstairs, replacing September's Feast of Mabon displays with Samhain displays. Not every witch celebrated the sabbats (my family wasn't particularly observant), but the holidays still generated a decent amount of business for us every year. And tourists ate it up. Even with the reward money from the Animal Pox, we still needed every penny of business we could get.

I probably could have found shop tasks to keep myself busy all day—cleaning up after Broomhilde was a chore that kept on giving—but finally Mama dragged me upstairs to join them on the couch. "No child of mine will disrespect the honored tradition of Lazy Sundays," she told me.

Work had been my attempt at distracting myself from my jittery anticipation for the date tonight. Dinner at Fitz's house seemed like a significant step forward in this ill-conceived relationship of ours. Even thinking of it as a "relationship" sent a streak of panic through me. I had no idea what I was doing, yet I was powerless to stop myself from running headlong into the mistake. I actually wished my parents were pushier when it came to my life decisions. If they told me I should stop seeing him, I might be able to make myself do it. But other than the occasional gleeful innuendo, they kept their real opinions about my dating choices to themselves.

At least the movie marathon kept me suitably distracted for the rest of the day—so much so that I lost track of the hour and barely had time to brush my teeth and change out of my pajamas before hopping into the car.

Fitz's house was a bungalow nestled near the northern edge of the town limits. I wasn't sure why I had envisioned him in a sleek modern apartment constructed entirely of glass and stainless steel, because of course we don't have any of those in Owl's Hollow. The house was gray brick with faded blue shutters and picturesque vines wrapping around the cast-iron railing on the small front porch. Similar, but not overly so, to every other house in the neighborhood.

I marched up the front steps, holding the box with my paper butterflies close to my chest. It was an unseasonably warm night, and I'd opted for a loose cream-colored tank top tucked into a pair of high-waisted brown linen shorts—which is to say, those were the first clean and (mostly) unwrinkled clothes to fall out of my closet during my rush to get dressed.

Fitz answered the door in jeans and a T-shirt with a toothbrush sticking out of his mouth.

"Sorry, I lost track of time," he garbled around it.

I chuckled as he stepped aside to let me in. The sight of him somehow both soothed and stoked my nerves. He said something else that I could only assume was to make myself at home, then disappeared around a corner. The floors were aggressively polished wood that made me terrified of scuffing them, so I slipped off my boots by the door to continue snooping in my socks. A small dining room to the left held a glossy round table for four with a chandelier overhead. There were generic land-scape paintings in ornate gilt frames, and on the credenza was an honest-to-god taxidermy pheasant, poised with wings out-stretched.

I dropped my box and bag on the table and, careful not to make eye contact with the pheasant, headed through to the living room. It was a big space, set up for entertaining with a couch and several chairs—including a velvet armchair that was a hideous shade of puke green—arranged around the redbrick fireplace. The mantel was bare except for the flatscreen television, but it was flanked by built-in shelves filled with various old books and knickknacks. I moved in for a closer look at the contents—there was a miniature Victorian bust, a couple tacky decorative plates, and a porcelain chicken that I couldn't resist picking up to examine.

"If you're looking to rob me," Fitz said from behind, "I don't think any of it's valuable."

I turned, still holding the porcelain chicken, which was patterned with blue and yellow flowers that reminded me of the wallpaper in my abuela's kitchen.

"I have to admit," I said, struggling for a way to say this tactfully. "None of this is how I imagined your house would look."

"Is that so?" He cast an appraising glance around, as if he were seeing it all for the first time. "Why?"

"I don't know," I hedged. "Your office is completely different."

"You don't like the decor?" He nodded toward the chicken in my hands. "Or the giant stuffed pheasant in the dining room?"

"No, it's all great," I said hastily. "I just meant it doesn't seem very . . . you."

He was regarding me with a straight face, so I had no idea what he was thinking. Wow, it had taken me less than five minutes in his house to insult him. I wondered if maybe I should show myself out.

"That's because none of it's mine." He cracked a grin. "I rented it fully furnished. It's awful, isn't it?"

"You asshole," I cried, resisting the urge to throw the chicken at him. "I was trying so hard to be nice!"

"And you were doing a commendable job."

"You're the worst." I returned the chicken to its perch, before it became an unwilling participant in homicide. "Why did you rent this place if you don't even like it?"

"I like the location." He gestured for me to follow him to the kitchen. "And I'm not here much anyway. It didn't seem important at the time. I'll find another place eventually."

"I'm getting a better idea of why Elinor didn't want to live here." He'd told me that she found an apartment with roommates because she wanted to have the full postgrad twenty-something experience, but I was beginning to think it was because she didn't fancy being haunted by the ghost of someone's dead grandmother wandering around in a housedress and curlers.

"She has referred to it as the 'Kitschy Nightmare' on several occasions," he said, pulling open a kitchen drawer. "And she named the pheasant Gordon Ramsay."

I laughed and leaned my elbows on the center island. The kitchen was less terrible than the rest of the house, because it had been updated recently with all new stainless-steel appliances, spotless white cabinets, and marble slab countertops. I did spy a few prancing cherub figurines tucked into the corners that tied well into the rest of the house's decor.

Oddly enough, I felt as if I'd been cheated out of something. I'd hoped for a glimpse into Fitz's life but instead was met with the veneer of someone else's. Even the gloriously tacky porcelain chicken was a small consolation.

Fitz laid a stack of papers in front of me and spread them

across the island. Take-out menus for at least a dozen different places in a twenty-mile radius.

"Take your pick."

"Now, wait a second," I protested. "You're not even going to cook me dinner?"

"I thought about it, but then I figured you'd want something edible."

"Come on, you can't be that bad." I skirted the island to open the fridge door and survey the contents. "Oh my god, do you eat *anything* other than apples and Greek yogurt?"

"Sometimes I have soup." He reached over my shoulder to push the door shut. "Would you also like an itemized list of my pantry to critique, or can we order dinner?"

I spun around and found him much closer than I expected, looking down at me with his hand still propped against the fridge beside my head.

"I'm not critiquing; I'm observing." I tilted my head back to meet his gaze and caught a whiff of mint that must have been his toothpaste. I had a sudden desire to taste it on his mouth. Then my stomach grumbled mutinously. Judging by Fitz's grin, he heard it too. "*Fine.* But if we're ordering takeout, we're doing it the right way."

I ducked under his arm to start picking through the menus.

"And what way is that?" He leaned back against the refrigerator, arms crossed.

"We order way too much food and pair it with cheap wine and a terrible movie." It was a time-honored tradition in my house.

"I have wine, but I'm not sure it's going to meet your standards." There was a butler's pantry separating the kitchen from the dining room. He pulled a bottle from a rack and two glasses from the cabinet. I didn't recognize the label, but it was gold embossed script on a creamy white background, all in French.

"You're really going to make me drink expensive, quality wine?" I took the glasses from him so he could work the corkscrew.

"I know, I'm a terrible date. We could make up for it with an extra terrible movie."

"I'll try to suffer in silence."

"That'll be a first."

I swatted him with a handful of menus and he laughed, popping the cork free. I recognized one of the restaurants as a Thai place I'd heard good things about. He'd already marked the dishes that contained coconut, so it didn't take long to make our selections. While he called the restaurant, I tried the wine and grudgingly had to admit that it was pretty damn delicious. Mama always insisted that there was no difference in taste between a ten-dollar bottle and a hundred-dollar bottle, but I was beginning to suspect that might be a lie that people who can't afford high-end wine tell themselves. How bourgeois of me. Lucas would be appalled.

While we waited for the food to be delivered, we settled on the couch with the wine and my box. I removed the lid and explained the concept for my parents' anniversary gift. I wanted the butterflies to flutter out of the box when it was opened, as if they were alive. My cheeks flared with self-conscious heat as he gently removed a paper butterfly and examined it.

"Why?" he asked, his eyes bright with fascination.

"They met at a campground in Tennessee during the monarch butterflies' fall migration, but they haven't been able to go back in years." I'd hoped the gift might spark that same joy they always exuded when they recalled the tale of seeing each other across a field, the air between them flashing orange and black with thousands upon thousands of monarchs in search of warmer climes.

I still hated that I hadn't been able to figure it out for myself, but in the end, I decided the look on their faces would be worth asking a mage for help. Fitz was quiet for a while, studying the delicate paper butterfly in his hand.

"I know it's cheesy," I said, trying not to fidget.

"It's not." There was a warmth about him, tinged with a soft sort of wistfulness that I hadn't seen before. "I think it's an amazing idea."

Glancing down at the full box, I realized I had no concept of how much magical effort it would cost him to do this favor for me. I didn't want him to exhaust himself to the point of collapse, like he had during the Animal Pox, and by now I understood him well enough to know that he would do so without a word of protest. Elinor would murder me.

"If it's too much trouble to animate all of them," I started, but he shook his head. He held out his hand with the butterfly on his palm. I watched breathlessly as the origami wings began to twitch and flutter, and then it took flight, rising upward in lazy spirals. Seconds later the rest of the monarchs followed suit, rising in a whisper-soft cloud. The sight was exactly how I'd imagined it, and as they swooped gracefully around our heads, tears began to well. I blinked them away, willing myself to keep it together.

"I have to feed them magic continuously to keep them going," Fitz said. "Not much, but they won't remain animated for more than a few minutes without it."

The spell I'd tried to craft would have kept them in motion indefinitely. But I hadn't been able to coax even a flutter out of them, and Fitz had brought them to life without breaking a sweat, so I wasn't about to complain.

I studied him for a few seconds, trying to make sure he really hadn't broken a sweat, in case "not much" magic was more than he was letting on. He seemed perfectly at ease, his features relaxed in a way that made me realize I'd never seen him relaxed before, not truly. But he was now, here, with me. And that new awareness settled over me like a cozy blanket.

"Is this your way of angling for an invite to the anniversary party?" With some effort, I managed to keep my voice light and level.

"Am I that transparent?"

"I'll try to get you on the waiting list." A butterfly perched on my nose, sending a thrill of delight through me. My well of sarcasm dried up, replaced with pure gratitude.

"They're perfect." My voice was barely above a whisper, so as not to disturb the butterfly. "Thank you."

Fitz said nothing. There was a new kind of warmth in his eyes, and it raked across my skin and sparked in my bloodstream. I brushed the butterfly from my nose, ready now for a new kind of touch. The empty box was between us on the couch, and I pushed it to the floor, not breaking eye contact—afraid that if I did, it would also break the taut desire stretching between us. I pushed up onto my knees to move closer. He cupped a hand behind my neck, and our lips met.

I was filled with a *want* that reverberated through my body like a second pulse. Fitz wrapped his other arm around my waist, and then I was straddling his lap, running my fingers through his hair, down his face, across his chest. God, he was a good kisser. Just the right amount of tongue. I liked having him under my hands, loved the shudder that ran through him as I slid them beneath the hem of his shirt. His fingertips rasped along my bare thighs, leaving trails of goosebumps in their wake, as he explored my jawline and neck with his lips, somehow both gentle and demanding.

He was stirring between my legs, and I rocked against him, capturing his moan in my mouth like it was rare wine. The crush of our bodies together was raw and simple, like nothing between us had ever been before. I didn't want it to end, didn't want to think about what might lie on the other side.

"Charlie." His voice was thick with need, his breath hot against my lips. I curled my fingers into the waistband of his jeans. "Charlie, wait."

Quiet as it was, the word cut through my haze. I pulled back, blinking hard to bring his face back into focus, trying to bring my breathing back under control.

"What's wrong?"

"I like you so much. And you're so fucking sexy, but this— I can't—" He shook his head, frustrated at his own fumbling. My heart pounded painfully against my ribs. *But.* That was not a word I wanted to hear. He took a shallow breath and tried again. "I just got out of a relationship in April. I need . . . to go slower."

Relief washed over me, cooling me down to a more functional state. *Slower* was not an ending. *Slower* I could handle. I twisted off him and sat back down on the couch. I leaned my head back and took a few seconds to collect myself.

"Shit, I'm sorry," he said into the silence. "I shouldn't have—"

"No, don't apologize." I patted his leg in what I hoped was a reassuring manner. "I get it. We can take things slow. It's okay."

He searched my face for a few seconds before his frown began to dissipate.

"Thank you." He draped his arm around my shoulders, and I obligingly scooted closer, pleased with how perfectly our bodies aligned. I rested my head in the dip of his shoulder. Now that my body temperature was almost back to normal, I could think a bit more clearly.

"You realize that's the first personal thing about yourself you've ever told me?" I asked, careful to keep any hint of accusation out of my tone.

"I've told you lots of things."

"Nothing I couldn't find by googling you."

"You've googled me?" he asked, amused.

My cheeks flushed with new, much less enjoyable heat, but I refused to be sidetracked.

"That's not the point."

He actually considered my point for a while, a small furrow forming between his brows.

"I'm not trying to hide anything," he said at last. "I guess I didn't think there was much worth telling."

That was like a pinprick to my heart, minuscule but painfully sharp. I cupped my hand against the side of his face, my thumb brushing against the spot where his dimple would be, if he were smiling.

"Every part of you is worth knowing," I said.

I don't know if he believed me, but without breaking eye contact, he turned his head to press a kiss against my palm. I wanted to pull him toward me again, to wrap myself around him and lose myself again in the fever of raw and simple desire. But I restrained myself to interlocking my fingers with his. A different kind of simplicity.

The doorbell rang shortly after, and—once the butterflies were safely tucked back into their box—we were able to lose ourselves instead in the wonders of Thai food and bad cinema. To be fair, the movie probably would have made more sense if we hadn't talked through most of it. We occasionally held off on talking long enough to make out some more, though we kept it strictly PG this time. The shrieking C-list actors and horrible special effects on the screen helped tremendously in mitigating the mood.

By the time the credits rolled, I was stuffed full of Thai and wine, my ribs hurt from laughing, and I was ninety-nine per-cent sure there was a hickey on my neck that my parents would never let me hear the end of. I was blissfully content with life, the universe, and everything.

I had curled up on my side, with my head on a throw pillow that I'd propped against Fitz's hip. He was combing his fingers through my hair in the most delicious way, sending shivers of sensation across my scalp and down my spine. I wasn't sure why I was compelled to ruin the moment. Possibly I could blame the wine, but more likely I'm an incurable snoop.

"Was it serious—with your ex?" I asked.

His hand stilled. The silence stretched longer and longer. I was on the verge of saying never mind, it was none of my business, when he started stroking again.

"We were together three years," he said. "Her name is Gwen. She cheated on me the night after we got engaged."

"Fuck, that's awful."

"It was." He wound a strand of my hair idly around his finger. His voice, when he spoke again, was brittle to the point of breaking. "I didn't find out until a month later who she slept with. It was my father."

"*Fuck.*" What else was there to say? I sat up, drawing his hand from my hair to clutch it between both of mine. "You don't have to talk about it, if you don't want to."

He shook his head. Judging by his expression, his mind was a million miles away—or maybe just however far Boston was. I realized that the truth about Gwen's affair partner was probably the impetus for his decision to abandon the family firm and strike out on his own.

"I can't say it was a huge surprise," Fitz said. "He could never stand the thought of me doing anything he couldn't do—having anything he couldn't have. I think the idea of me being happily married when his own marriage had crashed and burned was unbearable for him."

"He cheated on your mom," I said, without thinking, as if

pointing out that the second Sterling's divorce was his own damn fault could make any difference. The trouble with being a celebrity public figure was that all your dirty laundry, including the specifics of your nasty divorce battle, were served up for public consumption.

"He did, several times." Fitz gave a mirthless smile. "In all fairness, she cheated on him too. They were not well-suited. Or maybe they were perfectly suited. I guess it depends on how you look at it."

I knew our small town had its own share of sordid secrets and betrayal, but at least here those incidents stayed in the gossip mill, rather than being splashed across tabloids and web pages. If I remembered correctly, he'd been fourteen when they got divorced. I couldn't imagine how overwhelming that upheaval and scrutiny must have been. Then there was the fact that Mrs. Fitzgerald had not even contested her husband's bid for full custody of their children. Being left behind with your dick of a dad while your mom moved to Italy with her new boyfriend—I couldn't even begin to wrap my mind around it.

"Your father's an asshole." I was confident in that much at least. I wanted to say the same about Gwen, but insulting his ex-fiancée after I'd spent half the night with my tongue in his mouth seemed unnecessarily petty.

"I'm guessing Elinor already told you about him?" he asked.

"Some," I admitted. "But nothing about Gwen."

"He and El were always butting heads. She loved trying to get under his skin."

Elinor had told me that when their father was yelling at her, then at least he wasn't yelling at Fitz, and I wondered if Fitz had ever seen it that way. I wasn't sure it was my place to say anything.

"She hates how he treated you," I said at last.

"She thinks I should denounce him completely and never

speak to him again." He rested his chin on top of my head and let out a sigh. "She's probably right."

"But you don't want to?" I tried to keep my tone neutral, even though my knee-jerk reaction was to exclaim that of *course* she was right.

"I can't hate him the way she and Vic do." There was an undercurrent of defeat in his voice. "I know I should, and I've tried, but sometimes I still think that if I could say the right thing, if I could just do *enough*, then he'd finally want to change. I know it's stupid. My therapist says it's natural to feel that way about an abusive parent, and that recognizing it and examining it is the first step to letting it go. But I guess I'm not there yet."

I squeezed his hand more tightly between mine.

"It's not stupid," I said. "No one else can tell you how to feel."

"He wasn't always bad, you know?" Fitz slipped his hand free and shifted so that his arm was around me again. I nestled against him, pulling my knees up to my chest. "He was so excited the first time I used magic. He taught me everything. He's extremely powerful, and so many people would have killed to learn from him, but I'm the only pupil he ever took on."

"Not your sisters?"

"Victoria isn't a mage. She left home when she turned eighteen and never looked back. Elinor was a late bloomer. She was in high school the first time she used magic, and even then, she never wanted anything to do with it. She only recently started practicing in earnest."

"By disappearing your wallet."

"That is her favorite lesson these days." He chuckled. "I guess I brought it on myself, since I was the one who taught her how to do it."

"You know," I said, craning my neck to look up at him, "it's possible she's only ready to learn now because she has you to teach her." I hadn't met the second Sterling, but I could say with

certainty that I would prefer Fitz as a teacher over him. I'd prefer a sentient pickle as a teacher over him.

"Maybe." He was clearly turning the thought over in his
mind. Some of the heaviness in his features evaporated. "She
tends to be enthusiastic about most things, but she really loves
doing magic. She lights up every time, like it's the most wonderful experience in the world, no matter how drained she is
after."

I nodded, because that was exactly how I felt about witchcraft. The unique exhilaration it gave me was unparalleled.
Something about his phrasing bugged me, though. It took me a
few seconds to figure out what it was.

"But that's not what magic is like for you?" I asked.

He hesitated, caught off guard by the question.

"Maybe when I was a kid, but not anymore." He rubbed the
back of his neck with his free hand. "My dad doesn't think
magic and emotions should mix, so I guess it's just a job to me
now. I don't hate it, but usually I'm ready to get it over with."

I had no doubt his father's constant criticism had something
to do with that, but I held my tongue. Unbidden, the image of
his final tarot card sprang into my mind. The World in reverse,
signifying emptiness and disappointment. A painful knot constricted at the base of my throat.

I told myself to relax. Didn't I tell customers before every
reading that the future wasn't a fixed point? That it is constantly
evolving, influenced by our decisions and the decisions of others?

Still, I wished I could do another reading for him, so I could
know. But even if I convinced him to let me try, I knew it
wouldn't do any good. It would be impossible for me to clear my
intentions and interpret the cards without bias. I cared about
him too much. I wanted only good things for him. The tarot

would not appreciate me trying to manifest my own desires into the spread.

I needed to put it out of my mind. There was a reason I normally only did readings for customers, not for family or friends. Insight into the future wasn't always a good thing.

"Honestly," Fitz went on, and my attention snapped back to him. I was grateful that for once he was oblivious to my inner turmoil. "Animating those butterflies tonight was the first time magic has made me happy in years."

"Because of my excellent origami skills?" I asked dryly.

"Because it made *you* happy." He pressed a kiss against the top of my head.

Damn, he was making it really difficult to not jump his bones.

CHAPTER TWENTY

I woke up with a desert-dry mouth and a dull headache thudding in the back of my skull. I blinked blearily, disoriented by the unfamiliar ceiling I was staring at. After a few seconds, I realized I was on Fitz's couch, and the events of last night came rushing back to me, momentarily replacing my headache with a giddy whirl. We'd stayed up into the wee hours of the morning, talking and touching and soaking up each other's company. I'd kept saying I needed to get home but never managed to make it to the door. I didn't remember falling asleep, but it wasn't a surprise.

I rolled onto my stomach to hide my face from the sunlight streaming through the windows. Beneath my head wasn't the same round throw pillow I'd been using last night. It was a regular pillow with a soft cotton case. I breathed in the fresh, bracing smell of eucalyptus that I now recognized as the scent of Fitz's shampoo and smiled. I was considering drifting back to sleep when a panicked thought struck me. It was *Monday*.

I grabbed my phone from the coffee table where I'd left it last night after texting my parents to let them know I wasn't dead or dying. It was almost ten. I should have opened the shop two hours ago.

"Shit." I bolted upright and scrambled to disentangle my legs from a blanket that had appeared at some point in the night. My head was pounding with a new ferocity. As I pocketed my phone, I noticed a glass of water on the table beside a bottle of ibuprofen. *Bless you, Fitz.*

I gulped down some water and pills and climbed to my feet. As I rounded the arm of the couch, I kicked the butterfly box and it tumbled over, losing its lid. The butterflies fluttered free in a cloud of orange. I stared in astonished confusion as they dispersed. Fitz had said they wouldn't stay animated for long after he stopped feeding them magic. Maybe he was underestimating his own power.

At any rate, I didn't have time to figure it out. I snatched a few butterflies out of the air, careful not to crush the paper, but soon realized I also didn't have time to round them all up. A few were already lazily flapping their way to the ceiling.

I took a hesitant step down the corridor toward the bedrooms, wondering if Fitz was awake yet. I didn't want to run out—and leave his house infested with origami butterflies—without saying goodbye.

I heard his voice and took a few more steps. One of the doors was open a crack, and I realized he was talking on the phone. It wasn't a pleasant conversation by the sound of it.

"That's not fair, and you know it," he snapped. I could almost picture him pacing and running his hand through his hair. "No . . . no . . . I don't want to talk about this right now."

I retreated to the front of the house, deciding not to interrupt. But I also didn't have time to wait for the call to end. I dug a pen and old receipt out of my bag. I scribbled a note and left it on the coffee table. As an afterthought, I added *P.S. Sorry about the butterflies.*

When I got home, there were two cars in the customer parking lot, and my heart sank. But according to the sign, the witch was in. I opened the door to find Mim explaining the difference between two spell jars to a woman with a wriggling toddler. Near the back, a couple of men were chatting and laughing while they looked at wands.

Mim grinned when she caught my eye and waved me upstairs.

I ran up, knowing I at least needed to brush my hair and teeth, and probably put on a fresh shirt, before I could help any customers. Mama was elbow-deep in suds at the sink. She gave me a smile that could only be described as wicked.

"Hello, daughter," she said in a singsong. "Congratulations on your first walk of shame. I'd always planned to have a cake for you, but after so many years I'd given up hope the day would ever come."

"I hate to disappoint you, but I accidentally fell asleep on his couch. Nothing happened." Well, a lot had happened, but I wasn't about to go into detail.

"Sure, and that hickey on your neck is from holding hands too hard."

I clapped my hand over my neck and briefly considered packing my bags and fleeing the country.

"I think I'm entitled to some privacy," I said, mustering the last bit of dignity I possessed.

"I'll have you know that I'm not above stopping by Maven Enterprises and demanding to know his intentions with my daughter." She reached out to flick my ear with a sudsy hand. "And now that my daughter has shown up for work, I have some free time on my hands."

"Don't you dare." I knew she would have no qualms doing it, and she'd enjoy the hell out of it too. "You know, normal parents don't want to hear details about their daughter's sexual exploits."

"So there *was* sex," she crowed.

"No! Oh my god." I threw a tea towel at her and marched down the hallway. "I'm changing, then I'll take over for Mim. And then I'm going to look up how to retroactively emancipate myself."

"You know you love me," she said, resuming her singsong voice. "And there's no need to rush. We finished balancing the books on Saturday night."

I ignored her. Changing clothes took longer than I intended, because I had to dig up a shirt with a collar that would cover the bright red hickey. No doubt Mama's motherly intuition told her that I wasn't going to sit down for a meal, because by the time I returned she'd prepared a thermos of coffee and heated up a breakfast burrito.

I planted a kiss on her cheek and made it back downstairs in time to sell the couple some amethyst crystals and a jade wand. Mim was still in conversation with the woman, though it sounded like they'd meandered from spell jars into the rising price of eggs, so I had a minute to breathe.

My mouth was full of burrito when my phone rang. I stared down at Fitz's name for a while, debating internally while I chewed. Every time I was with him, the Cottage was all but forgotten, and then every time I was back at the Cottage, I swore to myself I wouldn't forget again.

If I was going to keep seeing Fitz—and after last night, I dearly wanted to—then I had to keep my priorities straight.

But also, it was just a phone call. And considering how I'd run out that morning, it would be rude to ignore him, right?

Pleased with my own bulletproof reasoning, I chased down my bite of burrito with a gulp of coffee and answered.

"Sorry for my disappearing act," I said. "I was late for work."

"No, I'm sorry I didn't wake you. I got caught up with something."

I remembered his fraught tone on the phone call before I left. I wanted to ask about it but told myself to let it go. He'd opened up last night, but that didn't mean he was ready to share every detail of his life with me, no matter how nosy I was.

"Were you able to wrangle the butterflies?" I asked instead.

"Eventually. I guess you figured out your spell?"

"What do you mean?"

"To make them fly?"

"I didn't do anything. They were still animated when I opened the box this morning."

"I told you last night, unless I'm actively feeding them magic, they won't stay animated for longer than a couple minutes."

"Well, clearly they did." I took another drink of coffee and smiled at Mim, who was dancing with the toddler and Broomhilde while the mother took advantage of the short reprieve to browse in peace.

"Then what are these markings on the wings?" Fitz asked musingly.

"The runes I tried to use originally, but like I said, they didn't work."

"A spell for perpetual motion?"

"Yes." I could practically hear his thoughts whirring, and I tried to catch up. "My spell wouldn't randomly start working overnight."

"Could my magic have activated yours somehow?"

"Like a jump-start?" My initial reaction was that my spellwork didn't need a mage's help, but when I forced myself to consider it objectively, it did make sense, sort of. I'd never heard of magecraft working in tandem with witchcraft, but that didn't mean it was impossible. Magic was magic.

"Maybe," Fitz said. "It's definitely not me keeping them in the air."

I wasn't sure what to say. There was something both exhila-rating and unsettling about the thought of Fitz's magic working with mine. I wondered if it was a phenomenon that could be replicated.

"I had fun last night," Fitz said, once my silence had stretched long enough to be awkward.

My heart thrummed faster. His voice was disarmingly inti-mate, and heat rose on the back of my neck. Any second now I'd be twirling my hair around my finger and giggling like a high schooler. I turned my back on the others to preserve a modicum of privacy.

"Me too." I managed to keep my tone casual, mostly.

"Want to come over again tonight?"

Yes. Yes. Yes.

I bit back that response. I couldn't be late two days in a row, and I clearly couldn't be trusted to keep a reasonable curfew. The woman approached the counter with a basketful of items, saving me from my own indecision.

"I've got a customer," I said. "I'll call you later, okay?"

We exchanged goodbyes, and I spun around with my cus-tomer service smile to ring up her purchases. Sensing that their visit was coming to an end, the toddler had a meltdown. It was a bit of a production helping the poor woman pack her bags and screaming child into her car. My ears were ringing by the time Mim and I made it back inside. At least the tantrum would forestall any hints about grandchildren she might have been planning to drop.

I flopped forward onto the counter, pressing my forehead into my arms.

"I can't believe I was late again," I said into the wood. "I'm so sorry."

Mim laughed and patted my back.

"I kind of figured you would be when you still weren't home at six this morning."

It didn't make me feel any better. If anything, my distress intensified. I'd been trying so hard to convince myself that dating Fitz wasn't a terrible idea, that it was possible to separate our business rivalry from our personal relationship. But despite a lifelong spotless work ethic, in the past month I'd repeatedly shirked my duties. When I was with him, the rest of my life was so far away.

"I'm sorry you had to cover for me."

"Charlie, it's not a big deal," Mim said carefully, as if she had just figured out I was genuinely upset. I had no doubt my aura was broadcasting my emotions to her right now. "I don't mind."

"You should," I insisted, raising my head. "It's my job. How are we supposed to save the shop if you can't even count on me to show up?"

Mim laughed again, and I twitched with irritation at her levity.

"First of all, you being late to work is not going to plummet us into bankruptcy. Second, you seem to forget that your mom and I ran this shop for years before you were born."

"Well, it's a relief to know that I'm completely redundant," I said testily.

"You know that's not what I meant." She set to work refolding some altar cloths the toddler had pulled from the shelf. "Your mom and I have been talking, and we think it would do you some good to take some time off. Maybe a little staycation?"

The prospect of lounging around upstairs in pajamas while my parents worked to keep our failing business afloat made me want to laugh. And cry.

Except it's not our *business, is it?*

"Bonnie, Jen, and I did that road trip to Lake Michigan in

May. I don't need any more time off." Logically, I knew that working nine hours a day, six days a week wasn't the healthiest work-life balance. But the time to reassess my priorities was not while we were on the verge of bankruptcy.

"You know," she said, tucking the last cloth into place, "just because this is the family business, it doesn't mean you have to work here forever. Maybe you could use a staycation to clear your head and think about other options."

I froze. How had a discussion about my tardiness become a suggestion that I make a career change? This particular concern wasn't a new one, but she and Mama hadn't raised it for at least a decade. I'd thought that leaving for college had satisfied their worry that I felt trapped in Owl's Hollow. After college, I'd even had a couple job offers, but I turned them down. I had chosen to come back.

"Is this because of Fitz?" I asked. "You think that because I've been on a few dates with a mage I must be yearning to escape my provincial life?"

"It's not about him." She shooed Broomhilde away from the crystal display before joining me at the counter. "Well, it's not *entirely* about him. I don't like watching you beat yourself up for having a nice time and forgetting about work for a while. You've always been too hard on yourself."

I didn't think that was true. Maybe if I was a little harder on myself, I'd be a more accomplished witch than I was now. Sure, I'd figured out the cure for the Animal Pox, but clearly I was still lacking, or my parents would have let me buy into the business by now, instead of coming up with reasons why I should leave.

"If you want to fire me, then you should just come out and say it." My tone was snappish, but there was a lump building in my throat, and my eyes were burning with the promise of tears.

"Baby, that's not what I'm saying." Mim reached across the counter to give my hands a squeeze. "I'm sorry, it's coming out all wrong. I mean that if you *do* ever want to try something else, you shouldn't worry about me and Mama. Being born a Sparrow doesn't mean you're stuck in the Cottage for the rest of your life."

"I don't feel stuck," I said, once the reassurance that I was not being fired had settled in and I could breathe again. But then something occurred to me. "Wait, do you?"

"Do I what?" She released my hands and started reorganizing the small rack of informational pamphlets we kept on the counter, even though I knew for a fact they were perfectly in order because I'd checked them yesterday.

"Do you feel stuck here?" I repeated, not willing to let this drop.

Mim had been only twenty-four when both her parents died in a car accident. She must have grown up knowing that the Cottage would be her inheritance, like I had, but she never could have anticipated it becoming her sole responsibility so soon. I'd never given much thought to what that must have been like, losing her parents and gaining the burden of the family legacy all at once. I guess she could have shut it down or sold it or tried to find a relative who might be willing to take it over, but she hadn't. Maybe she didn't think she had a choice.

"I love the Cottage." Mim was very purposefully not looking at me.

"That's not an answer," I said, more gently now.

She removed a stack of pamphlets, flipped idly through them, and returned them to the same spot.

"You can love your life and still feel stuck sometimes." When she looked up, there was a network of thin wrinkles in her face that I'd never noticed before. She and Mama were ageless to me, preserved in my mind as an unchanging memory. Whenever I let myself look at them, truly look at them, it was a shock to realize that they weren't immune to passing time.

"I don't feel stuck," I repeated. "If I wanted to leave, I would, but I don't want to. I wish you and Mama would believe me."

She offered me a smile, but there was something sad about it. Unease crept into my stomach, and I wished desperately I could read her mind, glean some idea of what she was thinking. Even her aura was a mystery to me right now. My sixth sense had always been less reliable than hers. Mine was tied strongly to my emotions, which meant when I needed it the most, like right now, it usually deserted me.

"I didn't mean to upset you, baby." She came around the counter to envelop me in a hug, which only made the tears threaten to reappear, even though my mood had improved now that I knew I didn't have to polish my résumé. "Your mom and I worry about you. That's *our* job."

I wanted to tell her to stop worrying, but I knew that would be as effective as telling the Earth to stop rotating. I also wanted to tell her that if they wanted me to be happy here, then they could let me buy into the business, and we could stop having this conversation once and for all. But I knew it wasn't the time.

"We have several spell sessions booked today." I pulled out the planner from under the counter. "We should probably start prepping."

Mim looked like she wanted to say something else, but instead she headed upstairs to fetch Mama so we could all get to work.

It was a pleasantly busy day, and I didn't have much time to dwell on my self-doubt. All our spell appointments went off without a hitch. I even handled a couple walk-ins on my own without incident. Maybe now we could put any talk of a staycation to bed.

Five o'clock rolled around. I had finished closing up shop

and was trying to attack a cobweb in the corner of the ceiling with a broom when my phone began to ring. It was Tandy. I answered with no little amount of trepidation. Tandy didn't call for friendly chats.

"Charlie, oh my gosh, I'm so glad you answered. You will not *believe* where I am and what I just heard."

I had a strong suspicion I didn't want to know, but I sighed. "Where are you?"

"I dropped by Maven Enterprises, because you know I like to keep an eye on things." She'd lowered her voice conspiratorially. This already did not bode well. "I'm outside right now, but earlier I went inside, and Elly wasn't at the front desk. I poked around a little—not snooping, you know, perfectly innocent—then I heard the two of them talking in the mage's office. And you know I'm not one to eavesdrop, but I heard your name, and so obviously I had to find out what they were saying about you, and Charlie, you will not *believe* the *audacity*. He said you spent the night *at his house*. What a filthy, rotten liar."

"Tandy," I broke in. "Don't worry about it. It's fine."

Fitz and Elinor's conversation had probably been similar to the one I had with Mama, along the lines of "*Nothing happened, so for the love of god stop asking about it.*" Not that Tandy would have bothered to listen for any more context.

"It is absolutely not fine. You can bet he's spreading that nasty rumor all over town, making you out to be some kind of floozy."

"Tandy—"

"It's a *disgrace*."

"Tandy—"

"But don't you worry. I'm going back in there right now, and I'm going to give him a piece of my mind."

Oh, for fuck's sake.

"Tandy, no. Don't you dare—"

"It's okay. I don't mind. We ladies have to stick up for each other."

"Please listen to me—"

"Don't worry. I'm taking care of it."

"Tandy!" I shouted into the phone, but she'd already hung up. I called her back immediately, but it went straight to voicemail. I tried three more times before I gave up.

"Dammit," I said aloud, resigning myself to a mess. Sure enough, a couple minutes later, my phone rang again. Elinor Fitzgerald.

I'd barely gotten out my hello before she started in.

"That obnoxious witch Tandy is in my brother's office ranting at him about, like, slander laws or some shit, and Fitzy is too nice to kick her out, but I swear, Charlie, I'm about to drag her out by her hair. *Please* tell me you didn't send her here, because she's saying you did."

I could hear the muffled sounds of Tandy's diatribe in the background. My head was starting to ache.

"I definitely did not. Put her on the phone."

"She just called him a lying bastard and threatened to hex him. Hold on, I'm going to strangle her with the straps of her ugly Gucci bag."

"Elinor, please let me talk to her," I begged. "No need for strangling."

"Fine, but the bitch is on notice."

There was almost a minute of shuffling and garbled voices before Tandy's voice, breathless with righteous indignation, sounded in my ear.

"I told you I was taking care of it. He's acting like he doesn't know what I'm talking about, but don't worry, I'm not letting him get away with that."

"Tandy," I snapped. "For fuck's sake, will you listen to me for a second?"

"What?" she snapped back.

"I tried to tell you before: Fitz isn't spreading rumors or lying about me."

"But I *heard* him say—"

"Tandy," I said firmly, with my last iota of patience. "He. Is. Not. Lying. About. Me."

"But—oh." She was silent for a few moments, and I could practically hear the gears turning in her head. "*Oh.* Well, good gracious, why didn't you say so before? Are you sure that's a smart idea? What will Ruby and Alicia think?"

Only Tandy would storm into someone's place of business to yell at them, then take the time to question my dating choices while she was at it.

"Please just leave them alone," I said wearily.

"All right, but we're going to need to have a talk about this." She didn't sound ashamed of herself in the least. "I find it concerning."

"Bye, Tandy."

More muffled noises, and then Elinor was back on the phone.

"I'm sorry about that." I pinched the bridge of my nose. "She thought she was—never mind. It won't happen again."

I wasn't sure that was a promise I could make, but it was too late now.

"No offense, but your friend is insane." Elinor at least seemed to have calmed down somewhat. I heard Fitz in the background saying that Tandy was a reluctant colleague, and I smiled.

"I'll make it up to you guys."

"I'd rather you let me cover her face in warts," said Elinor. Fitz said something I couldn't make out, and she shot back, "Yes, I *do* know how."

"I'd rather you didn't," I said. "Would some pizza for dinner appease you?"

"I suppose so. As long as there are no olives. Meet us at the office in an hour?"

"Okay, see you then." I ended the call, still smiling to myself. I phoned my favorite pizza place to order a large pepperoni with extra cheese and headed upstairs. The cobweb would get another day's reprieve.

CHAPTER TWENTY-ONE

My moms were in the middle of arranging chairs around the living room for their monthly book club, which was really an excuse to sit around with their friends and air their grievances about anyone and anything. Normally I would steal some of their snacks and hole up in my room, but for once I had better plans.

"I'm taking the car," I announced, as I went back to my bedroom to change.

"Ooh, does someone have special plans tonight?" Mama asked. I could practically hear her eyebrows waggling suggestively.

"As a matter of fact, yes. I'm going to hire a contractor to build me a house of candy in the woods so I can finally have some peace." I shut my door, though I could still hear strains of their giggles from the living room.

I pulled on a fresh shirt, reapplied deodorant to be safe, and touched up my hair and makeup. By the time I reemerged, the mood in the house had dampened considerably. My moms were both standing at the stove, staring down mournfully at a tray of smoking, nearly black cookies. They'd both forgotten to set a timer. Being proficient at witchcraft unfortunately did not always protect you from the horrors of the mundane.

"I'm sorry for your loss." I went into our pantry and pulled a bottle of certifiably cheap wine down from the top shelf.

"Why must bad things happen to good people?" Mama crossed herself in lament, even though she hadn't been a practicing Catholic since she was a teenager.

"I'm calling Keisha," Mim said, already transitioning into fix-it mode. "Maybe she can stop at that bakery by her house. The one with the good muffins."

I wished them luck and grabbed my bag to head downstairs, cradling the wine bottle in the crook of my arm. Dusk was falling by the time I arrived at Maven Enterprises. I couldn't see through the mirrored glass panes, and the door was locked, but Elinor let me in before I had a chance to knock.

"You're a lifesaver," she said, as she took the pizza from me. "I'm starving. Fitz is on the phone, but he should be done soon."

We set up on the low table in the lobby, sitting cross-legged on the rug. I'd been able to sweet-talk the cashier at the pizza place into giving me paper plates, cups, and napkins. I had unfortunately forgotten a corkscrew, but Elinor was more than happy to show off her magic skills. With some concentration, and her tongue sticking out adorably between her teeth, she drew the cork out with a wave of her hand. I applauded, duly impressed, and we toasted to pizza, the great peacemaker.

Fitz's call took longer than expected, so Elinor made the executive decision that we should start without him. I was pretty hungry myself, so I can't say I put up much of a fight. As we dug in, she kept casting glances down the hall toward Fitz's closed office door. Her attitude was not one of impatience but worry.

"Is something wrong?" I asked.

"What? No." She blinked and offered me a grin that seemed

forced. Less than a second later her gaze was drawn back down the hall. "I mean, well . . . if I ask you something, can it stay between us?"

"Sure," I said, my curiosity piqued.

"Has Fitzy said anything to you about maybe going back to Boston?"

"You mean to visit?"

"No, like moving back."

"Oh." My heart skipped a beat. "No, he hasn't. Why? Is he thinking about it?"

"No—I don't know." She picked at a piece of pepperoni. "I don't read his emails, but I have access to his inbox in case I need to find something and he's unavailable. I saw some emails from the director of human resources at our dad's company. The subject line was 'Salary negotiations.'"

"Oh," I said again.

"Dad has called a few times recently." She poured herself more wine. "I'm afraid he's trying to convince Fitz to come back and work for him. And I—well, I'm not sure, but a woman called the other day asking to speak with him, and I swear it was his ex, Gwen."

"Did you ask Fitz about it?"

She gave me a look like I'd just asked if she'd chatted with any aliens recently.

"He wouldn't tell me anyway," she said, which I gathered meant no. "He hates when I bring up Dad or Gwen. He always changes the subject."

"It's probably nothing." Surely he would have told Elinor if he was considering moving back to Boston—after all, it affected her too. She couldn't run Maven on her own. And I liked to think that he would have mentioned it to me too.

"Maybe." She didn't look convinced in the least. "Could you ask him about it? But like, subtly, so he doesn't know I told you?"

"I don't think that's a—"

"Please, Charlie?" She flashed me puppy dog eyes, which was hardly fair. I thought about it for a few seconds and decided there was nothing underhanded in asking him about it, if the topic happened to come up.

"Fine, I will *try*," I said. "But no promises."

That must have satisfied her because she breathed a sigh of relief.

"You're the best."

"We're not going to make a habit out of this, though."

"Make a habit out of what?" Fitz asked, as he came down the hall. I hadn't heard his office door open.

"Waiting on you to finish your boring work calls," Elinor said smoothly.

"Doesn't look like you waited at all," he pointed out. He sat down beside me and loosened his tie.

"Sorry." I leaned over to press a kiss against his five o'clock shadow. "Pizza waits for no man."

"I guess I should be grateful there's any left." He reached for a slice while I poured him some wine. I watched for his reaction as he took his first sip, and I was not disappointed. He made a face and looked down at it, as if to check he hadn't accidentally drunk toilet water.

"Do you like it?" I asked, all innocence. "It's my family's favorite vintage."

He gave me an appraising look, and I guess I wasn't as skilled at keeping a straight face as he was, because he smiled wryly.

"This feels like a trap. I'm pleading the Fifth."

"It's magic wine," I said. "The more you drink, the better it tastes."

"Isn't that all wine?" Elinor asked.

"Exactly."

Elinor and I giggled. Fitz was still smiling, but I could tell something was distracting him. I wondered if it had to do with the phone call.

"Everything okay?" I asked, nudging him with my shoulder.

"Everything's great." Damn, he was really good at that poker face. "Now, are you going to tell me why Tandy DiAngelo came in here yelling at me about slander laws?"

I groaned and downed the rest of my wine. Even though none of it was my fault, my cheeks were hot as I explained Tandy's misunderstanding. By the time I finished, Elinor was clutching her stomach and laughing so hard she could barely breathe.

"Oh my god," she said, between gasps. "Oh my god, she is a madwoman. I think I love her now."

Fitz was less amused.

"I told Elinor you slept on the couch," he said quietly, with a faint frown, while Elinor flopped onto her back, still laughing. "That's all."

"I never thought otherwise." I reached up to brush my fingers through his hair, mussing it in the way I liked. "I'm sorry if Tandy freaked you out."

"I was mostly just confused." His lips crooked. "I know you don't think of her as a friend, but I've never met anyone who would go that far to defend the honor of a colleague."

I hadn't considered that before. Great, was I going to have to be nice to Tandy now?

Elinor managed to get herself under control enough to sit up and drink more wine, which I didn't think would help with the irrepressible laughter. But I was glad she saw the humor in it, and I was relieved that no one had been hexed—or strangled with a Gucci bag. Best-case scenario.

I'd only planned on staying for dinner, but the three of us talked for hours. Elinor showed off more of her magic skills. First, she made her nail polish ripple through a rainbow of colors. Then she levitated a stray piece of pepperoni for almost thirty seconds before it ended up stuck to the ceiling, which she insisted was on purpose. After that, we used sticky notes to play several rounds of the Forehead Game. It ended in scandal when Elinor and I realized Fitz was cheating.

When we ran out of pizza, Elinor remembered she had a box of Twinkies in her car ("Don't ask," she told me) and went to fetch them. I managed to keep my hands and mouth to myself for all of ten seconds after she left, and then I was half in Fitz's lap while he tugged me closer with his left arm around my waist, his right hand tangled in my hair. The wild fervor of a brand-new relationship was one of my favorite feelings. I couldn't get enough of his deft touch, his clever tongue, his perfect way of holding me, like I was something both precious and irresistible.

We were so wrapped up in each other that when his cellphone rang, we both nearly jumped out of our skins. With his arm still tight around my waist, Fitz dug it out to see who was calling. He grimaced at the screen.

"It's Councilman Munch." His voice was low and strained. "I don't know why he's calling so late."

"Answer it," I told him, pulling back to a respectable distance. "Elinor will be back any second anyway."

He ran a hand down his face, trying to compose himself, and answered, only sounding a little winded. I climbed to my feet to get a drink from the water cooler in the corner. As I filled the white paper cone, my phone dinged with a text message. It was from Mim.

Linda Hibbert called. The council had a meeting tonight.
Apparently Munch has talked a majority over to his side re:
Maven's license. Doesn't look good for us.

I bit my lip and looked at Fitz.

"That's great news," he was saying.

I was such an idiot. Pretending like this thing between us was somehow entirely removed from the reality of our situation was childish and naïve. The Cottage was barely scraping by, and if Maven Enterprises was here to stay, then our chances of survival plummeted even more drastically. What made it worse was that I *wanted* Fitz and Elinor to stay. But I couldn't have them without Maven, and as long as Maven was here, the Cottage was in peril.

I drained the water in one gulp and tossed the cup into the trash. Fitz was still talking to Munch as I grabbed my bag and gave him a wave.

"Charlie, wait." He moved his hand over the receiver. "What's wrong?"

"Nothing, I've got to go." I gestured for him to return to the call and made a beeline for the door. Tears were brimming, and I desperately wanted to be safe in my car before they erupted.

"Larry, let me call you back." I heard Fitz scramble to his feet behind me. He caught up with me on the sidewalk.

"Nothing's wrong," I said, a little too loudly. I dug around for my keys while I walked. I'd found a parking spot at the end of the block, so my salvation was close at hand. "I need to get home."

"I don't believe you." He stepped around to face me, forcing me to stop short. "Please, just tell me."

"I know what Munch was calling about." I was glad the search for my keys gave me an excuse not to look at him. "I know you got the votes you need to renew your license."

"The vote isn't until the end of the week."

"So what?" I snapped. He recoiled at my tone. I gave up on my keys and pressed my palms to my eyes, trying to get hold of myself. "I'm sorry. I'm happy for you and Elinor, I am. But I need to go home."

"Charlie," he said, almost pleading. But he didn't seem to know what else to say. Because there *wasn't* anything else to say.

"Good night, Fitz." The back of my throat ached with the need to cry, but I held myself together as I moved past him toward the car. I didn't want pity or promises that everything would work out. I wanted to be alone.

I knew he wouldn't go back inside until I'd driven safely away, so I started the car without giving myself any time to cry into the steering wheel, like I might have done otherwise. I slammed it into drive and sped away, putting as much distance between me and Maven Enterprises as possible.

That night, Fitz wrote me a message, asking if I was awake. I stared at it for a long while before finally closing my grimoire and pushing it under the bed. I buried the silver pen in one of my desk drawers to remove myself further from the temptation. Then I double-checked my alarm and went to sleep.

CHAPTER TWENTY-TWO

With my parents' anniversary party coming up on Friday, I was able to throw myself headlong into the welcome distraction of preparations. It was going to be an evening lawn party, with a buffet of snacks and drinks. Almost twenty guests had RSVPed, which was a surprise to Mim, as Mama had told her she only invited five people.

Fitz tried calling a couple times throughout the week, but I texted back that I was busy. It wasn't a lie—between running the shop, worrying about the shop, and figuring out what size cake served twenty people, I didn't have a lot of free time. I knew I would have to talk to him eventually, but not until I had something worth saying. Currently all I had to offer was a lot of frustration and confusing emotions.

On Friday morning, despite my overflowing to-do list, I insisted on opening the shop as usual, since we couldn't afford to lose any business. We were still enjoying an increase in popularity after the Animal Pox, and for the first time in a while I didn't have hours to kill between customers. I was at the register, working through a line three people deep, when Anthony Hawthorn walked in. I looked past him, expecting his mother to come striding in with more complaints, but he was alone.

Anthony waited until the last customer left before he came forward.

"Hi," he said, shuffling his feet awkwardly, his hands tucked into his pockets. "I'm sorry about the other day."

"It's okay. It wasn't your fault."

He cast a nervous glance around the shop, and I guessed that he wasn't just here for an apology. He had a haggard look about him. There were dark circles under his eyes that were alarming on someone so young. I could sense something strange about his aura, but I couldn't put my finger on it.

"I, uh, I was wondering—you sell spells here, right?"

"I guess that's one way to put it." I regarded his antsy demeanor for a few seconds. "Does your mom know you're here?"

He shook his head fervently and immediately glanced around us again, as if he thought speaking about her would summon her out of thin air.

"I came straight from school. She thinks I'm at soccer practice."

Great, next I was going to be accused of turning her son into a delinquent.

"Well, I've got work I need to do," I said.

"Wait, please." He stepped up to the counter, pressing his hands together in supplication. "I need your help."

"With what?" Unless it was help changing a flat tire, I knew there was probably nothing I could do for him. We don't sell magic to minors, and even if he wanted something mundane like crystals or herbs, I wasn't sure I was willing to risk his mother's wrath.

"I've been having trouble sleeping. I have these weird dreams about—about—" He cut off, stricken, and looked around like he was afraid we were being watched. "Weird stuff. It doesn't matter. When I wake up, I'm still tired. I'm *always* tired, like I haven't slept at all."

"I think a doctor could probably—"

"My mom took me, but the pills don't make any difference. My mom keeps telling me to give it time." He gave me a hopeful look. "My friend Jason Cho said that his mom came here when she was having trouble with nightmares and you guys fixed her."

"I wouldn't say we *fixed* her." We'd sold Kathy Cho a magic-infused dream sachet with chamomile, catnip, cedar chips, and an amethyst. They were useful for healing the subconscious during sleep, and by the time the charge wore off, her dreams were back to normal. We had some clients who insisted on paying to regularly recharge their sachets, but in my experience, it wasn't usually necessary. Anyone who we suspected had chronic or severe sleep problems was directed to see a doctor. "I'm sorry, Anthony, but I can't sell you any spells without your mom here."

"But she'd never go for that." He dug around in his pocket. "I have money. I'll pay extra."

"I can't."

He looked on the verge of tears, which broke my heart, but no matter how much I wanted to, I couldn't make an exception. Sophie, who had been napping in the back room, came trotting out and jumped onto the counter. At the sight of her, Anthony perked up the slightest bit.

"I didn't know you had a cat." His voice was a little hoarse, like he was still trying not to cry.

"Her name is Sophie," I said, seizing on the distraction. "She spends most of her time sleeping."

"My mom won't let me have a pet." He inched closer. Sophie ignored him and lifted her paw to clean between her pink toe beans. "Not even a fish or a hamster. She thinks all animals carry diseases."

Somehow, I wasn't surprised, but I didn't want to badmouth his mother.

"Maybe when you're older." As soon as I spoke, I knew it was the wrong thing to say—I'd forgotten how much it sucked to have clueless adults trying to appease you. I never felt so ancient as when I was talking to teenagers.

Anthony reached out tentatively to pet Sophie, but before he could touch her, she arched her back and hissed, puffing out her fluffy tail even more. He stumbled a couple steps back.

"Sorry." I snatched her off the counter, ignoring when she directed her hissing at me. "She's temperamental." Although normally she only took a dislike to people when she sensed my family disliked them, like creepy repairmen or rude customers. Maybe she remembered Anthony's mother and considered him guilty by association. The bell on the counter rang, signaling the imminent arrival of another customer.

"I guess I should go," he said, his shoulders sagging with defeat.

"Tell your mom she can call if she has questions about what we do here." I highly doubted Mrs. Hawthorn had any interest in expanding her horizons on the subject of witchcraft, but it was worth offering.

Before he could respond, the door flew open, startling us both. There stood Morgan Hawthorn, like some sort of movie villain in Ann Taylor chic. Maybe talking about her really had summoned her out of thin air.

"How dare you," she shouted, which seemed like an overly dramatic way to enter a room, regardless of your temper.

"Um," I said. Sophie yowled in equally dramatic fashion and bolted from my arms and up the stairs.

"*Mom.*" Anthony's ears were turning bright pink. "What are you doing here?"

"I should be asking you that question." She shoved her phone screen toward him. "I was in the middle of an important call for work when I saw that you were here instead of the soccer field. What do you think you're doing?"

"You tracked my phone?" he cried.

"I pay the bill, so it's my phone."

"Can I help you, Mrs. Hawthorn?" I interrupted. I had no desire to stand here awkwardly while mother and son went at it.

She whirled to face me, obviously primed for a fight.

"You can explain what gives you the right to sell your witchcraft to my son."

"I haven't sold anything to him," I replied. "Other than the ritual that saved you from spending the rest of your life as a ferret—but since you never paid for that, I'm not sure it counts."

She stared at me, thunderstruck by my calm refusal to be cowed.

"You're a liar," she said finally. She marched forward, pulled something from her enormous purse, and slammed it on the counter. "What's this? I found it under his pillow."

"Looks like an amethyst. Classified as a silicate with a Mohs hardness of seven. I believe the majority of the world's supply is produced in Brazil and Uruguay. Anything else you'd like to know?"

Her glare intensified. I was beginning to think it was time for another white fire limpia.

"I know you sold this—this *black magic* charm to him. Tell me what it's for."

"Mom." Anthony tugged helplessly on her sleeve. "She didn't—"

"Be quiet," she snapped at him. "Adults are talking."

"First of all," I said, picking up the smooth amethyst and rolling it between my fingers, "this is neither black magic nor a charm. It's a crystal. It's a natural product of the earth and possesses no inherent magic. Second, we don't sell magic to minors."

"Oh," she said, with a sarcastic sneer. "I suppose all of these are natural products of the earth as well?"

She reached back into her purse and started piling items onto the counter: two wands, a few used spell jars, and three books on spellcasting. Each piece of merchandise had a sticker with a price and *Chanterelle Cottage* printed on it. I stared down in confusion, trying to figure out how he could have gotten his hands on all this. Had other people been purchasing things for him?

More important, *why* did he have all this? Had he been dabbling in magic on his own? It wasn't unheard of for young witches to try teaching the craft to themselves, especially if their family couldn't afford to hire a witchcraft tutor or, in Anthony's case, if their family had something against magic altogether.

"That's what I thought." Morgan crossed her arms in smug victory. "You have no right to push your dangerous practices on my son, and after this I'm going straight to the sheriff."

"Mom," Anthony whispered, horrified.

That was when it occurred to me why this exact collection of items seemed vaguely familiar. They were the inventory that had been stolen during the break-in three months ago, minus the specialty tea bags. I looked over at Anthony, who was looking back at me with wide eyes. We hadn't even bothered filing a police report, as the total monetary loss didn't even approach the deductible on our insurance, and we doubted the sheriff would put any real effort into tracking down the culprit anyway. Of course, that meant I couldn't prove I hadn't illegally sold the items to a minor. Only the spell jars would be considered "magical items," but that infraction would be more than enough to lose us our license.

Now would have been an excellent time for Anthony to confess and save us all the trouble, but he kept his mouth firmly shut. With a mother like that, though, who could blame the kid?

"You'll have to ask your son where he got these," I said coolly, hoping that at least Anthony wouldn't outright lie. He radiated pure terror, and his haggard features painted a pitiful sight. I couldn't bring myself to rat him out right now—not that his mother would believe me if I did. "I can assure you that we don't sell magic to minors."

"You're not going to duck responsibility for this." She bit down angrily on each word. "I came here to get an apology from you for going behind my back and trying to drag my son into this toxic environment."

"I don't have anything to apologize for. Anthony came here asking for my help. He's been having trouble sleeping. Maybe you should be more worried about that."

"I don't need *you* to tell me what's going on with *my* son," she said. Anthony tried to say something—probably to complain that she was talking about him like he wasn't there—but she shushed him. "He is my child, and I decide what's best for him."

"What on earth is going on down here?" Mim rounded the corner from the stairs. I have to admit, I was relieved. I'd dealt with my fair share of angry customers, but Morgan Hawthorn was her own special brand of exhausting.

I watched as Morgan took in Mim, in her pale green shift dress and convincing fake pearls, with her blond hair falling down her shoulders in perfect curls.

"Are you in charge here?" she demanded.

"What's going on?" Mim repeated, sidestepping the question. She and Mama did their best to never undermine me in front of the customers.

"I want an apology from this girl." Morgan gestured at me like I was a roach crawling up the wall. "She is being rude and disrespectful."

"Are you sure you don't deserve it?" Mim asked, joining me behind the counter.

Morgan blinked, as if she wasn't sure she'd heard correctly.

"I know for a fact she sold this witchcraft paraphernalia to my son without my permission. That is a crime."

"So is your haircut, but I doubt you charged into your salon, insulting your hairdresser and demanding an apology." In contrast to her words, Mim was the very essence of civility. "We don't sell magic to minors. I'm sure Charlie has told you that, and if she says she doesn't have anything to apologize to you for, then I believe her."

"I thought the customer was always right," Morgan snapped.

"Customers can be as wrong as anyone else—and usually are, in my experience," Mim replied equably. "Now, you've said your piece, so I'm going to ask you to leave."

Morgan looked between us, chin trembling with impotent rage. I guess it finally dawned on her that her "I want to speak to your manager" tone wasn't going to get her anywhere here. She propelled Anthony toward the door.

"Fine." She scooped all the items back into her bag. For evidence, I guess. "But I'll be seeing you in court. You'll be lucky if all they do is revoke your license."

"Bye now, drive safe," Mim said sweetly.

Anthony shot me a pathetic glance over his shoulder as his mother herded him out. Maybe he would find the courage to tell the truth rather than let this escalate all the way to the sheriff's office. I didn't have particularly high hopes. At any rate, it wouldn't take Morgan long to start spreading the news of the evil Chanterelle Cottage witches corrupting innocent children.

"Remind me again why I don't use hexes," I said, once the door shut behind them.

"They give you hives," replied Mim. "Now, please tell me that awful woman was lying, and you didn't sell anything to her kid?"

"That awful woman was lying, and I didn't sell anything to her kid." I filled her in on the story. When I told her that the

items were the ones that had been stolen from the shop, she
made a face.

"Damn, he's just a baby."

"Yeah, but if he doesn't tell the truth, we're going to be up a
creek."

"I guess we'll have to wait and see. I'll call Barry to give him
a heads-up." The mention of our lawyer gave me a twinge of
panic. If this did make it to court, it might not matter what the
outcome was. The legal fees alone could bankrupt us once and
for all.

"Are you okay?" Mim asked, stroking my hair.

"I'm fine." I massaged my temples. "But cleansing all her
bullshit energy is going to be a chore."

"Maybe we should close early today."

Normally I'd be against losing even the possibility of profit,
but the Hawthorns' visit had worn me out. I still had a lot of
work to do for the party tonight too.

"Good idea," I said. "Let's knock out a cleansing spell, then I
can get started on party prep."

Mim clapped her hands together, all business.

"You get the candles. I'll get the Taylor Swift and the wine."

The joys of modern witchcraft.

CHAPTER TWENTY-THREE

The number of guests at the anniversary party ended up being closer to forty, because for all the grief she gave Mama about sending extra invitations, it turned out Mim had a bad habit of inviting anyone and everyone she happened to cross paths with. We'd set up in the backyard. Pastor Dale had let us borrow tables and folding chairs from the church, and we'd strung white Christmas lights along the gazebo and all the tree branches we could reach.

Tandy had come early to help, bringing along her yapping Pomeranians, dressed in matching pink vests. Once the bulk of the setup was finished, she still didn't leave, despite my assurances that she could head home to get dressed and come back later with Carl.

"Carl's not coming," she said, with a deliberate flatness that gave me pause.

"Oh?" I tried to sound casual about it as I stacked plates onto the food table.

"I guess you might as well know." She was sorting the silverware into cups with a focus and vehemence unwarranted by the task. "I'm sure the gossip will be all over the party. I told him I wanted a divorce."

"*Oh.*"

"He moved into a hotel." She grimaced. "All he had to say when he left was that I could have at least done the laundry first."

"What a bastard." I hoped it was the right thing to say.

"You've got that right," she muttered. "Be careful who you end up with, Charlie. Fifteen years is a long time to share a bed with someone who despises you."

I thought about the magazine-perfect photos lining her upstairs hallway, and that one snapshot in the handmade frame of the younger Tandy and her brand-new family. An oblique sense of loss expanded in my chest.

Her dogs started weaving around her ankles, yipping for attention, and she stooped down to scratch behind their ears. Her sad smile, so out of place on her usually self-assured features, gave me a pang.

"I'm sorry you're dealing with this," I said. "If you ever need to talk or anything . . ."

She shook her head and straightened up, brushing her hands on her pants as if to rid herself of the conversation entirely.

"I shouldn't have even brought it up. This is your moms' night! Now give me those napkins; you're stacking them all wrong."

By the time the party had started in earnest, she was her normal self, flouncing around like she was the party planner and therefore in charge of everything from refills to conversation starters. I had a hunch that it was her version of a gift to my parents—not to mention a way to take her mind off her own problems—so I didn't interfere with her work. In fact, after so much stress leading up to the evening, it was nice to be free to relax and enjoy myself, as much as that was possible, with Mrs.

Hawthorn's threats hovering like a dark cloud, not to mention my ever-present worries about finances and lingering doubts about Fitz. To top it all off, Bonnie and Jen, who might have been able to cheer me up, had sent their regrets at the last minute. Jen's sister was sick and needed help with her abundance of children.

Despite everything, I did manage to moderately enjoy myself, at least for the first half hour of the party. Then I turned around to find both the Fitzgeralds coming around the corner of the house. Elinor was in one of her usual chic all-black ensembles and carrying a gift wrapped in silver. Fitz was in jeans and a blue button-down that I had no doubt would look amazing with his eyes, if I was to get close enough to find out— which I wasn't planning on doing.

I surveyed the crowd until I spotted Mama and went to grab her arm, smiling apologetically to her conversation partners as I dragged her away.

"Did you invite the Fitzgeralds?" I demanded.

"What? Oh!" She looked across the yard to spot Elinor and waved gleefully. "So what if I did? It's my party."

"You could have at least *told* me."

"Well, I assumed Fitz would tell you," she said, with an innocence that was all lies, because my parents had sussed out almost immediately that something had happened between me and Fitz, even though I refused to acknowledge or talk about it. I guess this was her method of revenge.

"You're lucky it's your anniversary, and I have to be nice to you."

"And you're lucky to have a mother who is cool enough to invite hot boys to parties for her daughter to flirt with."

"I don't want to flirt with anyone; I want to celebrate your anniversary with you."

"The great thing about anniversaries is that they happen

every year." She paused to wave and say hello to a couple of passing guests, and then she returned the full force of her motherly intuition onto me. "You two clearly have some things to work out, and you're not going to be able to enjoy yourself until you do. So be an adult and go talk to him, then kiss him or kick him to the curb—whichever the situation calls for. And *then* you can come back and celebrate with us."

"But—"

"You know the party is going to last all night. Go." She gave me a little shove and went back to her previous conversation, leaving me with the unwelcome decision of whether to defy her and attempt to avoid Fitz as long as possible, or suck it up and get it over with.

If only he didn't look so damn good in blue.

I stopped by the drink table to pour two cups of punch from the spiked bowl. Mama had insisted we label the two bowls *Fun* and *Not Fun*. The fun bowl contained enough liquor to light a bonfire and had a taste somewhere between cherry limeade and jet fuel. I took a gulp to steel my nerves and made my way to Fitz, who had already been abandoned by his sister and looked a little lost at the edge of the crowd. His hands were stuffed into his pockets, a stance that when I first met him I'd interpreted as casual and aloof. But I'd since realized that the habit signaled when he was nervous or uncertain.

My heart twinged with guilt at my immature avoidance techniques. I told myself that no matter what happened, for once I was going to comport myself with grace and aplomb, and with that determination in the forefront of my mind, I closed the distance between us.

"Thanks," Fitz said, when I handed him the cup of punch.

"Be careful," I said, as he started to take a drink. "That recipe can also be used to strip paint."

He swallowed and immediately began to cough, tears springing to his eyes.

"Holy shit," he rasped. I couldn't help a tight smile as I waited for him to catch his breath.

"I didn't know you were coming." It was a safe statement, not exactly an accusation, not exactly a warm welcome. "A party full of strangers doesn't seem like your kind of scene."

"I wanted to see you." The simple sincerity of it took me off guard. His tone carried no accusation either, even though my dodging his calls all week was not a shining example of maturity. "If you want me to leave, I will."

"I don't want you to leave," I said, before my brain could even make an executive decision on the issue. "Besides, I'm pretty sure one drink of that punch raises your blood alcohol above the legal limit."

He took another measured sip and winced.

"I hope you don't find occasion to throw this particular beverage in my face." He swirled the bright pink liquid around in the cup. "I might not survive it."

I wanted to laugh, but there was still a pressure in my chest that I needed to release—even though it was the last thing I wanted to do. As long as we didn't have the conversation, then our relationship existed in a glorious stasis, with no complications and, more important, no conclusion.

"I know we need to talk." I rolled my citrine pendant between my fingers, trying and failing to convince myself to make eye contact. I was aware of the surreptitious glances of other guests, no doubt waiting for either a repeat of our display in the graveyard or, even better, a knock-down drag-out fight. I threw back the rest of my drink and tossed the cup into the garbage. As tempting as a second round was, I needed to be sober for this. "Let's go into the shop so we can have some privacy."

His hands were out of his pockets now, but as usual I couldn't divine any of his thoughts, which hardly seemed fair, since I was sure he could read all of my nerves and uncertainty like a book. I snatched the shop's bell off the food table, where we'd put it before the party to warn us if any guests missed the signs directing them to the backyard. I had no desire to alert the entire party that Fitz and I were sequestering ourselves in the empty shop.

Once inside the Cottage, I turned on the lamp, bathing us in a warm amber glow. In here, I was marginally more at ease. Whether that was because I was in my element or because of the freshly cleansed air, I didn't know.

I leaned back against the counter and crossed my arms, wishing I'd used the walk here to come up with something to say. Fitz kept distance between us, standing at the edge of the light, which I both appreciated and hated, because his shadowed expression was even more of a mystery than before.

"I'm sorry I ran off the other night." I pushed the words out in a rushed jumble. "And I'm sorry I never called you back."

"You were busy," he replied, which was kind of him, since we both knew that wasn't my real reasoning.

"Please." I shook my head and stared at my feet. "Don't be nice about it—that makes this so much harder."

"You think we should stop seeing each other." His calm, grave certainty filled me with incongruous panic. I looked up sharply.

"What? No!" I took a short breath. *Grace and aplomb*, I reminded myself sternly. "Is that what you want?"

"No." He frowned and took a half step forward. The light brought his features into sharp relief. "But after Monday night, when you wouldn't return my calls, I just assumed . . ."

I shook my head again.

"I don't—that's not what I want." Even though I honestly hadn't realized it until this exact second.

"Then what do you want, Charlie?" he asked, his tone still infuriatingly calm. "I never seem to know what you're thinking."

"I could say the same to you," I shot back. "You're not exactly an open book."

He studied my face for a few seconds, the furrow of concentration deepening between his brows. He finished his drink and tossed the cup into the garbage can.

"So ask." He lifted his hands, palms up, in a gesture of surrender. "I'll tell you anything you want to know."

My heart skipped a beat. There were hundreds of things I wanted to know, but the question that sprang to my lips was: "Are you planning on moving back to Boston?"

He was obviously taken aback. Classic me, full of surprises.

"No, why would you think that?" he asked. I bit my lip, remembering my promise to be subtle. Unfortunately, Fitz caught on anyway and sighed. "Elinor."

Sorry, El, I thought. But at least he seemed more weary than upset.

"I can neither confirm nor deny my source," I said. "But she said your father offered you another job."

"He did. He's been trying to convince me to come back since I quit, but I'm not going to."

"Has Gwen been trying to convince you to go back too?"

He jerked at the mention of her name like he'd been struck. Guilt rankled in my chest, but he had said *anything*.

"I haven't talked to Gwen since . . ." His Adam's apple bobbed with a swallow. "I don't want to talk about her."

"I'm sorry." I tugged fretfully on a lock of my hair. "You're really not considering going back?"

He shook his head no, and I relaxed, unaccountably relieved.

"Shouldn't you want me to go back?" he asked, his frown returning. "If I leave, then you don't have to worry about Maven anymore."

He had a point. If anything, I should be trying to convince him to head back to Boston posthaste. How convenient it would be if Maven Enterprises closed its doors before the council even had a chance to vote.

"It's not that simple." I was frustrated—with myself, with him, with everything. I wanted him to stay, but I wanted Maven to close. Yet I couldn't have both. "That's the whole problem. I want to keep seeing you, but I can't keep pretending like everything is fine. Whatever our relationship is, there's a countdown clock on it. Can't you see that?"

"No, I don't see it." He stepped closer. I could reach out now and touch him, if I wanted. "I know everything won't be fine forever, but right now it *is*. I don't see why we can't enjoy it while it lasts and ignore all the rest."

"I can't just ignore it," I said. At least not anymore. "'All the rest' is my home, my family, my livelihood. If the Cottage closes, then I lose everything."

Frustration was building in his expression too, spilling into his words.

"You don't know that the Cottage will close, even if Maven's license is renewed."

"You don't know that it won't." I pressed my palms into my forehead, fighting the headache that was threatening. "Unlike you, I can't take my trust fund and start over wherever I want. This is all I have. This is my life."

"Charlie." His fingers clasped gently around my wrists, and I let him lower my hands. Our eyes locked. "You can't keep wrapping your identity and emotions up in this place. It's just a job. It's not who you are."

The utter certainty with which he spoke grated on me like a

raw nerve. As if he could possibly understand what the Cottage was to me. I yanked my wrists free.

"Is that you talking or your father?"

My words cut like a razor, and he fell back a step. So much for fucking grace and aplomb. I crossed my arms again and looked away, pushing down the guilt that reared its head while I waited for his retort. It was a long time coming, and the silence built up between us, thick and heavy.

"You're right." His reply was so subdued, at first I thought I might have imagined it.

I looked at him again, at the bleakness draining the light from his features. *Goddammit, Fitz.*

"Don't agree with me," I snapped, and he blinked owlishly. "For fuck's sake, I'm not right. I'm being an asshole."

"Can't it be both?" he asked, with a glimmer of dark humor. He stuck his hands back into his pockets. "The truth is, I'm more like him than I care to admit."

I hesitated, wishing there were a way I could wipe away the plaintive resignation in his expression and hating myself for being the one to put it there.

"How so?" I asked instead, my voice soft.

He cast a glance at the shop around us, draped in shadows and cluttered with the tools of my trade.

"When I look at this place, all I can think about are all the ways it needs improving, all the things you're doing wrong. How much that damn front porch needs a new coat of paint." A smile crossed his lips, dim and mirthless. "When I'm teaching Elinor, I can't stop thinking about how she should be further along than she is, how she lacks the discipline to be a truly great mage, how she's not—"

Without thinking, I reached up and pressed my fingers against his lips, stopping him short. He stared back at me in bafflement.

"Have you ever said any of that to Elinor?"

He waited for me to move my hand, and when I didn't, he shook his head no. I could see that he was stricken by the thought.

"I don't know your father, but I know you." I kept my fingers firmly in place, forcing his attention, demanding that he listen to every word. "You're kind, generous, and caring. You deserve to be reminded of that every minute of every day. I'm sorry if anything I've ever said made you feel otherwise."

He tried to protest, but I refused to move my hand.

"If you're going to argue instead of accepting my apology, then I'm going to make you stand there and listen while I say more nice things about you."

Beneath my fingers, his mouth twitched with a smile—a real one this time, that glinted in his eyes and ignited warmth in my chest. Gently, he pulled my hand down, and I let him.

"You are confusing as hell, Charlie Sparrow," he said, twining his fingers with mine. "I think I like it."

My heart was beating a jackhammer rhythm against my ribs as the simple link of our hands sent a wave of desire through my bloodstream.

"I thought I was surprising." I could barely push the words out past the lump in my throat.

"That too." His voice was husky. My own desire was reflected in his face, bright and burning. "I want to kiss you right now."

"Then do it," I said, barely a whisper.

"What about the countdown clock?"

My body ached with the effort of keeping myself in check. The public forum was tomorrow night, when the citizens would be free to argue for or against the renewal of Maven's license in front of the council. I wasn't sure how much it mattered if Munch already had his votes, but if anyone could persuade the councilors to rethink their position, it would be Mama. She would be speaking on behalf of the Sparrows.

After the vote, either Maven would be forced to close, or the Cottage would effectively be on notice. Regardless, the clock would be ticking down to the inevitable implosion of whatever this was between me and Fitz. Maybe we would have weeks. Maybe months. But it couldn't last.

I stared down at our interlaced fingers. I thought about the night at his house, when he told me that animating the butterflies was the first time magic had made him happy in years, because it had made *me* happy. I raised my gaze to meet his.

"I'll take every second I can get."

I don't even know who closed the gap, but our mouths met a second later, all heat and desperation. We'd kissed so many times before, but I knew immediately that this was different. Finally acknowledging the reality of our situation had left us raw, and that vulnerability throbbed between us, tender and aching to be soothed.

I slid my hands behind his neck and pulled him closer. I was heady with the tart cherry taste of his tongue. His hands skated over my hips, sparking rivulets of sensation that merged into a molten core of need. Then his grip tightened, and I braced my forearms on his shoulders as he lifted me, our kiss unbroken. I was sitting on the counter now, tugging him between my legs until there was no more space left between us. I was at the perfect height now to hold him, to kiss him, to do everything I wanted to do to him.

A deluge of excitement and terror and pure, unadulterated *want* swelled inside me, drowning out my heartbeat, my breath, and finally the little voice in my head insisting this was a bad idea, a terrible idea, the worst idea. It was too late for common sense. The floodgates were open now.

His fingers traveled up my ribs as his mouth moved down my neck. He tongued the hollow of my throat while his thumbs swiped under the curves of my breasts, teasing at the underwire of my bra. A hum of pleasure vibrated in my chest, and I arched toward him, wanting more. But he stymied me, his hands moving instead to cup my cheeks as he pressed his lips again to mine, softer this time, drawing out each kiss with delicious deliberateness, as if we had all the time in the world. He was driving me fucking wild, and I savored every moment of it.

We broke apart, and he rested his forehead against mine, our breath mingling in short, fervid gasps.

"I want you, Charlie," he whispered. "I want you so much."

I wanted to say something cool and sexy. Something surprising. But words were beyond my reach, so I kissed him again, hoping that would be enough to convey my intention of giving him exactly what he wanted.

I hooked my ankles behind his back to keep him close, although I didn't think I had to worry about him wandering away at that point. His left hand slid into my hair, cradling the back of my head, and I didn't even care that he was messing up the effortless beachy waves that I had achieved with much effort, because his right hand was charting an intriguing course beneath the hem of my dress and up my bare thigh.

I had a moment of panic because I couldn't remember if I'd shaved above my knees that morning, and then I decided that was a stupid thing to worry about when his fingers were already questing so close to brand-new territory for us. I wanted to tell him to stop being so provocative and rip my clothes off already, but I didn't want to detach my mouth from his for that long, not when we'd found such a perfect rhythm, when the connection between us was more intimate and yet more fragile than it had ever been before.

Hoping to nudge things along—*God, did I even remember to*

lock the shop door behind us?—I ran my hands down his chest, forgoing the buttons of his shirt in favor of his pants. I hadn't left much space between us to maneuver but refused to surrender any ground. I managed to undo the button and was reaching for the zipper when suddenly he wasn't kissing me anymore. He'd pulled his hand back so that it was now resting on my knee in disappointingly chaste fashion.

"Sorry." I yanked my own hands back in reflex. They were trembling with the same adrenaline that laced my voice. Reluctantly, I dropped my legs so that he was free to step back. "Too fast?"

Fitz didn't step back. His other hand was still tucked behind my head, holding our faces so close that his rapid breaths fluttered on my lips.

"No, it's not that," he said, with a hint of ruefulness. "I don't have a condom."

Well, at least one of us had managed to retain some common sense. I racked my memory, but I knew I didn't have any either, and my parents had no reason to keep rubbers on hand.

"Fuck," I said.

"Not without a condom."

I gave him a little shove for being a smartass, then decided I didn't actually want him to back away, so I grabbed the front of his shirt to keep him close. He was smiling, though there was an unmistakable strain of need in his features that I could relate to. Every inch of my skin was hot and tight, like the pulsing desire inside me was about to burst.

"Can't you, I don't know, summon one out of thin air?" I tried my best to keep the peevishness out of my tone, but honestly, what good were mages anyway?

His smile twitched wider with some secret amusement that I didn't care for one bit, but then he was brushing his lips along my clavicle, and my annoyance evaporated.

"I probably could." He punctuated each word with a ghost of a kiss on my neck, traveling upward until he could murmur directly into my ear. "If only the Cottage weren't spelled so that only Sparrows can do magic on the property."

Goddammit. The realization ruined my moment of toe-curling bliss. Witchcraft could do many things, but conjuring contraceptives out of nowhere was not one of them. I vented my disappointment with a groan that probably made me sound like a dramatic toddler but nonetheless made Fitz chuckle.

He started to move back, but I kept my grip on his shirt.

"Wait."

Clarity tried to seep back into my brain, reminding me where we were and that my parents' anniversary party was still in full swing in the backyard and that I definitely hadn't locked the door behind us. But I'd already shut down the critical-thinking part of my brain, and I wasn't ready to open it for business. Not when the tick, tick, tick of our countdown clock was ushering us inexorably toward the end of whatever this was, whatever it had a chance to be. Timing was something that Fitz and I never managed to get quite right, but maybe just this once I could change the rules.

"I can turn off the spell temporarily." I released my fistful of his shirt, because the material seemed expensive and prone to wrinkle, and I needed to stop destroying pieces of his wardrobe. In the beginning, I'd thought of his magic as effortless, because he always made it seem that way, fixing things with a wave of his hand, no fuss, no fanfare. But ever since the day of the Animal Pox, when I'd seen what too much of that no-fuss hand waving could do to him, I'd been cognizant of how dangerous magic could be for a mage, especially one like Fitz, who thought it was his responsibility to give and give and give until his heart gave out.

"Really?" he asked, not like he was skeptical that I could do it, but like he was surprised I would be willing to do it for him—for us. "Are you sure?"

"I mean, if you want me to." I couldn't account for my shyness, when sixty seconds ago he'd had his hand all the way up my skirt. But maybe he'd changed his mind, decided we were moving too fast after all, and the condom was a convenient excuse.

"Yes," he said immediately. His hand was on my knee again, or maybe it had never left and I hadn't noticed because his skin was the exact same degree of fever-hot as mine. "If you want to."

God, yes, I wanted to. So much that I wasn't even sure I could vocalize it in a coherent way. Instead of trying, I slid off the counter, grabbed his hand, and led him up the stairs.

CHAPTER TWENTY-FOUR

The house was a mess, every spare surface covered in odds and ends left over from party planning. I pretended I didn't notice in hopes that Fitz wouldn't either. This was the first time he'd been in my home, and it wasn't exactly the first impression I would have hoped for, but my shame lived in the same part of my brain as my critical thinking, so for now I didn't care about much more than getting my hands on him again.

We kept the jar that housed our specially formulated counterspell in the exact center of our home, which happened to be in the cupboard underneath the microwave.

"Turn around," I told Fitz. "No peeking."

He was clearly amused by my furtiveness, but he obliged, wandering off to examine the magnet collection on our fridge. Alongside various wedding, baby, and graduation announcements—most of them at least a year old—were a few remnants of my childhood, including an A+ book report I'd written on Agatha Christie's *Death on the Nile* in ninth grade and a dinosaur finger-painting I'd done when I was four. It was supposed to be a brontosaurus but strongly resembled a dick with legs. Artistic talent did not run in my family.

I opened the cabinet and moved aside some bags of pasta and an old cookie tin to find the spell jar. We had canceled out the spell a few times before, when other witches assisted us, like during the Animal Pox, or when Mim or Mama agreed to give a few lessons to a young local witch. This would be the first time horniness had been the driving factor. I was pretty sure this wasn't what Mama had intended when she told me to either kiss him or kick him to the curb, but play stupid games, et cetera.

I opened the jar and eased out a little bundle of dried heather. Removing one of the ingredients was all it took to interrupt the spell, though unfortunately resetting it wasn't as easy as putting the heather back. Tomorrow, I'd make up some excuse and ask Mim and Mama to help me reset it.

Tonight, anticipation had crowded everything else out of my mind. There was no point in pretending I had any clear reasoning or plan beyond getting Fitz into my bedroom.

I shut the cabinet door and joined him at the refrigerator, where he had moved aside an expired car wash coupon to reveal the full glory of my Dickosaurus (Mama's terminology). Judging by the pure delight on his face, he was not admiring my artistry.

"Any chance I can convince you that's not mine?" I asked.

"Considering you signed it, no."

"The '*h*' is backward, so that's not legally binding."

"Hang on." He started to pull his phone out of his back pocket. "I need to send a text. Totally unrelated."

I maneuvered between him and the fridge, blocking my art from view and putting us toe-to-toe. The inches of air between us were instantly charged. I placed my hand flat on his stomach and a shiver ran through him at my touch.

"Do you want to study my childhood artistic journey," I asked in a low voice, "or do you want me to take my clothes off?"

In response he leaned in and kissed me, bracketing my body with his. My shoulder blades knocked against the cool surface behind me, and I registered the clatter of some magnets falling to the linoleum. Maybe if I was lucky the Dickosaurus would slide under the refrigerator and be lost forever.

I took Fitz's hand again and pulled him toward the hallway. My heartbeat was pounding so hard that I could feel it in my fingertips. I wondered if he could feel it too. We stumbled gracelessly toward my bedroom, with me trying to concentrate long enough to lead us there and Fitz doing his level best to distract me at every second with his mouth and hands.

Somehow, we made it. I fumbled for the switch on the standing lamp in the corner, casting the room in a golden hue. Fitz shut the door, leaning back against it while he surveyed my bedroom. I wasn't interested in providing a tour or giving him time to see how lax I was about putting clothes back in the closet or removing empty tea mugs from my nightstand.

Without a word, I kicked off my shoes and removed my citrine pendant, setting it carefully on my overcrowded desk. Then I yanked my dress over my head. Judging by the way Fitz's hungry gaze locked on to me, I don't think he would have noticed if my walls had been papered with Dickosaurus paintings. I was wearing my boring beige bra, but at least my underwear sported some lace. Despite my hurry to strip, my shyness had returned. I was self-conscious of his eyes cataloging every inch of me. (I had definitely neglected to shave above my knees.)

"Fuck, Charlie," he breathed. "You're gorgeous." And in that moment, I was pretty sure he would have had the exact same reaction whether I'd been wearing burlap underthings or the best lingerie that Victoria's Secret had to offer.

My pulse was a runaway stampede as he moved closer. His fingertips skated around my thighs, his thumbs teasing at the edges of my waistband.

"For the record," he murmured, lowering his head to glide his lips along the edge of my jaw, his words featherlight on my skin, "I would have also loved to study your childhood artistic journey."

"I could always put my clothes back on."

"Don't you dare." He was kissing me now, starting at my clavicle and working his way up my neck, each point of contact raising a new ripple of goosebumps.

I started working on his buttons, trying to balance my resolve to not ruin another one of his shirts with my need to get the damn thing off already. I think I managed it without losing any buttons. He removed his hands from my body long enough to shuck it off. Some absurd part of my brain thought that he might take the time to hang it up or fold it neatly—he was always so tidy—but he left it crumpled on the floor where it fell. Then he was cupping my breasts, and I wasn't thinking about much of anything except how I could make sure I never had to be without his hands on me again.

Or my hands on him, for that matter. His skin was flushed with heat, the same heat that was burning across my body and gathering in my core. I slid my hands down his shoulders and along his rib cage, memorizing the shape of him. His muscles tightened and twitched under the pads of my fingers. He breathed a sound into my neck that might have been my name, but I couldn't be sure because my blood was a torrent in my ears.

Gently but insistently, I pushed him toward the bed. When the backs of his legs hit the mattress, he sat down, and I immediately clambered into his lap. I held his face between my palms and our lips met again while he unhooked my bra. I slipped my arms through the straps and flung it the way of his shirt, and in the next second his mouth was on my right nipple. I gasped as he worked with his lips and tongue and teeth until I was so sensitive that the slightest tickle of his breath had me digging my nails into his shoulders and biting back a moan—and then he did the same thing on the other side.

The heaviness between my legs was nearly unbearable, and I rocked against him in a vain attempt to find satisfaction. His groan reverberated in my chest, through my stomach, and lower.

The tiniest sliver of clarity lanced across my mind, and I seized it while I was still capable of coherency.

"Are you sure about this?" I was panting so hard that I had to pause in the middle to catch my breath. Maybe it was a stupid question considering where his mouth was, but it was less than a week ago that he'd told me he wanted to take it slow, and the last thing I wanted was for him to be pressured by everything I'd said about the countdown clock.

He must have understood what I was asking, because he straightened up. There were bright slashes of color across his cheekbones. His pupils were blown wide, and his irises were so dark in the dim light that I was afraid I could fall into that enticing darkness and never find my way out again. He licked his swollen lips, and my thighs clenched reflexively. He looked so sexy, I was about to lose my goddamn mind.

"I want this." His voice was low and threaded with need. "I want *you*. More than anything."

"More than world peace?" I teased, as if my entire body hadn't just erupted into fireworks.

"Fuck world peace," he said, without a moment's hesitation, and we were kissing again, and I was fairly certain I never wanted to taste anything but him for as long as I lived. Truffle fries be damned.

He gripped my hips and twisted until I was on my back, and then he crawled up beside my legs. His fingers were ten individual brands where they dug into my skin, curling into the hem of my underwear and tugging it down. His eyes were on mine the whole time, like he was waiting for me to tell him to stop. Fat chance of that. Instead I reached down to yank it the rest of the way off myself, startling an abrupt laugh out of him.

"Patience is not your strong suit, is it?" he asked, moving between my legs. It was only when denim scraped against my skin that I realized he was still wearing his pants. We would need to remedy that soon.

"I'm incredibly patient." I pushed my sweat-dampened hair from my face. So much for perfect beachy waves. "I wanted to kiss you since our trip to the market in August and look how long I waited."

Fitz smiled, his hand resting idly on my thigh, his index finger drawing a lazy circle that forced my entire consciousness to zero in on that single sensation in a way that was not conducive to *patience*.

"It was the day of the picnic for me," he said, and despite the currents of electric desire coursing through my body, I scoffed.

"And was that before or after I dumped a margarita on you?"

"After." He was unperturbed by my skepticism. "When you referenced *You've Got Mail*."

"Kind of a low bar, don't you think?"

"You broke the bar, Charlie." He leaned down and murmured the words against my skin, triggering an avalanche of shivers across my whole body. "I never stood a chance."

Before I could think of something—anything—to say, he laved his tongue along the ridge of my hip bone. I arched against him, and he planted his hands on the tops of my thighs, holding me firmly in place while he took his precious time tracing the curves and contours of my body with his tongue. Cool air kissed the trails he left behind, creating a maze of goose-pimpled pathways along my skin.

He circled lower and lower between my thighs, never quite reaching the aching core of me, in a way that felt deliberate and, frankly, diabolical.

"You know," I managed between shaky breaths, "if you're trying to find my clit, you're not even close."

He flashed me a wicked grin that made my whole body pulse with longing.

"What was that you were saying about your incredible patience?"

"I'm trying to be helpful." I stubbornly ignored the exodus of his hands to my breasts, which was distracting at best and torturous at worst. I was successful too, at least until he tweaked my oversensitized nipple, and an undignified cross between a yelp and a whimper escaped me. As revenge, I injected extra condescension into my tone. "I know some men need a road map."

"I'm aware that your clit is not on your thighs," he said dryly.

"Could've fooled me."

I don't know what is wrong with me that I couldn't resist being a smartass in the middle of what was undeniably effective foreplay. Maybe it's an only-child thing. And in true middle-child fashion, Fitz didn't seem the least bit annoyed. Instead, his smirk reappeared, and he sat back on his heels.

"Okay, then."

"Okay what?" I asked, dizzied by the loss of his hands.

"Show me." His eyes were fever-bright, his voice a scrape of desire that left me raw and exposed. "Touch yourself."

Oh fuck.

For a couple seconds, my mind was black except for those two words popping and sizzling like the lights of a marquee. My body was all in, desperate for pleasure, but the rest of me wasn't sure. Embarrassment threatened to rear its head, but there was something about the quality of Fitz's attention that empowered me, something about the way his warm, gentle hands rested again on my thighs that made me feel safe.

Slowly, I slid my right hand down my stomach, where minutes ago his tongue had been conducting a symphony of sensations. I let my legs fall open wider and found my rhythm, my head falling back against the pillow. With my left hand, I rolled my nipple between my thumb and forefinger, pinching hard enough that the pain merged with the ache between my legs then expanded into pleasure that curled my toes and knotted in my chest. Glimmers of bliss radiated from my core, chased by a frisson of frustration, because the edge was still a long way off.

Fitz's hand encircled my wrist, and my eyes sprang open. I had no trouble reading his features now. Pure, unbridled hunger. Before I could formulate any words, he drew my fingers into his mouth, one by one, sucking them clean.

Oh fuck oh fuck oh fuck.

"Oh fuck," I whispered. There were truly no more words left in my vocabulary. He had wiped the slate clean.

"My turn," he whispered back.

Maybe I'd wounded his pride because the first swipe of his tongue was a bull's-eye. Patience was overrated anyway. More expletives caught in my throat, coming out instead as a strangled moan while he consumed me. He hooked my right leg over his shoulder for better access. The swirl of his tongue was precisely calibrated with my pleasure, and with a heady rush I realized that he was mirroring the motion of my fingers, demonstrating what he'd learned. On cue, his hand snaked up to my breast and latched on to my nipple.

I grasped the comforter on either side of me and writhed helplessly while all my nerve endings sang in chorus. He was playing my body like a fiddle, as meticulous and perceptive as he was in every other aspect of his life. I teetered on the verge of climax, every iota of my being primed and desperate for release.

He gave it to me, a riotous eruption, catalyzed by his mouth and hands. I bucked against his grip, biting into my knuckles in an attempt to muffle my cries. As the onslaught of pleasure subsided, he only leaned into me harder, like he was determined to devour every last aftershock. Under the ministrations of his tongue and lips and teeth, one of those aftershocks lingered and intensified and all at once my body wrenched with a second orgasm, scorching white-hot through my blood vessels until I was incandescent.

My consciousness was still floating, untethered to my body, when I registered that Fitz, apparently satisfied with his work, was lowering my leg that had been hiked over his shoulder. He collapsed on his stomach beside me, his right arm a comforting weight across my waist and the fingers of his left hand threading through my hair. He pressed a soft kiss against my temple, and the contact brought me back to myself.

"You're a fast learner," I said, and a low laugh rumbled in his chest. He rolled onto his side to face me, and I turned my head so that I could catch his mouth with mine, tasting him, tasting myself on him. I would have thought I'd be exhausted, but my body was still keyed up, flushed and twice as hot in every place our skin touched. I wanted more of that, and he was still in his jeans, which couldn't be comfortable. That was a level of self-control that I would never understand.

I rolled on my side to face him and undid the zipper, pushing his pants and underwear down his hips. When my hand closed around him, he sucked in a sharp breath, a jolt like electricity lancing through his muscles. His arm around my waist tightened, drawing me closer.

"Fuck, Charlie." His voice in my ear was taut with strain, and

I was pleased that he was reduced to the same range of vocabulary as I had been.

I kept my grip purposefully loose, a whisper of friction, because two could play at the game of patience. His hips rocked in search of the stimulation I denied him.

A shaky sound escaped him, not quite a laugh.

"Not very neighborly of you," he managed.

"Oh, am I doing something wrong?" I asked innocently, as I swirled my thumb around the head.

He lurched against me, his fingers digging into my side and twisting in my hair. He said my name again, rasping it into my ear like a curse, like a prayer, and just like that, I was undone.

"Condom." My voice was a breathy squeak.

It took a few seconds for the word to penetrate the daze of his arousal, but finally he blinked and refocused. He unclenched his fingers from my waist. A flick of his wrist, and suddenly he was holding a square of plastic. It reminded me of when I was a kid, and my uncle would pretend to pull quarters from behind my ear. Judging from the new, ragged quality of Fitz's breaths, this had taken more energy than a simple sleight of hand.

"How difficult is that to do?" I asked, and then, because I knew he hated anyone fretting about his health, I added, "Maybe you can rustle up some gold bars or rare gems while you're at it."

"Hilarious," he said. A pause. "I'm fine."

Guess I wasn't as subtle as I'd hoped. The reassurance meant literally nothing—he'd said the same thing the day of the Animal Pox, when he'd been dead on his feet. But he wouldn't appreciate my badgering, and the desire between us was palpable and pressing to the point of distraction, so I decided to let it go.

"Good." I gave him another stroke. "Because I suspect I may not be very patient after all."

He huffed a laugh. His aura was effervescent right now,

shimmering with a rainbow of colors. I sat up and threw my leg over to straddle him, and the next few seconds were a flurried rush to kick his pants off and get the condom on, until finally, *finally* I was sinking down onto his length. His expression was downright indecent, as were the sounds issuing from his throat while I rode him, as was the searing sensation of his fingers digging again into the flesh of my hips, the rippling of his muscles beneath my hands as I slid them along his sweat-slick torso, the shivers of pleasure cascading from the place we were joined together. Deliciously obscene.

He pushed up from the bed and pulled me into his chest. A dizzying twist and roll, and then I was on my back and his hands were on my breasts and our mouths were locked together and the symphony of our movements carried me to exhilarating new heights. We were fitted together like puzzle pieces, perfectly aligned. He bore down on me, his pelvis grinding and sparking flickers of possibility that caught me off guard.

Fitz drew back slightly from the kiss, my bottom lip caught between his teeth for a tantalizing second.

"I want to make you come again." His breath tickled my chin.

"Overachiever," I said with a smile, even as his words corkscrewed straight to my core.

He nuzzled the side of my neck.

"Tell me how to get you there."

"Slower," I said, and tried to remember to breathe.

He obliged. I slid my hand between us and angled the knuckle of my thumb until every thrust brought a paroxysm of pleasure, building and building toward a dreamy crescendo.

"A little faster."

Our mouths were so close that my lips brushed his as I spoke. We breathed each other in as we found our rhythm. Orgasm roiled through me, quieter than before, but no less satisfying. I arched against him and let out something between a whimper and a sigh. He captured it with his tongue like he loved the taste of it.

Fitz rocked his hips against mine, drawing out my pleasure while he chased his own. He climaxed with my name on his lips. I slid my hand through his hair and held him close, inhaling the scent of eucalyptus and wishing I could suspend us in this moment, so that the countdown clock would never resume, so that I never had to let him go.

CHAPTER TWENTY-FIVE

Fitz and I did eventually manage to return to the party, after we'd cleaned up and gotten dressed and I had banished Fitz downstairs to the shop to wait for me while I fixed my hair, because he kept touching me in ways that were not conducive to cooling off. I was pretty sure I heard the click of his phone camera as he passed through the kitchen. Goddamn Dickosaurus.

Sadly, most of the good food was gone, but there was plenty of Fun Punch left. I didn't set out to get drunk. It was an unfortunate side effect of the number of innuendos my parents lobbed in my and Fitz's direction, thinking they were being so clever, except both of them were already three sheets to the wind and not nearly as subtle as they thought. Even Pastor Dale and Martha managed to catch on, and they were the kind of people who thought "Netflix and chill" was a family activity.

The cherry-limeade-flavored jet fuel was the only balm for my embarrassment. Elinor took pity on her older brother and offered to be designated driver, freeing Fitz to join me in the refuge of too many refills. The punch lived up to its name and soon the jagged edges of the night had smoothed into a stream of joyful, if slightly blurred, memories.

Someone set up cornhole, which prompted full-blooded rivalries that were unwarranted by a game composed entirely of tossing bean bags from one hole to another. Sweet old Harriet Wharburton was shockingly ruthless in her conquering of all who dared oppose her.

At some point, several of the guests ended up doing increasingly difficult yoga poses in the grass with Tandy in the lead, like a bizarre Simon Says, but with the distinct possibility of broken hips.

Even more bizarre was when someone connected their phone to a pair of speakers, and Pastor Dale took it upon himself to teach everyone the steps to "Cotton-Eyed Joe." After fifteen enthusiastic minutes, half the group was too tired to move anymore, and the other half was laughing too hard to continue.

My parents opened my present and were enchanted by the cloud of paper monarchs that rose around them, swooping and fluttering in an almost perfect imitation. Mim started crying immediately, while Mama sniffled and claimed her allergies were acting up. All the guests oohed and aahed appropriately, and I was so happy that I didn't even mind giving Fitz his due credit, though I didn't try to explain the strange circumstances around the butterflies' perpetual motion. I wasn't sure yet how I felt about the idea of his magecraft jump-starting my witchcraft—or if that was even what had happened.

Mama, once she had recovered from those pesky allergies, regaled everyone with the story of her and Mim's first meeting. The otherworldly beauty of half a million monarchs in flight, all aimed instinctively toward a singular purpose, and the mundane, yet somehow rarer, beauty of two people locking eyes across a field and knowing with similar instinct that they were destined to find each other.

I found myself swaying to the rhythm of the story, which to me was as familiar and comforting as a lullaby. I didn't think I could be happier until Fitz intertwined his fingers with mine, and I rested my head against his shoulder, and for once, our timing was in perfect harmony with the universe.

Sobering up was like waking from a particularly pleasant dream, but even so, I found I didn't mind reality all that much. It was only eleven, though it felt much later, and Fitz and I were lying on our backs in the old gazebo, staring up at the peeling paint and emerald leaves of the wisteria vine on the beams overhead. We had started off in chairs but had given them to Harriet and Mark when there weren't enough for all the guests. After that, the slip from sitting to reclining had been inevitable. There was a sheen of sweat on my skin and a satisfying ache in my muscles from the rigors of yoga and "Cotton-Eyed Joe"—and our earlier activities, of course.

I shivered in the cool autumn air but wasn't willing to move elsewhere in search of warmth, not when Fitz's fingers were still interlaced with mine and lazy, lulling conversation drifted so easily between us. Elinor and my moms were lounging in chairs and chatting up a storm about various magical theories. Everyone else had been gone for a while, with Tandy being the last to leave, toting her sleeping dogs in her arms like infants.

"Do you want to spend the night at my place?" The gentle cadence of Fitz's voice sparked a shiver up my spine.

"That depends," I said, with forced nonchalance. "Do you have condoms at your place?"

He chuckled, then brought my hand up and pressed his lips to my knuckles. The unspoken promise coiled in my stomach and curled my toes. It took all my self-control not to hop up right away and drag him to his car. I wasn't prepared to be *that* obvious in front of my parents and his sister.

Fortunately, Mother Nature provided me with a much more subtle excuse to get out of there. It started to rain, a fine mist at first, then heavy drops that threatened to soak us all to the skin as we carted armfuls of leftovers, tablecloths, and presents. At least the paper butterflies had long since been safely tucked away in their box. We made it inside the Cottage right before the heavens opened up, and we fumbled around in the dark for a few seconds.

"Shit, what did I just step on?" Elinor asked. Even through the rain and general commotion, there was a distinct crunching sound, followed by a second one. "Shit," she said again.

Mim finally flipped on the overhead lights. My vision didn't even need to fully adjust before I knew something was wrong.

The shop was in ruins.

That was my first panicked, apocalyptic thought when I saw the shards of spell jars littering the floor, along with the crystals, dried herbs, salt, and other ingredients that had been the result of hours of precise spellwork but now were a useless pile of detritus.

I took a few stumbling steps forward, ignoring the broken glass beneath my shoes. I peered down the first two aisles, and the longer I stared, the more the picture before me worsened. Almost all the product on the shelves was now on the floor, as if an earthquake had hit, but it hadn't merely fallen—a lot of it was broken, dented, or smashed. It looked like someone had taken a baseball bat to our entire stock.

All of us were silenced by shock, no one quite able to wrap their minds around what we were seeing.

"Oh hell no." Mama shoved her armload of leftovers onto the counter and yanked open the drawer where we kept our stun gun. (Witchcraft was a decent enough deterrent to intrud-

ers, but sometimes you needed a higher voltage.) She stomped
up the stairs, presumably to make sure the vandal hadn't continued their rampage there. Mim was right on her heels, demanding that she stop right this instant.

The door to the storeroom was open, and my heart dropped
further into my stomach. I headed back and only made it a
couple steps before Fitz was at my side. He gave me a look but
was wise enough not to suggest that it was too dangerous or
that I let him take the lead.

"Shouldn't we call the cops?" Elinor sounded uncharacteristically nervous, though that didn't stop her from following close
behind us.

"Whoever did this is gone." I had spotted Sophie curled up
on a high shelf. She was mostly useless as an anti-intruder measure, but she wouldn't have been sleeping without a care in the
world if there were still a stranger skulking around the Cottage.

I reached inside the doorway to turn on the light. No ski-
masked burglars lurked in the corners, but the storeroom was
trashed too. My feet took me forward into the room unthink-
ingly, and I turned in a circle, forcing myself to take in all the
damage. Most of the apothecary drawers had been yanked out
and dumped on the floor, and one of the cabinets had been
tipped over entirely.

In the middle of it all, splintered in half among a scattering
of loose straw, was Broomhilde. I was surprised at my visceral
reaction to the sight. Like I'd been punched in the gut.

I swore under my breath. My numb stupefaction was gone,
replaced with a stiff-backed outrage. I was trembling with the
sheer violation of it. Who could have done this? Who could
possibly hate us this much?

"Do you not have a security system?" Fitz asked.

There was no reproach in his tone, but my hackles went up

anyway. All that indignation festering under my skin had to escape somewhere.

"No, we don't," I snapped. "You can add it to the long, long list of things wrong with our business."

I sensed, rather than saw, him and Elinor exchange a startled glance at my vehemence. I regretted it immediately but was in no mood to apologize. I righted one of the chairs, the first distraction I could find. The other chair was missing one leg, and a second came off in my hand when I tried to flip it over.

"Charlie," Fitz began softly. "I didn't mean—"

He was cut off by my parents tramping down the stairs, and I brushed past him to meet them in the front.

"All clear," Mama announced.

"I don't think they went up there," Mim said.

"I don't see how they even got in." Mama picked her way around the edges of the shop. "None of the windows are broken. The door isn't damaged."

"We should have heard the bell." Mim rummaged through the stuff we'd brought from the backyard. "Is it not working? Where is it?"

Shit.

"I brought it in earlier." I circled the counter, using the chair leg to poke at the assortment of items that had been knocked to the floor. I found the bell under a dust cloth and scooped it up. "I must have forgotten it."

"But how did they get in?" Mim was winding and unwinding one of her curls around her finger, a telltale sign of nerves. On our way inside she'd been giggling with gleeful abandon, but there was no hint of that mirth left in her features. "No windows are broken. You locked the door, didn't you?"

I scanned the shambles of our livelihood, an ache blooming in my chest.

"Yes," I said, with zero conviction. I racked my alcohol-addled brain, trying to remember. I hadn't locked it on our way in, too distracted by the trepidation of our upcoming talk. But on our way out . . . I still hadn't locked it, too distracted by the need to steal one more kiss before we returned to the public gaze. That ache in my chest had become an unbearably tight knot. "No."

"Oh." Mim took a breath like she was about to speak but then seemed to lose track of what she meant to say. Finally, she gave another little "Oh" and fell silent.

"What's done is done," Mama said, in a tone that I think was supposed to be stoic and comforting, but she wasn't able to keep her frustration from leaking through the cracks. "We'll call the sheriff in the morning. There's nothing else we can do tonight."

And just like that, I was a teenager again, in trouble for missing curfew or leaving my bike out in the rain to get rusty. I was standing in the wilted ruins of the fairy ring, confused and alone.

It was the awful humiliation of being in the wrong and knowing you're in the wrong, but your parents aren't angry, just disappointed. Except anger would be better because even though anger burned hot, it also burned out quickly. Disappointment was a never-ending simmer, easy to forget about until it bubbled over and scalded you, then it kept right on simmering.

I wasn't a teenager anymore. I should have known better. I should have *been* better.

"We should go." Fitz broke the unbearable silence. And I could have kissed him for understanding that the best thing he could do to help right now was leave. The last thing I wanted was for anyone else to bear witness to my self-recrimination, to the soft underbelly of my relationship with my parents.

But, of course, kissing Fitz (among other things) was how I'd landed myself here to begin with.

We offered our lackluster farewells while Fitz tugged Elinor out the door. I couldn't even bring myself to meet his eyes one last time, which only made me more miserable once the door closed behind them. On top of that, I hated making them drive home in the middle of the night in the pouring rain without at least offering to let them stay, not that anyone in their right mind would want to linger in the middle of this mess. The fact that Mim hadn't insisted on them sleeping over was evidence of how truly fucked up this night had become.

Mama pointedly locked the door behind them.

"I'm sorry," I said into the silence that followed their departure.

Mama ignored my apology.

"Whoever did this used magic."

"I can feel it too," Mim said.

I pushed through my inner turmoil and tried to focus on my sixth sense. With my emotions in upheaval, it was hard to tune in to the vibrations of the shop, but I definitely noticed *something* different in the air. Something chaotic and . . . angry. Again, I wondered who would do something like this to us.

Then I realized no one *should* have been able to do this to us. The counterspell should have prevented any magic being done in the Cottage. Except that I'd turned it off tonight.

Mim and Mama were both watching me now, probably thinking about the counterspell too.

"I had to interrupt the spell." My voice was scratchy and painful in my throat as I forced back tears. "I was planning on resetting it in the morning."

I couldn't bring myself to tell the whole, messy, damning truth. I'd been so caught up with my own libido that I'd turned off the spell, forgotten the bell here where it was useless, then left the door unlocked for anyone who wanted to waltz into the shop and destroy it.

"I'm sorry," I said again, into the unending silence.

The words were pointless now. I wasn't sure what my moms could have said in that moment to reassure me. Maybe "Accidents happen" or "We all make mistakes" or anything to suggest that they still trusted me, that they didn't see my increasingly terrible decision-making over the past few weeks as evidence that I didn't deserve a stake in the business.

"We should get some sleep." Mim took the bell from my hands and trudged up the stairs.

"Yes, we'll want the sheriff here bright and early so he can scribble 'no sign of a break-in' into a report and file it in the trash." Mama's acerbic tone was salt in the wound, and I had to dig my fingernails into my palms to stop myself from retorting—or, more likely, bursting into tears.

I watched them disappear up the steps. I made no move to follow, and they didn't call down to make sure I was coming. When the door at the top of the stairs closed, I headed for the back room. I told myself I was going to start taking inventory, since Sheriff Daniels would want to know if anything was missing. But instead, I sat on the single intact chair in front of the workbench, which had conveniently been cleared off for me, and buried my face in my arms. My shame and anger burst like a bubble, and I finally let myself cry. It was a release but not a satisfying one.

I tried to organize my whirling thoughts into something approaching rationality. I wanted to unravel what was happening. I wanted to figure out who would do this to my family. An apology was useless, but if I could get to the bottom of this then I could make things right. Then Mim and Mama would have to forgive me.

But my brain wouldn't cooperate. My thoughts wouldn't settle. Mama had been right. There was nothing else to be done tonight.

An hour later, when I was sure both my parents would be in bed, I climbed the stairs to get ready for bed myself. I needed a shower, but I was so tired that I was afraid I would end up sitting on the floor with my knees hugged to my chest, sobbing while the water rained down on me, an embodiment of that *Arrested Development* meme. I brushed my teeth, washed my face, and pulled my hair into a bun on top of my head.

"Good enough," I said to my blotchy, red-eyed reflection in the mirror. She did not believe me.

My rumpled bed, which hours ago had been the site of such heightened joy, now filled me with a crumbling sense of despair. I crawled under the covers in a morass of self-pity. Without thinking, I grabbed my grimoire from the nightstand and tugged it under the blankets with me. As I opened it to the last page where Fitz and I had exchanged messages, I told myself that he would have gone straight home to bed, not spent himself further using magic. But I couldn't resist a peek. And there it was, a new line of handwriting, the ink still glistening where it hadn't even had time to soak into the paper.

It wasn't your fault.

More tears welled up, and for the few precious seconds I was able to let myself believe it, the iron fist gripping my lungs loosened the slightest bit, and I could breathe properly again. If I couldn't hear it from my parents, I guess Fitz was the next best thing. But already the relief was being eclipsed by reality. I picked up the silver pen.

I'm the one who left the door unlocked.

Whoever did this, I doubt a locked door would have stopped them.

Maybe true, but if I'd remembered the bell, it would have warned us the second the intruder stepped foot on the porch.

And if I'd left the counterspell intact, they wouldn't have been able to trash the shop with such rapid ease. The two together might not equal an expensive security system, but they served their purpose.

I shouldn't have been so careless.

The tears I had just managed to quell were falling again, smearing the ink. I shouldn't have let myself get so distracted by a mage, no matter how irresistible he was. I'd made a commitment to the Cottage and my family, and I'd let them down. But even with that certainty, I couldn't bring myself to regret my time with Fitz. I couldn't bring myself to stop wishing I could have *more* time with him. My conflicting desires were playing a game of tug-of-war in my chest, and the only thing I knew for sure was that no matter which side won, the ultimate loser would be me.

Fitz's reply came a few seconds later.

Don't cry, Shopgirl. Don't cry.

The quote from *You've Got Mail* shocked a laugh out of me, except that I was still crying, so it came out more like a strangled sob. I wasn't sure if the tear-splotched ink had somehow translated onto his page or if he just knew me that well. My warring emotions quieted, not completely, but enough that I managed to regain a sense of equilibrium. I scrounged around the bedside table for my tissue box and blew my nose before I could drip anything else onto my grimoire. Once I was dried out, I pulled the book back into my lap.

I'm sorry I snapped at you earlier, I wrote.

I shouldn't have said anything.

He had told me he would stop criticizing our business, but that was hardly the point here. I was trying to be a nice person, dammit.

Please just accept my apology so I can go to sleep.

Does that mean if I don't accept, we can keep talking?

I imagined I could see the wry smile on his face. He was probably in bed too, writing by lamplight. I bet his pajamas were an expensive matching set. A little classier than my faded, oversized T-shirt featuring Powerline from *A Goofy Movie.*

Imagining him in bed—and what he was or was not wearing—didn't seem conducive to sleep. And I desperately needed some rest if I was going to face the wreckage of the shop in the morning.

I'm really tired, I wrote. *I'm not sure how much longer I can write coherent sentences.*

We could always resort to pictographs.

Before I could come up with a reply, lines took shape on the bottom half of the page, slowly coalescing into a picture. I watched in bemusement until I realized he was drawing the Dickosaurus, with far too much accuracy to be from memory. I knew he'd snapped a photo.

He was clearly determined to get every detail just right. By the time he was finished, my shoulders shook with suppressed laughter and my eyes were filled with tears again. I could barely hold the pen steady.

Sir, this is copyright infringement. You'll be hearing from my attorneys.

I have it on good authority that the original signature isn't legally binding, so I'm not sure how well your copyright claim will hold up.

All my inner turmoil had evaporated. The realization fueled a spark of affection for Fitz and how effortlessly he was able to lift my spirits. To hell with my exhaustion, I was ready to hop into the car (I'd probably put on pants first), buy a box of condoms from the nearest twenty-four-hour convenience store (to be safe), and go straight to Fitz's house. Our countdown clock was winding steadily down—so why would we waste time with sleep?

I did seriously consider it but then realized that Mim and

Mama would be so on edge tonight that there was no way I'd make it to the front door without waking them. And explaining myself was the last thing I wanted to do. I finally understood the appeal of living alone.

A litany of less-than-virtuous responses paraded through my mind, but I managed to resist.

I can probably be convinced to settle out of court, but I need to sleep on it first.

In that case, I accept your apology. Can I call you tomorrow?

Tomorrow. The day of the council forum. It wasn't until six P.M., but I had to spend the day cleaning the trashed shop—our amazing timing at work once again. The spark inside me had been smothered by reality, but I still couldn't bring myself to say no.

Not if I call you first.

Good night, Charlie.

Good night, Fitz.

CHAPTER TWENTY-SIX

"And is anything missing?" Sheriff Daniels asked, scratching beneath the brim of his hat with his pen.

"Hard to tell when most of our inventory is smashed on the floor." Mim had managed to remain calm and collected thus far, but only barely. "It's thousands of dollars in damages."

"Mm-hmm." Daniels scribbled away in his little notebook. He'd already walked the perimeter of the property and picked his way through the shop. All that was left was taking our statements for his report. As Mama had predicted, he was especially interested in the fact that there was no sign of a break-in.

"It's still illegal to enter private property and trash it," Mama said tersely. "Even if the door is unlocked."

"True, but . . ." Daniels trailed off, perhaps concluding that blaming three witches for their own misfortune, even indirectly, was a bad idea. "Anyway, that's what insurance is for."

"And here I thought crime was what law enforcement was for." Mim's tone was so sugary that it took Daniels a few seconds to catch on.

"Now, hold on, I'm not saying I won't investigate," he said

defensively, though he had indeed been in the process of putting away his notepad. He flipped to a new page instead. "Any angry customers recently? Anyone threaten you?"

Morgan Hawthorn, I thought, and looked at Mim. I could tell she'd had the same thought, but neither of us spoke. If Mrs. Hawthorn hadn't already filed a complaint with the sheriff accusing us of selling magic to minors, then I wasn't about to put her on his radar. Besides, I couldn't imagine her showing up in the middle of the night to smash the shop to pieces. Way too hands-on. Revenge was what attorneys were for.

"There are plenty of people in town who hate magic and would be happy to see us go out of business," said Mama.

She was right. Larry Munch had a whole brigade of anti-magic citizens at his beck and call, some more unhinged than others. The confrontation with Eddie Hightower and his ramblings about the magic mafia sprang to mind.

"But whoever did this used magic," Mim pointed out. "We could sense it last night."

"The mages from Maven?" Daniels asked, his interest piqued. "The Fitzgibbons?"

"The Fitzgeralds," I snapped, "and no. It wasn't them."

I hadn't meant it to come out quite so vehemently. All three heads swiveled toward me. I released my irritation and tried to channel nonchalance.

"I mean, they were with us the whole night."

"Might've been a mage friend of theirs. Or maybe they hired someone," Daniels said. "They sure could afford it."

Hiring someone to destroy the shop while they celebrated my parents' anniversary with us in the backyard would be a particularly nefarious scheme. And distracting me with mind-blowing sex so that I interrupted the counterspell and forgot to lock the door would be a true stroke of evil genius. The only problem was that neither Fitz nor Elinor was nefarious. I knew them well enough to know that in my bones. Even a lifetime of distrust for mages couldn't convince me otherwise. But I wasn't sure how or if I could explain it in a way that Sheriff Daniels would understand.

"They wouldn't do that," I said weakly, and looked to my parents for support.

"She's right," Mim said, and Mama nodded along. "They're not that sort of people."

I breathed a sigh of relief. I wasn't sure what sort of people *would* do this to us, but at least I wasn't alone in my conviction that it wasn't the Fitzgeralds.

"If you say so." Daniels's head bobbed as he scribbled away. He didn't look like he'd been listening to us.

I wanted to keep arguing, and I think Mama must have known that, because she cut in before I could speak.

"What are the next steps?"

Sheriff Daniels finished up his notes and slid the notepad into his chest pocket.

"I do my job, and you call your insurance company. I'll have my report ready for you to send to them in a few days."

A wave of frustration and helplessness engulfed me, and I couldn't stand being out here anymore. Without a word, I went back into the Cottage. I closed the door and stood with my back against it for a long moment, surveying the wreckage. If I thought too hard about it, the sheer magnitude of what needed to be done would overwhelm me, so instead I shut down my brain and went on autopilot.

I grabbed the nonenchanted broom and picked up where I'd left off the night before, sweeping the remains of our inventory into piles. Broomhilde's pieces had been carefully gathered and tucked into a box that morning. I wasn't sure if my parents would go so far as a funeral, but I wouldn't put it past them. Whenever I found a crystal or other item that looked undamaged, I put it carefully aside. Crystals would have to be purified before we could sell them. Hell, the whole shop would have to be cleansed before we could reopen. Nothing would ruin spellwork faster than lingering bad energy.

I was halfway down the first aisle when my parents came inside. They had a low conversation that I couldn't hear, and then Mama announced they were going to put on some work clothes and find the insurance paperwork. I was almost finished with the second aisle when Mama trotted down the stairs to join me. Apparently Mim had drawn the short straw to deal with the insurance claim. Mama disappeared into the store-room for a few minutes and returned with the dustpan and a garbage bag.

We worked in silence, but it wasn't the comfortable silence I was accustomed to with my parents. The quiet was a subtle pressure, building from my toes to my head, until the words burst out of me.

"It wasn't my fault."

Mama paused in the middle of dumping some rubbish into the bag and blinked at me.

"What wasn't?"

I pursed my lips, immediately wishing I'd kept quiet, but there was no stopping now.

"This." I gestured to the mess. "I mean, I know I should've remembered the bell, and turning off the counterspell was a bad idea"—though I'd had a hard time making myself regret it— "but how was I supposed to know that someone out there hates us this much?"

It could have been a mage or a particularly powerful witch. I didn't know of any spells that could cause this kind of damage, but that didn't mean it was impossible. Or it could have been someone with enough money to hire an unscrupulous mage or witch. Knowing that magic was involved didn't narrow down the list of suspects all that much, once the two most obvious ones had been eliminated. Unfortunately, I doubted Sheriff Daniels was going to bother adding anyone else to his list.

"You think we blame you for this?" Mama asked with a frown. "Of course we don't."

"But you seemed so upset."

"Walking into a disaster zone will do that to you."

"I meant at me."

Mama straightened and wiped the sweat from her forehead. "Charlie, what's this about?"

"You know what it's about." I massaged my temples. Hearing that they didn't blame me didn't console me. Probably because I still blamed myself. "You and Mim are aware of what I've been doing with my free time lately."

"Don't you mean *who* you've been doing?"

I didn't laugh.

"Are you going to pretend it doesn't bother you? That it's not a terrible fucking idea?"

Mama set down the dustpan and redid her sloppy ponytail before replying. She was stalling for time, trying to figure out what she wanted to say.

"Do *you* think it's a terrible idea?" she asked at length.

I leaned against the broom. My limbs were suddenly heavy, and I wanted to follow Sophie's lead and curl up in a corner somewhere to sleep.

"I don't know what I think."

"So what do you want from me?" Mama's tone was mild, without a hint of accusation. "Do you want me to tell you to stop seeing him?"

My stomach was twisted into tight knots.

"I want you to be honest with me. If you don't trust me, if you think I'm too irresponsible to ever be part owner of the business, then I'd rather you just tell me."

"Why do you think we don't trust you?" Mama frowned again but then seemed to realize the obvious. "Because of last night?"

"Yes, because of last night," I said testily, though I knew my frustration was misplaced. "Or because of what I did to the fairy ring, or because I'm dating the competition. Any number of things. Take your pick." I should've insisted we have this conversation a long time ago. Ignoring the issue all this time had been a ridiculous way to cope, but it was the sort of problem that once you started avoiding it, it was almost impossible to stop.

"Obviously we weren't happy about how the fairy ring turned out, but you made a mistake. We've all messed up spells before. We're not holding that against you."

Her words injected me with cool relief, though not enough to ease my frustration.

"What am I supposed to think, when you refuse to let me buy into the business, even though it's the only thing I really want?" A little voice in me whispered that that wasn't strictly true, not anymore, but I pressed on. "You never give me a real reason, and I'm tired of trying to prove to you that I'm good enough."

"It was never about you not being good enough." Mama grabbed both my cheeks to look me in the eye. "You're a brilliant witch. You love the Cottage. And we'd love nothing more than to keep you here forever, but we want to make sure you know what you're getting into."

"I know what I'm getting into," I insisted. "I've known for years. How can I make you believe me?"

Mama dropped her hands and stepped back, crossing her arms. She was worrying her bottom lip between her teeth.

"Look, Charlie, you want me to be honest, so I will." She drew in a long breath, and for a second, I thought she was going to change her mind and fob me off again with vague excuses. But she forged on. "There's no other way to say this. The Cottage is a sinking ship. I don't know if we can save it. And there's no way Mim and I are going to throw your life savings away."

My heart skipped a beat. I already knew the Cottage was in trouble, but hearing it so plainly from Mama, with a finality that suggested she'd already given up, was like a slap in the face.

"And what if that money is all we need to save it?"

"Thirty thousand dollars are deep roots to put down."

"What's wrong with roots?"

She offered a weak smile.

"Nothing, as long as you're in the right place."

"This is my home," I said, frustration building again. "Where else would my roots be?"

Mama picked up the dustpan and scraped her nail against a rogue sticker that had attached itself to the plastic. I could tell she was formulating her thoughts, so I waited in silence.

"Did I ever tell you that before I met your mom, I had a job lined up in Texas? It was my dream job, at a reptile sanctuary. My road trip following the monarch migration was a last hurrah. But then I met Ruby, and I know it's a dumb cliché, but I finally felt complete. Like I'd found the last missing piece of a puzzle I'd spent my whole life putting together. She felt the same way. She was even going to move to Texas, and you know how much your mom hates humidity. But then her parents died, and she had to take over the Cottage, and I had to make a choice." She finished peeling off the sticker and rolled it absently between her thumb and forefinger. "Obviously, I chose her. And I've never regretted that. I only regret that I didn't do a better job of keeping in touch with my family, of making sure they were a part of your life. I regret that when my mother was dying, she was surprised to see us in her hospital room—she hadn't expected me to show up."

There was a catch in her voice, and Mama swiped the back of her hand across her face.

My abuela passed away when I was in college. I hadn't seen her often growing up, since she lived in Texas with the rest of Mama's family. But I had a collection of discrete memories about her that I treasured—mostly pleasant, like the jungle of potted plants and herbs on her tiny front porch and her endless array of little glass perfume bottles, each filled with a different condition oil, and the warmth of her tiny floral-patterned kitchen, where she showed me how to roll out the dough for empanadas.

Some memories were less pleasant, like the time she'd pulled off her chancla and flung it at my primo Daniel's head when he backtalked her, or how pale she was in her hospital bed the last time I saw her, beads clasped weakly in her hands while she prayed the rosary and then offered a final prayer to La Santa Muerte. I remembered seeing Mama mouth the words along with her mother, even though I'd never seen her pray before or since.

Mama still gripped the dustpan tightly in one hand, and with the other she touched the lump under her shirt that I knew was her own Caravaca de la Cruz. Her eyes were watery, but she had managed to keep the tears in check so far. She cleared her throat roughly.

"My point is, when you choose a path in life, you can't always find your way back to other paths you might have chosen, even if you want to. The older you get, the faster time flies, and you don't always realize what you're missing until it's too late." She set the dustpan aside and gripped my shoulders instead, like when I was a kid and she wanted to file away a mental snapshot of me from head to toe. "You need to understand that staying here and investing everything you've earned in the Cottage will close the door on so many other opportunities you might have had. Your mom and I don't want our choices to dictate yours."

Her age showed less plainly on her face than Mim's, but this close I could see the permanent crow's feet at the corners of her eyes and the laugh lines around her mouth. My throat burned, like I'd swallowed red-hot coals. The fire of conviction raged in my chest.

"Mama," I said, my voice scratchy but firm. "I need *you* to understand that my only regret would be walking away from the Cottage. Our life here—it's what I want. More than any-thing."

When I was here, there were no pieces of me missing. I was everything Mim and Mama had raised me to be, and every-thing I had figured out for myself in the subsequent years. I was neither a Bruja nor a Druid, but my craft was descended from both and informed by every other witch who had ever shared their wisdom with my parents or me. I was a Sparrow and a Vega and a witch of Chanterelle Cottage, and I'd never wanted to be anything else. I knew, in my bones, that this was where I belonged.

Mama pulled me into an embrace, and I laid my head on the dip in her shoulder where I'd laid it so many other times before. My brain was a cacophony of worry and doubt, but in that mo-ment, my heart was at peace.

Then my phone rang.

Begrudgingly, I pulled it out of my pocket. Mama kept one of her arms wrapped around me, and we both looked down at the screen. Fitz.

"I know you like him, mija," she said, pressing a soft kiss against the side of my head. "Mim and I like him too. But I'm afraid he and the Cottage are on different paths. You might want to start thinking about what that means for you, if our life here is what you want."

I hesitated, my finger hovering over the screen. Of course I'd thought about it, at least long enough to decide that I didn't want to think about it anymore and shove it to the back of my mind. I knew I should answer, if only to warn him that Sheriff Daniels was going to accuse him of being a criminal mastermind. After what had happened between us last night, I couldn't blow him off.

But Mama's meaningful gaze was on me, and I needed to prove that I knew what I wanted, that I knew what I was doing—to her and to myself. I sent the call to voicemail and slipped the phone back into my pocket.

"We're going to need another bag soon." I started back with the broom. Mama watched me for a few seconds longer but then went back to work without saying anything more.

It was another hour before Mim trudged down the stairs. She had worn one of her nice sheath dresses with pearls and heels to meet with the sheriff, but at some point since his departure she had traded in the heels for her fluffy slippers and put on a checkered housecoat over her dress. At her arrival, Sophie appeared out of nowhere and trotted up to her, meowing pitifully, as we'd been cruelly neglecting her.

"The good news is that we're covered." Mim bent down to scratch Sophie behind the ear. "The bad news is that the idiots who bought the policy selected a ten-thousand-dollar deductible."

"Unfortunately, I think those idiots were us," Mama said. "It was the only way we could afford the coverage."

"And are we also the idiots who scheduled that appointment with First National Bank today?" Mim raised her phone. "The calendar alert went off a few minutes ago."

Damn, I'd forgotten about that. Back when the council forum was the only other thing we had to worry about today, the appointment had been inconvenient but doable. The VP's office was in a branch two hours away. With the meeting at two and the forum at six, they wouldn't be able to make any detours, but they could still attend both. Now, on top of everything else, we had this mysterious malefactor on the loose.

"We should cancel," Mama said.

"But it could be another few months before he can meet with you," I said. "What about asking him to do the call over Zoom? Then you don't have to drive out there."

"No way," Mama said. "If I can't shake a man's hand and look him in the eye, how am I supposed to convince him of anything?"

"Then we cancel," said Mim. "We can make it another month or two without defaulting on the loan."

"No." I grabbed the trash bag from her. "This meeting is too important. I'll take over here."

Mim twisted one of her loose curls and looked at Mama. They had a swift, silent conversation and came to a conclusion. Mim sighed.

"If you're sure . . ."

"I'm sure. You two go get ready. As charming as the forlorn housewife and broke college student looks are, I don't think the VP will be impressed."

"I'll start taking you seriously as a fashion critic when you stop stealing my clothes," Mama said, shooting me a finger gun.

I wanted to argue but looked down and realized that I was, in fact, wearing one of her shirts. Touché.

They went upstairs together, already bickering about whether they should make sandwiches for lunch or grab something on the way.

My phone started ringing. Probably Fitz again. He would offer to come help. He'd bring good food. It could be a nice final few hours before the forum. I reached into my pocket, sent it to voicemail without looking, and got back to work.

CHAPTER TWENTY-SEVEN

I had no idea what one was supposed to wear to a forum where the fate of your livelihood was at stake, but I figured it probably wasn't one of Mama's old T-shirts, now sweat-stained and coated in a fine layer of dust. (You don't realize how lax you are with dusting until all the shelves are empty.) I settled on dark jeans and a green flannel shirt that I decided was vaguely businesslike since it did have buttons and a collar.

I spent too long straightening my hair as a way of distracting myself from my own troubled thoughts. Fitz had called one more time, and I'd finally relented and texted that I was busy, so that he would know I was alive. He read my message (what kind of lunatic leaves on their read receipts?) but he didn't reply. I had absolutely no right to be salty about that, but I was anyway. Maybe that was the stress of the day getting to me. It was five-thirty, and I still hadn't heard from my parents. They were supposed to be back an hour ago, and all my calls were going to voicemail, so clearly something had gone terribly wrong, and they had driven off a cliff into a lake or the bank VP had turned out to be a serial killer or—

My phone rang, and I snatched it up from the counter, dropping my straightener in the sink in my haste. I tried to pick it up, burned myself, cursed, dropped it again, then finally yanked out the plug. At least the sink was dry.

"Hey," I said, a little winded.

"Sorry, baby," said Mim. "This is the first bar of reception I've found in this godforsaken wilderness."

I heard Mama's muffled voice in the background informing her that they were on the side of a highway.

"Who ever heard of a highway with no cell reception?" Mim demanded of her.

More muffled conversation.

"Mim!" I shouted into the phone, exasperated. "What happened? Where are you?"

"Someone rear-ended us. We're fine, but the car is not. I think we're about an hour out of town?"

An hour? My heart dropped. I'd thought she was calling to say they would be here in a few minutes.

"The highway patrol finally showed up," Mim went on. "But no word from the tow truck."

"Uber?" I asked weakly, even though I knew it was pointless. It was half an hour before the forum. They weren't going to be here in time.

"I'm sorry. You're going to have to do the speech at the forum."

My heart sank even further. I wasn't particularly scared of public speaking, but the town would be expecting to hear from the owners of Chanterelle Cottage. Everyone knew me, but they knew me as the shop girl. To say I didn't command the same respect as Ruby and Alicia Sparrow was a massive understatement.

Mim caught on to my hesitation.

"Maybe you can put us on speakerphone for the speech?"

"No," I said, even as I heard Mama saying that was a terrible idea. Handshake, eye contact, et cetera. "I can do it. I can . . . try."

There was some shuffling on the other end of the line, and then Mama's voice was in my ear.

"You'll be great, mija. I even have some notes written up. They're on the kitchen table."

That was promising. I darted into the kitchen, conscious of the time ticking away. I still needed to put on my shoes and feed Sophie, and now I would have to ride my bike into town. It was going to be a close call, and I would be a sweaty mess by the time I got there. Maybe I should rethink the flannel.

I found the stack of notecards and scooped them up. I scanned the first one, then flipped through the rest.

"Mama," I said, with the infinite calm of someone who already knows she is doomed. "You have written exactly one note, and it says, 'You got this, bitch.'"

A pause.

"Oh. Well. I might have had some wine beforehand."

I took a long, steadying breath that did nothing to steady me.

"Look on the bright side," Mama said. "You *do* got this, bitch."

More shuffling, presumably caused by Mim ripping the phone from her hands.

"Just do your best, baby. Speak from the heart."

Right. Next, she would be telling me to follow my dreams and shoot for the moon, because even if I miss, I'll land among the stars.

"They don't want to hear from me." Now I was stalling. I tossed the notecards back onto the table and went to my bedroom to find some shoes.

"Everyone loves you!"

"They love *you*. And Mama. I'm just the girl that rings them up at the cash register."

"What the hell are you even saying?" Mama demanded. Mim must have put me on speaker. "You're the one who figured out the transmutation spell—and the graveyard ritual was your idea too. You're a fucking goddess, and everyone knows it. Now I want you to walk into that forum and kick some mage ass."

Mim said something I couldn't quite make out.

"Fine," Mama said grudgingly. "Kick some ass *politely*."

Despite my growing distress, I huffed out a laugh.

"We've got to go," Mim said, raising her voice over the sound of an engine. "The tow truck is here. We'll be back as soon as we can. Sorry again. We love you, bye!"

"Love you," I said, and the line went dead.

I decided not to think anymore, because thinking would lead to panic, and panic would lead to me hiding under my blankets until all this was over. I put on some sneakers and changed into a T-shirt. It was chilly outside, but I knew the ride into town would warm me up plenty. I pulled my hair into a ponytail, then shoved my phone, wallet, a brush, and the flannel shirt into a backpack. I figured I'd slip into the restroom when I got there and spruce myself up.

The clock on my bedside table said 5:43. Even if I pedaled like the wind, I was still going to be late.

I shouldered the backpack and ran. I got halfway down the steps before remembering Sophie's dinner and ran all the way back up. She could survive a few hours without food, but that wouldn't stop her from punishing us by puking a hairball onto the rug or knocking some glassware to the ground.

"You're welcome," I told her pointedly, as I dumped a can of food into her bowl. She continued her languid cleaning of her silky coat and ignored me.

I went out the front door, checked the locks twice, skipped down the steps—and stopped short.

A familiar black Mercedes was idling in the parking lot. Fitz was standing behind the open driver's-side door, his hand resting on the top.

"Ruby texted that you might need a ride," he said, when I didn't move or speak. His tone and bearing were neutral, so I couldn't tell what he was thinking—whether he was confused or annoyed or completely indifferent.

I shifted my weight, wondering if I was about to outdo myself in stubbornness—and stupidity—and refuse a ride from him. On the one hand, last night he had given me a record-breaking three orgasms. On the other hand, I'd then proceeded to ignore him all day today like an asshole. If I'd had another hand, I would have considered that the town hall was less than a ten-minute car ride away, but also ten minutes can feel like an hour when the situation is awkward enough.

Perhaps sensing that he needed to save me from my own stupidity, Fitz walked around and opened the passenger door.

"Come on," he said, with a smile that seemed a little forced. "I'll let you push all the buttons you want."

I forced my own smile and climbed in, hugging my backpack against my chest like it needed protecting. Or I did. Fitz shut the door, and I watched as he rounded the hood. He was in a suit and tie, because of course he was. Owl's Hollow wasn't exactly a business formal kind of town, but Fitz wore it so naturally. There would be no question in anyone's mind which one of us was a bona fide business owner and which one was flying by the seat of her pants.

We left the driveway in silence, and it was immediately obvious that my fear of awkwardness was not unfounded. If anything, I'd underestimated it.

A few more minutes passed, and I was starting to consider a tuck and roll out of the car when Fitz cleared his throat.

"So, are you going to talk, or am I going to have to turn on NPR?"

"I don't know what you want me to say."

"You could start with how you're doing."

"About as well as I can be, considering I spent the day dumping half our inventory in the garbage."

"Is there anything I can do to help?"

"No." I watched the scenery through the window, the familiar rows of trees, interrupted occasionally by fences and driveways, all blanketed with the soft orange glow of sunset. I should say more. I should thank him for offering, for the ride, for giving two shits about me despite having every reason not to. But I couldn't make the words come out. All the thinking I'd been doing today had left me with a singular conclusion that I wasn't yet ready to face.

"And do I get a hint?"

"A hint?"

"About what I did to piss you off so much between last night and this morning."

"You didn't do anything." That would have made things easier, if he were a proper competitor, with insults and sabotage. It would be so much easier to hate him.

"Sheriff Daniels doesn't agree."

I winced.

"He called you?"

"Came by the office. I guess he wanted to interrogate me in person. I ended up having to reschedule two appointments."

Figures. Sheriff Daniels could barely be bothered to file a report on a good day, but give him the chance to horribly inconvenience someone while also stirring up town-wide drama, and he transformed into a supercop.

"I told him you and Elinor were with us all night."

"Allegedly I used my vast resources to hire a big-city thug—or possibly a gang? The sheriff didn't seem too clear on that part."

We pulled into the parking lot and managed to find a spot.

There were dozens of people milling around the town hall, but on a night like this, most of them had probably walked.

"Daniels is an ass," I said.

"I don't care about Daniels." He shifted the car into park and looked at me. "You know I had nothing to do with this, right?"

"Of course I know that." I pulled on the door handle, but it was locked. So much for my swift escape from the conversation.

"Then why are you acting like this?" Fitz asked, either not noticing or choosing to ignore my fight with his car door.

"I'm not acting like anything." I hit what I thought was the unlock button but only succeeded in lowering the window an inch. This fucking car.

"Charlie, please, look at me." He put his hand on my arm, a ghost of a touch. The note of pleading in his voice snagged me like a fishhook, and I abandoned my escape attempt. "Last night was—I had a good time. I thought you did too."

"Sure, right up until the whole ruination-of-my-livelihood thing."

My flippant tone prompted a flash of what looked like actual irritation across his features, which meant I was truly in rare form. Maybe I could afford to dial back the sarcasm a couple degrees.

"Sorry." I fiddled restlessly with my necklace. "Yes, I had a good time. But that was yesterday."

"And today?"

"Fitz, look where we are." I glanced toward the town hall, at the light spilling through the propped doors, beckoning every- one inside. "We've reached the end of the countdown clock."

"The vote isn't until tomorrow night."

"We're about to go in there and try to convince those people that only one of our businesses deserves to stay open. Then what—you want to come back to the parking lot for a quickie like nothing happened?"

"You know that's not what I meant," he said, with a hint of indignation. "And even if Maven's license gets renewed, that doesn't mean Chanterelle Cottage will close."

And even if Maven closed, that didn't guarantee that the Cottage would stay open. But I'd made my decision. If I was lashing myself to the mast of a sinking ship, then so be it.

"You've cut significantly into our revenue." I didn't bother to soften the accusation. "Revenue we need to stay open. That's the way it is, and no amount of optimism is going to change that."

"You should hire an accountant—there are some who specialize in small businesses in trouble—and try to—"

"Jesus *Christ*, Fitz, stop telling me what to do."

We were both shocked by my outburst. I hadn't meant to snap at him. I knew he was trying to help. I knew that most of his unsolicited advice was probably worth taking. But he was missing the heart of the problem, and my impatience was like needles under my skin.

"I'm sorry," he said, but I held up my hand.

"No, don't apologize, just stop." I took a second to gather myself, willing my voice to remain calm and steady. "Listen to me. We can't coexist in Owl's Hollow. I've never pretended differently. And tonight, I'm going to do everything I can to convince them that this town is better off without Maven Enterprises. That is what I have to do. And I can't do it if I think of you as a friend or—or something else." I forced myself to gulp down some air and squeezed my hands together in my lap until my bones hurt. "I need this to be over, okay? Please."

"Is that really what you want?" His voice was low and soft, with a shred of vulnerability that almost broke me.

No no no.

"It is."

I thought back to the last card in his tarot spread—the World in reverse. Emptiness and disappointment. I had never expected that the harbinger would be me.

He swallowed and broke from my gaze. For a long while he stared silently ahead, watching the last of the forum attendees trickle into the town hall. There was a tremor in his clenched jaw. Finally, he nodded. I released a breath, but it carried no relief with it.

"Thank you." I tried to sound casual, like I hadn't imploded everything between us. "Now unlock your stupid space car and let me out. We're going to be late."

He hit a button on his side panel. I yanked the handle again and practically fell out of the car. *Smooth, Charlie.* I put on my backpack and made sure I shut the door gently. Last thing I wanted to do was break something on his car, which probably (definitely) cost more than I made in a year.

I wanted to wait for him, which was a foolish instinct. I forced myself to walk away, though I couldn't stop myself from listening for his door to open. I didn't know what I wanted, for him to open the door and call after me, or to open the door and walk into the forum like nothing had happened, or to drive away and never be seen again. I couldn't decide before I was distracted by Tandy waving me down from the entrance. She was going to blow a gasket when she realized my parents weren't coming.

I squared my shoulders, pasted on my best approximation of a confident smile, and crossed the parking lot to break the bad news. Tandy herded me into the meeting hall, managing to simultaneously blow a gasket and take control of the situation. For once I didn't mind. My head was spinning with everything I needed to say and how I was going to say it. My nerves were a burning pit in my stomach.

The meeting hall was not as full as it had been on the day of the Whiteout, but empty seats were few and far between as the last members of the audience trickled in. Tandy led the way to the front row, explaining that she'd come early to reserve us seats. She was in a smart blue dress with a string of pearls that were probably real, although I wasn't sure how to tell the difference. Her sky-high heels clacked on the wood floors while my sneakers squeaked. The undercurrent of my inadequacy was becoming a riotous river.

Shit, *and* I'd forgotten to change into my nicer shirt and fix my hair. Too late for that now. We were sitting down, and the council members were filing onto the dais, where a long table and chairs had been set up for them, so that they could properly lord over the proceedings. On the floor in front, facing the dais, was a single black microphone stand. Bonnie slid the microphone free, fiddled with the cord for a few seconds, then turned to the crowd and greeted everyone.

Tandy, who was bad at sitting quietly and listening, immediately leaned over and whispered in my ear.

"After the mayor is done, the floor will be open for any citizens who want to speak their piece, then you and the Fitzgeralds will have some time."

I was pretty sure she was telling me the same things that Bonnie was saying, but I nodded along anyway. I wasn't sure how much it was going to help my nerves to sit through a bunch of random citizens talking either about how much they hate or how much they love Maven Enterprises. Especially if there were more of the latter than the former.

While Bonnie was admonishing everyone to remain civil and restrain themselves to three minutes each, I took a moment to let down my hair and run my fingers through it, so at least all that straightening wouldn't go to waste. By the time Bonnie returned the microphone and took her seat onstage, there was already a line forming in the center aisle. Tandy, of course, had sprung from her chair to be the first.

Gratitude was not something I associated with Tandy Di-Angelo, so it took me a while to identify the emotion. But knowing that she would be setting the tone for the evening in that tyrannical, no-nonsense way of hers helped to soothe my roiling stomach—at least a little bit. Tandy used more than her allotted three minutes, though she did manage to keep herself under five. She had a lot to say about witchcraft as the superior art form, none of which was especially relevant to the discussion of whether the council should renew Maven Enterprises' license, though near the end she did get around to mentioning that Belville, a town thirty miles east of us, had welcomed a magecraft firm last year and two months later a tornado took out their clock tower, and there was no way that was a coincidence. (It was.)

Specious arguments aside, I appreciated her effort and offered her a smile when she returned to her seat. She smiled back and immediately began texting for the rest of the session.

I tried to listen carefully to all the points being made by the fine citizens of Owl's Hollow, but the best I could manage was what I hoped was a vaguely interested attitude and the occasional thoughtful nod. In my head I was fervidly writing and rewriting my speech. There was a lot I could say about the value that the Cottage brought to the town and the research I'd done on how magecraft firms could be detrimental to small-town economies. Sheriff Daniels's little visit to Maven today was an obvious fact to mention. I could give people food for thought without technically accusing Fitz and Elinor of doing anything illegal.

Whether I could live with myself after doing so was a different matter entirely.

As unobtrusively as possible, I leaned farther back in my seat and tried to catch a glimpse of Fitz. He and his sister were in the front row as well, on the opposite side of the aisle. Fitz was

staring straight ahead. I couldn't decipher much from his profile, but I suspected he was paying as much attention as I was. I
must have stared for too long because he turned his head. Our
eyes met. A ghost of hurt passed over his features, and my heart
ached in reply. I needed to break the connection, but I couldn't
make myself do it. He looked away first.

The last person in line, an elderly gentleman, spent a couple
minutes extolling the virtues of magecraft and thanking Fitz
personally for curing his trick hip, which had been plaguing
him for a decade. Fitz must have been paying some modicum of
attention because he managed a warm smile for the man.

I wondered how much that appointment cost, both the man
and Fitz. Altering the human body was a dangerous business,
because of not only the possible complications but also the toll
it took on the mage. Few would agree to treat so much as a
stubbed toe. The magic malpractice insurance rates alone could
eat half the annual budget of a smaller firm.

I recalled the day I'd turned Councilwoman Hibbert from a
bobcat back into a human and got that nasty scratch on my arm
for my troubles. Fitz had been determined to heal me, despite
his exhaustion. No wonder Elinor worried about him. He might
have been a brilliant mage, but his judgment when it came to
preserving his own health was questionable at best. And mages
couldn't heal their own magical fatigue.

The old man returned spryly to his seat. Bonnie came down
the steps and announced a ten-minute break before the next
segment.

I jumped up and made a beeline for the restroom. I reached
the stall in time to drop to my knees and dry heave into the
toilet. My nerves must have finally gotten the better of me. Or
maybe it was the guilt.

"You have nothing to feel guilty about," I told the toilet water
sternly.

The restroom door opened, and I climbed to my feet and flushed. I exchanged polite smiles with the women who'd entered and went to wash my hands. My hair thankfully looked half decent, but my cheeks were pink and hot and my eyes slightly bloodshot, like I'd been crying. I wet a paper towel and dabbed at my face, to no avail. If I'd been smart, I would have brought my makeup bag with me for touch-ups. If I'd been smart, I would have worn something classier than jeans and a T-shirt. *Goddammit, I forgot my flannel shirt again.*

If I'd been smart, I wouldn't have waited until five minutes before the forum to torpedo my relationship with Fitz. I would have done it weeks ago. Or better yet, I would have never gotten involved at all.

I wanted to give myself a much-needed pep talk. But there were people waiting to use the sink, so I left.

Instead of standing awkwardly in the bathroom, I was now standing awkwardly in the middle of the hallway, and people were starting to stare. For lack of a better option, I returned to the meeting hall. I avoided looking toward the Fitzgeralds' seats and instead asked Tandy if she had anything to help my nerves. When I packed my bag earlier, I hadn't thought to include my satchel of emergency crystals. Not so long ago I would have rather chopped off a finger than admit weakness to Tandy Di-Angelo, but she'd somehow clawed her way out of the "reluctant colleague" category. Not a friend exactly, but close enough.

"I sure do." She began digging around in her purse. "I've got quartz, a vetiver talisman, and a bottle of Valium. I like to be prepared."

I was pretty sure she was joking about the Valium but decided not to ask.

"The quartz is fine, thanks." I hated the smell of vetiver.

"So do you know what you're going to say?" she asked, handing it over. "I'm assuming Alicia didn't leave you anything to work with, so I wrote up some notes you can use." She waved her phone at me. I guess she wasn't texting after all.

"I know what I'm going to say," I lied. I couldn't be sure that her notes would be any better than "*You got this, bitch,*" and the only thing worse than not using her notes would be reading the notes first and *then* not using them.

I pulled out my own phone to check the time and saw that I had two messages.

Mama: *Don't forget to kick ass.*
Mim: *Politely.*

Tears welled up behind my eyeballs, and I shoved the phone back into my pocket. We only had a couple minutes left. I held the crystal in a tight grip and tried to focus. Using quartz to drain negative energy is one of the first spells you learn as a witch, because it's so easy a child can do it. The problem is for most people it becomes exponentially harder the older you get. No one is sure why, although most witches assume it's because you stop believing that magic can solve all your problems. Magic *can't* solve all your problems, but if you want it to solve any of them, belief is a necessary ingredient—belief in the power of the magic and belief in your own abilities to channel it.

Tonight, I couldn't lighten the load on my mind even the tiniest bit. I told myself Tandy probably hadn't cleansed her crystal properly, but I was bullshitting. I was too wrapped up in my own emotions to focus properly. Too conflicted by impossible hope and awful reality to believe that there was any way to make this better.

I should have gone with the Valium.

Bonnie was back at the microphone, announcing that a representative of Chanterelle Cottage would be given the opportunity to speak first. Keeping the quartz in a tight grip, I stood up.

Bonnie gave me an encouraging little smile before heading back to her seat. There was technically no reason that a competitor should be given a special time slot to speak at the hearing for Maven Enterprises' license renewal, but that was one of the advantages of being friends with the (temporary) mayor.

I adjusted the microphone, stalling for time. But unfortunately, there's only so much fiddling you can do with a microphone stand before it becomes painfully obvious what you are doing.

"Hello," I said, trying my best to make eye contact with each of the council members while radiating charm and confidence. I did skip over Councilman Munch. It didn't matter how charming I was: I couldn't work miracles. "I'm Charlie Sparrow."

I felt a little silly introducing myself, since the council obviously knew who I was, but it seemed like the professional thing to do. In my jeans, T-shirt, and sneakers, I needed as many professional points as I could get.

"My parents wanted to be here, but they had some car trouble. I'm going to do my best to fill their shoes. First, I want to thank the council and everyone here for your time and attention tonight." The last part was the tiniest bit pointed, since Councilman Emerson's attention was clearly fixated on his phone on the table, as he scrolled with one finger in what I'm sure he thought was a subtle fashion. "And I especially wanted to thank everyone who had something kind to say about the Cottage or my family. It means a lot to me."

I'd had a hard time focusing on the exact words being said, but that didn't mean I'd missed the gist of the heartwarming sentiments. Maybe they were the minority, but there were people in Owl's Hollow who preferred the cozy warmth of witchcraft to the cold flash of magecraft. I wanted to turn to face them all, to make sure they understood my sincerity, but I didn't want to accidentally lock eyes with Fitz again. I wasn't sure I could recover a second time. Not even an hour ago I'd informed him in no uncertain terms that I was going to stand up here and do everything I could to run his business out of town.

So why now, with my breath echoing faintly in the microphone, was I frozen with indecision?

I squeezed the quartz so hard that it was probably going to leave permanent scores in my palm. Councilman Emerson was still absorbed in his phone. Councilman Huang cracked a yawn. Larry Munch was picking at a hangnail. What the hell was I even doing here? What could I possibly say to these people that would make any difference? I'd known for a week that Fitz already had the votes he needed. I was arguing against a decision that had already been made by politicians behind closed doors.

Sure, I could ramble on about the impact of Maven on local businesses—namely mine—but I was no expert. I couldn't even listen to Mim talk about bookkeeping without my head starting to hurt. I had my doubts about the qualifications of most of the council, but Bonnie had her master's in economics. She knew better than I did what economic risks Maven Enterprises did (or did not) pose to the town. Councilwoman Hibbert, who I was pretty sure was on my side on account of the whole bobcat incident, had been a small business owner for thirty years before retirement. She knew as well as I did the burden of carrying that dream on your back, the constant dread that one bad month would end that dream for good.

But wasn't Maven Enterprises a small business too? The Cottage's inability to withstand competition was not a good reason to deny Fitz his chance to build a new life here in Owl's Hollow.

If Chanterelle Cottage couldn't thrive on its own merits, then maybe we had no choice but to let it go.

Shopgirl deserved better.

"Charlie, is everything all right?" Bonnie asked in a low voice, her brows furrowed slightly. I probably looked like I was having a stroke, standing here in silence having an existential crisis while a room full of people stared at my ass.

"Sorry, I'm—yes, sorry." I took a steadying breath. I forced my fist to loosen around the quartz. "I don't have anything further to say to the council on behalf of Chanterelle Cottage. Thank you again for your time."

I turned away from the mic almost before the last word left my mouth. I was desperately glad for the front-row seat because it meant I didn't have far to go, but it did also mean that I was in prime position to absorb all the stares in the room. There was a ripple of shocked murmurs behind me, and the council members, even Munch, were exchanging confused looks. There was no confusion in the look Tandy was giving me, only pure indignation. I dropped her crystal back in her lap. Maybe she could get some use out of it.

Bonnie stood up uncertainly, like she was waiting for me to run back to the microphone and shout, "*Just kidding!*" I stayed where I was and offered her a helpless grimace. If anyone wanted me to explain myself, they could get in line. I, too, would have liked to know what the hell I was thinking.

Bonnie rushed to the mic and announced that in closing, a representative of Maven Enterprises was invited to speak. From the corner of my eye, I watched Elinor stand up, holding a stack of papers. She was stunning in a black dress and blazer with big brass buttons. I caught a glimpse of a brightly colored graph on one of the pages she was holding. Wonderful, she had handouts. And probably a killer speech planned that she would deliver easily with both charm and confidence. I was willing to bet even money on a standing ovation.

Right as she took a step toward the microphone, Fitz reached out and grabbed her arm. I was unable to resist tilting my head for a better look. He was whispering something fervently in her ear while Elinor shook her head repeatedly. In turn, she whispered even more heatedly back at him. He gave a final, abrupt reply, and she made a noise of pure frustration before tossing the handouts into his lap and strutting over to the microphone.

Again, my attention lingered too long on Fitz, and again, he caught me staring. I had no idea what he was thinking, and there was no way he knew what I was thinking either—because I didn't even know. This time we both broke away simultaneously.

"Good evening," Elinor said into the microphone. I must have gotten to know her better than I thought over the past three months because I immediately recognized the saccharine lilt of her voice as the tone reserved especially for when she was annoyed at her brother. "On behalf of Maven Enterprises, I also don't have anything to say to the council. *Apparently.*"

She shot a glare over her shoulder at Fitz, who, in the way of all big brothers, was completely unfazed. The meeting hall erupted again into astonished whispers as Elinor flounced back to her seat and plopped down with her arms crossed in an obvious sulk. What a waste of a perfectly good handout.

Bonnie looked unsure whether she was the victim of some elaborate, pointless prank. When neither Elinor nor Fitz moved, she returned to the microphone.

"Well," she said, in a falsely cheery voice. "That was—umm, that's everything I guess. Thank you everyone for coming and sharing your, um, insights with us. The council will vote tomorrow evening and post our decision on the town website by eight P.M. Please drive safely!"

I think she probably had planned a more elegant closing speech, but the inexplicable turn of the evening had thrown her off her game. She was going to corner me the first chance she got, but I wasn't in the mood for a lecture on how she'd gone to bat for Chanterelle Cottage with the council and I'd let her down. I loved Bonnie, but when it came to politics, she was as irritatingly tenacious as they come, and she wasn't a big fan of the "It wouldn't have made a difference anyway" argument. Coward that I am, I had every intention of bolting as soon as she dismissed us, but Tandy had an iron grip on my arm before I could budge.

"What was that?" she hissed. "You told me you knew what you were going to say."

"I said everything I wanted to say." I decided it was better to pretend that I'd known what I was doing all along, rather than admit that I had short-circuited in the moment.

"Maybe I should talk to Bonnie," said Tandy, mostly to herself. "I can type up my notes and email them to the council."

"That's a good idea." I sensed my opportunity to escape. "You should do that."

Tandy released me and went in search of Bonnie. I slung my backpack over one shoulder and headed for the door to the left of the dais, which led to the council chamber and offices, as well as a rear exit. I had no desire to play twenty questions with every curious citizen between here and the parking lot, and more important, I didn't want to face Elinor and Fitz. Maybe on the way home I could take a detour down the yellow brick road and ask the Wizard for some courage.

I left the town hall through the back, but the second I stepped into the crisp night air, I remembered that in my infinite foresight and wisdom, I'd dumped my ride home on arrival. I shivered and finally remembered my flannel shirt in my backpack. While I was putting it on, the door behind me opened.

"There you are," said Bonnie. She must have eluded Tandy. "Are you okay? What's going on?"

"I'm fine. I'm about to head home."

She radiated skepticism and leaned back against the closed door, clearly not planning on taking me at my word.

"So you're going to pretend all of that was totally normal and you expect me to go along with it?"

"That's the plan."

"Cute." Bonnie crossed her arms and didn't move. "I was expecting you to decimate Maven Enterprises up there. Or at least say . . . something."

"I did thank everyone for their time."

"Are you and Fitz together now? I can't think of any other reason why both of you would wave the white flag like that."

"We're not together." I slung my backpack over my shoulder again. "Not anymore."

"But you *were*?" Her eyebrows shot up. "Since when? You haven't told me anything since your first date at The Blue Spoon."

"Sorry, I guess we've both been pretty busy." Bonnie had her hands full with her new mayoral duties, and I'd been distracted by my concerns for the Cottage—as well as my ill-fated romance. And of course, we'd both been preoccupied with first the Whiteout, then the Animal Pox. I sighed, irritated at myself for letting the friendship fall by the wayside. One more thing I could feel guilty about. I gave her the broad strokes of the situation, not because I didn't want her to know everything, but because I wasn't sure I could go into details without crying. And that would be the icing on top of tonight's towering cake of failure.

Before I was even finished, Bonnie threw her arms around me in a hug. That was probably for the best because I didn't even have a broad strokes explanation for why I had thrown away my last chance to convince the council that the town was better off mage-free. I hugged her back.

"That's it," Bonnie announced, coming to some decision. "We're going for ice cream."

"I haven't had dinner yet."

"We'll get a couple extra scoops."

"I need to get home." I wasn't particularly convincing, even to myself.

"I'll drive you home after." Bonnie leaned back to give me a look. "Now stop arguing. I'm the mayor, so you have to do what I say."

"Good to see the power hasn't gone to your head."

"Meet me at my car. I need a couple minutes to finish up inside."

"Shake some hands and kiss some babies?"

"The usual."

Bonnie went back into the town hall, and I took the sidewalk to the front parking lot, though first I peered around the corner to see if Fitz's car was still there. It was gone, which was a relief. At least I think it was.

Bonnie had a reserved spot in the front row. I kept my head down as I walked, hoping to avoid interactions. Perhaps sensing my mood, the people trickling out through the front door gave me space. I had almost reached Bonnie's car when Elinor stepped in front of me. I braced myself for some outrage—Fitz must have filled her in by now.

"I'm not even going to ask what happened." She was tapping away on her phone but spared me a glance. She seemed like her normal, breezy self. Maybe with a bonus dose of irritation. "Fitz told me to check if you needed a ride home."

"Is he still here?" It slipped out before I could stop myself. It was a stupid question, not least of all because I'd seen for myself that his car was gone. You can't dump a man unceremoniously in a parking lot, then expect him to hang around for a chat.

"No, he left right after. Said he had somewhere to be." Elinor gave me another look, longer this time, like she was waiting for me to say something. When I didn't, she went back to her phone. "My car's parked down the street."

"No thanks. Bonnie is taking me home."

"Okay, but Fitz also told me to make sure you weren't lying." She finally put away her phone. "Which I thought was weird. Why would you lie about something like that?"

Because I would rather walk home than accept help from Elinor right after I'd dumped her brother. The fact that Fitz knew me well enough to foresee that only made the whole situation more miserable.

"I don't know," I said lightly. "Maybe you should ask Fitz."

Elinor's lips twisted in contemplation. She lowered her voice.

"I know I said I wasn't going to ask what happened, but what the hell happened?"

I was saved from having to answer by Bonnie's arrival, with her briefcase in one hand and her keys in the other.

"Hi, Elinor," she said. "Doing all right?"

"Never better." Elinor flashed a grin.

"Have you thought about my offer?"

"Sorry, I've had a lot going on."

"It's still on the table," Bonnie said, hitting the unlock button. "Have a good night."

"You too." Elinor gave her a little wave, shot me one more look, and walked off.

"What offer?" I asked as we climbed into the car and buckled up.

"I asked her to be my campaign manager for the special election."

"Why?"

"I figured if she could bring most of the town on board with a magecraft firm, she'd be able to convince them to elect me for a full term." Bonnie started the car then winced. "Sorry."

It took me a second to figure out that she wasn't apologizing for starting the car, but for reminding me that the council was going to vote to renew Maven's license tomorrow. Like I could have forgotten.

"I meant why do you need a campaign manager?" I asked. "I thought you were unopposed."

"So did I," Bonnie said grimly. "Larry Munch is going to announce his candidacy after the vote. Bringing in Maven Enterprises wasn't an evil plot to run Chanterelle Cottage out of business after all. I guess his anti-magic schtick wasn't giving him the political advantages he was hoping for, because now he wants to distinguish himself as the hero who brought modern magic to Owl's Hollow. Next stop, mayor's office."

"Magecraft isn't more modern than witchcraft," I said. "Just more pretentious."

"I know, I know. But that's how Munch is going to spin it."

"Guess we both have a reason for extra ice cream, then."

CHAPTER TWENTY-EIGHT

Bonnie and I stayed at the ice cream parlor until it closed. I broke down and told her the whole story about Fitz, including our interlude in the shop the night before, sans details. It's easier not to cry when you're stuffing your face with ice cream.

When we arrived back at the Cottage, my parents' car was there, which meant there was no more putting off the inevitable. I had no doubt that Tandy would have called them immediately. Even so, I couldn't quite make myself open the door. We sat idling for a while. I studied the shadowy exterior of the Cottage in the illumination of the headlights. Fitz was right. It probably could use a new coat of paint. How annoying.

But we weren't on the verge of bankruptcy because of poor maintenance. Unfortunately, that was the least of our problems.

"Look," Bonnie said into the dismal silence. "I don't know if the Cottage is going to survive this or not. But what I do know is that no matter what happens, you're going to be okay. Got it?"

"Let me guess. I have to agree with you because you're the mayor?"

"For another few months at least."

"Fine, I will agree with you as long as you agree that you're also going to be okay, no matter what happens with the election." I reached over and squeezed her hand. "If you can't be the mayor, then we'll have to get started on your Senate campaign."

Bonnie smiled.

"If you insist."

"Thanks for the ride," I said, opening the door. "See you tomorrow?"

"Yeah." She stifled a yawn. "I'm going straight to bed. I've been up since four this morning."

"Sleep tight." I hopped out with my backpack and waved while she did a three-point turn out of the driveway.

The upstairs windows were dark. Mama and Mim must have already gone to bed. I paused before I reached the front steps. The thought of going inside right now and being faced with the quiet shop, the bare shelves, and the trash bags filled with the remains of our inventory strewn along the aisles was too much to bear. I decided to use the back stairs, but once I made it to the backyard, I found myself wandering toward the gazebo instead.

The wood was still damp from last night's rain, but I lay down anyway, using my backpack as a pillow. As long as I didn't think too hard, it was nice to be here, in the last place where I'd still believed everything might work out for the best. A breeze skimmed across the wisteria vines, making the leaves flutter.

I hugged myself tightly against the chill. Despite that, my eyelids started drooping. Before I could drift off and freeze to death, my phone rang. Probably Mama or Mim wanting to know where I was. I picked it up to let them know that I was busy brooding in soap opera fashion, and I'd be in soon. But it was Elinor.

"Hello?" I said uncertainly.

"I like you, Charlie," she said, without a hello. "So I'm going to do my best to stay civil here. Now, please, will you tell me what the *hell* you said to my brother?"

The cat must be out of the bag.

"I told him that we couldn't see each other anymore. I don't think it's a good—"

"Yeah, yeah," she interrupted. "Star-crossed lovers, parting is such sweet sorrow, et cetera, et cetera. Now, what else?"

"Nothing." I was a little unsettled by her vehemence. Even Fitz hadn't been this upset. "I wasn't exactly nice about it, but other than that—"

"You must have said something else." There was rising panic in her voice. "He's decided to move back to Boston."

"What? Why?"

"I don't know. I mean, I know our father has been trying to convince him to come back to the firm. He's retiring, and he wants Fitz to take over as CEO. But I don't know why Fitz suddenly decided tonight that he's taking the job, when up until a few hours ago, he was consistently telling the old man to go to hell."

I would have liked to pretend that I had no idea either, because that was much easier than admitting to her—or myself— that I had been the cause of his change of heart. But also, what did it matter, *why* he changed his mind? It wasn't my concern anymore. It couldn't be.

"Well." I cleared my throat uncomfortably. "If it's what Fitz wants."

"Of course you would say that. It would work out great for you if he shut down Maven and went back to Boston."

"That's not what I—" I cut myself off and started again. "Your family's firm is a thousand times bigger than Maven. If your father's retiring and Fitz would be in charge, then how is that so terrible?"

"Except my father won't retire. He's stepping down because he's an old fart who can't even magically peel a potato anymore without hurting himself, and no one wants a CEO who can't do all the big, flashy magic. Instead, my father will stay on the board so that he can keep controlling Fitz and making him miserable, and Fitzy will stay there and take it, because—because—I don't *know* why. That's what I'm trying to find out. So I can fix it."

"I'm sorry, Elinor," I said quietly. "I don't know what he's thinking. I wish I did."

It wasn't exactly a lie, but it certainly wasn't the truth either. For a few seconds, there was only the sound of her strained breathing.

"I've gotta go," she said at last.

"Goodbye," I said, but she'd already hung up.

I stared at the screen for a while, then called Fitz. It rang three times before going to voicemail, which meant he'd *sent* me to voicemail. My finger hovered over the call button, but I didn't try again. I climbed to my feet, scooped up my backpack, and trudged to the back stairs. I was newly exhausted and couldn't think of anything except bed.

I crept through the house, which was dark save for the light above the stove. There was a note taped to the vent hood in Mim's handwriting.

Pizza in the fridge. We can talk in the a.m. ♡

I filled up the kettle and grabbed a slice to eat cold while the water boiled. I licked my fingers clean and brought a mug of chamomile tea back to my bedroom to steep while I got ready for bed. By the time I was bundled in bed, sipping the last of my tea, I was ready to fall asleep sitting up. I shoved the mug to the far side of the nightstand where two other mugs had been languishing for who knows how long, then reached for the lamp switch. I hesitated with my hand hovering over my grimoire.

I knew it was stupid, but I couldn't resist flipping it open to the last page of my conversation with Fitz. The Dickosaurus rendition brought a smile to my face, followed by a pang of loss. There was no new message, and I told myself I wasn't allowed to be disappointed. I closed the book, flipped off the light, and curled up under my blanket.

And, of course, as soon as I was finally able to fall asleep, I was no longer even the tiniest bit sleepy. I tossed and turned and tossed some more. I rolled over periodically to check the clock. 10:43 P.M. 10:59 P.M. 11:12 P.M. 11:38 P.M. 12:14 A.M. 12:51 A.M. I wasn't sure if I was trying to reassure myself that I still had enough time for a decent night's sleep or if I was intent on torturing myself into submission.

I was finally, *finally* drifting off when my ringtone jolted me awake. I swore and pressed my hand to my chest while my heart rabbited wildly. I scrambled to grab my phone before it could wake up my parents. Why was I so popular tonight?

It was Jen. I'd barely gotten out my hello when she said, "Oh, thank god, you're still awake."

"Barely," I muttered. "What's wrong?"

"We've had three patients from Owl's Hollow admitted in the past couple hours. They're unconscious and mostly unresponsive. According to family, they went to sleep normally but couldn't be woken up again."

My brain rushed to keep up with what she was saying. I'd fallen into a parallel world where I was a doctor being called in the middle of the night for a consult, except I'd never graduated from medical school.

"Like . . . a coma?" I asked weakly.

"Almost, but not quite. We can wake them up for brief periods with extreme stimuli, but they fall right back into the stupor."

"Okay, that seems bad." I yawned. "But why are you telling me?"

"These people don't have any similarities—different ages, different backgrounds, different parts of town. Two have been at home most of the day, the other one was at the forum tonight. The only thing they have in common is that they're from Owl's Hollow. I think there's something bad going on there. Something magic."

CHAPTER TWENTY-NINE

Half an hour later, I was pacing the kitchen with Mama. We were both on our second cup of coffee and making our way down the contact lists in our phones. Mim had already been fast asleep when I hung up with Jen, but luckily Mama had been dealing with the same bout of insomnia as me. We tried waking up Mim. Like Jen had said, extreme stimuli (when Mama poured some ice water on her face) woke her up for a couple seconds. She grimaced and batted us away, then rolled over and went right back to sleep.

We decided the best thing we could do for her was figure out what the hell was going on. The first order of business was rallying the troops. Unfortunately, it was nearly two in the morning, so the troops were all asleep. Jen's sister, who lived a few towns over, was on her way to check on Bonnie, but I already knew she would be in the same magic sleep as everyone else. Bonnie's phone was an extension of her body, and she would have answered if she was awake. Tandy and the Wharburtons didn't answer either. Lucas's voicemail was full, which wasn't a surprise. He tended to forget he had a phone. Maybe we'd get lucky, and instead of sleeping he was astral projecting and would solve the mystery for us.

I called Fitz and Elinor again. I hadn't mentioned it to Mama, but I'd called them first, though I hadn't left voicemails the first time. This time when I got Fitz's voicemail I waited for the beep.

"If you get this, please call me right away." I tried to sound urgent but not desperate. I wasn't sure I succeeded. "There's something going on—just call me. Please."

I ended the call, then shot off a text saying basically the same thing. If he was awake, I knew he'd call me back, regardless of how I'd ended things. If he didn't call back, it meant he was already asleep. Which meant Mama and I had to face this newest threat alone.

Once we'd run out of people to call, we grabbed our grimoires and sat down at the kitchen table to start brainstorming cures. I was jotting down the list of our ideas, but after a few minutes, Mama's suggestions started to slow down. I looked up and saw her eyelids drooping.

"Mama," I snapped. "Don't even think about it."

"I'm sorry." Her words were slurred slightly. "I took my sleep medication like twenty minutes before your heroic rescue. In the cage match between coffee and prescription benzos . . . I'm too sleepy to finish the metaphor."

She stood up and went to refill her coffee anyway. I swallowed my unease and tried to focus on what I was writing.

Sleeping spell in reverse?

Custom sigil?

Mass cleansing?

I crossed through the last one. The spell in the graveyard had only worked because we had a coven's worth of witches casting in unison. There was no way Mama and I would be able to cast anything half as potent.

The obvious solution was the fairy ring. Assuming we could figure out the source of the curse, Mama could use that information to bind the wild magic of the fairy ring to her will. She could blanket the whole town with a spell reversal by herself.

If only *someone* hadn't wasted the magic a year ago and left the fairy ring wilted and powerless. Without it, a town-wide spell was out of the question. Mama was kind enough not to bring it up, but I knew who would be to blame if we couldn't save Owl's Hollow. I tried my best to keep the self-recrimination compartmentalized in the back of my brain. It wasn't helpful, even if it was deserved.

Trying to awaken every citizen individually was another option, but that was hardly a workable plan. There were people out there with medical conditions who needed to be able to wake up when their bodies demanded it, and people who had drifted off with a candle burning or an infant in the next room or—or—if I let myself think about it too much, the panic began to overwhelm me.

Mama came back to the table with her mug, and I eyed her skeptically.

"Maybe you should keep doing laps."

"My back hurts," she complained. "These old bones don't work like they used to."

I gave her a pointed glare. She dutifully started to pace from the kitchen through to the living room and back again. "If this thing is only affecting people in Owl's Hollow, then what if we drove out of town? We could find a hotel, get a couple hours of sleep."

"No such luck. Jen said that at least one person who'd come from Owl's Hollow with a family member fell asleep in the waiting room at the hospital and now they are in the same not-quite-coma as the others. Whatever this magic is, it's affecting anyone who was in Owl's Hollow when it was cast, no matter where they fall asleep."

"Wonderful." She trudged her way through the kitchen and back to the living room. "Maybe instead of a spell for waking we should focus more on healing."

"It's black magic, not a sickness," I murmured to myself, but wrote down the idea anyway. It wasn't like we could afford to be choosy right now.

I don't think she heard me, but she followed up with: "Or a curse removal. A basic one wouldn't be any good against this magnitude of magic, but . . ."

"We could modify one." I started flipping through my grimoire so I could bookmark a couple of my more successful curse removal spells. They weren't in particularly high demand in Owl's Hollow. There were only a few of us witches, and none of us had the time or inclination to go around hexing people. Of course, if this magic was the work of a mage, like Fitz suspected, then I wasn't sure a curse removal would do any good. I didn't know if magecraft had the same distinctions between white and black magic that witchcraft did. Their magic was graded more on the damage it did to the mage who cast it, so their rubric could range anywhere from "Easy-Peasy" to "Fuck Around and Find Out."

I found my most basic curse removal, but I was pretty sure I had a better one. If only I kept my grimoire in bullet journal format like Tandy did. Hers didn't fit the witchy aesthetic as well, but she never had trouble finding what she was looking for.

I was focused on thumbing through pages when it occurred to some distant part of my brain that Mama hadn't paced back through the kitchen in a couple minutes. A horrible certainty struck me that it was way too quiet in here. I jumped to my feet, nearly toppling over my chair, and sprinted to the living room.

I prayed I would find Mama standing at one of the bookshelves, lost in thought. Instead, I found her sitting on the couch, where she'd no doubt thought she would rest her back—and her eyes—for a second. I shook her shoulders once, in case she hadn't quite drifted off yet, but I knew before I'd even touched her that she was fast asleep. She looked so peaceful. It was hard not to resent that.

"Dammit, Mama." I did my best to at least maneuver her into a semicomfortable position. It was easier to be mad than anything else right now. I tucked her under the throw blanket, and she let out a contented sigh. Whatever this curse was, at least it was giving people pleasant dreams.

I grabbed her lukewarm coffee from the side table and downed it in four gulps, then went to use the bathroom and splash water on my face. I considered hopping into the shower, but I wasn't quite that far gone yet. And there wasn't time. At some point, no amount of cold water in the world was going to keep me awake. Then what would happen to Owl's Hollow? A town-wide sleeping curse would surely make the news, and every coven and magecraft firm in the tristate area would descend in hopes of capturing the glory of saving an entire town.

But for how many people would that be too late?

I grabbed my grimoire and my meager list from the table and moved them to the countertop so that I could stand while I worked. I wasn't going to take any chances. I flipped back through my grimoire, jotting down any ideas that came to me, no matter how half-baked. Every thirty seconds or so, I'd jab the silver pen into my palm until it hurt, to make sure I was still awake. If I somehow fell asleep without realizing it, I'd be damned if I was going to keep working in my dreams.

Soon I was going to have to stop writing down ideas and try

something. But the enormity of that task was too much to face right now. With Mama, our odds had been astronomical but not impossible. Alone, I wasn't sure I had enough hope in me to cast even the simplest of spells.

The page I was staring at blurred, and I fiercely scrubbed the tears away, even though there was no one here to witness me crying. Hell, that was *why* I was crying.

I reached the end of the useful pages in my grimoire. The last few were my conversations with Fitz over the past several weeks. I wanted to read them too, not because they would contain anything useful, but because maybe they would at least give me some fleeting joy before I failed miserably and doomed the whole town. Instead of reading, I flipped to the last page and wrote on a new line.

Please be there. I need you.

God, that was pathetic. And pointless. But I didn't care anymore. I was too sleepy to care about anything. Maybe Mama had the right idea. Maybe I needed to sit down for a second and rest my eyes. Maybe then a brilliant epiphany would hit me, and I wouldn't have to give up.

But that wasn't a useful line of thinking. Some part of me still realized that, which was a good sign. I stabbed my palm again with the pen, so hard I almost drew blood.

"More coffee," I told myself sternly. "Then you're going down to the work room to try some spells."

When ink letters started to form on the page beneath my shakily penned plea, I almost dismissed it as a trick of the light and slammed the book closed. But I blinked and rubbed my eyes, and the letters were still forming.

What's wrong?

I laughed out loud, mostly from exhaustion-induced hysteria. The sight was a jolt of adrenaline into my system. I snatched up the pen and scribbled, barely legible:

Check your fucking phone.

I started a new pot of coffee. I realized I was humming to myself, which seemed a little ridiculous, but also why not? At least now if I was going to fail, I didn't have to do it alone.

A minute later my phone rang, and I answered it before it had even finished the first ring.

"I turned off my phone because Elinor wouldn't stop calling me." Fitz sounded perplexed but not panicked, which meant that wherever he was—probably his office—he was oblivious to the town's newest peril. "What's going on?"

I gave him the spiel as quickly as I could manage, which was not very quick at all because a superabundance of caffeine could only keep me conscious, not coherent. I missed my college days, when my body could take three hours of sleep and an energy drink and turn it into enough inspiration to research and write a ten-page paper overnight.

Once Fitz understood everything, he was quiet for a long while. I already knew what he was going to say before he spoke.

"I need to check on Elinor."

"Okay." It wouldn't make a difference to him that I'd had no luck reaching her by phone. "After that, meet me at the Cottage. We haven't reset the counterspell yet."

"I will," Fitz said. I could hear his car starting in the background.

"And please don't fall asleep." I tried to keep my tone light and airy, like I had no doubt we would be able to reverse this latest magic conundrum, but I was pretty sure I just sounded bleak.

"I won't." The gentle cadence of his voice was more comforting than it had any right to be. "Bye, Charlie."

"Bye, Fitz."

CHAPTER THIRTY

I figured I had at least an hour before Fitz arrived. Reversing the spell on the town couldn't be done from the comfort of the warm kitchen. I wasn't sure yet what we were going to do, but whatever it was, we were going to need a lot of magic. Possibly more than either of us had to offer.

I shed my pajamas and hopped into a cold shower for a few minutes before putting on the same jeans and T-shirt I'd worn to the forum. I slipped on my sneakers and checked on Mama and Mim one last time. Still sleeping soundly.

I headed downstairs with my phone, grimoire, and list in hand. I flipped on the lights and was momentarily stunned by the pitiful state of the shop before I remembered our visitor from the night before. I groaned and scanned my list. Some of these rituals would require a lot of specific items and ingredients that I wasn't sure had survived the intruder.

I put my grimoire and list on the table and surveyed the work room, which remained a mess despite all my efforts today. I pulled my damp hair into a ponytail and got to work trying to bring some semblance of order to the chaos. Maybe it wasn't the best use of my time right now, but at least I would stay awake. After forty-five minutes, I had sweated off any freshness my shower had given me, and the work room, while not exactly neat, was now organized into neat piles. I'd even lit some sandalwood incense to help clear negative energy.

Fitz would be here any minute, so I went back upstairs to use the bathroom—all that coffee was going straight through me— and fix my hair yet again. With my bladder empty, I was ready for more coffee. My mug from earlier was still mostly full. It was tepid, but I wasn't about to waste it, since caffeine was at a premium now. I heard the muffled sound of the bell in the shop, so instead of sticking my mug into the microwave, I dumped in a handful of ice cubes and some extra cream. Starbucks, eat your heart out.

I headed downstairs, careful to keep the mug level. I was a few steps from the bottom when Sophie emerged from wherever she'd been hiding and darted under my feet in what I can only assume was an attempt to murder me. I tripped down the last steps, but fortunately, my body regained its sense of self-preservation in the nick of time, and I caught myself with one hand on the banister and the other braced on the wall. Unfortunately, that meant my coffee ended up flying through the air—and right at Fitz's head.

He did catch the mug before it collided with his face. The number of beverages I'd flung at him since we'd met must have really honed his reflexes.

"Sorry," I said. Sophie meowed and headbutted the back of my ankle, and I nudged her away with my toe. I knew better than to think she was apologizing. More likely she was trying, ineffectively, to finish the job.

"I guess I should be glad it's not hot." Fitz swiped a hand

across his dripping face. His white collared shirt had a huge brown stain on it now. At least he wasn't wearing one of his expensive ties.

"How's Elinor?" I figured there wasn't any need to waste time with more apologies when he had proved more than once that a beverage in the face wasn't any undue hardship. My resolution to stop ruining his shirts was obviously no match for my mom's homicidal cat.

"Asleep," Fitz said, which wasn't a surprise. I took the empty mug from him and led the way to the work room. "I managed to wake her up for almost a minute but then she was out again."

"That makes you more successful than a glass of ice water."

"Her roommate works the night shift, so she was still awake. She promised to keep an eye on Elinor."

"That's good." I couldn't bring myself to look his way again. There was something off about him. His uncharacteristic terseness was unsettling. Had I pissed him off that much? He'd seemed fine on the phone but maybe he changed his mind on the way over here. Or maybe the fourth drink I'd thrown on him was the straw that broke the camel's back. I knew I should probably address it, but ignoring it seemed like a much easier option, so I went with that instead.

"I've got a pot of coffee upstairs that should still be warm." I flattened out the list of spells on the table, then flipped idly through my grimoire without any particular purpose in mind. I needed something to do with my hands. "I think we should probably set up down here, though, so I have all my supplies."

More uneasy silence. It was hard to remain nonchalant when he still hadn't said anything. I shut my grimoire. We didn't have time to stand around being awkward. "Let's grab some coffee and get to work."

"I think I need to sit down for a minute first."

I finally turned, ready to tell him he was absolutely not allowed to sit down for even a minute, because if he dozed off
before we'd even gotten started, then I would do worse than
pour iced coffee on him. But now I saw that he hadn't magically
erased the previous cup of coffee yet. Under the bright overhead
light, he was blanched of all color—in both his face and his
aura—and swaying on his feet.

"Shit." I scanned the room for a chair, but the only unbroken
one was currently stacked high with the books and boxes of
inventory that I'd been sorting. Fitz staggered back to lean
against the wall and slid to the floor. I gave up locating a chair
and ran to help him make it to the ground without a concus-
sion. Leave it to Fitz to waste away in polite silence while I
flung coffee at him and wasted time poking around my grimoire. I wanted to yell at him for not saying something sooner—
for even risking the drive over here when he was obviously
half-unconscious himself. But I decided, in a rare moment of
maturity, that maybe the situation called for a little more compassion. "Exactly how hard did you try to wake Elinor up?"

"I'm fine," he murmured, rubbing his hands over his face.

I couldn't tell if he was purposefully sidestepping my question or if he was having trouble concentrating on what I was
saying.

"You're an idiot." So much for compassion.

"She's my sister." His tone might have been defensive, if he'd
had any energy to put behind it. "I had to try."

Be nice, Charlie. For fuck's sake, is it really that difficult?

I took a long, deliberate breath, willing my raging nerves to
settle.

"I know." And I didn't even point out that if Elinor were
here, she'd be calling him an idiot too. Maturity. "You need to
rest, but don't fall asleep."

"I'm fine," he said again. He looked like he was thinking about trying to stand, so I planted both hands on his shoulders. His eyes were a little bleary but otherwise he appeared lucid enough. That had to be a good sign.

"Don't move." I tried to strike a balance between nice and authoritative. "I can help."

I didn't actually know if I could help, but I had to try, didn't I? He hadn't even looked this bad on the day he ended the Whiteout, and Elinor said he'd gone home and slept for two straight days after that. He was on borrowed time right now.

I found the apothecary drawer labeled *Peppermint* and was relieved to see that there were still a few dried leaves in it. Normally I'd make a tea, but no time for that.

"Here, chew on these." I pressed them into his hand. He stared blankly down at his palm, like he was having trouble processing what I'd said. No time for that either. I took the leaves and held them up to his lips. "Open."

He did as he was told, probably more from reflex than anything else, because when I deposited the leaves on his tongue, he seemed startled, first by my fingers in his mouth and then by the bite of the peppermint.

"Chew," I said. "It'll make you feel better."

But not by much and not for long. When I was certain he was chewing and no longer on the verge of passing out, I retrieved my grimoire and opened it on the workbench. I had plenty of spells for healing and renewed energy, but I decided on the more potent restoration spell. We used a lesser version of it in a spell jar, one of our most popular products, so I knew we probably had all the necessary ingredients on hand, even if some of them had been rescued from the remnants of smashed jars that morning.

I scurried around the shop and work room, sourcing my materials in a jittery, caffeine-induced haze. At this point I wasn't even sure I'd be clear-minded enough to cast a simple blessing, much less a powerful restoration. On the other hand, without the caffeine I'd probably be facedown on the floor in an enchanted sleep right now.

By the time I knelt back down beside Fitz with my armful of treasures, his eyelids were dangerously heavy.

"I'll be okay," he said, with wincing effort. "I just need a minute."

I ignored him and tied my red ribbon around my wrist. I retrieved the incense stick that was still sending up lazy spirals of smoke from the table so that I could cleanse the space around us. At this point, I was pretty sure he wouldn't be able to move, even if he tried. When Fitz coughed, I figured the space was cleansed enough and pressed the tip of the stick into the metal holder to break off the ember. I pushed the holder aside to set up my makeshift altar. Normally I would have used a table, because usually Fitz would have been sitting across the table from me. We would have to make the best of things.

Most of the handheld mirrors in the shop had been smashed, but I'd found one with only a single crack down the middle that I hoped wouldn't hurt anything. I placed the mirror on his lap and put a green pillar candle on top. The wax also had a crack in it. With forceful optimism, I decided to hope that the symmetry would improve the spell.

I fished two tiger's eye stones out of my pocket and tucked one into each of his hands. His grip wasn't exactly iron, but he didn't drop them. I unscrewed the cap from a small vial of rosemary oil and tipped a few droplets onto my finger. His breath stuttered as I leaned closer, and my heart skipped in response. I anointed his forehead with the tilted X of Nauthiz, a rune for strength and endurance. While I was at it, I anointed my own forehead with Isa to calm my mind and focus my will. It was a vertical line, so I didn't need to fuss with drawing any complicated shapes in reverse.

I patted down my pockets before realizing I'd forgotten to grab a book of matches. Before I could climb to my feet, Fitz made a feeble gesture, and the candle sparked to life.

"Stop that," I said.

"I told you I'm fine."

"Yes, several times now, but somehow I still don't believe you." I picked up my malachite stone and pointed it at him meaningfully. "Maybe it's the way you're drifting ever closer to unconsciousness."

He frowned faintly at the altar I'd set up in his lap.

"Is this going to hurt?"

"Only when I cut out your heart. Once the actual sacrificing starts, you won't notice."

He made a wheezing sound that I thought was a laugh.

"I need to meditate for a while," I told him. "Please don't fall asleep in the middle of this. It would be a waste of perfectly good magic." I didn't think this spell was strong enough to break the sleeping curse, although I guessed if he drifted off then we would find out.

"I promise." There was a distinct lack of conviction in his tone, but the only thing to do was forge ahead.

With the malachite clasped tightly between my hands, I closed my eyes and searched for a quiet center within myself. The Isa rune was already working, smoothing the jagged edges of my caffeine high and honing my intentions to a sharp point.

Normally for a spell like this, I would have meditated for at least ten minutes before trying to channel any magic, but time was of the essence. I had to balance the level of focus needed to cast the spell with how much longer Fitz could stay awake.

When I opened my eyes, he was watching me, and I almost

lost all that hard-earned focus. Using the malachite, I traced a cross through the flame, delineating the four cardinal directions. The nice thing about working in the shop was that I knew where true north was without using a compass.

"Stare into the flame," I said, not quite looking at him. When he finally shifted his attention from my face to the candle, it was like I'd dropped from sunlight into shade. I had to clear my throat before I could speak again. "Squeeze the tiger's eyes as hard as you can and imagine you're drawing warmth from them. Feel the warmth travel up your arms, across your chest, and into your heart."

As I spoke, the malachite in my hand was warming as well. I purposefully blocked myself off from the flow of the energy—it wasn't for me. When the malachite was close to burning my skin and the directionless energy churned like a rushing river against a dam, I pressed the tip of the crystal to Fitz's chest, right over his heart, and opened the floodgates.

His head snapped back like he'd been struck, and his whole body tensed. He sucked in a lungful of oxygen, his eyes squeezed shut. Magic settled over him in a fine mist, shimmering on his skin, clinging like dew to his eyelashes and lips.

The spell was so potent that ripples were washing over me even as I channeled it toward Fitz. As it tapered off, every fiber of my being vibrated with restored energy.

"Fuck," Fitz whispered. "That was . . . incredible." When he opened his eyes, they were clear and shining. I hadn't realized how close we were, breathing the same air. He smelled of mint and rosemary and the distinct tang of magic. At some point, I'd pressed my hand flush against his chest, my fingers grasping his shirt, the malachite cooling rapidly against my palm.

I told myself I had to let go of him, but my body wouldn't obey. *Just let go.*

I released his shirt and sat back on my heels.

"How do you feel?" I asked.

"Normal." He opened his hands to examine the tiger's eyes curiously. "Better than normal."

"You don't have to sound so surprised about it." I blew out the candle and took the stones from him.

"I'm not." He set the mirror and candle to the side so he could stand. "Well, maybe a little."

He extended a hand to help me up. I took it, against my better judgment.

"Careful, I might decide to reverse it." I expected him to drop my hand but instead his grip tightened slightly.

"Thanks, Charlie," he said softly. His thumb brushed against my knuckles in a way that sent tingles all the way up my arm. Vestiges of magic. Probably.

"You're welcome." I dropped one of the tiger's eyes into his shirt pocket and slid the other into the back pocket of my jeans. They would be charged with good energy for a while yet, and we could use the extra boost tonight. Making Fitz fighting fit was the easy part. Now we had a town-wide curse to lift. "Consider it payment for the butterflies. I'd say we're even now."

"Technically, the butterflies were how I paid you back for dinner on our first date." The corners of his lips tugged with a smile that didn't quite materialize. He still hadn't let go of my hand.

"I guess you owe me one, then." My voice stuck a little in my throat. I wished he hadn't brought up our first date. It made me think of everything that came after, the good and the bad. I'd told him it was over between us. I'd told him I *wanted* it to be over. It felt like years, but it was only hours ago. Nothing had changed. *Let go. Let go.*

I pulled my hand free and turned away from him, pretending to be invested in putting away the materials from the spell. I wanted to fill up the charged, uncomfortable silence with more rambling, but I didn't trust my voice not to wobble. I kept my hands busy and tried to marshal my composure, which was hard when my mind kept drifting back to that night on his couch, the first time he'd opened up to me, and how it had only whetted my appetite to know more of him, to know all of him. And now I'd never get the chance.

Despite my malaise of regret and self-pity, something clicked into place in my brain.

"The butterflies," I said aloud.

"What about them?"

I didn't even know, at first. My brain raced to catch up with itself. The perpetual motion of the butterflies was not something that either of us could have accomplished alone, but his magecraft had jump-started my witchcraft.

I thought about the wilted fairy ring. My parents had always thought there might be a way to recharge it manually, but to my knowledge, no witch had ever succeeded.

Could a mage?

Fitz was still waiting patiently for me to explain myself. I met his gaze and was once again struck with the feeling of perfect harmony. Maybe our lives—and our hearts—were doomed to be always out of rhythm, but for this one night, we had managed to be in the right place at the right time.

"Have I ever told you how Chanterelle Cottage got its name?"

CHAPTER THIRTY-ONE

Before we could try regenerating the fairy ring, I needed to use the scrying glass. There was no way around it. Tarot and tea leaves were too vague for my purposes, and pendulums were too narrowly specific. Since I didn't want to guess at what the cards were trying to tell me or play twenty questions with my pendulum, scrying was the best method for finding the truth I sought.

We weren't even sure if Fitz would be able to bring the mushrooms back to their full potency, though he was willing to try. But the magic would be useless to me if I didn't uncover the source of this sleeping curse. I needed absolute clarity on what I was trying to accomplish if I wanted to bind the magic to my will. I couldn't afford to make the same mistake as last time.

I figured that even if my idea to recharge the ring didn't work, knowing who had cursed Owl's Hollow—and why— would be useful information in itself. So that should be the first order of business.

The problem was that I disliked the scrying glass under the best of circumstances, wide awake and with both my parents on hand to keep me from straying too far into the void. Right now,

I was wired with anxiety, buzzed on caffeine and remnant magic, and alone, except for a mage who knew next to nothing about witchcraft in general, much less the delicate and dangerous art of scrying. A mage I had dumped a few hours ago in a public parking lot.

But it wouldn't do any good to dwell on the negatives of this situation. There were far, far too many, and I would only succeed in damaging my focus beyond repair. I cleared my mind as best as I could while I knelt in front of the obsidian glass, which had thankfully survived the intruder's rampage.

I'd already drawn my sacred circle and lit the white candles on either side of the glass. I'd used matches this time, much to Fitz's annoyance. I don't think he was accustomed to feeling so useless. I did cast the circle around both of us. I wasn't sure how much help Fitz would be if I got into trouble, but it wasn't like I had any other option.

"Will you get the light?" I asked Fitz, who was kneeling across from me. He shot me a look like he suspected I was patronizing him but made a gesture and cast us into darkness. A bit dramatic, considering the light switch was five feet away, but I didn't say anything.

I waited a minute for my vision to adjust to the wavering candlelight. I'd forgotten how creepy the scrying glass was, the way it seemed to swallow the light rather than reflect it.

"Are you sure this is safe?" Fitz asked.

I didn't know if he'd caught on to my own trepidation or if he could also sense the vague hint of menace beneath the obsidian's surface.

"It's . . . mostly safe." I only saw flickers of his face in between shadows, but I could guess what he was thinking. "I'll be fine. I've done it before. Just don't let me get lost in there."

"What do you mean?" he asked with alarm. "How the hell am I supposed to do that?"

"Relax." I reached out to pat his hand where it rested on the floor. "I'm joking."

I wasn't joking. I think he knew that. But he also knew he couldn't talk me out of it, and so he thankfully didn't try. He did shift his hand to interlace his fingers with mine, and I let him. Maybe it was a potential distraction, but I couldn't give up that single point of connection in the darkness. I didn't want to be alone.

I took a deep breath and bent forward to stare into the glass. My vision unfocused, sending me down, down, down into the blackness, until I was floating in it, untethered. In the past when I had attempted scrying, I always let the glass take me where it willed. It was easier and safer that way. But tonight, I needed specific answers to specific questions, which meant I had to exert my own will onto the void.

It was too vast to search—somehow both empty and fraught. I tried to call the answers to me, sending out my questions, demanding a response. For a long time, the incorporeal universe was unyielding, uninterested in my presumption, but I kept pushing. I could be stubborn too. More stubborn than the universe itself? I guessed we would find out tonight.

At last, there was a stirring in the firmament, a hint that maybe I was being heard. I leaned into it, pushing so hard that the edges of my consciousness were fraying with the strain.

Who is doing this to Owl's Hollow?

I ripped through the thin veil of shadows and fell back into reality. But I wasn't in the Cottage. I was in an unfamiliar bedroom. The scene was hazy and streaked with shadows, like I had swiped a hand over a soot-covered windowpane to peer through. Judging by the posters on the wall, the assortment of sporting equipment piled in the corner, and the stack of textbooks on the desk, the room belonged to a teenager. I blinked, and the scene clarified further. There was someone on the bed, curled on their side and hugging a pillow. At first, I thought they were asleep, but then I saw that they were shaking with body-racking sobs. I blinked again, and everything was clear now. It was Anthony Hawthorn.

My heart broke a little at the sight of him. He was somehow even more pale and gaunt than he'd been yesterday before the party. The dark circles under his eyes were cavernous. He'd told me that his sleep was plagued with nightmares, but right now it looked like he hadn't slept for days.

This was all starting to make a terrible sort of sense. Fitz had predicted that the culprit was a young mage lacking control of his magic. At sixteen, Anthony would be bursting with nascent power. Was it enough to send an entire town into chaos thrice without killing himself from the strain? I was skeptical.

But then again, he'd stolen those spell jars and magic-infused tea bags from us, among other assorted witchcraft paraphernalia. My restoration spell had been enough to bring Fitz back from the brink. Maybe the Cottage's wares had done the same for Anthony. Even considering the magnitude of the Whiteout and the Animal Pox, that might have been enough to keep him out of the hospital, barely. From the look of him now, he'd run out of spells to co-opt.

The last time I'd used the scrying glass, Fitz had sensed me spying on him in his office. I wondered if Anthony might be able to sense me too. Tentatively, I reached out to him with my mind, worried that if I caused too much disruption, I'd snap out of the scene entirely. Anthony shot upright and looked around wildly like someone had called his name.

I tried to let him know it was me. I didn't want to scare the poor kid, but if I could convince him to come to the Cottage, maybe he could do something to help us fix this. Or at least maybe there was something we could do to help *him*. But I had no idea where he lived and doubted Fitz would either.

"I'm sorry," Anthony wailed. He was still shuddering with sobs. "I'm so sorry. I didn't mean to. I didn't mean for any of this to happen."

I believed him. A teenager accidentally unleashing enough magic to cripple our town was frightening, but it wasn't un-heard of. When a mage was first coming into their power, the magic manifested in odd ways, often unconsciously mirroring the mage's desires—turning dinner into ice cream, for instance.

Anthony must have figured out that the Whiteout and the Animal Pox were his doing. He'd fought with his mother about doing his homework, and all the written words in the town vanished. His mother refused to let him have a pet, and people—including his mother—started turning into animals. Now he was desperate for sleep, and Owl's Hollow couldn't wake up.

But considering his mother's antipathy for magic, it was no surprise he hadn't told her what was happening. No surprise that he would rather suffer in silence—and burgle the local witches—than tell the truth. Judging from his current state, his attempts to deal with this on his own had cost him dearly.

He wiped some of the tears and snot from his face with a sleeve and went on, voice quavering.

"When I went to Chanterelle Cottage last night, I only wanted to talk to you, I swear. I wanted to apologize about my mom and bring back the stuff I stole. But then the shop was empty, and I saw you all in the backyard having a party and—and—I was so tired. And so angry. I haven't been able to sleep in days, and no one will help me, and when I saw you there, laughing and goofing off—it just happened, and I couldn't stop it. And I tried to fix it, but I was even more tired than before, so I left. I'm sorry."

A mage had been responsible for the sabotage of the Cottage after all, but not the one that the sheriff suspected.

I tried to express to him that it was okay, that everything was going to be okay, even though I wasn't sure I believed it myself. But I was falling backward out of the scene. I'd meddled too much, made a nuisance of myself, and now the void was pulling me away. I tried to hang on, but I'd lost any control I had, and soon I was drifting aimlessly in the darkness again. I needed to return to the physical world. I had no idea how long I'd been scrying, but I knew instinctively that it was too long. My iron will was eroding, and I was at the whim of the universe now.

Images flitted past me, and I was tossed on waves of emotions, from the crest of ecstasy to the depths of sorrow. I struggled to right myself, to shake off the cacophony of visions and return to my body.

But in the distance, so far away it was a pinprick of light on my consciousness, I saw the answer to the question I hadn't meant to ask but nonetheless had been radiating like the Bat-Signal into the darkness.

Is Chanterelle Cottage going to survive?

Even as I swam toward that distant shore, I heard Mim's voice in my memory, warning me to not seek out the future in the glass. *The universe doesn't give answers for free.*

I was going too deep, too far without a tether. I knew I wasn't going to be able to find my way back, but still I dove deeper and deeper, chasing the light that remained just out of reach. My thoughts were ragged and painful. My mind was closing in on itself, like it was starved of oxygen and shutting down.

There was a tug on my hand, faint as a ghost. I looked down, only to remember that I was outside my body. I didn't have a hand here, only a consciousness that was sailing ever further away from the Charlie who was kneeling in the shop.

Another tug, harder this time, insistent but still easy to ignore. I was so close to my answer. The light was gleaming ahead of me like a guiding star. If I stretched a little further, if I disconnected entirely from the anchor of my body, then I could reach out and—

"Charlie!" Fitz's voice resonated inside me, so loud that it hurt.

I was flung backward—no, not flung. Pulled. I was being yanked back through the void with dizzying speed. When I reached the edge, the universe tried to keep me, tightening the cords of darkness that I hadn't even realized were coiling around me. But there was one more almighty tug, and I snapped out of the trance and into my body with a force that knocked me flat on my back.

My head spiraled from the shock, and my stomach lurched with nausea. My lungs were so constricted that even a few deep breaths didn't completely ease the ache in my chest. It took me a few seconds to even register that the overhead light was back on, and a few seconds more to realize that the reason everything was blurry was that my eyes were filled with tears.

"Charlie, are you okay?" Fitz's face swam into view, his concern palpable.

I bolted upright, and Fitz dodged out of the way in time to narrowly avoid our foreheads colliding. I slammed my hand down on the obsidian.

"We're done," I told it. Relief filled me as the last traces of darkness faded from my head. I blew out the candles.

"You said this was safe." There was no missing the accusation in Fitz's tone. He was glaring at me like I'd kicked his dog.

"It is."

"Are you fucking kidding me right now?" he demanded. "You stopped *breathing*, Charlie. For almost a full minute."

That would explain my dizziness and the faint ache in my lungs. The surface of the obsidian glass was flat and harmless in the garish light. There had been a moment when I was ready to lose myself to the siren call of the void. Fitz's fingers were close to mine on the wooden floor, and I thought of the tug I'd felt, the unrelenting pull that had been stronger than the darkness I was mired in. Belatedly, I realized that what I'd interpreted as his anger was in fact worry, sharpened to a razor's edge.

"I'm safe now," I said.

"You're unbelievable." He pulled his hand away and stood up. "You shouldn't have done that."

Any comfort I'd taken in his solicitude evaporated. Irritation sizzled under my skin, and I scrambled to my feet.

"First, you don't get to tell me what to do, and second, why do you even care?"

He shot me a confused frown.

"What?"

"Elinor told me you're moving back to Boston. Owl's Hollow isn't your problem anymore, and neither am I."

He shook his head.

"This town is—it was supposed to be my new home." He ran a hand through his hair and paced a few steps away from me. "Owl's Hollow has never been a problem to me."

"And me?" I asked, staring at his back. He didn't turn around.

"The real question is why do *you* care? I thought you'd be happy." He took a deep breath, but instead of relaxing, the line of his shoulders stiffened. He turned slowly. "I'm shutting down Maven. Isn't that what you wanted?"

"Is it even what *you* want?" A tremor ran through my voice, and I had to take a moment to steady myself. "Do you want to work for your father again?"

"He's retiring."

"Elinor said—"

"Elinor doesn't know anything about it," he said, with a flash of pique, "and neither do you."

His uncharacteristically blistering tone gave me pause, but not for long.

"You told me that you weren't going back." I found that I couldn't hold his heated gaze and dropped my eyes, fiddling with the hem of my shirt. Between his father and his ex-fiancée, Fitz hadn't left Boston—he'd escaped. And last night, he'd been so sure that he was never going back. Only one thing had changed since then.

"You told me that the two of us can't coexist in Owl's Hollow." Accusation laced his words again, softer this time, but unmistakable. He took a tentative step in my direction. "You told me you wanted it to be over, Charlie. And now, what, you've changed your mind?"

He sounded more annoyed than hopeful, which stung. I was tempted to ask if going back to Boston also meant going back to Gwen, but I pushed the thought aside. I didn't have any claim on him, and I didn't have any right to tell him how to live his life.

Even though I knew logically that was true, and even though I knew that I couldn't have it both ways—that if I wanted to protect the Cottage, I couldn't be involved with Fitz—there was still a not-insignificant part of me that wanted to beg him to stay. I cared about him. I didn't want him to go back to living under his father's thumb, even if he was the competitor running my family out of business.

I didn't want him to leave but couldn't ask him to stay.

He was watching me intently, and I realized he was waiting on my answer. But "yes" was impossible and "no" was a lie. I wasn't sure what else there was to say.

"We don't have time for this." My voice cracked on the last word, and I swallowed hard. "I figured out who's responsible for the sleep magic—for everything. It was Anthony Hawthorn."

He searched my face for a few moments longer, and my cheeks flushed under the weight of it. I wished I knew what he was looking for.

"The kid?" he asked finally. "Are you sure?"

It was a tremendous effort not to heave a sigh of relief when he accepted the change in subject. I willed my voice to steady and told him what I'd seen and what Anthony had told me.

"We have to help him," Fitz said.

"We have to help the town first." I picked up my grimoire from the table and hugged it to my chest, hoping to soak up some solace from the familiar weight of it. I had all the knowledge I needed to use the fairy ring, but that didn't mean that I had the strength to bind the magic to my will. Some cowardly, treacherous part of me hoped that Fitz wouldn't be able to recharge the mushrooms, because then I'd never have to face my own ineptitude.

But more than that, I wished my parents were here, to save me from the possibility of my own failure.

You got this, bitch, I told myself.

"Are you okay?" Fitz asked. All the ire from before had drained from his voice, leaving behind a dull weariness that wasn't necessarily better. I realized my trepidation must be written on my features and tried to reset my expression into something approaching confidence. Shopgirl was made of sterner stuff than this.

"Yes," I said, and I almost believed it.

CHAPTER THIRTY-TWO

Before we could leave, I had some preparations to make. It took me close to an hour (and a fresh pot of coffee) to draw up plans in my grimoire and gather the necessary materials from the shop. By the time Fitz and I made our way into the backyard, the dark sky was softening at the edges with the first blush of dawn. I readjusted the tote bag straps on my shoulder and led the way to a hidden path behind the gazebo. We didn't put much effort into upkeep of the trail, so it was overgrown and only slightly easier to traverse than the woods around us.

"I feel like I should have brought hiking shoes," Fitz said. "Or a machete."

I wanted to give a witty reply, but my stomach was a wreck of nerves, and my brain was too focused on the upcoming task to offer me anything approaching cleverness.

"It's not far," I managed.

We walked for another few minutes in tense, awkward silence. The acres of forest behind the Cottage were my family's property, though we didn't begrudge the occasional local forager or young couple looking for a secluded rendezvous spot. In warmer months, Lucas would hang a hammock and spend a few weeks communing with nature. But everyone who ventured into the woods knew to avoid the clearing where we were headed. We hadn't put up a sign or fence, but we didn't need to. The glen itself emanated a strange, subtle sense of warning.

The clearing was carpeted with fallen leaves and decaying wood, damp from rainfall and interspersed with patches of grass and clover. Delineating the glade was a fifty-foot circle of mushrooms.

"Golden chanterelles," I said, as Fitz stopped at my side to survey the scene.

Right now, they were brown instead of their usual vibrant yellow, but the effect of the ring was still striking. The mycelium of this particular fungus system had been expanding since my many-greats-grandparents had first purchased the land and planted the spores they'd brought from Ireland. There was no reason this precise species of *Cantharellus cibarius* should have been able to grow this far away from its natural habitat, but that didn't stop the mushrooms from springing back year after year.

Fitz eyed the chanterelles with a mix of interest and suspicion.

"It's one of the largest rings in the country," I added. I wasn't sure why I'd devolved into tour guide mode when there was work to be done. I found a nearby tree with a broken branch where I could hang my tote bag and started rifling through the contents to ensure I hadn't forgotten anything.

"Elinor is going to be furious that I saw this before she did. She's obsessed with these things."

"My parents are shamelessly susceptible to flattery, so I wouldn't be surprised if they already showed her this and swore her to secrecy."

Fitz crouched down for a better look at the mushrooms, though he didn't seem inclined to move any closer.

"I won't pretend I understood all of Elinor's thesis, but according to her, fairy rings can be dangerous."

I paused and looked up from the bag.

"You read her thesis?"

"Yes," he said with a touch of defensiveness. "So?"

"Nothing. It's sweet." I needed to stop discovering how much this man loved his sisters. It was catnip for a single child like me. I'd told him it was over between us, and I'd meant it. Or at least I wanted to mean it. "Anyway, fairy rings aren't dangerous. They're . . . finicky."

He stood up and gave me a look that spoke volumes, which I ignored.

"Don't step inside the ring until I tell you to, and you'll be fine." I started around the circle in a clockwise direction. "Now come on. We have to circle it nine times."

"Are you serious?"

"I told you—finicky."

He regarded me with slightly narrowed eyes, like he wasn't convinced that this wasn't some kind of hazing ritual. When I kept walking, he finally fell in behind me.

"Am I at least allowed to ask the point of this?"

"What's the point of any tradition?" I double-checked that my red ribbon was still secure around my wrist. "You can't expect to make use of nature's magic without showing a little respect first."

"So why nine times?"

"Because ten is one too many."

"You're doing this on purpose."

"I don't know what you're talking about," I said airily. I used my fingers to keep track of our progress, not trusting my sapped brain.

"Is this even going to work?"

I bristled at the question, though I could tell from his tone that he wasn't questioning my competence, but rather the enormity of the situation itself. I took a deep breath. Even in their wilted state, the mushrooms emitted a faintly fruity smell, like apricots.

"I hope so."

After our ninth circumnavigation of the fairy ring, I retrieved the materials from my tote bag. I had to pile some of them into Fitz's arms, which he accepted without comment. I steeled myself and stepped inside the ring. Fitz hesitated at the edge but followed suit. When he didn't immediately burst into flames, he relaxed marginally.

I'd given it some real thought earlier, and I decided to set up the components of the ritual before Fitz tried to recharge the ring. There wasn't exactly an instruction book on this—as far as I knew, it had never been tried before—but I hoped that the structure of the compass round would help the mushrooms retain the magic that Fitz would feed them.

I oriented myself in the circle using the sunrise. Instead of finding suitable representations of the elements in the disorganization of the shop, I'd grabbed my tarot deck. The mango wood box had been thrown out of its drawer during Anthony's episode, but the cards and crystal inside were untouched. Despite the time crunch, I took the time to draw a single card, hoping for some guidance. The Two of Swords in reverse, suggesting confusion, uncertainty about the future, and being caught between a rock and a hard place.

"A little on the nose," I muttered.

"What is it?" Fitz peered over my shoulder at the card.

"Nothing." I shoved it back into the deck. Strictly speaking, I should have taken some time to meditate over the card, tried to glean some wisdom for how to best handle my rock and hard place. Maybe later.

I flipped through the cards to pull out the Ace of Swords,

which I placed face up in the grass on the eastern edge of the ring.

"Will you hand me the celestite?" I extended my hand toward Fitz, who was holding the pouch of crystals I'd packed.

"Am I supposed to know what that is?" he asked dryly.

"In the bag. It's the light blue one."

He fished it out and handed it to me. I'd already cleansed all the crystals in a bowl of black salt, but they still needed to be charged. I held the smooth piece of celestite in my palm and blew on it softly, then set it on top of the Ace of Swords.

"The ruby next." I thumbed through the cards to locate the Ace of Wands. "It's the red one," I added, but Fitz was already holding it out to me with an expression that suggested he didn't appreciate my condescension.

I placed the card on the southern edge of the circle, then patted my pockets in search of the book of matches that I'd evidently forgotten to bring.

"I don't suppose you could provide a little fire for this?" I asked, holding up the ruby.

"What are you doing exactly?"

"Each of the cardinal directions corresponds with an element." It was an effort to keep the impatience out of my tone. There was a reason I didn't like casting spells with a lay audience. "I need to charge the stones with their respective elements."

"More pointless traditions?" His tone reminded me of the first day we met, and not in a nice, nostalgic way, but in an I-can't-believe-I-forgot-how-smarmy-and-absolutely-infuriating-this-man-can-be way.

"Look, if you can't help, then I'll go get some damn matches." I whirled on my heel.

"Charlie, wait." He caught me by the elbow. "For fuck's sake, you don't have to bite my head off. I'm trying to understand. This stuff doesn't make much sense to me. It never has."

I shook his hand off and turned on him.

"This *stuff* is not a parlor trick. It's not a game."

"I know that."

"My magic is just as serious as yours." I tried to calm my racing heart. He was right that there was no need to bite his head off. But my nerves were so brittle, it was like my composure had been snapped into pieces. "I don't have to justify any of it to you."

"I'm not asking you to justify it." He held out his hand, palm up. For a second, I thought he wanted me to take it, but then a small orange flame appeared, hovering a few inches above his skin. "I just want to understand."

I pressed my lips together. Part of me still wanted to storm back to the house and retrieve the matches, but that would be needlessly contrary. I couldn't do this on my own. And maybe if Fitz understood what I was trying to accomplish, he'd have an easier time regenerating the fairy ring to make it possible.

Or maybe it didn't matter regardless, and this was all an exercise in futility. But that wasn't a useful line of thinking. We were running out of time.

I held the ruby between my thumb and forefinger and passed it back and forth through the flame until it was warm. I also took a moment to recenter myself. I wouldn't be able to cast even a beginner spell with my current state of emotional imbalance.

"Thanks," I murmured, not meeting Fitz's eye. I placed the ruby on the Ace of Wands. "The dark blue crystal is lapis lazuli."

"Water, I'm guessing?"

"Gold star for you." I shuffled through the deck. "Water is also associated with the west and the tarot suit of Cups."

I slid the Ace of Cups from the deck and put it on the ground. By the time I turned around, Fitz was already holding out the lapis lazuli and the water bottle that I'd handed him earlier. At least he caught on fast, when he wasn't busy being a judgmental ass.

I poured the water over the crystal, rotating it carefully. Once I was satisfied, I shook off the excess liquid and set it carefully on the card. I searched the deck for the last card.

"Ace of Pentacles," I said, pulling it free. "Associated with the element of earth."

"There aren't any more crystals."

I reached into his shirt pocket to retrieve the tiger's eye. It was warm to the touch, though I couldn't tell if that was from residual magic or his body heat. I lingered too close to him for a second too long, until heat crept up my own back and neck. I could feel him watching me, feel the moment stretching between us, taut as a rubber band about to snap. I forced myself to retreat.

I knelt at the northern edge of the ring and dug through a layer of dead leaves to reach the damp soil. I scooped some out with my fingers and rolled the crystal in it, then placed the tiger's eye on the card and stood up, not bothering to brush off my jeans.

"I'm laying a compass round." I felt a little foolish narrating my work out loud, but he had said he wanted to understand. "It's a sacred, liminal space that blocks out negative energies. It will contain the magic of my spell until I'm ready to release it."

Fitz looked unsure as he surveyed the withered fairy ring around us. It wouldn't seem any different to him, but I could already sense the change in the air, like the moments before a storm. I paced the inside edge of the circle, setting the boundary more firmly in my mind. I was having trouble concentrating with Fitz watching me, but I didn't want to admit that by asking him to stop staring. Finally on the third iteration, I was content with the barrier I'd created.

I slipped my athame from my back pocket and removed it from its sheath. I eyeballed the center of the ring and knelt down again, facing north.

"Could you please?" I squinted up at Fitz and pointed to the dirt across from me. "I can't focus with you hovering over me like that."

Fitz joined me on the ground without complaint, even though his black slacks were going to be way more expensive to clean than my jeans. In the peachy morning light that filtered through the trees, I could see the faint shine of the rune on his forehead. Hopefully mine was still in place too. I could use the mental reinforcement.

"What's next?" Fitz's voice was hushed. Maybe he *could* sense the shift in the atmosphere, or maybe he was nervous about the knife in my hand.

"The runes." I injected unearned confidence into my voice. "Algiz, the rune of life. It can be used for both protection and banishing negative energies." I sank my blade into the soft earth between us to carve out the shape as I spoke, a Y with an extra arm in the center that was supposed to represent the horns of an elk.

"And Sowilo, the rune of the sun. It symbolizes action and triumph. More important, it will amplify the effect of Algiz."

"Looks more like a lightning bolt," Fitz said, as I carved the second shape in the dirt.

"Well, take it up with Odin."

"Odin, like the one-eyed Norse god?"

"He was the one who gave us the Elder Futhark runes, if you believe the legends."

I could tell by the way he was watching me, with a slight quirk in his lips, that he dearly wanted to ask if I believed the legends. But he refrained. I found a clean patch of denim and wiped the flat of the blade on my thigh. Briskly, because I knew Fitz would stop me otherwise, I brought the edge to my left thumb and drew blood. Fitz made a noise of shocked protest, which I ignored. I probably should have done something more to disinfect the knife, but there would be time to worry about that later. And anyway, it was barely more than a paper cut, though it stung like hell. Normally when I thought a spell called for a piece of myself, I would use saliva or a strand of hair, but I wasn't about to risk the efficacy of this working because the universe decided I wasn't invested enough. I'd slice open a vein if it meant saving my family, but hopefully that wouldn't be necessary.

"Have you done this spell before?" Fitz asked, with only the slightest hint of reproach as I squeezed out a couple drops of blood over each of the runes.

"No," I said, and then, in response to his troubled frown, added, "It's not like I have a page in my grimoire dedicated to instructions for when every citizen in town gets turned into Sleeping Beauty."

"Then how do you know it will work?"

I don't. I bit back the truthful response. I didn't want to lie to him, but I also didn't want to admit the creeping fear I had spent all night trying to quash—that I didn't know what I was doing. That no matter how much I meditated or which crystals I used, I wasn't skilled enough, strong enough, talented enough to reverse this curse.

I couldn't think like that. Witchcraft was predicated on belief. If I didn't believe this spell was even possible, then we were dead in the water. I pressed my thumb against my jeans to stop the bleeding.

"Look," I said softly. "Witchcraft is about harmony and balance and learning how to work within the cyclical flow of the universe, but more than anything, it's about intention and intuition. There are as many ways to cast a single spell as there are witches in the world. I can use ancient traditions and crystals and runes to boost my power and guide my intentions, but at the core of every working, it comes down to me—just me. Showing the magic where I need it to go, what I need it to do, and trusting the universe to listen."

I looked down at my knees. Unfolding the layers of my craft had left me feeling exposed and defenseless. In a strange way, I was laid bare. After an interminable moment of quiet, Fitz reached out and took my left hand. He swiped his thumb across mine, sealing the cut and leaving a fizz of magic in its wake.

"When you put it that way, it doesn't sound so different from magecraft."

I stared at my hand in his. My knee-jerk reaction was to disagree, to argue that our crafts were nothing alike. But weren't we banking on that to make this scheme work? His magecraft and my witchcraft, working together?

But maybe we were kidding ourselves. Maybe this was always going to be a total disaster. As politely and unobtrusively as possible, I freed my hand from his. I knew I should probably thank him for healing me, but I didn't trust myself to not also point out that wasting his energy on something so trivial was another stroke of idiocy on his part. Better to say nothing and preserve the modicum of goodwill that existed between us at the moment.

"It's your turn," I said. "I need the fairy ring at full strength if my ritual is going to reach the entire town."

"I should warn you that I have no idea what I'm doing. This is the first time I've even seen a fairy ring in person."

"Can you try to bring the chanterelles back to life?"

He nodded thoughtfully, surveying the circle around us.

"But don't hurt yourself," I added. I knew he wouldn't listen to me, but it needed to be said.

He pressed his hands on the ground, on either side of the runes, and dug his fingers into the dirt. He closed his eyes and went still. I was reminded of the day in the council chambers when he'd reversed the Whiteout. He had the same uncanny tranquility about him now, a peaceful sort of emptiness like he had gone somewhere else entirely. I wondered if the act of magic was as serene on the inside for him as it appeared on the outside. Was it anything like the powerful stirring I experienced whenever I cast a spell? The buzz of sensation across my skin? The ever-faster crescendo into a fever pitch? I wished I'd thought to ask him at some point, but as with so many other things between us, I'd run out of time.

For a long while—it could have been seconds or minutes or hours for all the good my internal clock was doing me—nothing stirred but the familiar vitality of the compass round, pulsing with potential, but nowhere near potent enough for the task at hand.

Then Fitz's eyes sprang open, and in the same moment, his magic rippled through the earth like a tremor. I could sense the trajectory of it, twisting and diverging into thousands of directions at once, and I realized he was feeding into the mycelium, the complex network of threadlike roots beneath us that was as old as the Cottage itself.

One by one, the chanterelles revived, their color vibrant as the sunrise. And in the wake of Fitz's magic, came an older, wilder magic, drawn back to its rightful place by the resurrection of the fairy ring.

Holy shit, it worked, I thought, but said nothing. I didn't want Fitz to think I'd doubted him.

"Holy shit," said Fitz. "It worked."

A laugh escaped me, but the levity of relief was short-lived. Fitz had done his part, but I still had to do mine. My thrill at the fairy ring's new vitality sharpened into anxiety at the memory of how my last attempt to harvest this magic had ended. And the stakes were so much higher now.

"What's wrong?" Fitz must have noticed the shift in my mood. He wiped his hands off on his pants, though it was a futile effort with the dirt caked under his fingernails and in the creases of his palms.

I tried to say that nothing was wrong, but those weren't the words that came out.

"The fairy ring is the spell I told you about before, the one I fucked up so badly." I swallowed hard around the lump in my throat. "I've never successfully done a ritual here. I don't know why I thought this time could be different."

Fitz studied me with a slight furrow in his brow. I wondered if he was upset that I'd neglected to mention the fact that I had no idea what the hell I was doing.

"I really hoped it was turning a car into a pumpkin," he said at last.

I surprised myself with another breathless laugh, half-strangled by the ache of shame in my chest.

"Sorry to disappoint." I had the horrible realization that I was about to start crying.

"Do you know what went wrong last time?" he asked, more serious now.

I nodded, not trusting myself to speak lest I release the floods.

"Then why don't you think it will work?" His tone was gentle with genuine curiosity. "You were the one to figure out how to reverse the Animal Pox. People in town are constantly talking about what a powerful witch you are—it's pretty annoying actually."

Elation surged in my chest but was tempered immediately with cold doubt. He was probably just trying to cheer me up, and I wasn't sure how to explain to him that even if it was true, even if the whole town thought I was some kind of wunderkind, it didn't change the fact that I knew I wasn't. I was intimately acquainted with all my failures and shortcomings. I was the only one aware of the constant specter of wasted potential at my back. I was the only one who could see the stark, unimpressive reality of who I was.

"Thanks," I said briskly. "Now that I know how high everyone's expectations are, all my worries have disappeared."

I waited for him to tell me I was too hard on myself or that I needed to think positive or fake it till I make it, or any of the other hundreds of inane things that people had told me in my life, as if it were that easy, as if all I needed was an attitude adjustment and everything that I knew to be true about myself would suddenly cease to be.

"I know what it's like," he said instead, "to feel like you'll never be good enough. It's terrible."

I envisioned the life he'd had before Owl's Hollow, doing everything he could to please a father who only ever gave criticism in return. How different that was from my own life, with two parents who acted like I'd hung the moon, who had been telling me since I was in diapers how special, how talented, how gifted I was.

Two completely divergent paths and yet somehow we'd both ended up here, face-to-face, with this terrible, mutual understanding between us.

He went on, and the comforting cadence of his voice thrummed in my chest like a second heartbeat.

"According to this very powerful and annoying witch I know, no one can tell you how to feel." He leaned in to rest a consoling hand on my knee. It was a soft touch but set off a chain reaction of fireworks in my body. "But just because your feelings are real, that doesn't make them true."

I know that, I wanted to say, but my lips remained sealed. If I knew that, then why was pain blossoming in my chest? His words were an incision, a clean cut straight through to my core, exposing to the light a part of myself that I'd let fester in darkness for so long, unexamined—unable to hurt me, but also unable to heal. Maybe I'd known it in the way that I knew there were no monsters under my bed when I was twelve. Of course I was safe, but I could only really believe it after Mim or Mama had checked and told me so.

My own vulnerability in that moment scared me, and I reached automatically for humor, in hopes of deflecting even an iota of the intensity in his gaze.

"That sounds like a line you stole from your therapist." I tried for levity, but my voice was strained with the persistent threat of tears.

"I pay her a lot of money for the privilege." Despite the quip, his intensity never wavered. The warmth of his hand seeped through my jeans. I wished I could throw myself into his arms. I wished a lot more than that.

"For what it's worth," I said, "it's obvious to me that you're pretty fucking incredible."

His lips curved in a rueful smile.

"For what it's worth," he said, and I had to force my attention up from his mouth, "you're pretty fucking incredible yourself, Charlie Sparrow."

"I still don't know if I can do this."

"Since when has that ever stopped you from trying?"

I couldn't help a smile, because he had me there. Maybe I wasn't particularly gifted, but by god, I was stubborn. Even more stubborn than the universe itself, as of tonight.

I took a deep, centering breath and settled back on my heels. Fitz removed his hand from my knee, and I tried not to miss it.

"I'm going to try a cleansing spell." Explaining my work to him was no longer cumbersome. If anything, it sharpened my focus. "It's similar to the one we did in the graveyard." My mind had to tiptoe delicately around that memory, because if I lingered too long, I would start thinking about our first kiss. That kind of dangerous reminiscing would not be useful right now.

"You're going to make it rain?"

I was pretty sure I wasn't imagining the skepticism in his tone, but I decided to give him the benefit of the doubt. It was a fair question anyway. I was no weather witch, and the ritual in the graveyard had taken seven of us to accomplish.

"No rain. I'm hoping the fairy ring will amplify the spell enough to cover the whole town." "Hoping" being the operative word there.

Fitz clearly didn't miss my choice of vocabulary either, but he only nodded in reply. We were past the point of second-guessing.

I had forgotten to bring my quartz, so I grabbed the tiger's eye out of my pocket instead. It wasn't as versatile, but it would serve well enough. More than anything, I needed something tangible to focus my nervous energy on. I closed my eyes and rolled the smooth stone between the fingers of my left hand. In my right I still clutched my athame.

It wasn't so much a meditation as a gathering of will. Without opening my eyes, I used the knife to trace Algiz and Sowilo in the air above their carven counterparts. The ritual was flawless. I knew that in my bones. The cleansing magic built into a steady, insistent hum. It thrummed in rhythm with my heart-beat, effervescing in my blood. But it wasn't enough.

I sought out the foreign, untamed magic that coursed through the fairy ring. I threaded my will through it, tentatively at first, but then with increasing resolve. I built up the picture in my mind of the spell I wanted to unleash, a cleansing magic to blanket an entire town, to reverse a curse that had been created—not intentionally through malice, but accidentally through fear and confusion and loneliness—by a young mage who had too much power and no one to help him harness it. The clarity of the situation strengthened my intention, and the fairy ring's magic bent to my control. It was intoxicating. It was terrifying.

The new flood of magic rushed around us like a riptide, amplifying and whirling around the circle in a cyclonic frenzy. The energy had crossed into the physical world now, raising a wind that pelted us with dust and leaves, snarling my hair and whipping tears into my eyes, even though the grass and trees outside the ring remained eerily placid.

I swiped my right arm across my face to clear my vision and found that Fitz was watching me with a calm expression at odds with the furor around us. I wished I could siphon some of that calm for myself. At the rate the spell was intensifying, I was no longer convinced that either of us was going to survive this unscathed. I was petrified by the magnitude of this new magic, at how mercilessly it beat against the boundaries of the compass, eager to burst free.

Was I really going to unleash this chaos on Owl's Hollow? Why did I think I was capable of guiding this much power with nothing but the force of my singular intention, my solitary will?

This is a mistake. As soon as the thought crept into my head, the edges of my spell began to unravel.

I can't do this. The subtle shadow of decay spread through the air, bringing with it a clammy chill and the distinct scent of rot.

From the corner of my eye, I could see the golden chanterelles droop and darken.

It was happening again, and there was nothing I could do to stop it. The entire working was about to collapse around us. *I can't do this.*

A brush of something against my cheek brought me out of my paralyzed stupor. My gaze locked with Fitz's as he slid his fingers softly along my jawline to cup the side of my face. Another point of connection between us, delicate but strong. He didn't say a word, but I could hear him with every fiber of my being.

You can.

I tightened my grip on my athame and aimed it upward. I envisioned it piercing the invisible sphere around us. The magic siphoned out in a ribbon of pure energy, rustling through the treetops, lancing toward the rising sun. Instinctively, I didn't struggle against it. I stopped trying to bend it to my will. Instead, I sought out the dark, calm center inside myself. I whispered my intention one last time into the void, and I trusted the universe to listen.

The casting of some spells resonates more deeply with your soul than others. There's no use trying to predict it. Sometimes the planets and the stars align perfectly. Sometimes it has to do with the nature of the spell or who you're casting it for.

Or who you're casting it with.

I was electric with the buzz of the magic, with the thrill of Fitz's skin against mine. I breathed in the scent of coffee and rosemary oil and a hint of peppermint, and before I could breathe out, his lips were against mine. I dropped my athame so I could slide my hand behind his neck, tug him closer, until there was no space between us, until we were moving in perfect synchrony.

I have no idea how long it lasted but by the time we broke

apart, the magic had all but deserted the compass round, leaving behind only a faint crackle in the air and the crisp, sterile smell of ozone, like the seconds after a lightning strike.

"How do we know if it worked?" Fitz murmured. Our foreheads were still touching, and I wasn't eager to pull any farther back, not with the way my lips were tingling and my heart was trilling, not with the way his fingers were tangled so enticingly in my hair. Not with the way his eyes, star-bright and burning, were locked on me.

My phone started ringing, and I nearly jumped out of my skin. I'd forgotten I even had it in my pocket. Before I could reach for it, Fitz's started ringing too.

"I think it worked." I tried to sound pleased instead of begrudged as I straightened up and dug out my phone.

Fitz offered a thin smile and pulled his out as well.

"Hi, El," he said, rising to his feet.

I checked my screen. There were simultaneous calls coming in from Mama and Bonnie, along with some incoming text messages. I answered Mama on speaker so that I could type out a message to Bonnie that I would call her soon.

"Morning, sunshine," I said in a singsong voice.

"Good morning." The sound of Mama's voice produced an unexpected wave of emotion, and I had to blink hard a couple times to clear away the tears. "Can I assume that you did not abandon your loving parents here in order to go to a wild party?"

"No party." I stood up, hopping a little when I discovered that my left foot had gone to sleep. "A few cocktails. Some light recreational drug use. Why, is something going on?"

I limped to the inside edge of the ring and started walking it counterclockwise to close down the residual magic of the compass.

"Excuse me." Mim's voice came over the speaker. "As hilarious as your little comedy routine is, I would like to know exactly what is going on and where my daughter is, thank you."

I heard Mama say something like "buzzkill," and I smiled.

"Fitz and I are out back," I said, completing my circle. "We'll be home in a minute."

"Oh? And what, pray tell, are you and Fitz doing out there?" Mama asked in a gleeful tone that prompted me to mash the screen in a desperate attempt to turn off the speaker. I accidentally ended the call instead. Served her right.

I turned and nearly walked right into Fitz. He was wearing a smirk that told me he'd overheard my beloved mother. Before I could do anything, like deny my heritage, he offered me his phone.

"Elinor wants to talk to you."

I brought it to my ear and said hello in reflex, only belatedly realizing that I had no idea what Elinor could possibly want to say to me.

"Hi." Elinor still sounded a little groggy. "I need you to be totally honest with me right now."

"Okay?"

"Is my brother all right? Really?"

Fitz was watching me with a knowing, weary look. I covered the mouthpiece with my hand.

"Are you all right?" I asked. "*Really?*"

He glanced briefly heavenward.

"I'm fine."

"He says he's fine," I reported.

"He's a dirty rotten liar."

"She says you're a dirty rotten liar," I repeated innocently to Fitz. "I am inclined to agree with her."

"Give me that." He reached for the phone, but I danced back out of his reach. "I barely used any magic. Most of it was your spell."

I gave him a once-over and had to agree that he did seem fine. Nothing like earlier when he'd first arrived at the Cottage. "He's okay, Elinor. Really."

She was quiet for a moment, maybe trying to decide how likely it was that I, too, was a dirty rotten liar.

"I've got to check on some friends," she said finally. "I need you to not let him drive until he's had some sleep. Confiscate his keys if you have to. Can you do that?"

Fitz made another swipe for the phone, probably guessing at his sister's intent, but I dodged him again.

"I can do that."

"Thank you." Her relief was audible.

"If you're done conspiring," Fitz said, hand outstretched, "can I have my phone back?"

I handed it over and let him finish arguing quietly with his sister while I gathered up my crystals and tarot cards, tucking everything safely back into my tote bag. I could tell from Fitz's increasingly resigned tone that he was losing. I was putting away the last ingredients when he said goodbye.

"In my defense," I said, in response to the peevish look he gave me, "Elinor is very persuasive."

He put his phone away and stooped down to pick up the plastic cap from the empty water bottle that I'd overlooked.

"I would remind you that I'm a grown man and can take care of myself, but I'm guessing that's not going to make a difference here."

"Would it be the worst thing in the world to let someone else take care of you for a change?" I took the cap from him. The brush of our fingers sent a tingle up my arm, and I lingered despite myself, wondering if he felt it too.

"I guess not," he murmured, his attention flicking briefly down to my mouth.

I swallowed hard, wondering how long we had before Mama

or Mim came out here looking for us. Before I could make any ill-advised decisions, like kissing him again, my ringtone cut through the tension as neatly as a hot knife through butter.

I checked the screen. Fucking Tandy, of course. I hit ignore.

"Come on," I said. "Our couch is comfortable. Get a couple hours of sleep, then Elinor is happy and as a bonus, you don't end up in a ditch on the way home."

If Fitz was disappointed—or relieved—by the interruption, he didn't let on, just stuck his hands into his pockets. I stepped over the row of fungi, half expecting there to be some kind of stir as we crossed the threshold, but the magic was placid, for now.

At the Cottage, we took the back stairs into the laundry room. I'd left a mess downstairs in the shop, but it could wait. I'd earned a few hours of sleep myself.

We were greeted first by the clatter of pots and pans. Mim was bustling around the kitchen barefoot, wearing a polka-dotted dress and a frilly apron, and her hair in curlers like a parody of a 1950s housewife. It was her usual Sunday morning routine, and for a split second I wondered if I'd dreamed the last twenty-four hours, and I was about to wake up in my bed to the smell of bacon.

Mama was leaning over the counter, still in her pajama pants and old T-shirt, though she'd thrown her robe over the ensemble. She was drinking a glass of water, probably hoping to counteract the multiple cups of coffee from last night.

"The prodigal children return." She tried for a dry tone, but her smile broke through. She was obviously pleased as punch.

Mim moved aside so that Fitz and I could wash up at the sink, but the second our hands were dry, she jabbed her spatula in the direction of the couch.

"You two sit down. You look like death warmed over."

"Thanks a lot," I said, though I obeyed, grabbing Fitz's sleeve to drag him along with me. "Is that any way to talk to the town's conquering heroes?"

"And is there any chance of you telling us what exactly you've saved us from?" Mama asked. "Should we be worried about a recurrence?"

Anthony. I'd forgotten about him in all the hubbub. Someone needed to check on him. Help him navigate the fallout of all this with his mom, with the town. I wasn't even sure myself how to deal with any of this. And I was too tired to try to figure it out right now.

"Can I explain later?" I asked.

Mama was primed to argue, as patience was not her strong suit (what can I say, I come by it honestly), but Mim piped up from the kitchen.

"Whatever you need, baby."

Mama stuck out her tongue, and I stifled a giggle, which immediately turned into a yawn. Sitting down might have been a mistake. It had given my fatigue a chance to catch up. Exhaustion settled into my muscles, snuffing out the last of my magic-induced adrenaline high. I also shouldn't have sat right next to Fitz, our arms close enough to touch with only the slightest shift.

I slouched down a little farther in my seat, angling to get more comfortable, even though I knew it was only going to make it harder to stay awake. I was finding it hard to care at this point.

"Fitz, hon," Mim called, "do you want eggs or pancakes?"

"I'm okay, thanks."

"Wrong answer," I whispered.

"You're getting both, then," Mim said. Anticipating his protest, she added, "And the more polite you are, the more bacon I'm adding to your plate."

"I wouldn't test her," Mama said. "Not sure your arteries could take it."

Fitz gave me a bemused look, and I shrugged.

"What can I say? She's a menace."

"But a cute one," Mama said.

"Thank you, my love," Mim said. "You get Charlie's bacon."

I started to protest but yawned again instead.

"You should go to bed," Fitz said. He was sitting with his cheek propped in his hand and his elbow resting on the back of the couch. When I tilted my head back, our faces were perilously close.

"I'm not leaving you here alone with them." My phone dinged with a new text message. I pulled it out, silenced it without looking, and dropped it onto the coffee table. I'd spent all night figuring out how to wake up Owl's Hollow. I'd earned a couple hours of peace. "They can't be trusted not to embarrass me."

"They can hear you," Mama said mildly.

"I know." I shot her a look over my shoulder. "Am I wrong?"

She flashed a wicked grin.

"No, but as your parents, we have every right to embarrass you as much and as often as we see fit."

"See?" I turned back to Fitz to find him smiling. "What?"

"Nothing," he said, and I had an up-close view of the dimple in his cheek, the crinkling at the corners of his eyes. "It's more . . . inviting here than I expected."

"Were you expecting us to drop you into a bubbling cauldron?" He shook his head.

"I guess I should say it's more inviting than I'm used to." His smile had faded somewhat.

I didn't want to think about the kind of home he was used to, because that was the kind of home he had in Boston. And I didn't want to think about Boston right now. It was easy enough to push the thought aside, when sleep was rapidly becoming the only thing I *could* think about.

I burrowed deeper into the couch, tucking my legs beneath me. My knees knocked against the side of Fitz's thigh, but he didn't move.

"I'm sorry about your pants." I wiped uselessly at the dirt stain on his left knee, then realized his shirt was still splotched with dried coffee. "And your shirt. They're probably dry clean only, aren't they?"

"I don't use dry cleaning," he said, with a touch of amusement.

"Oh, right. Perks of being a mage."

"For the record, I would still prefer if you refrained from spilling any more beverages on me."

"No promises." I had to clench my jaw against another yawn.

"You should get some sleep."

"So should you." I rested my head on the back cushion. Not as comfortable as my bed, but I wasn't picky at the moment. "Are you trying to get rid of me so that you can sneak out?"

"Never crossed my mind."

I held out my hand.

"Give me your keys, and I'll go to bed."

"How about I keep my keys, and instead I'll give you my word that I won't leave without getting some sleep?"

"You drive a hard bargain, sir." I wasn't sure at what point my eyes had closed, but I was finding it difficult to open them again. "Either that or I'm too tired to argue."

"Go to sleep, Charlie." His soft voice settled over me like a blanket.

"Promise you won't leave?" I meant to add "until you get some sleep," but the words didn't quite form.

"I promise."

When I first woke up, the world was a bleary watercolor. I was too warm and snug to even think about moving. I was curled against Fitz's side, my head tucked into the crook of his neck and shoulder, his head resting atop mine. His chest rose and fell in the measured rhythm of sleep. Someone had laid a quilt over us both.

The house smelled of breakfast, and I could hear the faint clinking of silverware and my parents' hushed conversation over the dining table. The sheer perfection of that moment, with its permeating sense of home, lulled me gently back to sleep.

When I woke up a second time, I was still curled up on the couch, but I was alone.

CHAPTER THIRTY-THREE

The week after the final salvation of Owl's Hollow was a haze of phone calls and visitors. I was sure that the media had come up with a catchy name for the latest mysterious catastrophe to befall the town, but I hadn't been paying attention. Some of those phone calls and visitors were reporters. They were hungry for the story, but I wasn't eager to go on record about any of it, so I had been dodging all attempts to schedule an interview. I knew my parents would have liked me to speak to at least one reporter, though they would never have pressured me. A feature news story would undoubtedly boost business for the Cottage. But I was afraid that telling the story would cheapen it somehow, that the perfect, crystalline memory of the fairy ring, saturated by sunrise and teeming with magic, and of our impulsive last kiss, would be irreparably tarnished. I couldn't stand the thought of that, not when it was all I had left.

And I especially didn't know how I was supposed to protect Anthony's anonymity if reporters were digging around, short of flat-out lying to them about the origin of the town's bad luck. We'd been telling any citizens who asked that there was no reason to think that Owl's Hollow was still in danger, but I doubted the media would simply take our word for it. Anthony was only a kid. He didn't deserve to have his life ruined over this.

When I wasn't avoiding reporters, I was sprucing up the shop in preparation for our grand reopening, and when I wasn't in the shop, I was in my bedroom, sitting cross-legged on the floor with my grimoire open to a page that was blank except for a single line in neat, familiar handwriting.

Goodbye, Charlie. I'm sorry it had to be this way.

I was saved from my obsessive rereading of the ten words by an alert from my phone. I snatched it up, a little breathless, but it was just a reminder that I had a lunch date with Bonnie. She'd asked me to stop by her office first and to "wear something nice." She refused to give any more details, except to remind me that she was still mayor, so I still had to do what she said. Grudgingly, I put aside my book of shadows and pulled on a sundress and cardigan. I spent two minutes halfheartedly curling my hair before I gave up and pulled it into a messy bun. Nice enough, I decided.

My abbreviated beauty routine meant I had some time to kill, so I went down to the shop to finish the work I'd started last night of organizing the crystal display—alphabetically, in defiance of both my parents. After my success with the fairy ring, I decided I had earned sufficient capital to start putting my foot down on some things around here. Maybe next I'd see about replacing that god-awful billboard.

I was halfway through my work when the bell on the counter rang. I dropped my handful of rose quartz to see who it was. We were closed on Sundays, but there were a few regulars for whom we were happy to fudge our business hours when necessary. I peeked through the window but didn't recognize the car in the driveway. An odd kernel of disappointment settled in my stomach, which I ignored. I was about to close the blinds and go back to work when I saw who was walking up the front steps. Anthony Hawthorn.

I unlocked the door and pulled it open, trying to project a cheerfulness that I didn't feel.

"Hi." I opened the door wider. I started to invite him inside but then saw that his mother was standing by the car, her arms crossed and face dour. Since she wasn't storming after her son, I assumed she had given him permission to talk to me. I decided we'd stay on the porch anyway.

"Hi." His hands were stuffed into the pockets of his hoodie, and despite the shy hunch of his shoulders, like a turtle trying to retreat into his shell, he looked much healthier than I'd ever seen him. The dark circles under his eyes had paled considerably, and there was color again in his complexion and his aura.

"You seem better," I said hopefully, and he nodded.

"I've been sleeping more, since—since that night." He scuffed his toe against the peeling paint of the deck. I wondered if the spell Fitz and I cast had inadvertently helped Anthony as well. Or maybe his confession while I was scrying had eased his guilty conscience. "Mr. Fitzgerald talked to my mom and explained everything to her. She didn't want to listen at first, but she finally gets it, I think."

"That's great." It was an effort to remain stoic at the mention of Fitz, but I was getting pretty good at it these days.

"The principal is letting me transfer into the magecraft class instead of PE, and my mom even said I could start seeing a private magic tutor online, if I keep my grades up. Mr. Fitzgerald promised he would recommend me to this mage who's a professor at Harvard. My mom thinks it will look good on my college applications."

While he was talking, Sophie slipped out through the crack

in the door. Whatever hostility she'd held for him in the past was long forgotten as she wound through his legs, purring so loudly they could probably hear her in the next county. He seemed a little baffled by her attention but mostly pleased, so I let her be.

"That's so great to hear," I said. With the right instruction, it wouldn't be long before he had a handle on his powers. Soothing that inner turmoil would make accidental town-wide curses—and hopefully the nightmares too—a thing of the past.

"Thanks." He shot a look over his shoulder, and his mom gave him a "hurry it up" gesture. She may have come to reluctant terms with her son being a mage, but that didn't translate to open-armed acceptance of all magic-wielding folks. "I wanted to tell you again how sorry I am about the shop. My mom said you weren't going to tell the sheriff it was me."

"I know it was an accident. No hard feelings, I promise." I tried to repress my amused smile. We wouldn't have pressed charges anyway, but Mrs. Hawthorn had made sure of it by deploying her lawyer to explain, in the sleaziest terms possible, that even though we had no proof of her son's culpability in the break-ins and damages, she was willing to drop her complaint about us (allegedly) selling magic items to a minor if we would sign an agreement to not pursue any criminal or civil action against her or her son. It was all very official and unnecessary, but after conferring with our own attorney, we decided that it was worth signing the documents if she would drop her complaints. Sheriff Daniels would be relieved to not have to do any more legwork on either case.

"And, um—" Anthony looked over his shoulder again, beseechingly, and Morgan gave him an imperious glare that was Mom-speak for "*Stop stalling.*" He stooped over to pet Sophie, and she purred even louder, if that was possible. "My mom said I have to—I mean, I want to help out in the shop until I've paid you back for everything I broke. I don't know anything about witchcraft, but I can sweep and stuff."

"That's nice of you to offer, but you don't have to do that."

Through his shaggy bangs, he gave me a beleaguered look that told me he had no choice in the matter. Clearly his mother was as relentless in her personal moral code as she was in her dislike of everything and everyone who existed outside that code.

"I want to do the right thing." He might as well have been reading off a script. "I can come for a couple hours after school on Tuesdays and Wednesdays, and every other Saturday, once soccer season is over."

Mrs. Hawthorn was now giving me that same imperious glare, one hand propped on her hip, the other tapping impatiently on the hood of her car. I realized I had about as much choice in this as Anthony did. Maybe it would be nice to have some help around here while I whipped the place into shape. He could come for a month or two and then I'd let him off the hook, assuming his mother didn't decide sooner that his debt was paid.

"All right." I bent over to give Sophie a scratch behind the ears too, and she responded by swatting my hand away. Apparently within the past couple of minutes I had been ousted from her affections and replaced by Anthony. "I guess I'll see you on Tuesday?"

"Yeah, okay. Thanks, Charlie. For everything."

"You are very welcome." I leaned to the side and gave his mom a cheerful wave. She issued a tight-lipped smile in return and climbed back into the driver's seat. Anthony jogged down the steps and back to the car before she could start honking. He gave one last wave through the window. It was nice to see a smile on his face, and I found myself smiling too.

Once the crystal display was finally organized (possibly for the first time in its existence), I borrowed the car to go into town. When I reached the town hall, there weren't any more cars than usual for a weekend, which was a relief. I had been half-afraid I was going to arrive at a media circus. I trusted Bonnie, but it was possible she thought that an onslaught of press would be a favor to me.

Bonnie was behind her desk, typing away at her computer. When she saw me, she immediately jumped up and came around to give me a hug.

"Thanks for coming," she said. "I'm starving. I was thinking The Blue Spoon? My treat."

The thought of returning to the site of my and Fitz's first date made my stomach flip, but I wasn't about to become one of those people who had to avoid every place they'd ever been with their ex. I pushed aside the agitation.

"Sounds good."

"But first things first, this is yours." She shuffled some papers around on her desk until she found a blank white envelope, which she handed to me with a little flourish. She was beaming.

I opened it and pulled out a check from the city, made out to Chanterelle Cottage. It was for ten thousand dollars.

"What?" I asked, staring at it. I couldn't think of anything else to say.

"I talked to the council and convinced them that even though we didn't technically hire you to fix the latest fiasco, we still owed you the going rate for saving the town."

"Thanks, Bonnie, but I can't accept this."

"Of course you can."

"No, I mean, Fitz deserves half of this." There was an uncomfortable lump in my throat.

"Believe me, I tried to give it to him," she said with a touch of exasperation. "When I called him, he told me that you did all the work."

I started to protest, but she gave me a dismissive wave and started moving around the stacks of paper on her desk again.

"I know, I know. You told me what happened already. I mailed him a check anyway. He ripped it in half and marked it return to sender."

A chuckle escaped me, although I was more annoyed than amused. I wasn't sure why I found the concept of an extra five thousand dollars *annoying,* but it wasn't the first time Fitz had managed to annoy me without trying, solely by virtue of being himself. He was strict about being paid (a lot) for his work, and I wouldn't have been able to cast that spell without him, so his refusal to accept the money wasn't a matter of generosity to the town but to me, specifically. Which was annoying.

"Thank you," I told Bonnie. "This means a lot."

"You earned it." Bonnie grinned at me, but she was still rifling through her desk. "You earned this other thing too, but I can't find it."

There was a knock behind us, and I turned to find Elinor standing in the open doorway.

"Looking for this?" She held up a black-framed certificate.

"Thank god," Bonnie said. "I was afraid my desk had eaten it."

"Hi," I said to Elinor, trying my best to sound like a normal person. I'd known she was still in town, but I hadn't heard from her since the morning that Fitz left.

"Hi." Her poker face wasn't usually as good as her brother's, but today it was flawless. I had no idea what she was thinking.

"Elinor is my new right-hand woman," Bonnie said, taking the certificate from her. "With the campaign, and hopefully beyond, assuming all goes according to plan."

"You're a shoo-in." Elinor pulled out her phone. "The campaign practically runs itself. Are we ready?"

There was something off about her. She was more subdued than normal, but I couldn't tell if she was angry, sad, distracted, or a mixture of the three.

Bonnie rounded the desk to stand next to me.

"Charlie Sparrow," she said, using her official politician voice. "I am pleased to present you with this certificate of commendation, in recognition of your tireless efforts to protect Owl's Hollow and its citizens."

"What." My shining wit was certainly on display today.

"Take the certificate and smile for the picture so we can go eat." Bonnie had reverted to her normal voice. She shook the framed certificate in front of me.

I did as I was told, holding it in my left hand so that I could shake Bonnie's hand with my right. We both smiled for Elinor as she snapped a few photos.

"Perfect," she announced, after taking several horizontal and vertical.

"Excuse me, hi, what just happened?" I stared down at the city's insignia embossed on the creamy paper; beneath it was my full name in elegant script. I didn't even know our town gave official commendations.

"You're a hero," Bonnie said. "Heroes deserve fancy certificates. It's not that hard to understand."

"And did Fitz mail back one of these ripped in half too?"

Something like a laugh escaped Elinor, but she covered it with a cough. She was typing rapidly on her phone and studiously avoiding my gaze.

"I'll get the press release out today," she said, and I had a hunch that unlike the check, this certificate was more for Bonnie's sake than mine. Reminding everyone that she was a long-time friend and supporter of the town's savior would undoubtedly boost her polling numbers. I didn't mind. I was glad I could help, even indirectly.

"Thanks," Bonnie told Elinor. "We're headed to The Blue Spoon. Want to join us?"

Elinor's eyes flicked up at that, meeting mine for a split second before she busied herself again with her phone.

"No thanks, I've got a lot to get done."

"Your boss sounds like a real bitch," Bonnie said.

"I plead the Fifth." Elinor smiled and left.

Bonnie retrieved her purse from her desk drawer and her jacket from its hook on the back of the door.

"Civil service makes me so hungry," she said, right as the phone on her desk started to ring. "Dammit."

She gave me a look that was half pleading, half apologetic.

"Answer it," I said with a wave. "There's something I need to take care of anyway. I'll meet you out front."

I hurried to catch up with Elinor, who was moving surprisingly fast considering the height of her heels. She was in her usual witchy aesthetic but with a business professional spin. I was relieved that she'd landed on her feet with this job, even though it wasn't my fault that Fitz had decided to shut down Maven. Or not entirely my fault, anyway. I should have known he wouldn't leave Elinor here unless she had other options.

"Hey," I said. "Do you have a second?"

She stopped and turned. An emotion flickered over her face, gone before I could identify it.

"Sure."

It was only when we were face-to-face that I realized I had no idea what I wanted to say.

"How are you doing?" I cringed inwardly at my own awkwardness.

Her lips quirked with a sardonic smile.

"Been better, been worse. How about you?"

"Same, I guess. I wanted to apologize to you."

"For what?"

"For—" *Shit, for what?* I hadn't done anything to Elinor, but I was plagued by this cloud of abstract guilt, and I wasn't sure how else to assuage it. "I don't know. I'm sorry about how everything turned out, I guess. I want us to be friends, but I understand if you don't—"

She threw her arms around me before I could finish. I blinked in shock for a few seconds, then hugged her back.

"I'm so glad you said that." She sounded like her old self again. "I feel the same way, but I didn't know how to say it."

We separated, and she was smiling back at me. I hadn't even realized how tightly wound I'd been until now, as the knot in my chest loosened and I could breathe easily again.

"Come to lunch with us," I said. Bonnie had finished her phone call and was locking her office door. "Please?"

"I have a lot of work to do." She gnawed for a second on her bottom lip.

"Bonnie," I called, "will you please order her to have lunch with us?"

"This isn't a military dictatorship." Bonnie handed me her purse while she pulled on her jacket.

"Then why do you keep ordering me around?" I asked.

Bonnie made a face at me before taking her purse back and turning to Elinor.

"You're free to join us or to tell Charlie to stop bothering you."

"Rude," I said. "You just lost my vote."

Elinor laughed.

"Okay, okay, I'll come for a quick bite. Every vote counts."

"I thought I was a shoo-in." Bonnie was clearly affronted.

"That was before you started alienating your core constituency." I grinned and linked arms with both of them to hurry us along. Those truffle fries were calling my name.

When I returned home a few hours later, Mim and Mama were watching some obscure eighties horror flick and sharing a big bowl of popcorn on the couch.

"How was lunch?" Mim asked, her attention glued to the screen. I guessed that meant Bonnie hadn't told them the news. I started to hold up the certificate, then changed my mind. It had been a good day, but I was tired and unaccountably sad for reasons I didn't want to think about. Celebration with my parents could wait until tomorrow, when I'd hopefully be in a better mood.

"It was fun."

"Watch with us." Mama patted the spot next to her on the couch.

"Maybe later," I said. "I'm beat."

I went to my room and tossed my purse onto my desk chair. I stared at the certificate for a while, trying to make sense of the pride and self-doubt jockeying for dominance in my chest. I set the frame facedown on my desk, then changed my mind and propped it upright against a stack of books. I'd earned it, hadn't I? I was the witch who'd saved Owl's Hollow.

But the surge of confidence was short-lived, and in its wake my fatigue returned.

I kicked off my shoes and flung myself backward on my bed. I wanted to go to sleep. A nap seemed like a better option than stewing in my own murky emotions. But I was keenly aware of my grimoire next to my head, and I couldn't resist the siren call for even thirty seconds. I might be the witch who'd saved Owl's

Hollow, but I hadn't done it alone. I sat up and pulled it into my lap. It fell open obligingly to the page with Fitz's last message. I stared down at it, torturing myself by reading and rereading until the words were a nonsensical blur.

Every few minutes, I'd pick up my rune-carved pen, preparing to scrawl out a reply—the mood and content of which I could never quite decide on. I was pretty sure it was only a matter of time before I broke down and did something stupid, like beg him to come back.

In a fit of good sense, I slammed my grimoire shut and hopped off my bed. I crossed the room, shoved my window open, and flung the pen as far as I could.

Okay, maybe not *particularly* good sense, but at least it was done.

"Wonderfully dramatic. I approve."

I whirled to find Mama in my doorway.

"Hey." I rubbed my eyes, which were welling with unwelcome tears. "What's up?"

"Mm-hmm, super convincing." She moseyed over to sit on the foot of my bed and patted the comforter beside her.

I considered insisting that I was fine, and we didn't need to talk about it, but I didn't think I could get the words out without bursting into tears. I gave up and sat down next to her, leaning into her side when she wrapped an arm around me.

"I feel so stupid," I whispered. My throat ached with the effort of holding back tears. I'd known he was going to leave. I was the one who ended things in the first place. I'd all but told him that I wanted him to go.

So why was it a kick in the gut every time I remembered he was gone? Why did my heart leap every time my phone buzzed or the shop bell rang, like I was expecting it to be him on the other end of the line or walking through the door? Stupid.

"I wish there were something I could do to make it all better." Mama planted a kiss on top of my head. "But there's no spell to mend a broken heart."

That wasn't strictly true. There were spells to make a memory fade, spells to temporarily soothe your chaotic emotions, and spells to give you better discernment when it came to love. But I didn't want any of that anyway, and I knew what she meant. Magic wasn't a cure-all. There were some things in life you just had to live through.

"I prefer when your lovers behave badly," she said ruefully. "Then your mom and I can plot to hex them."

"He wasn't my lover."

"Right, and you haven't been mooning over him every spare minute for the past week."

"I haven't been mooning. I've been . . . thinking. A lot. About everything."

"And what conclusions have you reached after all that thinking?"

"That my parents spend entirely too much time eavesdropping at my bedroom door, for starters."

"Slander!" came Mim's voice from the hall.

"Oh my god." I buried my face in my hands.

"In my defense," Mim said, peeking into the room, "the door is open."

Perhaps she decided my lack of response was an invitation, because she came in and sat on my other side.

"What else is on your mind?" Mama asked, with a rare note of seriousness in her tone, and I realized that I wasn't going to be able to cut this conversation short with my fantastic wit.

"Wondering if it really had to be this way." Misery constricted my voice into a whisper.

"Baby," Mim began uncertainly. I was pretty sure she exchanged a look with Mama over my head. "If you need to take some time off, you know we support you, right?"

"Time off for what?"

"I don't know, a vacation?" Great, not this again.

"To Boston, maybe?" Mama added. Subtle.

"I don't need time off. I'm not going anywhere." I'd be lying if I said I hadn't considered it: hopping into the car and driving until I reached the East Coast, finding Fitz and convincing him to return to Owl's Hollow, dragging him back by the ear if I had to.

But he'd said it himself. He was a grown man. He could take care of himself. And he'd made his decision, however much I disagreed with it. My incivility aside, no one had forced him out of town. If anything, with the council vote in his favor, he was being welcomed with open arms.

If Fitz wanted to be in Owl's Hollow, then he'd be here. If he wanted to talk to me, then he'd pick up the phone.

I wasn't going to pretend otherwise. It wasn't fair to either of us.

Mim and Mama were trading another silent look, which was getting old fast. I guess I couldn't blame them for being worried, what with all the not-mooning I'd been doing lately.

"Well, in that case," Mim said, "we have some good news that might cheer you up."

"But if you're not in the mood to be cheered up right now, that's okay too," added Mama.

"Tell me."

They each grabbed one of my hands, which gave me an un-settling sense of déjà vu. This had been the exact position we were in when I was ten and they told me my hamster had gone to hamster heaven. Sometimes I forgot how much history was built into every square foot of this house. But they'd said *good* news.

"We want you to buy into the business," said Mama. "If you still want to, that is."

"Are you serious?" My heart leaped into my throat. "I mean—yes! Yes, I still want to." Some part of me wanted to add "No takesies-backsies" like a third grader. I'd been waiting for this moment for so long; I was almost afraid to believe it was happening, in case it was some kind of sick prank or spontaneous hallucination.

The joy had barely crystallized when panic broke through, giving me whiplash. I couldn't pretend anymore that proving myself to my parents was the only thing between me and some storybook happily ever after. It was my own unreasonable expectations that had been dogging my steps through my whole adult life. I was the one who had weighed myself down with all my mistakes and set a bar for myself that could never be cleared. A bar that rose higher every time I came close.

But I was ready to stop chasing that moving target. It was time to rest on my laurels.

There was still a small, quiet part of me that lamented all my wasted potential, but it was easier to ignore now. As a very powerful and annoying mage once told me, feelings could be real without being true.

"If we're doing it, then we're doing it right," Mim said. "Lawyers, contracts, the whole nine yards."

"If you insist." As if I didn't already have a list of attorneys in the state who handled business deals tucked into my desk drawer. "What made you change your mind?"

"It wasn't a matter of changing our minds." Mim rubbed my back in slow circles. "I told you before, it's never been about you, baby."

"The bank agreed to restructure the loan," said Mama. "The vice president was charmed by my magnetic personality."

"I'm sure all the work I put into our business plan had nothing to do with it," Mim said dryly.

"I don't see how; it was excruciatingly boring."

"The point being," said Mim, as she reached behind me to flick Mama's ear, "between the restructuring and the . . . um, uptick in business, the Cottage is in a good place now. Better than it has been in years, honestly. It's worth investing in."

"It was always worth investing in," I said, but I took her point. The uptick in business she was referring to was more than the wave of new customers from the press we were getting. Now that Maven Enterprises was closed, all the regulars we'd lost over the past three months were back on our books. And I hadn't even told them yet about the ten-thousand-dollar bonus that came with my fancy certificate.

"Well." Mama clapped her hands together. "If we're doing this right, then we need champagne. I may or may not have put a bottle in the fridge this morning."

"Ah yes, I noticed you'd broken the bank on that exquisite twelve-dollar vintage."

"Champagne is champagne," Mama said. "Don't be a snob."

"If I were a snob, I'd tell you that technically it's only champagne if it comes from the—"

Mama snatched up one of my pillows and walloped me in the back of the head. I hopped off the bed. Laughter bubbled inside my chest, heady and tinged with relief. Maybe all was not right in the world, but all was right in *my* world—or almost all.

It was enough, I told myself. It had to be.

CHAPTER THIRTY-FOUR

Three weeks passed. October became November, and I found my way back to the normal rhythm of life in Owl's Hollow, for the most part. We observed Samhain with a funeral pyre for Broomhilde in the backyard. It was a somber affair—despite myself, I missed my broom-sibling—but we all agreed that she had lived a good life and deserved to rest in the Great Janitorial Closet in the sky. And after the funeral, the bonfire provided us with an excuse for consolation s'mores.

For the sake of the Cottage as well as Bonnie's reelection campaign, I capitulated to a couple of interview requests and gave an official account of the thrilling conclusion to the town's magic troubles. We kept Anthony's name out of it. There was no guarantee that other news outlets would respect his anonymity, but I pitied anyone foolish enough to cross Mrs. Hawthorn.

Anthony had been true to his word and was a surprisingly enthusiastic employee. With his help, I managed to return the shop to its former glory and then some. My parents pitched in when they could but spent most of their time getting our new accounting software up and running, complete with an iPad and card scanner we could use at the till. Mim was against it at first—she loved her spreadsheets—but after I showed her the demo video, she was ready to take the plunge. My next goal was to implement some actual inventory software. Mama would be a harder sell, suspicious as she was of newfangled technology (read: anything invented in the past two decades). But I was confident I would win her over eventually.

I tried not to think too hard about why I was suddenly so keen on updating the shop. I told everyone—and myself—that it was because of my new ownership stake, but it was an excuse that only everyone else believed. I could never admit to Fitz that some of his unwelcome suggestions for how to improve our business were useful, but since he wasn't here, I was free to make the changes and take the credit. It was a good plan, as long as I never admitted it to myself either. That felt too much like missing him.

Even though I had a long to-do list that only grew longer whenever I had time to sit and think about it, my parents insisted I start taking Mondays off to relax. I slept in, had a big breakfast, watched some TV, but still only made it to eleven A.M. before I was bored out of my mind. I'd tried to sneak into the shop but had been chased back upstairs, much to the bemusement of a couple of customers.

Left with no other recourse, I holed up in my bedroom, blasted an old high school playlist on my phone, and practiced my origami animals. I had a lot of paper left over from my butterflies and realized I enjoyed the folding process when I wasn't on a time crunch or worried about making them perfect. I had mastered the technique for the cat and dog and was working on the frog. It did call to mind the Adam Scott meme from *Parks and Rec.* *"Do you think a depressed person could make this?"* But my growing menagerie was the only thing keeping me from moping under a heap of blankets during my free time, so I was content to fold away, trusting that the desire to mope would fade eventually.

I was sitting at my desk, so engrossed in my folding that I almost didn't register the noise behind me. But there was a pause between two songs, and the flutter of paper caught my attention. I turned to find my grimoire on my bed, as I'd left it, lying open—not as I'd left it.

My heart lurched in my chest, and I accidentally crushed the delicate, half-formed frog in my hand. I let it fall to the floor as I stood up. I told myself this was nothing, that I must have forgotten I'd left the book open, but still I crept gingerly across the room, like if I made too much noise the grimoire would change its mind and slam shut.

I pulled the book toward me, holding my breath as the inked letters appeared on the page, one by one, in his neat, careful hand.
Hi, Charlie.

I tried to breathe normally and debate whether I should answer, but that was a lost cause and a foregone conclusion. I dug through my nightstand and my desk for Tandy's overpriced pen before remembering, with a muttered curse, that I'd flung it dramatically out of the window weeks ago. How long would it take me to bespell a new pen? It hadn't taken long the first time, but now I was distracted and nervous and increasingly out of breath and there was no way I'd be able to so much as carve a rune in this state.

Easier to find the original pen. I wasn't an athletic person, so I doubted it had landed too far. I'd make Mama and Mim help if I must, as soon as I came up with a good excuse for why I so desperately needed that specific pen.

I put on one sneaker and searched fruitlessly for the other one before giving up and changing into my boots instead. This did not bode well for my powers of detection.

I rushed down the stairs, though not so fast as to tempt Sophie to try to murder me again. The shop was empty of customers, and Mim and Mama were behind the counter, poking at the iPad screen—hopefully not doing any irreparable damage. The last time Mama had tried to use it she ended up crashing the app. I decided not to worry about that right now. It was my day off, after all.

I yanked open the door, and my momentum nearly carried me into the person standing there. I halted with an inch to spare. It took a second for my brain to catch up with what I was seeing, and even then, I had trouble believing it. After a few more seconds, my mouth finally caught up with the rest of me.

"Hi, Fitz," I said, breathless.

"Lose something?" He was holding up the silver pen, but I barely noticed. I couldn't take my eyes off him. At the reality of him in front of me, casually understated in jeans, a blue shirt (god, he looked so fucking good in blue), and a black wool coat, with his sunglasses perched on top of his head, pushing his hair back from his forehead.

"Thanks," I managed, taking the pen. Our fingers brushed, and it was like an echo of the fairy ring magic, shooting through my veins and thrumming in my heart. I hadn't even realized how much I missed him until right this moment. That was scary enough for me to tamp down my emotions. I didn't even know why he was here. He was probably in town to visit Elinor and figured he'd stop by for a quick hello before jetting back to his penthouse office. (I had no idea what the offices of his family business looked like. I assumed that all CEOs must work in a penthouse with floor-to-ceiling windows, leather couches, and an artificial putting green.)

"You painted the front porch," he said, with a touch of smugness that I couldn't even bring myself to find annoying right now.

"And our business tripled overnight," I said. "A true small-town miracle."

"Congratulations, by the way, on becoming part owner."

Elinor had probably told him, if he hadn't heard it from the rumor mill first. I finally had the thing I wanted most in the world, which of course meant there was room for something new.

"Thanks." I had to take another moment to gather myself into a semblance of calm. "Come in."

I opened the door wider so he could enter. In the deafening silence that followed, I realized my parents had disappeared from the shop floor—far too efficiently for me to believe they had no idea Fitz was going to show up today.

I shut the door with my hip and ran a hand surreptitiously over my hair. Perhaps if my dear parents were not such traitors, I might have been tipped off to wear something other than sweatpants and an old band T-shirt that was so faded I didn't even remember which band it was. Not that it mattered what Fitz thought of me. Not that I cared. I was beyond all that now. I had ascended into the realm of beginner's origami and left all other worldly concerns behind.

With this new transcendence, I rounded the counter and leaned my elbows on it.

"What can I help you with today, sir?" I asked in my best shopkeeper voice.

He smiled, and my heart beat a little faster, even though I kept reminding myself that I didn't care. I didn't care.

"How about a tarot reading?" he asked, slipping off his coat.

I laid out the black silk cloth on the counter, then retrieved my deck and shuffled it, doing my best to focus on the cards instead of on Fitz, even though I desperately wanted to ask why he was here and for how long. If he didn't want to share, I wasn't going to pry.

"Draw three cards, please." I fanned the deck out for him. "They will speak to your past, present, and future."

He obliged, and I showed him where to place each card in a horizontal row. I set the rest of the deck aside and took some time to collect myself and soothe my frenetic energy before I started the reading.

I flipped the card on his far left and tapped it in thought, but before I could say anything, he closed his hand gently over mine. I let out an embarrassing cross between a hiccup and a gasp at the unexpected contact. Despite the late autumn chill outside, his hand was warm.

"Can I try?" He was still smiling—such an open, earnest expression. I recalled his smug, cool demeanor the first time he came into the Cottage, how immediately he had rubbed me the wrong way. But I just hadn't met him yet, not the real him anyway.

"Can you try . . . reading your own tarot?" I asked in confusion, and he nodded. I hesitated, not sure where this was going, but withdrew my hand. "Sure."

He leaned down to study the first card. My deck had little Roman numerals at the top but no words, so I was curious what exactly he was hoping to glean.

"The Ten of . . . Sticks?"

"Swords."

"That's what I meant. So this is my past?" He appeared so deeply contemplative that I had to bite back my own smile.

"Yes," I said, then after a long pause: "Do you need a hint?"

He shook his head and tapped the card like I had earlier.

"I grew up in a broken household—broken even before my parents divorced. My mother is an alcoholic, and my father is an abusive control freak. Both of them are textbook narcissists." His smile had faded, but his tone was light, purposefully so, like he didn't want to lend the subject any emotion. "I probably wouldn't have stood a chance, but I'm lucky enough to have two sisters who are only half as annoying as they are wonderful."

"This is amazingly specific for tarot reading," I said.

"I guess I have a talent."

"And what else does your magnificent talent see in this card?"

"A few months ago, I left the family business and started over in a town I'd never heard of before. And everything was great, except for this local witch who took an extreme and irrational dislike to me." I snorted, and he ignored me. "But I won her over in the end—for a while at least."

There was a lump forming in my throat, and I swallowed hard. I didn't know what to say, so I didn't say anything.

"She was convinced that we couldn't coexist in Owl's Hollow, or at least our businesses couldn't. And I guess she was right." He let out a resigned sigh. "It seemed to me that the choice was between staying here and ruining her life or going home and picking up where I left off. And the more I thought about it, the more I realized that—even though I hadn't known her very long, even though it didn't make any sense—there wasn't much I *wouldn't* do for her at that point."

I marshaled my courage enough to look up, but he was still staring at the Ten of Swords, like it really did hold the entire story in its smooth surface.

"I went home, and I told myself it was the best thing for everyone, and that it was what I wanted. But the problem was that it didn't feel like home anymore. It hadn't for a long time. I missed Owl's Hollow, and I missed that damn witch."

My stomach was somersaulting in a way that made it difficult to concentrate.

"She missed you too," I said. He raised his eyes to mine. They were shining with something between delight and relief. We were close enough that if I pushed onto my toes, my lips would reach his with no problem at all, but I resisted, for now. "At least according to the card," I added.

He chuckled and flipped the second card, which signified his present.

"The . . . dancing man?"

"The Fool."

"That doesn't sound promising."

It was, actually. The Fool suggested possibilities and new beginnings.

"You're the one doing the reading." I struggled to keep my
face and tone neutral. "You tell me."

"I've moved back to Owl's Hollow. For now. Or for good. I
don't know yet. I have another few months on the lease for my
house."

My chest twinged.

"Are you reopening Maven?"

"No," he said, without hesitation.

"You should—" My voice cracked, and I had to take a second
to compose myself. I couldn't believe I was about to say this.
"You should reopen. I don't want you to give it up for me."

He studied me with the same intensity he'd shown the cards.

"You'd be okay with me reopening Maven? What about the
Cottage?"

"I want you to be happy." I didn't hesitate either. It was the
one thing I was sure about. "Whatever else that means, I can
live with it." I just wished I'd realized that earlier. Maybe I could
have saved us both a lot of grief.

He fiddled idly with the card. It was strange seeing someone
else touch my deck, but Fitz didn't evoke the same sting of violation as when a client randomly grabbed a card during a reading.

"I didn't close it for you—well, maybe at first." A faint frown
wrinkled his forehead. "It took going back to Boston for me to
figure out that my father isn't the only reason I wanted to leave
the family business. I don't like how mercenary my magecraft
has become. When I watch you performing a spell, you're so
blissful, so alive. I used to enjoy magic the way you do, the way
Elinor does, but it's been a chore for me for so long that I forgot
it could be anything else."

He placed the Fool back in its spot and took my hand instead.

"I don't know what I'm going to do yet, but I'm not reopening Maven. The landlord had interest from someone who wanted that suite and two adjoining ones that had been vacant for a while, so he let me out of the lease early. There will be a frozen yogurt shop there by this time next year."

My thoughts were spinning round and round in a carousel of disbelief. Fitz was back. And he was staying. And he was no longer the competition. He was just some guy that I knew. That I really, really liked. And he was here.

"I didn't realize froyo was still a thing," I said, because I couldn't think of anything else that wasn't incoherent or embarrassing or both.

His aura was a beautiful sight, practically iridescent. And he was smiling again. I'd missed that dimple so much.

"I guess that leaves the future." He reached for the final card, but I slapped my hand over it before he could reveal it.

One of the rules of tarot is to not ask questions to which you already know the answer. The universe doesn't like to be tested. And I was certain, with every fiber of my being, that I knew exactly what the future held.

"Reading's over." I swept the cards to the side. "I want to kiss you right now."

I could tell I'd surprised him. Classic me. Though in this instance, I wasn't sure how that was possible. Surely at this point my desire was coming off me in waves.

He recovered swiftly.

"What are you waiting for?"

"For my parents to stop eavesdropping from the top of the stairs."

There was an unmistakable flurry of whispers, shuffling, and then finally the sound of the door clicking shut with painstaking care, as if there were any chance they could maintain plausible deniability.

"Well, that's embarrassing." Fitz's cheeks flushed pink, and it was so cute I could barely stand it.

"Welcome to my world," I said, and then I grabbed him by the collar and kissed him.

The heat between us was searing and fed by such desperation that it was like he'd been gone for years, but our connection was so seamless it was almost like he'd never left. I hated the counter separating us but was also grateful because it was the only thing keeping me from turning this whole reunion pornographic. I wanted to keep kissing him forever. I wanted to do a lot more than that with him.

Instead, I forced myself to break away, giving us both time to catch our breath, to regain some semblance of self-control. We had time now. I had to keep reminding myself of that. The countdown clock was stopped—smashed to smithereens—and we finally had *time*.

The thought filled me with a dizzying euphoria, and I put my trembling hands to work stacking the cards and tucking my deck back into its box.

"That will be forty dollars for the reading," I said, resuming my shopkeeper voice.

He took his sunglasses off his head and ran a hand through his hair, which was unfairly sexy.

"Technically I did the reading," he said, grinning. By now, I was convinced he knew how much I loved his dimple and had begun to weaponize it against me. I forced my attention away from his mouth. Therein lay only temptation.

"Technically, you don't know anything about tarot, and they're my cards."

"How about I meet you halfway at twenty?"

"Thirty."

"Twenty-five and dinner's on me."

I made a show of hemming and hawing.

"Deal, but only if the wine is the super expensive stuff. Like at *least* eighteen dollars."

"Do you think I'm made of money?" he asked. When I started to reply, he added, "Don't answer that."

I decided to withhold any snide remarks about trust funds, for now. After opening and closing a business over the course of a few months, then leaving his father in the lurch, it was possible he was as poor as the rest of us common folk now, though somehow, I doubted it. Fitz seemed like the type of person who had contingencies.

"You could always apply at the frozen yogurt place," I said, rounding the counter.

"I could do worse. Providing froyo to the masses seems like a noble occupation."

"Oh, I agree." I took his hand and led him toward the stairs, remembering at the last second to grab the bell, in case any customers arrived. "Now come say hi to my parents. I learned a long time ago that the only way past the embarrassment is through it."

"This feels like a trap," he said, but didn't resist.

Before my foot hit the first step, I turned, because there was one thing I hadn't yet said, and I wanted to make sure it was perfectly clear to him, so there was never any doubt.

"Fitz," I said. His gaze met mine, and I was back in the fairy ring, with the stars and planets in perfect alignment, reverberating in my soul. "I'm glad you came home."

His eyes flashed with something both satisfied and hungry. Without a word, he tugged me back toward him. Then my arms were around his neck and his hands were at the small of my back, drawing me closer until there was no more space between us, until our bodies were slotted together like the two final pieces of a puzzle. Our lips met again, softer than before. Our kiss was deliciously deliberate, as if we had all the time in the world. Maybe we did.

ACKNOWLEDGMENTS

As always, thank you to my agent, Taylor Haggerty, for being my advocate and cheerleader. Thanks to Sarah Peed for seeing the potential in this not-so-little pandemic book, and thanks to Emily Archbold for taking it across the finish line.

All my love and gratitude to my family, especially my parents, who love and support me through thick and thin.

To all my friends (you know who you are) who gift me with their love, time, and expertise: You are my heroes.

Dr. Emily Naviasky, you get a special mention, because you singlehandedly dragged this book out of the mire of my terrible (lack of) plotting. Thank you, thank you, thank you.

Kara, maybe next time I'll manage to be an iconoclast. I don't have enough caffeine left in my bloodstream to figure out a clever way to express my gratitude for your love and friendship, so this is what you get. Thanks for being you.

D. L. Soria is the author of *Thief Liar Lady, Iron Cast, Beneath the Citadel,* and *Fire with Fire.* She lives with a clingy cat and spends her time trying to come up with bios that make her sound kind of cool. She has yet to succeed.

destinysoria.com
Instagram: @thedestinysoria